THE PROGENIES
OF THE
BABYLONIAN EMPIRE

*The Origin, Migration and Settlement
of the Black Africans*

K J Liah

ISBN 978-0-6486541-6-2
© K.J. Liah, 2019

Published by Africa World Books Pty. Ltd.
(www.africaworldbooks.com)

Design and typesetting: Africa World Books

ACKNOWLEDGEMENTS

Foremost, a special thanks to the readers. For five years, I have received so many phone calls that came with encouragements and well wishes. It is good to know that you are all out there sharing the search for the origin of humanity and keen to know who the Progenies of the Babylonian Empire are.

My special thanks and love go to Nyamal Chuol, my wife and lifetime partner, my best friend who stood with me throughout this journey. I appreciate my children who have endured my absence: Nyajima, Nyapal and Buay, your endurance is always something special to me. My special thanks go to my parents, Jial Liah and Nyaneng Top who have given me so much education and lectured me on the Nilotic beliefs, particularly, the Naath generation of cultural practices. They still believe and cherish the Naath traditional practices and have minimal contact with the western concept of modernity.

A few individuals also deserve to be acknowledged. One of these people is Dr John Gai Yoh, a man whose quest for black history is unmatched. He constantly mentored and encouraged me to research the origin, migration and settlement of the ancient people who today we call Nilotic as part of the bigger debate on Black People. He constantly shared with me related articles and books on the ancient history of the Black people. His wide connections to black/African writers around the world is amusing and something that should be tapped.

Particular gratitude goes to the following friends who encouraged and supported me emotionally: John Gatyiel Chuol, Bachuy Dor

Madeng, James Keah Ninrew, Simon Bol Joluong, Dor Kubang Jiech, Sunday Jial, Majok Chuol Puok, Chawich Malual Diu, Gawar Wat, Dr Mabor Nyak, Dr Gai Riam and many others who put me in contact with invaluable resources and people across the world. Without their support, it would have been impossible to reach this far.

K. J. Liah,
Juba, South Sudan, December 2019.

CONTENTS

PREFACE   7
Part One – About this Work, 7
Part Two – The Preview, 13
Part Three – Westerners and Asians in Africa, 22

Chapter 1   **THE OUT OF AFRICA EVE**   32
Introduction, 32
The Human Evolution, 34
The Validation of Data, 50
The Migration Out of Africa, 53
The Progenitors, 58
Biblical Creation, 65
The Four Rivers of Gardens of Eden, 71
Pishon River, 73
Gihon River, 74
Euphrates River, 75
Tigris River, 75
Adam's First Wife, Lilith, 76
John Milton's Paradise Lost, 77
Journey of Gilgamesh, 79

Chapter 2   **THE PROGENIES OF THE EMPIRE**   81
Introduction, 81
Black Civilization in Mesopotamia, 87
Tower of Babel, 108

Chapter 3   **KEMET, THE LAND OF THE BLACKS**   116
            Introduction, 116
            The Ancient Land of Kemet, 130
            Herodotus Observations in Egypt and Ethiopia, 154
            Robbing the Royal Mummies, 162
            Destruction of Ancient Monuments:
                The Great Sphinx of Giza, 169
            Fighting over Ancient Kemet Monuments, 176
            Ancient Kemet Contribution to Sciences, 188
            Conclusion on the Scientific Evidence of
                Black Genesis in Kemet, 199

Chapter 4   **THE TERMS THAT DEFINED BLACK AFRICA** 207
            Discourse on the Word "Cush", 207
            Discourse on the Word "Africa", 217
            Discourse on the Word "Naath", 221
            Discourse on the Word "Nilotic", 234
            Discourse on the Word "Nuer", 241
            The Earth Master, 254
            The Cattle Master, 257
            Waathkhor, 259
            Kuarjuayni, 263
            Kuarthoay, 263
            Discourse on the Terms "Dinka," and "Jieng", 264
            The Nubians, 266

Chapter 5   **CONCLUSION**   274

            INDEX   289

PREFACE

PART ONE

ABOUT THIS WORK

This book is the result of over seven years of research. It comprises records of my visits to different countries to assemble documents and pieces of information that help put together the ancient history of the black people of Africa, particularly the Nilotic people. My visits took me to Egypt, Ethiopia, Iraq, Lebanon, South Sudan and Sudan to collect information which has helped to create this book.

Though I began my research in 2012, it was upon my return from Lebanon that I gained more insight into the subject. In Lebanon, I had been contracted as a humanitarian worker serving Syrian refugees who had been displaced by conflict. I learned plenty about fighting and displacement as I saw and heard about miseries from around the world. My heart ached as I listened to the stories from the children and mothers who had been affected by the cold conditions of the mountains in the Beqaa Valley and other misfortunes caused by powerful individuals and their own government. The government was not entirely responsible for pushing the country into the abyss, they shared the responsibility with other groups including opposition groups and other Islamic states who supported the escalation of the violence in Syria.

The Syrian conflict exploded in 2011, the same year that South Sudan gained its independence. Barely a year later, South Sudan also erupted and descended into conflict. Due to its effect on the people, this was one of the worst conflicts ever fought in Sudan. The same government that was mandated to look after the interests of South Sudan ended up causing misery in its people by orchestrating a coup without any reasonable basis. The politicians who were being targeted were also part of the people's suffering. While I understand the need to liberate South Sudan from dictatorship, I do not believe that the South Sudanese people were ready to accept change in that manner. My opinion is that an alternative route to liberation should have been the option.

To date, a majority of South Sudanese people and the international community continue to contest the government's claim that Riek Machar, the SPLM/A-In Opposition leader, orchestrated the coup. When South Sudan descended into conflict in December 2013, instead of taking off to another country where my services would still be appreciated, I decided to remain in South Sudan. I understood that my country was not only vulnerable, but also in need of humanitarian aid due to the potential famine that was looming. Here we were, only a few years into independence and South Sudan was already embroiled in a man-made internal crisis, throwing the country into a vicious cycle of violence. The people of South Sudan should have been allowed to rest after decades of fighting for liberation from the abusive regime in Khartoum.

The truth is that since the Cushites were driven out of Babylon, which extended all the way to the Upper Nile Savannah basin over 5,000 years ago, the inhabitants of South Sudan have not rested. Sadly, the current internal fighting in South Sudan has no basis or justification whatsoever. Whatever the intention of the fighting, there has never been any rest for the people of South Sudan. History tells us that South Sudan was dominated by outside powers that succeeded in controlling her people through slavery, thus ruling them. The people refused to be dominated, resisting throughout the centuries that followed and creating a vicious cycle. The South Sudan conflict can be classified as an example, for those who never judge history, to read and learn from it. History is a reality that should always be revisited, the leaders of South Sudan who claim to be fighting to eradicate the fascist regime in Khartoum merely cast a cursory glance at recent history (the 19th century) without going further back. Many people, though angry, sought comfort from Biblical passages that focus on punishment under the illusion that these references were meant for South Sudan and its current generation. If that is the case, then the punishment has already been claimed by those who fought the wars in Egypt before the coming of the current Arab population.

The nature of the conflict blocked people from moving freely within the country, so I was forced to use other means to reach my informants. Those that succeeded in contacting me did so under humanitarian cover, as it was the only way to access areas with information about the people who knew the origins of the Nilotic people. I had great difficulty accessing the areas that were controlled by the informants from the eastern part of the Nile to the western part. It got to a point where I was detained and jailed at different airports including Rumbek, Bor, and Malakal simply because I am from the Nuer community. The Dinka and the Nuer viewed the violence that engulfed the entire country through tribal lenses. This is a shameful state of affairs that is obvious to other nationalities and to the South Sudanese who have become victims of this conflict.

This may explain why I felt the need to research on the origins of the Nilotic to contribute to the community's intellectual heritage. My contribution to this debate offers critical analysis and thinking, and could possibly guide the next generation on their history. This debate, however, may also be inaccurate given that I have used Biblical and scientific theories without discrimination. I believe that both ontologies are relevant, and subject to interpretation by readers from both worlds. My intention was to engage individuals with scientific and Biblical backgrounds, because of their references regarding the people of South Sudan and the Nilotic people in general.

As members of the Nilotic people, the Nuer are vocal about their traditional and cultural behaviors, which require close analysis and interpretation. This has resulted in confusion and erroneous information-gathering by those researching their origins. The research conducted by powerful individuals and those without any relationship with the Nuer relied on myths and theories from oral stories retold to children. They interpreted the information they gathered according to their own understanding, which may have resulted in negative perception of the customs and traditions of the community.

It is my belief that those foreigners who came to Africa and the Nuer people in particular, will never be able to understand them, even if they live among them for years. Access to information has limited indigenous people from presenting their own version of the truth regarding their origins, thus pitting them against these powerful individuals. The advantage I had during this research was that most of the people with the wealth of information had all been squeezed into the Protection of Civilians sites manned by the United Nations. The ongoing conflict had driven them into the protection sites and, though unfortunate, the situation was an added advantage to my research. While their destitute situation caused me great sadness, it made my work much easier, as I was able to capture the information I needed in the shortest time possible. To maximize the available time, I conducted the interviews on weekends, late evenings, and during field missions. This proved to be quite challenging, to the point where my health and family life were compromised. I had little time with my children, as most of it was spent transcribing the data I gathered. My movements within the Malakal, Bentiu, Bor, and Juba Protection of Civilians also provided me with ample time to gather more data.

In this book, I have thoroughly explained why the Nilotic cannot discuss their origins without mentioning or discussing the regions of east, west and north Africa, because such places define their origins and migrations. The genesis of the Nilotic is closely tied to that of the black Africans who were the first inhabitants of Earth, as proven by science. The migration that follows the Nile is also critical to this debate.

Entire African civilizations and origins are tied to ancient Babylon, Egypt, Central Africa and Sudan. Cheikh Anta Diop, Chancellor Williams, Ivan van Sertima, and other black writers brought the entire buried world of the blacks to the surface and reminded us once again that black people were responsible for the civilization of the whole world, and that what is offered as the civilization of the West is really just a photocopy of the stolen civilization of black Africans. They wrote that Western authors have entirely undermined black civilization and continue to hold on to what they know about that period.

According to history, blacks not only left marks on the surface of the Earth but also walked as far as the Americas, which are claimed to have been discovered by Christopher Columbus. During his famous voyage, Columbus acknowledged that he was informed by the Indians that black people had visited their land and he was shown the knives and spears used by the blacks. In addition, Columbus also saw portrayals of black people created in the mountains that acted as markers. There is plenty of evidence available to Western writers that is always buried, never revealed.

For a start, we know that the ancient Egyptians—who were part of building the earliest civilization—were black people who could be termed Nilotic and inhabited that country. More references are found when you read the Bible and learn of the presence of ancient blacks fathered a long time ago by Cush and Nimrod who inhabited modern-day Iraq. The modern sciences that guide the compass and entire elements of the universe were first brought to light in Babylon and Egypt, and most of the design of the Egyptian pyramids were built by the fathers of the blacks who inhabited the land, as indicated by the oldest name of Egypt, "Shem", which means "black". Most of the African countries inhabited and controlled by Asians were also initially black countries, and through the decline of the black power, the Arabs invaded and turned them into their own. These Arab countries in Africa include Libya, Tunisia, parts of Sudan, Egypt, Ethiopia, Morocco and Algeria, among others. They refer to themselves as "Arab" countries. These documented conclusions informed coherent theories that define the reality surrounding the way things work in Africa. Most of them had abused black people when their friends wielded power, causing collisions with the black populations.

As I have mentioned before, it is impossible to document the history of the Nuer without discussing the history of conflict in the olden days—and the more recent conflict in South Sudan. If I do so, I will have omitted a sizable portion of this history, which is necessary in defining the reality of what the Nuer and Nilotic people have been through and continue to face in contemporary society. I have classified history into several parts, in which I have narrated the origins of black people and their migration. The Nilotic people started in east Africa and spread to the Middle East. Prior to the emergence of the Nilotic, there were blacks, who were associated with their skin color and reflected the ancient world. I referenced the invasion and occupation of Sudan (or Cush) by the Arabs after they pushed black people away and squeezed them into the Upper Nile Basin; this is where the distinction of ethnic groups, including the Nuer from the Nilotic people, began.

PART 2:
THE PREVIEW

The early civilizations of black People were also confirmed by the Bible, by history, and by the remains that continue to stand in Iraq, Egypt, Sudan, Zimbabwe, and Ethiopia, and in the rest of the black kingdoms of Africa. In the Bible, the prophets and prophetesses have clearly demonstrated how the great-grandfather of the blacks is portrayed as part of civilization. Several Biblical books remind us about the importance of black people and the emergence of the Nilotic as the center of creation. One of these books is by the prophet Isaiah, who prophesied about the Sudanese people.

If you go back to history, it has been recorded by anthropologists and historians that black people, particularly the Naath or Nuer, fought off the Assyrians and other Asians who came to invade and colonize the blacks along the Mediterranean. They were engaged in this war for a century. The Kingdom of Kush is mentioned in the Bible, with its leaders ruling Egypt and also matching strongmen into Jerusalem. I found myself with two contemporary theories that explain human origin and existence. If you believe in the Bible and wish to take that perspective seriously, you will realize that Kush and his descendants are the key to creation, and that his forefathers were part of this history. God appreciated his bravery, hunting skills and building prowess. God also recognized the Tower of Babel as a magnificent and creative structure, leading to the emergence of different languages. The scientific discoveries discussed in this book will prove that black people were responsible for initiating civilization and the construction of magnificent structures that humans are still unable to comprehend. Blacks were known for their generosity and for advancing humanity. The first humans are said to have lived in central and east Africa before they spread across the face of the Earth; yet despite all of the visible evidence, black people are still viewed as backward, confused, and poor by those they educated. Africa was built and established in the middle of the Earth, which is technically part of the Garden of Eden.

As a young man, I used to wonder about where the Nilotic people originated, trying to pinpoint the exact location where the first man emerged before coming to the Upper Nile Basin and the rest of the places where the Nilotic people live in Kenya, Uganda, and Tanzania, and prior to dispersing from Kuer-Kuong and the early migration from Babylon and Egypt. I know that the majority of the Nilotic people in the Upper Nile, the land of black people, were not educated and could not document their great journey and migration in writing. Thus, the story of their journey was passed on from generation to generation through word of mouth. Gradually, this vital information has disappeared over time, with only a few people holding scanty details. It is worth mentioning that most of the generations who were fortunate to hear about this journey from their great-grandfathers passed on centuries ago. This means that the information has gradually changed from myth to legends until they are forgotten. The fact that our current location is not our original homeland encouraged me to conduct research and safeguard any further loss of information henceforth. The truth is that every Nilotic community has its own mythology that is different from others, and is believed to be the true origin of their presence in the occupied land of the Upper Nile Basin. These mythologies have poisoned the minds of younger generations for centuries, and people tend to believe them and cannot have any alternative explanation of where they came from except a few phrases I found used by the few Nuer elders (such as 'Mer' referring to Meroë). This reflects the coming of the great-grandparents before they possessed the term "Nilotic". Nilotic refers to the people of the Nile and continues to hold that character. Most of the Nilotic people continue to live along the Nile in the Upper Nile Basin. These groups include the Nuer, Dinka and the Luo who continue to settle along the Nile. The Nile shapes the life of the Nilotic people; they cultivate, fish, drink, and develop green pastures for their livestock along.

According to Nuer traditional stories and mythology, there are individuals who have the power to control the waters of the Nile.

These individuals are believed to possess totemic energy generated from the Nile. Diu Luony, a 79-year-old Jikany chief, stated that

> My totemic powers are generated from lilies; I can harm someone with it, if I remove it from the water lamenting that I am in conflict with someone. I will go further by sacrificing an animal to the gods of water and my powers will guide me toward the person and he cannot cross to the other side of the shore. I own the water and can prevent someone from drinking from rivers if I intend to do so.

This group within the Nuer community believes that their ancestor had the power over water and parted the lakes and rivers, just like the miracles in the Bible when the pharaoh was tested to allow the Israelites to leave Egypt. Both parties performed miracles, until in the end, the God of Moses succeeded and the Israelites were delivered from their bondage. Another group, called the Bar by the Jikany clan, believed that they had the power to use underwater creatures to prevent people from crossing the Nile. They sound like myths, but in reality, they were true.

Through these interviews, I was informed that the Nilotic people walked barefoot for many years when they were displaced in the north until they settled in the current Upper Nile Basin areas after encountering difficult times and attacks from enemies. While growing up, I was also informed that the Nuer originated from the current Koch County of Unity State, in a place called Lich Tree (commonly known as Tharjiath Lich). Even my own father, like many other elders in the community, believed the same. But the story is a bit different.

Ran Gam Rolnyang and his wife Nyawel Beeh were the first people to settle in Kuer-Kuong. When they arrived, Nyawel Beeh was pregnant, and when her time to give birth came, she knelt down and gave birth to their first child—a son, Gaw Ran—and this is the reason the Nuer consider this to be the place that holds their birthrights. The elders could not be wrong, because that was what they had been told; modern education was the latest thing in Sudanese society, given that the same attacks and intimidation from the foreigners and colonizers were still fighting the Nilotic people despite the abandonment of northern Sudan to invaders. I persisted with digging deeper to find out more about what others knew about the Nilotics, and I realized that there was conflicting and scanty information about their origins. All signs led to the origin of the black civilization and basically narrowed it down to the origin of the Naath people. To explain the Nuer's origins, different authors have published various theories twisted to suit their interests. Sadly, it is hard to undo what has already been produced and printed. For example, to write about the Nuer, you must consult the works of Evans Pritchard, Sharon Hutchinson, and Douglas Johnson, or risk your work being seen as questionable even if you are a Nuer and have conducted research within your own community. The West has controlled everything about Africa—something I refer to as neo-colonialism.

I am conducting research on a history of black people and I believe that I have authority over my culture and traditions because no one could tell it better than myself. Due to ignorance, undermining, and the belief that Western and Asian scholars are superior, we have undone the previous progress made by black people towards civilization. If we are aware that all human beings (white, brown, Asian, and black) in this world, originated in Africa, then why do we still doubt that Africa is the center of civilization? Africa denotes 'black,' which is an indication that this is the land of blacks, just as Sudan is. The Nilotic people are the true people of Africa, and if reflected and examined clearly, this knowledge completely defines the continent regardless of the crossbreeding which has generated lighter-toned people who have also become Africans in one way or the other. Do not get me wrong: "Nilotic" means those who lived along the Nile or came following the Nile in the olden days. The African black soil also reflects the people who inhabited the land before the term "Nilotic" was coined; we were once all black people living in a common place before dispersing to different routes to explore and colonize the earth.

As we will learn later on in this book, there are concrete records to indicate that all people were created black, and it was after dispersing to different locations that environmental conditions caused people to acquire different colors. In addition, the Bible tells us that all humanity descended from Adam and Eve, and through them, the other races of the world were created. If you study both texts properly, you will realize that there are similarities between the Bible and scientific findings; of course, there are differences, which are also huge, but both help in finding the truth around the origins of man.

Whenever I conduct fresh interviews with different categories of informants such as old men, women, elders, community leaders, and intellectuals, I notice that every time the topic of the origins of the Nilotic people and the Nuer in particular is introduced, those who are unfamiliar with the topic express surprise. Others jump to the Lich Tree in Koch County theory, which is the most recent historical event and the last settlement of the Nuer migration. Others with an interest in the topic encourage me to continue exploring this possibility and look forward to reading my findings. Generally, most Nuer have the feeling that the current Unity State is not the cradle of the Nuer man, and believe that they must have come from elsewhere. Sadly, that place is unknown to many people. The topic itself leads to thought-provoking discussions capable of drawing together many. Most of the people that I have talked to admitted after the discussion that this topic is worth studying and they were interested in learning about its results. A good number of people only know about the Great Migration of the Naath/Nilotic people from central and west Africa to north Africa, Babylon, and back to Egypt, and to Khartoum and then the Upper Nile Basin. This theory tells us that the Nuer and other Nilotic people once camped around Khartoum, where they grazed their animals. This notion was supported by the excavation conducted in the 1940s by Sudanese archeologists, who later found remains of the long-time camp settlement, which related to the current activities of the Nuer in the north. Approximately 90% of the Nuer that were interviewed, whether opinion leaders, academics, or ordinary subjects, concluded that they came from Khartoum before settling in their current location. Some also stated that their ancestors came from central Africa and could cite some of the ethnic communities in South Sudan who came from there. This involves coming directly to the current location of the Nuer without passing through north Africa, and Egypt in particular.

There are also those who link the origin of the Nuer to the descendants of Adam and Eve, as told in the Bible. These individuals have been indoctrinated by the Bible, as opposed to having actual knowledge about history of the Nuer. The floods during Noah's time and the Tower of Babel are also said to have a connection with origins of the Nuer. The Bible also refers to Sudanese men who were blessed and contributed to the liberation and wars during that time. They also think that we are descendants of Cush, who fathered Nimrod with his children and who had his Kingdom in the capital of Meroë. The older generation still remembers 'Mer' as the place where the Nuer originated. This 'Mer' is what we know to be Meroë. The Nuer are known for shortening long names when pronouncing them.

When I asked an 83-year-old man whose father was a chief of the Leek community in the Unity state of South Sudan about the origins of the Nuer, he stared at me for a long time and stated that this was a difficult question similar to coming from Mer, as I used to hear from my great-grandfathers. In fact, there are clues that indicate this is a scantily researched area with little information. Without evidence to support their claims, some of the Nuer and non-Nuer authors may have had great difficulty in drawing a clear conclusion on this matter, It has been clear to the Nuer and the Dinka who were once cousins and came through the Nile with their animals, that Khartoum is one of the locations they settled in when they left Egypt and Meroë.

Evans Pritchard's books on the Nuer are widely quoted in anthropological works on Africa. He was hired by the government of Anglo-Egypt, which was a joint authority exercised by Britain and Egypt in January of 1899 to restore Egyptian rule in Sudan, though part of his work was conducted because he was a research fellow of Leverhulme. The intention of the research he conducted was to study the Nuer and understand their political, cultural and social life to assist with governing them. The colonialists believed that they were aggressive, thus the need to study all aspects of their lives to make it easier for the government to manage them. Many other foreigners like him also penetrated into the heart of Nuer land through the main rivers of Sobat, the White Nile and the Bhar el Jebel. All of the writers who managed to penetrate into the Naath land wrote voluminous accounts of the Nuer that were later used by those with the intent to colonize the people. Different ways were used to make sure that every tiny aspect of the Nuer was documented and scrutinized, and one of these ways were the Sudan intelligence reports recorded from 1899 that detailed much about the people. Other publications include the Sudan notes and records that began in 1918 and were also used to record the customs of the people of Anglo-Egyptian Sudan. Some district officers were also mandated to collect comprehensive reports on the Nuer that were then used by the government to analyze the political situation. Some of these officers, with their erroneous behavior, were killed. Those eliminated include Major C. H. Stigand, who was killed in 1919 by the Aliab Dinka, and Captain V. H. Ferguson, killed in 1927 by the Nyuong Nuer. The murder of these two officers brought great devastation, as many Nuer and Dinka died because of a scorched earth policy conducted by the British government. Animals, which were the only source of livelihood for their families, were not spared, as houses were torched to the ground and men were executed.

As Evans Pritchard went about conducting his research in the heartland of nomadic Africa, he sent in his contributions regarding the Nuer for publication in academic journals. He said, *"I described the ways in which the Nilotic people obtain their livelihood, and their political institutions."* This information was then presented to the Anglo-Egyptian government to enable it to carry out forced interventions among the Nilotic people such as the Nuer. The information was never used to ensure peaceful engagements. Pritchard's findings further enumerated the similarities between the Nuer and the

Dinka, including their languages and physical looks, concluding that they may have had a common origin. He interpreted the differences and similarities through the lens of the Atwot language and culture among the Dinka, which is similar to that of the Nuer. All of these studies were carried out so that they could understand how to manage or conquer the communities for their own benefit. Pritchard made other wrong assumptions, including stating that *"the word 'Nuer' is sanctioned by a century of usage. It is probably of Dinka origin."* Reading his conclusion, I was a little embarrassed by this assumption. Pritchard, who was a well-known researcher, could have investigated this term correctly and come up with a well-grounded definition for his writing. As a native Nuer, I found this conclusion vague and devoid of research. Reading his work, I realized that the reason why he brought along a Dinka as his translator in Nuer land was because of the preconceived idea that the term 'Nuer' had its origins among the Dinka. Thus, a Dinka would know more of the Nuer than the Nuer themselves. Despite receiving a wealth of information on the community from the Nuer people he encountered during his research, his mind remained fixated on the documentation of previous writers who recorded that the Nuer were part of the Dinka. I am positive that as he went about visiting the villages, the people informed him that the two communities were completely different at the moment. Any Nuer child is aware of these differences.

The death of Captain V.H. Ferguson occurred when his translator interpreted his speech erroneously, which also led to the death of many of the Nyuong and Jagei people. The hostilities and wars between the Nuer and Dinka have always hampered their relationship as neighbors.

Pritchard confessed that studying the Nuer was a big challenge because of the reports he had read, and he further cautioned that whoever read his work must judge him fairly. He wrote,

> ... the reader must judge what I have accomplished. I would ask him not to judge too harshly, for if my account is sometimes scanty

and uneven I would urge that the investigation was carried out in adverse circumstances; that Nuer social organization is simple and their culture bare; and that what I described is almost entirely based on direct observation and is not augmented by copious notes taken down from regular informants, of whom, indeed, I had none.[1]

He further recognized that there were insufficiencies to his research, which were indeed revealed in his books. As he stated, when he first arrived in Yoanyang town of in the Leek County of Sudan in 1930, he had a hard time convincing the Nuer. Typically, the Nuer do not easily open up to outsiders. They first study the person before opening up, an important aspect that was skipped by Evans Pritchard when he first arrived. Other barriers to communication included the assumption that the Dinka and Balanda languages would ease communication, so he brought a long two servants (a Dinka and a Balanda) for interpretation, and to cook for him and carry his luggage.

The people we interviewed were not only Nuer, but were also drawn from different Nilotic communities. However, a large portion of the work was collected from the Internal Displaced Persons camps in the United Nations PoC sites brought together by the conflict in South Sudan. I have travelled further into the areas occupied by the Nuer in the Upper Nile, Jonglei and Unity states to speak with spiritual leaders, elders, singers of gods, and intellectuals, which has provided me with a wealth of information. I must say the motivation for this project came at the right time, because as soon as the idea came into my mind, I decided to implement it. I have also learned much from the experienced people who agreed to share with me what they know about the origins of the Nilotic people. I believe that my work will be used by future African generations, particularly the Nilotic people, as they dig further towards tracing their origins. I may have forgotten to

---

1   E.E. Evans-Pritchard, The Nuer: A Description of the Modes of Livelihood and PoliticalInstitutions of a Nilotic People. Published in 1969, Oxford University Press, USA. P.9.

include some vital information towards tracing the entire journey, but I hope that others will continue from where I stopped.

PART 3
WESTERNERS AND ASIANS IN AFRICA

As a young man born in Sudan at the time when Sudanese were trying to divorce themselves from the autocratic, Islamic, and authoritarian Arab regime in Sudan, I spent almost my entire youth in the military. I was given over to the SPLM/A movement when I was only seven years of age in 1987, and returned later in 2005 when the peace agreement was to be implemented by the warring parties. My duties in the SPLM/A were mainly two—to study, and then to join the struggle for liberation—so at the camp, the focus was on military training and education. There were numerous children my age, and masses that were fed by the humanitarian community in Ethiopia. To the SPLA, we were a garden to be harvested and then sent for military training to fight the Arabs in Sudan; while to the international community, we were unaccompanied children who had been displaced by conflict in Sudan. The real agenda was hidden from the international community, who did not realize that we had been conscripted and forcefully recruited to join the army. This truth only came out after we had grown up. In those early days, I did not understand the political environment that I was living in, and I was only aware that there was conflict in my hometown of Leer. The SPLA was also on the offensive trying to counterattack the policies of the government in Khartoum. They requested young people to be conscripted through village chiefs without informing their parents. It was as if the slavery trade controlled by Arab invaders had returned in the South Sudanese villages. This policy was implemented by SPLA to conscript all the children found looking after cattle in the grazing fields or on their way to visit relatives. That was the reality of the SPLA/SPLM era of the 1980s. It was a painful experience for a young man whose father was a chief to be taken into a distant land, not knowing if I would survive or ever see my parents again. My conscription into the SPLA nearly caused my parents to divorce, because my mother did not support me joining the SPLA. Her sources and the rumors circulating in the villages informed her that late John Garang, the leader of the SPLA, had borrowed a lot of weapons from the Ethiopian government. Since he had no money to pay for the weapons, a deal with the South Sudanese to contribute their children as compensation for the weapons was brokered. This turned out to be untrue, given the circumstances we found in Ethiopia. However, these rumors remained true in the minds of the parents who lost their children to the SPLA conscription.

Back at home, I joined my father who was leaving for Leer Town. For the first time, I saw Arabs wearing the white robes locally known as *jallabia* and enquired of my father who they were. I learnt that these were businessmen and women who hawked their goods around the town, while others owned shops where people from the surrounding areas could trade. Villagers came into the town to sell their cows, goats and chickens, and on their way back would purchase various items such as sugar, onions, biscuits, and clothes, among other things. The town was an active trading center where interactions among different people spoke different languages. As a typical village boy who had never visited a large town, I was surprised and observed a pleasant scene. I had spent most of my childhood like any boy, looking after cattle, goats, and other family animals. I had never thought about visiting Leer, which I thought was too far away. I knew that my uncle worked in Leer Town as a medical doctor, and had a home in Reekyuol, where the rest of my family often visited him. I was also aware that Leer was full of exotic things that could interfere with our normal pattern of life. Children were known to abandon their chores to spend time in town trying to get integrated into the town life through trade. I never wanted that to happen to me, so whenever I visited the town, it was always in the company of my father.

In one corner of the town, there was an Arab military barracks that reminded me of the gun battles that took place in the 1990s. I always wondered why the Arab traders in Leer were guarded by an armed military. The SPLA was also active and also had bases in places such as Padeah and Thonyor, which may explain why the Arab government was sensitive. While I did not understand the situation as a young boy, I was also afraid of being caught in a crossfire between the two groups. As soon as we got back home, my father would bring out a watermelon and slice it into pieces as I recounted my experiences of the day. I would ask him what brought the brown people to Leer, and why they carried guns around, and if they were aware that these weapons could cause danger to our people and animals. They looked menacing, as though they were prepared to fire their guns at anytime. I wanted to know whether, if they fired their guns, the shots would reach us at home.

My father explained that the Arabs had come to kill us. They lived in a place called Khartoum, and while we never travelled there, they kept coming to us. They had conquered and taken possession of the northern part of Leek, Jikany, and Bul, and some parts of Jagei. It was only a matter of time before they took over our land. I became scared and could not imagine where we would move to next. He added that if we refused to leave this land, we might be assimilated into their environment and become their people, and those who resisted would be killed. He also informed me that the SPLA soldiers camping in Padeah and Thonyor were planning to resist this assimilation plan, and that was the reason for the Arab military presence. He warned me not to travel to Leer alone in the event that fighting between the two forces would take place. I listened to his wise advice, and to this day I appreciate the good education that he gave me.

Based on the authoritative position of black authors who wrote widely about black civilization and how the land was conquered by the invaders, I realized that the same exact thing was happening as the Arabs sought control of towns in South Sudan. It was the same war that our ancestors fought to keep the invaders at bay in the Mediterranean for a century until they could not hold on any longer, resulting in the loss of Egypt. Now northern Sudan is in the same situation I faced in the early 1980s when I visited Leer Town with my father. Fifty years on, the regime in Khartoum still hangs onto the same policy of annexing South Sudan to make it a part of Arabic culture and civilization. Their assimilation policy was implemented, and the people of South Sudan were enslaved and taken to Arab areas to work for them as slaves.

The majority of the South Sudanese, including the Nubians, the people of the Blue Nile, and those in Darfur also suffered. This is one of the reasons why most of the black people living close to the Arabs converted to Islam. Once you are converted, they would spare you and you could even intermarry with them. Sadly, this intermarriage was one-sided, because the Arabs could marry your daughter, but blacks were not allowed to marry theirs. The blacks were assimilated and behaved like Arabs; they ate, slept and prayed like them, adopting the complete opposite of African culture. Following the mass armed resistance from the people of South Sudan and the liberation of towns under the Arab regime, a sense of being liberated from the Arabs emerged. Under the SPLA regime, one could sense total freedom, because you knew that your fellow black was the one carrying the gun and if anything happened, no one could manipulate the result of a court case. This was totally different from when the Arab regime wielded power and could do as they pleased. I finally understood why the Arabs kept coming to invade the small portion of land left for the blacks, especially the Nilotic people of Sudan. The indoctrination by the SPLA leadership explained why the Arabs wanted to colonize black people and what their vision for the next 100 years could be. They also explained the policies they had put in place to counter the ones enacted by the Arabs. Though I was conscripted as a young child and did not enjoy the love of my parents, I can attest that I benefited from the challenging education I got from those who liberated themselves from the shackles of poverty and Arab enslavement. I came to accept that it may have been my destiny to be part of the liberation of the people of South Sudan and the black people of Africa. I know that Sudan is Africa and Africa is Sudan; no one can differentiate between these two terms. The land is black and people are black. We may have

Arabs and other groups in Africa that are descendants of those who came to invade the land of the blacks; there is historical evidence to confirm this claim.

At some point in history, black people were almost annihilated and taken away from their land. No one is innocent of the violations committed against blacks, Sudanese or Africans. Slaves forcefully taken away from Africa are responsible for building the White House. There are 30,000,000 black Americans today, descendants of black slaves forcefully uprooted from their homes in Africa to work in the cotton fields of the United States. Many people lost their lives in this manner. In 1441, the first African slaves landed in the maritime town of Lagos in Portugal from northern Mauritania. In this town, slaves were being sold or taxed at one-fifth of every single slave that came to the town. In 1552, 10% of the population of Lisbon was comprised of slaves brought from Africa. The continent was considered to be a harvesting ground for slaves. These were the realities of the ancient practices on Africans. Due to the systematic exposure of Africa to outside invaders, the population became significantly reduced, and disintegrated as people ran away from the slave traders. Ancient empires that flourished for centuries disintegrated and were obliterated; thus, ancient history was buried or erased, leaving few clues. Further exploration to introduce and sharpen civilization was abruptly halted, living the entire continent to be humiliated by the one-time beneficiaries of our civilization. Finally, Ivan Van Sertima said that the most backward and inaccessible elements were left untouched to testify and give false witness to what they framed as the complexity of black evolution.[2]

Sudanese slavery is an ancient practice that began during a time when the fathers of the Nilotic Sudanese, who now occupy the Upper Nile Basin, were defeated from the northern part of the Sudan. They moved to the Upper Nile Basin where they built, protected, and defended their own territory. One of the advantages they had over

---

2   Ivan Van Sertima (1976). They Came Before Columbus. The African Presence in Ancient America.

their invaders was their understanding of the terrain, which hindered the invaders from penetrating deeper into the Upper Nile Basin. Thus, the area became the shield that blocked the entire south Sudan and other parts of Africa from the intruders. Black people were abducted, collected, and transported to north Sudan, where they were sold as slaves to either Egyptian masters or Sudanese Arabs. Women and girls were used as sex slaves, while boys and men were used as their army after they were castrated. Masters waited for their wives to step out and then forced the women and girls to have sex. Testimonies from those who escaped have been documented. One of these testimonies stated that in the 1940s, the mother of the interviewee's grandfather was captured in southern Sudan and sold to a wealthy landowner in Khartoum. She became his wife and bore him several children, one of whom was his grandfather.[3] Areas that were badly affected were the Nuba Mountains, the southern Blue Nile, Abyei, Aweil, Parieng, and some areas closer to the Nile such as Adok Port in Leer. The raiding involved burning houses and killing and terrorizing entire communities. The Arabs used guns, while the local community only had spears and sticks. It was a very traumatizing experience for those affected because the real intention was to depopulate the Nilotic people. When giving his own family's testimony, Fatin Abbas stated that the derogatory Arab term 'abid', which literally translates to 'slave', continues to be used in present-day Sudan and in other Arab countries when referring to black people. This was because slavery has been used to prune black people for centuries. The slavery in Sudan has shaped the way South Sudanese characterize the north as being bullies and inhumane. It also contributed to the way they fought the liberation war by annexing territory from northern Sudan. The people of South Sudan realized that historical inequalities characterized by

---

3   Fatin Abbas (2016). Coming to terms with Sudan's legacy of slavery. *Among northern Sudanese families, slavery continues to be a taboo subject, even though this history has shaped the Sudans for centuries.* http://africanarguments.org/2016/01/18/coming-to-terms-with-sudans-legacy-of-slavery-2/

slavery would never end, so they chose an independent South Sudan. Abbas further stated that,

> This not only points to the kind of discrimination that South Sudanese have had to suffer at the hands of northerners, it also indicates the extent to which the legacy of slavery continued to inform structures of economic, political, and social inequality long after the official abolishment of the practice in 1924, and the country's independence in 1956.[4]

While slavery had been officially abolished in Sudan, the practice continued until the Comprehensive Peace Agreement was signed in 2005. The Anti-Slavery Society documented the most recent cases of every single person raided in Sudan, and it was always the Arabs who believed that they were masters over black people. As I mentioned earlier, this misconception is not new. In recent times, as the Khartoum government fought the SPLA, they recruited armed tribal militias to counter its offensive. The areas most affected were Northern Bhar el Ghazel, Southern Darfur, and Kordofan. The government used this tribal entity to destabilize and exhaust the black Africans so that they could give up their dream of liberation. Eventually, the people would have been forced to submit to their rules and their religion. The benefits offered to the tribes that cooperated with the Khartoum regime included the items they looted during their raid, such as human beings, livestock and slaves.[5] More than 600 people were reported killed during the 1986 to 1988 raids, and another 400 were captured from the Abyei Area. The Dinka transport minister from the Sudanese

---

4   Fatin Abbas (2016). Coming to terms with Sudan's legacy of slavery. *Among northern Sudanese families, slavery continues to be a taboo subject, even though this history has shaped the Sudans for centuries. Accessed on 15 May 2019. http://africanarguments. org/2016/01/18/coming-to-terms-with-sudans-legacy-of-slavery-2/*

5   Slavery in Sudan. Cultural Survival Quarterly Magazine. Accessed on 20 May 2019. https://www.culturalsurvival.org/publications/cultural-survival-quarterly/slavery-sudan

government confirmed these numbers. The temporary holding facilities where the slaves were kept included Satep, Meram, Datelia, Kolek, Muglad, and Tibum.[6] These are the areas where those captured were gathered before being dispatched to their final destination, to be auctioned like animals and properties. The going price for a slave ranged between $30 and $60, cheaper than goats. They worked as farm laborers, sex slaves, cattle herders,and fetchers of water. The concept that man is free did not apply to them, and they were used like any other beast of burden.

Turks, Egyptians and Sudanese Arabs joined forces and implemented the policy of the term 'slave' referring to black Africans living in South Sudan. All the black people were seen as *'abid'* created by God to be slaves, and this policy was reflected in the treatment of black people by Arabs. From the 1840s, it was Europeans who came through the Nile trading, and they had dominance over the White Nile until they reached Gondokoro. It was in this place the Bari and other tribes that lived in the region were used to further the objectives of the traders, who were specialized in ivory and slaves. Some chiefs were appointed to further their goals. The alliances they made give the chiefs authority to recruit slaves from other tribes within the area, which allowed their people to stay untouched if they harvested other tribes for slavery. In 1883, the Machar Nyuon, the grandfather of Dr. Riek Machar, mobilized the strongmen from Southern Unity State and led them to form an alliance with the Dinka and fight the slave traders in Nyang Machar. The mission was to liberate the Dinka from the hands of Turkish slave traders. After fierce fighting, they managed to defeat the Turks. By then there was a very low resistance toward the Turks by the Dinka, and that is why they managed to penetrate from Northern Bhar el Ghazel to Nyang Machar and to the Port of Shambe. In the Equatoria region, the ivory and slave trades were rampant, and

---

6   Slavery in Sudan. Cultural Survival Quarterly Magazine. Accessed on 12 July 2019. https://www.culturalsurvival.org/publications/cultural-survival-quarterly/slavery-sudan

though there was resistance, it never stopped the trade. Many chiefs that were appointed collaborated with the traders and used others as their agents to harvest the locals for trade. They were empowered by the traders to do this dirty job for them. So it was that the slave trade later flourished among the tribes. In the olden days, one tribe would capture members of another and sell them as slaves. Chiefs were appointed in the districts, and they had absolute power over the community. These paramount chiefs had sub-chiefs who obeyed and implemented every order given to them, to the point of offering their dependents as slaves. The sub-chiefs' responsibility was to feed those under his authority, and in return, as long as they cultivated his fields, they were treated like any other family member. They acted as though they belonged to the chief. The women slaves were also placed in the same category as any other wives that the chief of the village might have. They were also sexually abused. They would be kept there to multiply by giving birth to children which would later grow and increase the number of the captives.[7] This was roughly how the people of the Nilotic tribes were divided by the interests of the slave traders and were used to garner them support—and to harvest humans for their own survival.

---

7   Alice Moore Harrel (2010). Egypt's African Empire. Samuel Baker, Charles Gordon and the Creation of Equatoria. Sussex Academic Press. P. 78

CHAPTER 1

THE OUT OF AFRICA EVE

INTRODUCTION

The generally accepted anthroplogical theory is that Africa is the birthplace of humanity. Evidence – such as the extinct hominid *Paranthropus*, put forward by Richard and Mary Leakey who conducted extensive fossil finds related to evolution in Olduvai Gorge, Tanzania, and the work of Christopher Ehret – traces the early origin of humanity to Africa, and from that origin, the migration of early people took place, making Africa the cradle of humanity. Some social scientists, such as Christopher Ehret, Cheikh Anta Diop, and Chancellor Williams, also referred to the people migrating out of Africa as "'Out of Africa' Eves" in reference to Garden of Eden as claimed by the Bible.

Archaeological evidence of exhumed traces, such as the fossil of Lucy that was discovered in Hadar, Ethiopia, could trace such early origins to the black people of Africa. This evidence was not surprising to many archaeologists, anthropologists, geographers, and historians; they had plenty of evidence that explained these facts. Africa has been proposed as the original homeland for all human beings. The origin's location has been pointed to East, Central, and West Africa, in which the people were referred to as 'black' regardless of their race and color.

As years passed, ongoing discoveries supported the same idea of a common origin within Africa.

The African migration discourses pointed out that black people were the first humans, and it was through them, in association with migration, that environment played a key role in determining the races that occupy the world today. Those who migrated out of Africa during the early phases of migration and colonized the Middle East and the Levant were ancestors of the people we refer to today as Nilotic peoples (from the ancient Ethiopians), which includes the Nuer (who call themselves the Naath), the Jieng (who called themselves the Dinka), the Shilluk (who called themselves the Chollo), the Luo, the Kalenjin, the Masai, the Sara, the Ateker, the Pokot, the Samburu, the Turkana, the Acholi, the Adhola, the Alur, the Lango, the Kumam, and the Maa-speaking people of South Sudan, Ethiopia, Kenya, Uganda, and Tanzania. West Africa also hosts some communities of Nilotic origin, which include the Serer people of Senegal, Gambia, and Mauritania. They established their presence in the ancient Babylonian Empire and were known as the Chaldeans, Akkadians, and Hittites at the time of the Mesopotamians (see Chapter 2 for more detailed discussion). Traces of their early presence can be felt in the Middle East even today.

One of the examples of the ancient presence of the Nilotic people in the Middle East is the remnant of an ancient settlement. Harran, an ancient city near Nineveh in Iraq, with its pyramid-shaped huts which directly resemble the current *luak* and *duel* (African traditional huts used commonly in South Sudan for animal shades and human dwellings) of the black people of Africa, still stands today as a testament to their early presence in the Babylonian region. After wars and environmental factors, such as the flooding of the established locations of their civilization, they migrated back to Africa, established their presence timidly in Egypt, and later founded their biggest kingdoms, such as the Cush kingdom in Sudan. The Naath people being part of the Nilotic group as an intact ethnic community, established themselves in the Cush kingdom, at Jebel Barkal (a mountain located at the town of Karima in northern Sudan), which had three temples and 13 palaces. Khartoum (including Tuti Island) was one of the ancient settlements that existed before displacement to the southern part of the country, which is South Sudan today.

THE HUMAN EVOLUTION

In this chapter, I am going to use two famous worldviews and theories of science and religion. The reason for deciding to use these two worldviews is that they are the most popular frames of ideology that have convinced us of the how we think of our existence in this world. Religion has a huge following, and so does science. I cannot discriminate by sticking with only one ontology while leaving the other alone. I must discuss both mindsets, and whatever you believe in

Group of Homo Habilis eating their hunt.
Courtesy Nairobi National Museum 2017.

will also inform you about the origin of black people, since the origin of Africans has been discussed at length. The aim is to capture both worldviews to encourage deeper comparative debates regarding the origins of Africans. It looks at Africa as the cradle of man, in which Nilotic is the community where the Naath people of South Sudan emerged.

Scientists are sure about evolution, and state that it started 15 million years ago; this was the time when the first man walked on Earth. It has taken humans different stages to develop from primates that are believed to be extinct. It started with primates who walked on four limbs and let to the humans of today that walk on two limbs; this has been a long process of evolution. Humans of today are called *Homo*, and man is called *Homo sapiens*. *Hominidae* is the family to which human beings belong. It was during the Miocene epoch that the family of *Hominidae* split from the *Pongidae* (ape) family. The family of *Dryopithecus* became the first to evolve into man, and it is believed to be the common ancestor of man and apes.

In the 1960s, Dr. Richard Leakey, who is a Kenyan paleoanthropologist, conservationist, and politician, was Director of the National Museum of Kenya; he and other scientists made groundbreaking discoveries at Lake Turkana, the Olduvai Gorge, and other sites in Kenya, Tanzania, and Ethiopia. These findings support the idea that the first humans originated in Africa. Most of the findings date back to the very beginning of human lineage, and Africa was seen as the "Eden" of all species on Earth that are related to us.[8] Christopher Ehret, Distinguished Research Professor at the University of California, Los Angeles, is an American scholar of African history and historical linguistics, acknowledged that the transformation process began about 5 to 8 million years ago in the forests of Central and Eastern Africa. It therefore appears that evolution, as a process, occurred a long time ago, and in stages that eventually defined the descendants of man.

---

8   Ehret, Christopher. *The Civilizations of Africa: A History to 1800.* Charlottesville: University of Virginia Press, 2002.

According to Jared Diamond, an American geographer and historian who has written extensively about Africa, the cradle of human life is Africa, a fact that is based on fossilized evidence which also indicates that human evolution began in Africa.[9] Jared Diamond added that "all of that human history, for the last 5 to 6 million years after our origin about 7 million years ago, remained confined in Africa".[10] Most historians are in relative agreement that there are no facts or archeological evidence that point to the possibility of the original habitat of humans being outside of Africa.[11] *National Geographic* wrote an article entitled "Modern human comes out of Africa, definitive study says." The article mentioned that humans are solely children of Africa, with no Neanderthals or island dwellers. A study conducted by scientists on modern humans to compare the skulls and DNA of human remains around the world concluded that modern humans (*Homo Sapiens*) had their origin in Africa. The rest of the human species in other parts of the world all originated from Africa. This study was conducted by the University of Cambridge and combined global genetic variations and compared more than 6,000 skulls from more than 100 ancient human populations.[12] East Africa is believed to be the cradle of mankind because of the work scientists have conducted in the area, especially the excavation of human bones over 200,000 years old. At Jebel Irhoud in Morocco, the remains of a much older ancient people dating back 300,000 years were found.[13]

---

9   Diamond, Jared., *Guns, Germs and Steel: The Fates of Human Societies*. New York: W.W. Norton, 1997 (p. 36)..

10   Ibid.

11   Diop, Cheikh Anta (edited and translated by Mercer Cook), *The African Origin of Civilization: Myth or Reality*. New York: Lawrence Hill and Co., 1974 (p.179).

12   Owen, James. "Modern Humans Came Out of Africa, 'Definitive Study says". *National Geographic*, July 2007. http://news.nationalgeographic.com/news/2007/07/070718-african-origin.html

13   Sample, Ian. "Oldest Homo Sapiens bones ever found shake foundation of human story". The Guardian, July 2017. https://www.theguardian.com/science/2017/jun/07/oldest-Homo-sapiens-bones-ever-found-shake-foundations-of-the-human-story

This has bypassed the discoveries in East Africa, and as stated, more discoveries may continue to surprise the scientific community.

Dr. Ahmed Osman, who has written a number of books on the ancient origins of Egypt, has also written on the origin of humanity. Like many other authors who have written on this subject, he states that "it is Science which has enabled us to explore the fascinating findings related to the fossil and genetic records of our ancient ancestors. So, to the fields of paleontology, anthropology, molecular biology and archaeology have vastly increased our understanding of human beings and the way they lived many thousands of years ago."[14] He added that science has provided tangible evidence on human progress, and most of the difficult questions attract responses associated with evolution and natural selection. He also wrote that "We are told that humans share a common ancestral heritage with apes and emerged from a primate past through a process of random genetic variations...there is a growing body of scientists who point to ever more reasons for doubting the standard evolutionary story and who provide cause to look in new directions."[15] As suggested, Africa is the cradle of mankind, and the findings should not be confined to East Africa alone, with Tanzania, Kenya, and Ethiopia as the main locations where bones have been excavated. The cradle should not be restricted to a small pool or lake, but it must be expanded beyond that understanding. When more research is conducted on a larger scale and when more results from different locations such as South Sudan, Central Africa, etc., are taken into consideration, there will be more enlightened understanding of this fascinating subject.

As widely noted by Cheikh Anta Diop in his writings, many West African legends state that humans originated from the East, leading to the belief that the 'Great Water' is the Indian Ocean. However, these same stories also state that while crossing from East to West, migrants

---

14 Osman, Ahmed. "Ancient Origin: Reconstructing the Story of Humanity's Past", 2017.. https://www.ancient-origins.net/

15 Ibid.

encountered pygmies; but the presence of pygmies is only recorded in Central Africa, thereby leading some to dispute this claim. These legends comprehensively summarize the origins of man thus: "The early arrival of the Negro on the road to civilization and the current reversal of the situation ... he is the man who comes down to Sennar [one of the states in Sudan], which, no doubt, is the plain located between the White Nile and the Blue Nile; the point of departure for the Meroitic Sudanese civilization. Sennar is also the name of the Mesopotamian plain, likely between two rivers: The Tigris and the Euphrates".[16] This is the area believed to be the location of the Garden of Eden, where according to the Bible, Adam and Eve were both placed by God after He created them. There are assumptions stating that since the era of the Great Flood, most of the rivers that came out of the Garden of Eden were wiped out, and this may have changed the physical arrangement. Hence, the explanations given in the Bible would not have fit the new topographical order. Nevertheless, the fallacy still remains that science points to East and Central Africa for the origin of man, while the Bible directs us to the Middle East. The two theories (scientific and Biblical) do not bring us to conclusion. It could also be the case that the Garden of Eden was not been a small place but covered a wide geographical area that could combine the Upper Nile in Sudan and the Mesopotamian plains.

There are other locations that have never been investigated and could be the departure point for humanity in Africa. Legends from West Africa assume that blacks migrated from the East – the region of the 'Great Water'. Some have identified this Great Water as the Indian Ocean, but there is no proof to support this assertion. Others have identified the Great Water as the River Nile, which gives life to South Sudan, Sudan, and Egypt.[17] As found by explorers after Herodotus, the genesis of the Nile lies in Central and East Africa. It is the same Nile that Herodotus described when he was in Egypt. Herodotus

---

16   Diop, p. 181.

17   Ibid.

was a historian who visited Egypt during the Persian occupation and described the nature of the flow of the water according to the seasons thus: "It begins to rise and continues to increase for another hundred days, and as soon as those days are passed, the river retires and contracts and continues low during the whole of winter."[18] Herodotus was not aware that the genesis of the river was in *Central* Africa, the land of the Great Water. He was keen to seek the cause of the fluctuations in the flow of the water at different time periods.[19] Herodotus was Greek, and he wrote about Africa in 450 B.C.E. He further explored Africa from north to south, describing whatever he saw and the opinions he listened to from the people he interacted with. The Great Water that was mentioned could be the Indian Ocean.

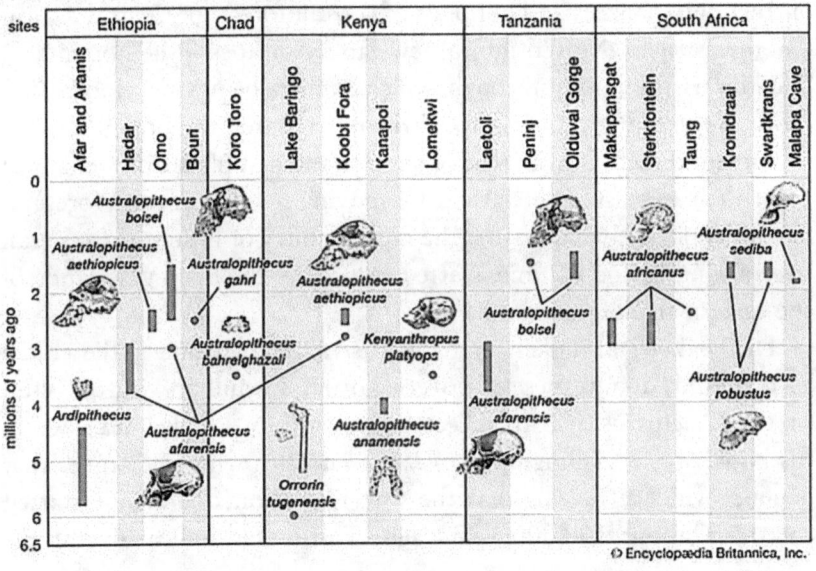

Locations of hominin fossil deposits

© Encyclopædia Britannica, Inc.

---

18   See Rawlinson.

19   Rawlinson, George, *Herodotus' Description of Egypt and Egyptians: The History of Herodotus, Vol. 2, Book 2* (New York. D. Appleton and Company, 1885), Chapters 5 – 59.

Human evolution is described as "the process by which human beings developed on Earth from now-extinct primates."[20] Current human beings belong to the group of *Homo sapiens*, which is seen as the developer and innovator of upright-walking species that live on the ground and evolved first in Africa thousands of years ago. Humans are the living members of the group many zoologists are reclassifying as *Hominini*.[21] There are the different stages of evolution as man became a refined human being who thinks and invents tools to extend his development.

It all began with the first apelike creatures, the size of modern-day chimpanzees. Evolution began to take effect after 5 million years, when the transformation of *Homo sapiens* into a wise and intelligent human occurred. Over a long period of time, one species of the apelike creatures, closely tied to the forest environment, gave rise to the current chimpanzees and bonobos of the rainforests of Central Africa. Another species evolved into a new family of apes – the hominids – and this is the family through which human beings developed into *Homo sapiens*.[22] According to Christopher Ehret, the hominids took a different direction from that of apes. In the first phase, they changed from their nearest ape relatives by moving away from the forest to live in wooded savannahs and the bush country of Eastern Africa and, over a long period of time, started to occupy the open grasslands of the eastern side of the continent.

Dr. Leakey's argument that the East African region is the cradle of mankind, due to these discoveries of an 18 million-year-old skull in 1959, helps us also to reflect on what John Reader discusses in his book *Africa, A Biography of the Continent*, where he argues that genetic evidence reveals that the first migration of humans started in Africa about 100,000 years ago. The fossils indicated that the

---

20 *Encyclopedia Brittanica,* "Human Evolution": https://www.britannica.com/science/human-evolution

21 Ibid.

22 Ehret, p. 17.

"hominid line" evolved in Africa for over 5 million years, and modern humans were around the continent for all those years.[23] It was at this period that the remaining humans migrated from Africa in search of better lives and spilled out into other continents. It has been assumed from here that the ancestors of the Naath people could be among this group, as they left Africa in search of more habitable places. This led them to such places as the Sumerian islands, where they settled. They moved away from their original settlements to explore the world around them. In more recent years, when Africa was being colonized by Western powers, no evidence existed to suggest that non-African colonizers were returning to Africa as a home they had earlier left or of being welcomed by the Africans who had remained behind.[24] They came to exploit Africa's resources, and in the process spilled blood, annihilating entire communities. *Dryopethicus* is the earliest known ancestor of man, and the *Encyclopedia Britannica* described it as:

> A genus of extinct ape that is representative of early members of the lineage that includes humans and other apes. Although *Dryopithecus* has been known by a variety of names based upon fragmentary material found over a widespread area including Europe, Africa, and Asia, it appears probable that only a single genus is represented. *Dryopithecus* is found as fossils in Miocene and Pliocene deposits (23 to 2.6 million years old) and apparently originated in Africa.[25]

The stages of the evolution of human beings began from this primate. Its distinct forms are well-documented, and included small, medium, and large gorilla-sized animals. It had larger canine teeth, but they were not well developed. Their limbs were not that long, and their skulls lacked developed crests. The creatures adapted an upright

---

23   Reader, John, *Africa: A Biography of the Continent* (New York: Vintage, 1997), p. 97.

24   Ibid.

25   *Encyclopedia Britannica*, "Dyropthicus": https://www.britannica.com/animal/Dryopithecus

posture and began walking for an hour to exercise, using their hind legs for locomotion. Describing how evolution took effect, it was argued that that:

> The upright bipedal gait of humans is a unique and highly ineffi-cient mode of locomotion, but the anatomy of modern apes, with 60 percent of their body weight carried on the hind-legs, indicates that the common ancestor of apes and humans was pre-adapted to bipedalism. Environmental circumstances in Africa explain why and how the fully upright stance and bipedal gait evolved in humans.[26]

In the third phase, they developed opposable thumbs that gave them the power to use manipulative tools.[27] These were the develop-mental stages that the first humans went through. Dr. Richard Leakey excavated the fossils of these hominids in Eastern Africa, and carefully analyzed them and recorded his findings. After *Dryopethicus* came another primate, named *Australopithecus*.

Australopithecus is a Latin word *australis*, meaning "of the south," and the Greek word *pithekos*, which means "ape". They acquired the name "southern apes" and were divided into two sub-groups, namely *Australopithecus ramidus* and *Australopithecus afarensis*. *Australopithecus ramidus* were about "1.2 meters tall, and the fossils show the *foramen magnum* that was large to indicate upright walking. The forelimbs were different from those of the earlier ape-like ancestors. They had teeth like humans." *Australopithecus afarensis* was the group from which the fossil of the famous Lucy belonged. They were described as a:

> ... group of extinct primates closely related to, if not actually ancestors of, modern human beings and known from a series

---

26   Reader, p. 55.

27   Ehret, p. 17.

of fossils found at numerous sites in eastern, north-central, and southern Africa. The various species of *Australopithecus* lived 4.4 million to 1.4 million years ago (mya), during the Pliocene and Pleistocene epochs (which lasted from 5.3 million to 11,700 years ago). The genus name, meaning "southern ape," refers to the first fossils found, which were discovered in South Africa. Perhaps the most famous specimen of *Australopithecus* is "Lucy," a remarkably preserved fossilized skeleton from Ethiopia that has been dated to 3.2 mya.[28]

They were able to walk on two slightly bowed legs, which made their walk slightly ape-like. They were able to climb and live on top of trees, and they had large teeth and jaws. *Australopithecus robustus* was taller than its predecessors, but still ape-like. They also weighed more than their ancestors.[29]

Australopithecus emerged between 1.5 and 4 million years ago and inhabited the region that lies from as far as the Red Sea, across the Horn of Africa, and toward the southern parts of the continent. They fed on a varied diet that included plants and meat.[30] The other group was *Paranthropus*, which also parted from the *Australopithecus* line of descent around 3 million years ago. It had a robust skull and a massive chewing dentition, which was suitable for grinding plant food, implying that it fed on a different diet compared to *Australopithecus*.[31] Dr. Richard Leakey argued that "the knowledge of preservation and fossilization processes we acquire from doing this helps us interpret and understand better the scattered and meager evidence that turns

---

28 *Encyclopedia Britannica*, "Australopithecus": https://www.britannica.com/topic/Australopithecus

29 *New World Encyclopedia*, "Australopithecus": https://www.newworldencyclopedia.org/entry/Australopithecus

30 Ehret, p. 17

31 Ibid.

up on ancient campsites."[32] He further argues that the discoveries from sites around Lake Turkana, in Kenya, Ethiopia, and Tanzania, combined with unearthed fossils, have immensely informed anthropologists about the human activities that occurred millions of years ago, providing new thinking about early human life. Traces and evidence of how human beings evolved based on fossil records and bone fragments that have survived over time continue to be discovered in sites located in Africa even today. The latest discovery, in Morocco where the oldest fossil of *Homo sapien* was found, is the latest discovery on the African continent. The fossil discovered in Morocco is believed to be the oldest than the East African ones, which date back to 195,000 years ago, by 300,000 years.[33] *Homo genus* became the next stage of evolution, and the first human of the genus was *Homo habilis*.

Homo habilis had some similarities to its ancestors such as *Dryopethicus* and *Australopithecus*. Its brain indicated that it might have been able to speak and conceive of ideas. It was also given the name "handy man" due to its ability to make tools. It was erect and around five feet tall. Another group of the *Homo* family is *Homo erectus*, which was also upright. His face was smaller and long, with a less prominent or absent chin, a larger brain size, and prominent speech. *Homo erectus* made and used tools, and also knew how to use and control fire. It was also carnivorous. The group began spreading from Africa to Asia and Europe. It has been noted that "the Java Man and Peking Man had brain capacities similar to the modern man at 1300cc. They were cave dwellers."[34] After this group came *Homo sapiens* and *Homo sapiens neanderthelensis*. This came as the result of Homo sapiens breaking into two groups.

---

32 Leakey, Richard E. & Roger Lewin, *Origins: The Emergence and Evolution of our Species and Its Possible Future* (New York: E.P. Dutton, 1977), p. 70.

33 "Oldest Fossils of Homo Sapiens Found in Morocco, Altering History of Our Species" (New York Times, June 7th, 2017; https://www.nytimes.com/2017/06/07/science/human-fossils-morocco.html.

34 *New World Encyclopedia*, Australopithecus: op. cit.

Africa has been designated as the cradle of mankind, but the war of words regarding the origin of man still persists. On Graham Hancock's website, it has been suggested that:

The Multiregional theory argues that the earliest hominins emerged in Africa and evolved to a stage known as *Homo erectus*, around two million years ago. *Homo erectus* then moved out of Africa and migrated as far as Southeast Asia. Around 500,000 years ago, somewhere in Eurasia, they underwent further adaptations, giving rise to various regionally adapted lineages. These migrants then evolved towards *Homo sapiens* from wherever they colonized and remained. In this model, all lineages were early *Homo sapiens*; modern humans emerging separately (but concurrently) in Africa, Asia, Europe, and Australia. Due to interbreeding on the edges of these regions, evolutionary adaptations were shared across the planet (genetic drift) and the species remained strongly homogenous rather than producing four evolutionarily distinct, anatomically modern human species. It has now been proven that several human forms were indeed interbreeding, just as multiregional theorists had long expected.[35]

It has been posited that *Homo erectus* migrated from Africa during the early period of the exodus, giving rise to hominin forms that could have become extinct. Scientific evidence continues to increasingly support the fact that *Homo sapiens* successfully colonized the planet starting around 70,000 years ago.[36]

Homo sapiens neanderthelensis "had a brain size larger than modern man and were gigantic in size." Their large head and jaw were powerful and muscular. They were hunters and carnivores, and their dwelling places in caves were well-organized. They had a powerful

---

35   Fenton, Bruce R., *The Forgotten Exodus: The Into Africa Theory of Human Evolution* (Self-published, 2017), https://grahamhancock.com/fentonb1/

36   Ibid.

food-collecting system. *Homo sapiens sapiens* is also known as "modern-day man" and is what we are today. If you compare *sapiens sapiens* with *Homo sapiens neanderthelensis*, they are smaller in size, and the brain size is reduced to 1300cc. The jaw also reduced, and the skull and chin were round. One of the earliest examples of this was the Cro- Magnon. They moved and spread widely into Europe, Australia, and the Americas. They were omnivores, with skillful hands, and developed the power of thinking and producing art and more sophisticated tools and sentiments.[37]

Cheikh Anta Diop concluded that the *Homo sapien* stage marked the end of further evolutionary development among human beings. The African origin of humanity may have remained, but without further evolution of humans as we know them today. Through this period, most of the migration of species and humans took place, and *Homo sapiens*, who are now living in Europe, were part of the people who migrated from Africa approximately 400,000 years ago. Diop wrote extensively about black civilization, which further enhances the argument against the origin of humans in Europe. He holds the idea that there were no indigenous Europeans, and those who embrace opposing views are most likely basing their arguments on false assumptions.

Edwin Sammy Achala, who wrote the book *The Origin of the Races and Destruction of Man by Man*, looked at human evolution through a Biblical lens and did not believe in evolution as described by sciencel he preferred to think of it as a fairytale designed to confuse people. It's very difficult to marry a Biblical theory of creation, as stipulated in the creation story, with the evolutionary theory believed by science to be the basic origin of humankind. As stipulated by Charles Darwin, this point of view stemmed from the perception that writers often politicize the concept of evolution. Achala states that "reviewing the different stages and periods of human existence on Earth, we find that theories of evolution in certain areas of science need to be challenged

---

37   *New World Encyclopedia*, Australopithecus: op. cit.

as being mythical and misunderstanding, as in the allegation that a black man evolved from an ape and, as in the theory by Charles Darwin, that man evolved from a lower form of life".[38] During his journeys across the world in 1859, Darwin made some discoveries on the origin of species and indicated that small changes taking place over time could cause large changes. After publishing his work on this subject, he formulated a theory on evolution by natural selection, in which he postulates that organisms mutate over time as a result of changes in hereditary physical and behavioral traits. An organism will better adapt to its changing environment, and that change will help it survive and reproduce in the existing environment. This is how adaptation to the environment enabled our ancestors to migrate and adapt to their new environments when they were moving from East and Central Africa to different parts of the world.

It has been noted that "the exact nature of our evolutionary relationships has been the subject of debate and investigation since the great British naturalist Charles Darwin published his monumental books *On the Origin of Species* (1859) and *The Descent of Man* (1871). Darwin never claimed, as some of his Victorian contemporaries insisted he had, that 'man was descended from the apes', and modern scientists would view such a statement as a useless simplification – just as they would dismiss any popular notions that a certain extinct species is the 'missing link' between humans and the apes. There is, theoretically, however, a common ancestor that existed millions of years ago. This ancestral species does not constitute a 'missing link' along a lineage but rather a node for divergence into separate lineages."[39]

The idea of natural selection is perhaps one of the most important scientific theories ever developed. Despite some shortcomings, this theory is convincing because it is based on findings from a variety of

---

38 Achala, Edwin Sammy, *The Origin of the Races and Destruction of Man by Man* (Indianapolis: Xlibris, 2011), p. 21.

39 *Encyclopedia Brittanica,* "Human Evolution": https://www.britannica.com/science/human-evolution

different scientific disciplines, such as paleontology, geology, genetics, and development biology. Scientifically, physical and behavioral selections are possible because of the natural changes that take place at the DNA level in the genes. Such changes, referred to as mutations, are in turn seen as the raw materials necessary for evolution. This is how the survival of the fittest occurs, and how many animals have managed to survive and thrive after such changes. However, species that lack strong coping mechanisms become extinct, or are replaced by stronger species. As can be recalled from our interaction with friendly animals, certain types of monkeys, such as gorillas, are not significantly different from humans in regard to biological functions. For example, based on existing research, some animals have been trained using sign language, and have managed to communicate using it to a certain degree. Bodie Hodge stated:

Koko is a fascinating gorilla but is far from being human. Koko has learned nearly 1,000 signs in American Sign Language, and Koko knows quite a number of voice commands. It has taken Koko nearly 32 years to learn all this. Other animals, like the bonobo named Kanzi, have also been trained to hear commands. These trained responses are similar to those of dogs and many other animals. They can be trained to do or respond to certain sounds or motions and even give a response in return. For example, the world's smartest dog, according to *Guinness Book of World Records*, can recognize over 1,022 commands, and respond to each accordingly; some are even math problems! Many of these commands are vocal or hand signals, much like the command Koko is given.[40]

There is some presumption that the cradle of humanity is in Asia, based on the discovery of *Pithecanthropus* in Java, *Sinanthropus* in China, and the Biblical story about creation (Adam and Eve), which

40   Hodge, Bodie, *Tower of Babel: The Cultural Heritage of Our Ancestors* (Green Forest, AR: Master Books, 2013), p. 72.

many theologians have traced to Mesopotamia (modern-day Iraq).[41] Scientists assured people of early migration, and it has been noted above that the ancestors of the people we call Nilotic today moved out and colonized the Middle East; and this supports the biblical idea of the Garden of Eden being on the Mesopotamian plains. If one were to critically analyze the Garden of Eden story at the moment, it would be obvious that the topography of the land of has changed since the Great Deluge or Flood that wiped out living organisms on earth. The indicators are still visible even today, and one of them is the Nile (referred to in the Bible as the Gihon), claimed as one of the tributaries of the river that is mentioned in the Garden of Eden story. However, the River Nile does not come out of Eden, but presumably flows into it. What is clear from archeological digs in South Africa, in addition to what is known about the Nubian civilization, is that the Great Water referred to in historical documents, is the River Nile,[42] the longest river in the world.

Analysis of fossils that have been excavated in various parts of Africa indicates that humans have been there for more than 100,000 years, which is a much longer period compared to humans on other continents. A case can be made that Africans, who migrated from Africa to start new lives elsewhere, became ancestors to humans on other continents, hence the age difference. Fossils from other continents suggest that the presence of humans in these places is much shorter compared to the presence of humans in Africa. For example, one of the *Homo sapiens* found in southern France in 1868, the Cro-Magnon man, was said to have occupied a rock shelter in the Dordogne region around 30,000 years ago.[43] The ancestors of Cro-Magnons evolved in Africa and had a bigger brain that conceived ideas. The oldest known fossil evidence of the existence of these ancestors was excavated from various places, including

---

41 Diop, p.197.

42 Diop, p. 179.

43 Reader, p. 90.

caves in South Africa, cliff shelters on the Indian Ocean shoreline of South Africa, and savannah grasslands of the Rift Valley basin in Ethiopia, Kenya, and Tanzania.[44] These excavations covered many African countries such as Libya, Morocco, Algeria, Sudan, Ethiopia, Kenya, Tanzania, Zambia, and South Africa. The specimens collected provided huge amounts of valuable information covering the period 500,000 to 30,000 years.[45]

Based on information from other fossils, there is evidence that modern humans also had a presence in the Middle East. The population that took the northern route toward Europe most likely settled there 40,000 years later. There was also another group that went east to Australia, and presumably reached it, 35,000 years ago, while those who went to China settled there 30,000 years ago.[46] The fossils of the oldest Neanderthals in Europe do not go beyond 800,000 years. In addition, carbon dating indicates that negroid *Homo sapiens* had voluminous skulls measuring up to 1,500 cubic centimeters on average and lived in South Africa from around 100,000 to 50,000 years ago, as confirmed by other authors.[47] There are numerous assumptions that, apart from Africa, Asia could also have been the origin of man, and to some extent, Europe. However, no proof in the form of concrete fossil evidence has ever been provided.

THE VALIDATION OF DATA

Martin Meredith reported findings from a study conducted at the University of California and Harvard, where UC Berkeley sampled 189 people, including 121 Africans from six sub-Saharan regions. Participants from Africa showed common mitochondrial DNA, which

---

44   Reader, p. 90

45   Ibid,, p. 91.

46   Ibid.

47   Diop, p. 31.

is similar to the DNA of human ancestors who lived in Africa between 166,000 and 249,000 years ago. Mitochondria are parts of cells that help in energy production systems within living organisms; they are the 'powerhouses of the cell' and help to stabilize its structure.[48] Another team from Harvard conducted a different but similar mitochondrial test, which produced a date of 220,000 years ago.[49] Similarly, in 2003, geneticists from the University of Maryland, led by Sarah Tishkoff, conducted a genetic analysis of more than 600 Tanzanians and found that "they belonged to one of the oldest known human DNAs in the world." Those whose genes were analyzed came from 14 tribes and four linguistic groups. They included the Sandawe, who speak Khoisan languages; the Burunge and Gorowa, who migrated to Tanzania from Ethiopia within the last 5,000 years; and the Maasai and Dotog, who originated from Sudan. These results suggest that an ancient genetic lineage originated in Africa some 170,000 years ago.[50] The mutations were passed from one generation to another without affecting the DNA, and mitochondria DNA carry the sequences of the history of the DNA. This is why fossils could be examined and recorded to reflect their lineages.[51] All the examined fossils, genes, and language structures indicated the origin of modern humans to be in Africa. The reality is that every single person alive today is a descendant of the humans that originated from Africa more than 100,000 years ago. They moved with their livestock and scattered across the rest of the world as their numbers increased.[52]

An article written by Bruce R. Fenton titled "Theory of Human Evolution" describes how Matthias Meyer from the Max Planck Institute for Evolutionary Anthropology led a team of scientists in

---

48 Reader, p. 91.

49 Meredith, Martin, *Born in Africa: The Quest for the Origin of Human Life* (New York: PublicAffairs, 2011), p. 179.

50 Meredith, p. 181

51 Reader, p. 93.

52 Ibid.

conducting detailed analyses of both nuclear and mitochondrial DNA from hominin fossils that were excavated from the Sima de los Huesos archeological site in Spain. The results of the analyses indicated that *Homo sapiens* and *Homo neanderthalensis* split from each other and had two main branches. This split occurred over 700,000 years ago, rather than 400,000 as previously thought. This understanding helps us reexamine conclusions made previously regarding the two hominins. The latest understanding is that *Homo sapiens* could be 800,000 years old. Analytical interpretations of previous records continue to be proven right or wrong, as studies progress and horizons of human understanding expand mainly because of advances made in modern technology. Geneticists Benoit Nabholz, Sylvain Glémin, and Nicolas Galtier reveal much in their latest studies. They think there is a problem with studies on genetic materials, which have been separated from the physical examination of fossils. Some studies led to strange conclusions regarding the hominin thus:

> The Indiana University project concluded that all the fossil hominins in Europe were either Neanderthals or directly ancestral to Neanderthals–not ancestors of *Homo sapiens*. We must under-stand that while respective groups in Africa match European hominin populations, this revelation discounted all known African hominins as being ancestors of modern humans. The morphological research also provided further shock–the divergence between *Homo sapiens* and Neanderthals had apparently begun as early as one million years.[53]

Archaeologists are continuously investigating fossil records to unearth the record of history and verify it. Chinese scientists who conducted archaeological studies recorded that they identified modern human fossil remains at the Bijie archaeological site that ranged from 180,000 years old, thus questioning what has been documented regarding the origin of man.

---

53   Fenton, op. cit.

THE MIGRATION OUT OF AFRICA

In the third millennium BCE (which corresponds roughly to the Middle Bronze age), some parts of Africa – especially the northern and western parts – dried up, and the areas that were wetlands turned to deserts. The lands that were once flourishing areas, sustaining lives, were not in a position to provide that service any more. Factors such as drying up of the land and movement of people to find suitable and habitable places were associated with changes in the environment, which also included the Ice Age and the subsequent drying up of the savannah areas. Black people started to migrate into the Nile corridors from the arid areas, which sustained their lives, and moved into the Nile Valley. Such movement to the Nile generated the term which the ancestors of the Naath people happened to be called: the Nilotic. This term becomes controversial because of the way the Western scholars assigned it. Different people gave the ancestors of the Naath people different names. Even the authors of the Bible decided to call them the children of Ham, a name associated with all black people who colonized the Middle East and the Levant. Such names are still controversial to the descendants of the Naath people. This is one of the areas where the Nilotic came to be known. The flow of the Nile sustained people and was rich in agriculture, and the people started to cultivate and domesticate a number of fruits and plants. Many agricultural advancements took place because of the Nile, and the Africans who revolutionized planting are not given the credit even today.

As mentioned, Cheikh Anta Diop, Christopher Ehret, and Chancellor Williams have stated that East and Central Africa were the origins of humanity, referring to it as "Out of Africa Eve" in reference to the migration of the first humans who colonized our planet. It was documented that there were four groups of hunter-gatherers who traveled southwest toward the Congo, Ivory Coast, and then south toward the Cape of Good Hope and northeast toward the Nile. Ehret also proposed that the group that went toward the Nile in 125,000 BCE and crossed into the Levant, only to perish when climatic conditions deteriorated around 90,000 BCE. Another group that started migrating in 85,000 BCE crossed the Red Sea to the south of the Arabian Peninsula. This group entered the Indian subcontinent, spread into Indonesia and reached southern China in 75,000 BCE, and in around 65,000 BCE spread to Borneo and Australia. This is why we have the current dark aborigines of Australia, because most of them moved out of Africa and camped in what we call Australia today. The warmer climatic conditions in 50,000 BCE encouraged another group of migrants to move northward through the Levant and cross the Bosporus into Europe. These are the ancestors of the Europeans and Native Americans who crossed to Alaska and then spread to America.[54]

Christopher Ehret, quoted above, talked about the desertification of some parts of Africa. He recalled in his writings that equatorial Africa has always been densely forested, thus attracting people from other areas to come and settle there, particularly around 7,000 BCE. Due to climatic conditions, blacks who lived in the area that later became the Sahara migrated to the Upper Nile Basin, which had a tropical climate. Some people were left behind but later migrated toward the south and further north.[55] This period was termed the Neolithic Era and lasted for six millennia. It was assumed that the best climatic conditions to support life existed between 5,500-4,000 BCE.

It was during this period that the first African population moved; this has been noted and documented by scientists from different disciplines.[56] When the climate deteriorated around 4,000 BCE, drought set in, lakes and rivers shrank, and water levels dropped drastically. These rivers had been flowing toward the River Niger

---

54 Bauval, Robert and Thomas Brophy, *Black Genesis: The Prehistoric Origins of Ancient Egypt* (Rochester, VT: Bear & Company, 2011).

55 Diop, p. 22.

56 Croegaert, Luc, *The African Continent: An Insight into its Earliest History* (Nairobi: Paulines Publications Africa, 1985), pp.15-16.

and the Atlantic, particularly the Bhar el-Ghazal and the River Nile. Due to uncontrollable grazing, vegetation decreased, and wildlife migrated in search of pasture.[57] The Nilotic people were among the first to camp and settle around the Upper Nile. It is likely that the first group found an indigenous black population in that region. It was the last ice age that brought dryness to the continent, and climate changes prompted cultural responses that forced people to migrate to search of better lives. Prior to the lakes and rivers drying up in the Sahara, hunting had been practiced for 18,000 years. As a result, competition for resources resulted in violence; existing evidence indicates that confrontations started about 14,000 years ago.[58] Climatic conditions had an adverse effect in the migration of people. The dense forests provided humans with plant foods and meat from wild animals. When the climatic conditions changed, the wild animals were forced to move near water sources, where they could find greener pastures. Similarly, people moved closer to water sources with their livestock.[59] When there were environmental changes, human migrations took place, and people went to camps near the water and food sources. The population that remained behind started to devise ways to survive. Some moved closer to the Nile, as it was the source of life, resulting in the establishment of the oldest kingdoms I recorded history.

Deliberate control of plant productivity dates back to 70,000 years ago, in southern Africa, and the world's earliest-known centrally organized food production system was established along the Nile 15,000 years ago – long before the Pharaohs – then swept away by calamities and changes in the river's flow-pattern.[60]

---

57 Ibid., p. 17.
58 Reader, p. 132.
59 Ibid.
60 Ibid., p. 145.

The climatic conditions in the African continent improved steadily about 125,000 years ago, and life became normal again. However, the earlier climatic changes had brought about new environmental challenges. The area that became the Sahara, for example, never changed into the forest again, and some rivers that had dried up never flowed again. One of the sites, Katanda, on the Upper Semliki River in the western Rift Valley of the Democratic Republic of Congo (DRC), in central Africa, became periodically cooler and drier. The invention of the spear is believed to have enhanced the hunting ability of the inhabitants, but unfortunately, widespread hunting led to the extinction of mammals. Earlier, people had fashioned barbed harpoons from bones and used them to catch catfish by spearing them in shallow rivers and lakes during rainy seasons.

The Katanda site is 90,000 years old and was occupied by people who manufactured specialized tools using sophisticated and complex techniques. They had formed large social networks and loved personal adornment, and often used symbols as a form of art.[61] In ancient caves, the drawings and symbols found on walls were signs of communication used by the group members. This was a common way of passing messages in ancient times. For example, when a man went out to hunt, he drew the 'hunting symbols,' which were understood by the community members to mean he was looking for wild game. Therefore, communication to alert members of the group about actions to be taken was more effective. They also planned and strategized effectively as a group, including designing appropriate tools for a variety of activities.

In the central and southern parts of the African continent, the dense African forest provided abundant and varied food sources. Combined with the huge size of the continent and the diversity of the environment, this resulted in high population growth.[62] As a result of these favorable conditions, the birth rate increased, and deaths declined; the living

61 Ibid., p. 136.
62 Ibid., p. 133.

conditions in Africa improved significantly. When climatic conditions deteriorated, the opposite happened. There were disruptions in human activities, and living conditions worsened. With little rain season after season, rivers dried up, plant and animal resources became scarce, the birth rate declined, and deaths increased, with young and old people being the first to perish.[63] As a result of all the poor climatic conditions, survival became a challenge, and there was nothing to eat.

The human fossils excavated in South Africa indicated signs of cannibalism, while fossils from the excavation site at the Klasies River mouth in South Africa show signs of de-fleshing (where someone scoops out the brain from the skull of a dead person using sharp, stone tools).[64] This must be taken on a case-by-case basis, because there are very few incidences where people in Africa have been reported to be cannibals. There are unverified historical reports of cannibalism in Africa, but most of the information is exaggerated. It could have happened a long time ago, but the cultural norms of communities living then would have quickly stopped the practice.

Following serious investigations into cannibalism among early communities in Africa, there was little hard evidence to support the wide existence of the practice. Although many authors report the disappearance of some species in Africa, according to their findings, such disappearances are attributed to hunting, which eventually led to the extinction of large mammalian species. The fossil records report the disappearance of 66 species from around 100,000 to 50,000 years ago, while 19 large *mammalian genera* disappeared around 1.5 million years ago.[65]

---

63   Ibid.
64   Ibid., p. 134.
65   Ibid.

THE PROGENITORS

Based on excavations conducted by British archaeologist A. J. Arkell along the Nile, rearing of livestock and subsistence farming existed in Sudan from the earliest of times. In excavations conducted near Khartoum and others conducted further south, unearthed materials indicated that ancient black people who had lived there grew grains and looked after cattle as early as 4500 BCE.[66] Pottery-making was also found to be an important activity of the time. Actually, the art of making pottery has been one of the chief activities associated with the black race for a long time. The Naath people today, in South Sudan and Western Ethiopia, make pottery and use it for cooking, storing grains, plates for eating, and keeping water. The accepted timeline suggests that black people occupied and lived in this territory long before any recorded invasion by the Arabs. Some Arab tribes, such as the Juhaynah, came to Sudan in the 11th century (1001-1100), which is considered to be the early part of the Middle Ages.

Upon their arrival from the north, the *Tharjiath Lich* (Lich Tree) became a focal point of departure toward the interior of Africa for all Nilotic people. More discussion on the Lich Tree will be presented later based on the way the Naath narrated it. In discussions on the origins of man, the elders often said that climatic changes, conflict, and expansion were the key factors that led to migration. Looking for sufficient rainfall, fertile soils, and opportunities for trade should also have been considered key factors for migration.

After a long time of settlement in North Africa, particularly Egypt and Sudan, the Naath people, together with the rest of the black people of the region, established the Kingdom of Cush, with independent leadership after other races came to settle in Egypt. Cush became a prosperous kingdom with lucrative businesses where many people came to trade across the region. Goods such as Ivory, gold, ostrich

---

66   Van Sertima, Ivan, *They Came Before Columbus: The African Presence in Ancient America* (New York: Random House, 1976), p. 117.

feathers, ebony, *tuok* and *nor* (palm fruits) were an attractive source of trade. Meroë was a wealthy metropolis in the ancient kingdom of Cush, located in what is now Sudan. The city flourished through trade between 800 BCE and 350 BCE. The Naath settled there for some time and became deeply involved in the management and construction of the city and control of its affairs. After shaky relations and the threat of conquest, the Nilotic people moved toward Khartoum.

Both oral tradition and historians narrated and documented the journey of the first man on Earth through Africa. It is within this belief that the Nilotic people trace their migration. Oral history, remembered by a few old men interviewed in South Sudan's Unity, Upper Nile, and Jonglei states pointed at central, western and north Africa – specifically, areas around Senegal, Cameroon, Mali, Ghana, Egypt, and Sudan – as the original lands of the people we today call Nilotic, including the Naath people prior to their migration toward the Middle East. This proposition may coincide with evolutionary theory via where the first human fossils were discovered. The Naath oral history was well-remembered by the older generations who are no longer alive, and they passed it down to their sons and daughters who later informed this writer. Only a few clues that were left behind helped to connect the dots in determining the narrative, and these were being told as stories where children gathered around a fire and a father began the story. It sounds like myth and legend. Certain tribes, like the Wolof in Senegal, have similarities with the Nilotic groups of South Sudan, especially the Nuer and the Dinka.

The second version of the oral history of the Naath was the version of the "Lich Tree," known as "Tharjiath Lich," which was believed to be the place where the first man was created. In fact, it may not be the first man who was created there, but it could be the place where the first Naath settled for the first time. There is no physical interpretation of the world "Chak," which is "creation" according to those who actually passed on the oral history, and there were no inquisitive minds to correct or provide evidence for that version of history. Elders I interviewed from 2014 to 2018, on the origins of the Naath people being placed on the Lich Tree, indicated that it was Ran Gam Rolnyang – with his wife, Nyawel Bhee, who was pregnant at the time with their son, Gaw Ran – who came with other migrants and chose to settle in the southern area of Kuerkuong. The area referred to as Kuerkuong includes the entirety of Koch County of the Jagei people, where the Lich Tree was later said to have been located, in Unity State of South Sudan. The Kuerkuong stretches from Lake No in the North of the state, Mayom in the west, Nyuong in the south, and Leer in the southeast.

Cheikh Anta Diop made comparative studies between the Naath (Nuer) and Jieng (Dinka) of the Upper Nile and Wolof in Senegal. The Wolof ethnic group could be found in West Africa around north-western Senegal, the Gambia, and southeastern coastal Mauritania. The only place they have dominated is Senegal, and in other locations, they are in the minority. From their physical appearance, skin color, names, and cultural practices, the Wolof are similar to the Nilotic community. It has been further stated that "Senegalese proper names still keep their meaning in the Upper Nile region, which they have completely lost in Wolof: *dieng* means rain in the Dinka language, etc. Some are in Upper Nile region compound names, which we can barely detect today in Wolof country. Many facts show their true Nilotic origin."[67] It has been noted that there was migration from the east in the Upper Nile that penetrated central Africa and headed to the west Africa region. The first arrivals happened in 102 BCE when the Sahara was drying up. History has it that the Wolof and others from Nilotic communities went to west Africa, leaving early when the Kingdom of Cush fell to foreign invaders. It has been further stated that the Bantu language was also brought by the Nilotic people: "The last ones during the protohistoric epoch might have consisted of the proto-Wangara of the Mandé language, where the tribes coming from the East brought

---

67 Diop, Cheikh Anta, *Civilization or Barbarism: An Authentic Anthropology* (Chicago: Chicago Review Press, 1991), p.181.

the neo-Bantu language."[68] The influence that lit up the interior of Africa was sparked in the Nile Valley, and matured in Egypt by the people we today call Nilotic. Black Africans penetrated back to central Africa through the White Nile, passing through Congo, the Blue Nile, and the coastal region of North Africa all the way to Senegal through Mauritania.

Pottery, cattle rearing, and agriculture were therefore part of the lives of Nilotic people in Sudan. There are some indications in Nilotic history, from the Naath and Dinka people, that Khartoum is a name that was associated with their local dialects and culture. Through migration due to wars and harsh environmental factors, people left Khartoum and the surrounding areas, but these areas were later occupied by Arab tribes who imposed their presence on that part of the land. A.J. Arkell found in his excavations interesting similarities among different groups of people living on the western side of the Nile in the Sahara Desert and what is now part of Darfur. This could be a pointer to the fact that agriculture in Egypt was introduced by the black people who inhabited it. It has been stated that "the Mandé people of West Africa created a center of plant domestication around the headwaters of the river Niger circa 4500 BC...Egypt gave nothing in the way of plants to Black Africa; Black Africans contributed the bottle gourd, the watermelon, the tamarind fruit, and cultivated cotton to Egypt".[69] The ancient people of Africa created the civilization and moved with it, and spread it to the Middle East as they traveled along Southern Arabia and the Mesopotamian plains.

After this development, the Caucasians realized that the Nile corridor had became a paradise, a land of abundance, and was a food basket; it attracted them and led them to come settle in the land. Tribes such as the Bedouins, Juhaynah, Ja'alin, Arab-Berber, Baggara, Hausa, and north African Arabs made it to Africa. This is confirmed by the Arab saying that "against the camel's mange use tar, and against

---

68   Diop (1991), p. 182.
69   Van Sertima, p. 118.

poverty make a trip to Sudan." To the Arabs, Sudan means Africa, because every corner of the continent was a paradise and a land of abundance. This trip to Sudan was not only for agricultural products, but also for tapping resources. Africans were also very generous and receptive to visitors. Oba Ewuare, king of the Benin Empire, ascended to power between 1280 and 1300 and was too receptive and willing to let guests dine in peace, and even said to "never make a stranger suffer and whatever else you may do to a foreigner, you must not kill him. Forgive his transgressions because he does not know the laws by which you live. Give him time and teach the laws of your land." As a result of that receptive statement, Chancellor Williams confirmed that "the Blacks were pushed to the bottom of the social, economic, and political ladder wherever and wherever the Asians and Mulatto offspring gained control. This scheme of weakening the Blacks by turning their half-white brothers against them cannot be overemphasized because it began in the early times and it became the universal practice of the whites and is still one of the cornerstones in the edifice of the power."[70] This is how Africa, the paradise, was nearly lost to invaders. The presence of Arabs in Africa had shifted the power balance and black Africans were displaced in the lands occupied at that moment by Arabs and pushed into the interior of Africa. Africa suffered from invasions from foreign forces. They occupied Africa and established their presence in north Africa, eastern Africa, western, central, and southern Africa. Their coming was not peaceful. Instead, they enslaved, murdered, and committed crimes of the highest order. The invaders harvested the people of Africa, shifted them into their countries and the Middle East, made them work on their plantations and militaries, and used them as sex slaves. It was the Arabs who captured Africans for slavery and later, this practice was followed by the West.

H.A. MacMichael, who wrote *A History of the Arabs in the Sudan*, confirmed that the Asians were also very proud of their mulatto sons

---

70 Williams, Chancellor, *The Destruction of Black Civilization: Great Issues of a Race from 4500 B.C. to 2000 A.D.* (Chicago: Third World Press, 1971), pp. 60–61.

with the black women they raped or took by force. It was a very confusing situation that women were used as sex slaves and gave birth to children whom their masters regarded as their own, and yet they didn't want to set their mothers free. The mothers had no freedom, worked as slaves, and were used as sex objects; yet their sons were widely accepted by their fathers and rewarded with total freedom. This enslavement resulted from the practice of slavery carried out by the Arabs and the people of the Middle East who came to North Africa. Common black African tradition and culture dictates that once you are in involved in a sexual encounter with a woman who becomes your wife by virtue of sleeping together, she will no longer be your slave, and you cannot mistreat her. Once you see her carrying your baby, she will no longer be seen as an enemy, but a member of a family. This humane behaviour of Africans was misconstrued by the West and Middle Easterners, such as the Arabs and the Persians.

There is also evidence showing that some groups of blacks never submitted to invasion and opposed enslavement. They fought to the death and were totally overcome and wiped out. Their traces are still visible thanks to the work of archaeologists throughout the northern part of Sudan. For many years, Africans held Upper Egypt while the Asians held Lower Egypt.[71] The first dynasty established by the pharaoh Menes after he defeated the Asians also resulted in the restoration of black rule in Egypt. After Menes, the fighting between Asians and Africans continued for 5,000 years. It was an unending pressure that exhausted the black people until they finally gave up the battle and the Nilotics moved down to Sudan.

The continent of Africa was called the black continent because of the inhabitants' color since creation, and because of the black cotton soil used for the cultivation of plants. It was the soil that gave energy to the Africans; it protected the people by preventing sickness. Some races took the name Black Africa and used it to refer it to what they thought was the backwardness of the people of the continent. This

71 Ibid.

came about because the history of Africa was written by outsiders rather than Africans, and there was a reluctant attitude from Africans to correct such negative branding.

There is growing awareness and consciousness of the past that was hidden by those who had the power to bend history to their will. Contemporary Africa is waking up and is tracing the early footsteps of the past and its ancestors who showed the world the road to civilization and made the black man's civilization known. More focus is being placed on writing history based on African lenses, and social scientists such as Cheikh Anta Diop, Chancellor Williams, and others have written extensively on the African origin of civilizations such as the ones we see today in Egypt, Sudan, Ethiopia, and Central Africa. They were products of the past and taught humanity. Luc Croegaert emphasized that those first Africans were not explorers, bold travelers, adventure-seekers, or scholars who were discovering new things for rarely read memoirs; nor were they officers who were tired of garrison life and who showed braveness in the jungle or looked for love and forgot their worries. They were distant pastoral hunters of the Neolithic period. They were there to find a suitable environment that could accommodate and sustain their lives.

As already argued, the west and central African regions are regarded as the location of the origins of mankind, implying that the origin of the earliest man is traceable to the Nilotic people. According to research conducted by Wyatt MacGaffey in Sudan in 1961, the people of Darfur, Dongola, and Kordofan seem to have the same origins, which in turn seem to lie in west Africa. An excavation conducted with the support from the Archeological Society of Sudan in areas of northern Sudan suggests that at one time, an invasion conducted by black people took place. This could well be the great invasion of North Africa/Egypt referred to throughout this manuscript. It is further believed that when the invasion took place, most people, especially the Nubians, were pushed toward South Sudan and eventually developed their own dialect and culture. We will read more in later chapters about how Nubians were descended from Mizraim and were the progenitors of those who established the ancient civilization of Egypt. They also developed strong social ties with the Nilotic people, who were the children of Cush – brother to Mizraim – as mentioned in the Bible. They were believed to have come from a country occupied by the Nilotic people, to which the Shilluk tribe belonged.[72] The various discussions given so far on evolution provide an alternative understanding of how humans emerged and migrated out of Africa to other locations. Those who purely believe in science strongly hold this view.

We now turn to the Biblical perspective of the creation of man, which is also held strongly by a sizable number of people interested in this field.

BIBLICAL CREATION

As you have read in scientific discussions of theories associated with the origin of man, religion looks at the spiritual and supernatural explanations of the universe's creation and origin. We could say that there shouldn't be a conflict between the two ontologies of religious faith and scientific understanding of our world. One of the unique characteristics of both ontologies is that they are searching for neverending knowledge, wisdom, and understanding of the universe. Let's read more about the Biblical theory of creation.

The Old Testament of the Bible tells us about the origins of the universe, in a sense that God's creation was done chronologically. He conducted the creation process, systematically making sure that He created different things every day for six days and rested on the seventh day. Everything He created had a purpose and a role to play. The main focus of His creation was the Garden of Eden, where He created the first man and his lifetime partner Eve (created from his rib). The

---

72 MacGarrey, Wyatt "The History of Negro Migrations in the Northern Sudan" (Chicago: University of Chicago Press, *Southwestern Journal of Anthropology*, Vol. 17, No. 2, Summer 1961), pp.178-197.

Garden of Eden was an earthly paradise and the home of Adam and Eve with everything He created, just like places discovered by scientists as being the cradle of man in specific locations in Africa. When God decided to populate the Earth, and the first man and woman were meant to colonize the planet, God created a situation that made them move out of the Garden of Eden.

Things started to change when God put man and woman in charge of everything He created. God told the couple that they could eat fruits from every tree in the Garden except the tree in the middle. This was a test He set for them, and He may have known that His creatures were going to fail the test. From that viewpoint, God wanted Adam and Eve to be "free" beings who could make willful choices and not be robots simply doing what they were programmed to do.[73] This was about independent choices that could make them choose between good and evil. It was done in consideration of the fact that the world outside would be cruel to His special creatures, so He had to devise a strategy to equip and prepare them for that life. God has no control over your independent choices, and only gives you guidance on the choices you make; and that's what was given to Adam and Eve in the Garden. Whether Adam and Eve had planned on the choice they made or not, it cost them their paradise, because the "fruit from the tree of knowledge of good and evil"[74] was eaten and this was an attractive fruit of a special tree that could hardly be resisted. The Bible, being a book of records of the past, was written to guide the actions of man and to bring him closer to God, with choices prevailing for Him. One of the important choices given to Adam and Eve focused on the tree, which was not to be tampered with. He also warned them about not eating the fruit, and if they did, they were "doomed to die."[75] Death, here, could mean banished from his creation as a sign of punishment, allowing them to live their lives without protectors such as the angels

73 Freedman, Sir Lawrence: *Strategy: A History* (Oxford: Oxford University Press, 2013).

74 Ibid.

75 Ibid.

who were guarding the gates of the Garden of Eden. The choice was provided, and the consequences of that choice were also stipulated. The test of their faith was part of the creation, and "if God really did not want Adam and Eve to lapse, it would have been simple not to put the fruit there in the first place."[76] The fruit became bait for their desire to leave the Garden of Eden. The serpent, the most cunning of all animals, was also part of creation, and could have been used as part of the plot to drive Adam and Eve out of the Garden of Eden. It approached Eve, trying to inquire if God had forbidden her from eating the fruit from the tree in the middle of the Garden. The serpent received confirmation that both Adam and Eve were not allowed to eat from the tree of good and evil. The serpent then informed Eve that God knew that if they ate from the tree of knowledge, they would become like gods; he then persuaded Eve to take a bite. Such statements from the serpent indicates that he was very much aware that God informed Adam and Eve not to test the fruit of the tree in the middle of the Garden. It could be inquired that if it was not a test from God, why did He place the tree in the middle of the Garden? Why was it created there, if it had no use for the creatures?

We know that "prior to the fall, the serpent was not only the most intelligent creature of all but perhaps the most beautiful also...the serpent did not crawl as it does today. It even had wings and stood upright".[77] We are further informed that the serpent was one of the creatures besides man that spoke in the Bible (Numbers 22:28). A donkey spoke too, and in Revelation 8: 13, an eagle talked; the serpent was a symbol of the treasury (Psalms 58:4; Matthew 23:33; Revelation 12:15). All these creatures had some distinguishing characteristic; they talked to each other and lived together in the Garden of Eden as creatures which were created for a purpose. If Adam and Eve could understand the language of the rest of creatures, this means that

---

76 Ibid.

77 Willmington Harold, *Willmington's Guide to the Bible: 30th Anniversary Edition* (Carol Stream, IL: Tyndale House Publishing, Inc., 1984).

they were all part of the same group of creation and had the same value in the eye of the Creator.

After eating the fruit, their eyes opened, and they realized that they were naked. They then sewed together fig leaves to cover their bodies. The test did not last. Eve was overcome by the persuasion of the serpent and ate the fruit. Realizing her mistake, she persuaded Adam to do the same. They both realized that they had sinned, and since Adam was at the center of creation, he blamed his ignorance and also pushed the blame back to God, looking at Eve as being his gift from God and the one who was deceived by the serpent, which resulted in their overall sin. Adam and Eve were created in the likeness of God and were in a position to differentiate between good and evil, and if they had not eaten from the tree of the knowledge of good and evil, they would have avoided death.[78] But since they did not comply, they were chased out of the Garden of Eden. Thus, began their migration to colonize the planet. The Bible is written in a way that you are meant to trust in God and obey his laws. If Adam and Eve had not eaten the fruit, they would have been immortal and lived forever – just like the angels, since they were created in the likeness of God and may not fall into sin – and the world would be a better place to live. Christians believe that after Adam and Eve were chased out of Eden, suffering became part of their survival as a punishment from God. Desertification, pestilence, and disease were the result of this punishment given to Adam and Eve.

The term "Eden" appears in several Sumerian texts that are written in that ancient language. Eden means "flat terrain" and refers to a particular place, which was reserved as the "garden of the gods" and located in Mesopotamia (modern Iraq) between the Tigris and Euphrates Rivers. The term "Sumer" in the ancient Sumerian language means the land of the "civilized kings," referring to Ham, Cush, Nimrod, and the rest of the ancient kings who made it great. It was also the land of the gods, with each god commanding almost a hundred smaller gods. The place was protected and guarded by the

---

78 Lawrence, op. cit.

gods. Humans and gods lived together, but humans were servants of the gods. The tablets of Nippur narrate the Sumerian creation story. The Epic of Gilgamesh (see below), which is believed to be the oldest written story on Earth, was one of the ancient Sumerian myths and was written originally on twelve tablets of clay in cuneiform script. The story talked about the journey of the historical king of Uruk, which took place between 2750 and 2500 BCE and resulted in the founding of the Garden of the Gods.

There are many assumptions regarding the exact location of the Garden of Eden, based on the narrative in the Bible. The Garden of Eden was the place where Adam was created as a human being from mud by God. The Garden comprised a dense forest of different types of trees, which produced a large variety of fruits. There were also different types of animals that freely roamed the garden. A big river watered the garden before it separated into four tributaries. The beauty of the garden was extremely pleasing to the eye, with all kinds of plants and creatures intermingling to produce a panoramic environment. It has been noted that in the middle of the garden, there was the tree of life and a tree of the knowledge of good and evil. According to Genesis 2:8–17, the Garden of Eden was home to humankind. The place was very fertile, since it was watered by the big river that had four tributaries flowing out of it. According to this explanation, it is highly unlikely that this was a small kitchen-like garden; it must have been a pretty huge garden that covered the entire region. The late Dr. John Garang, a Nilotic and the former leader of the Sudan People's Liberation Army (SPLA), commented on the size of the Garden of Eden, stating that:

> Many people will be surprised that in the Bible, in the Old Testament, the Sudan was part of the Garden of Eden, where it is stated in Genesis Chapter 2, Verse 8 to 14, that the Garden of Eden was watered by four rivers. One of them is the White Nile, [referred] to as Pessian in the Bible. The other one is the Gihon and note there is also Gihon Hotel in Addis Ababa, [which should hence mean] the Blue Nile. And to the East, [there were] Tigris

and Euphrates. So, the Garden of Eden was not a small vegetable garden. It was a vast piece of territory. My own village happens to be just East of the Nile. So, I fall within the Garden of Eden.[79]

Based on Garang's sentimental statements, one is convinced that the Nilotic people could have been part of the creation, if his description of the Garden of Eden happened to be true. They must have journeyed long and hard to reach where they live today. It is doubtful whether the Blue Nile was part of the four rivers that watered the Garden of Eden, but certainly the White Nile fits the Biblical description of the Garden of Eden.

Scholars and researchers have worked hard in trying to pinpoint the exact location of the Garden of Eden, but their efforts have not yielded much fruit. The descriptions of the rivers that are said to have watered the entire region covered by the Garden imply that these were big rivers that sustained lives. Most of the historical places that many writers perceive as part of the Garden of Eden have included Iran, Iraq, Turkey, and Israel. But as stated elsewhere, some evidence, both Biblical and scientific, gives the impression that central, east and west Africa resemble the Garden of Eden.[80] With such information, it could have been entire locations mentioned from the Middle East to Africa where the descendants of the black man lived since thousands of years ago until today. This is not stated here as a fixed position on the subject strictly set in concrete, but it is what some people with a different point of view believe to be the case. To rationalize their presumption, such people point out that central Africa historically refers to the region around the Ngorongoro Crater, where a great deal of archaeological work has been carried out.

---

79 Garang, John, "Garang's Speech at the Signing Ceremony of South Sudan Peace Deal", *Sudan Tribune*, January 9, 2005 (http://www.sudantribune.com/text-garang-s-speech-at-the,7476)

80 Jehovah's Witnesses, "Havilah", *Watch Tower* Online Library, retrieved June 24, 2019 (https://wol.jw.org/en/wol/d/r1/lp-e/1200001921).

THE FOUR RIVERS OF GARDENS OF EDEN

The first civilization of mankind was founded by black men along Asian borders, and it was centered between the Euphrates and Tigris Rivers. We are all aware where these locations are. These rivers flow from the mountains of Armenia at a southeast direction toward the Persian Gulf. The area is fertile because of lush deposits of soil brought down by the two rivers; and the civilizations of the rest of the world, including the Western and Eastern, were adopted from the black civilization. It is also believed that without black civilization, any other civilization would have been impossible. The Tigris and Euphrates regions were inhabited by many different tribes, and the places have had different names in the past, which included Sumer, Akkad (or Accad), Chaldea, and many other. The name of these locations was once known as Babylon. This is also the location of the Garden of Eden, and the people who inhabited this area were black people. According to the Book of Genesis, "[a] stream flowed in Eden and watered the garden; beyond Eden, it divided into four rivers. The first River is the Pishon; it flows around the country of Havilah. The second river is the Gihon; it flows around the country of Cush. The third river is the Tigris, which flows east of Assyria and the fourth river is the Euphrates." According to Rudolf R. Windsor, these were the four rivers that watered the Garden of Eden. Sudanese and Ethiopians are certain that Gihon, as mentioned in the Bible, is the River Nile, and it flows into Ethiopia (Cush) and Egypt. Interestingly, in ancient times, Ethiopia used to be two places: Eastern and Western Ethiopia (which literally mean Cush and Abyssinia, respectively). In the story of Babel, we understand that this tower was built by Nimrod, who was fathered by Cush, and the people who lived there were black. Again, in the areas watered by the four rivers where the Garden of Eden was situated lived the black people. According to Rudolf Windsor, "the people who reside in the lower part of the Tigris-Euphrates valley were Ethiopians, black in complexion." This is supported by evidence that Nimrod was the son of Cush and Nimrod was the mighty Ethiopian conqueror and builder of the land of Shinar, and he ruled over cities such as Babylon, Erech and Accad (Akkad). Cush had two children, Seba and Havilah, and Havilah became the name of a tribe which controlled a huge area of land. Different writers have located this land around the Persian Gulf.

We are further told in the Bible that Abraham was the father of the twelve tribes of Israel. The father of Abraham (Terah) came from the land of Ur of the Chaldeans, and this land was located at the southern part of the Euphrates. Chaldeans were one of the many tribes of Cushites, and it has been mentioned in this book that "Cush" meant "black" as well as referring to the land currently bordering Egypt. Cushites appeared to have spread from the Upper Nile to the Euphrates and Tigris Rivers, and more evidence indicates that nations such as Babylon, Akkadia, Sumer, and the Chaldea were inhabited by the Cushites. The kindred of the Sumerians or Cushites or Ethiopians were the people inhabiting Southern Iran, Afghanistan, Pakistan, and northwest India. The Sumerians founded cities that existed for more than 4,000 years, which included Eridu, Lagash, Nippur, Kish, and Ur. During ancient times (4000 BCE), Hamites controlled the great civilization soon after the flood. This civilization existed in Africa: the land of Canaan (Israel), parts of Arabia, Syria, Phoenicias, Turkey, Babylonia, southern Persia (Iran), and East Pakistan and most parts of India.[81]

The *Harper Collins Bible Dictionary* defined Babel as "Babylon," which is positioned as the Hebrew term. It was the site that recounts the origin of several languages when the people led by Nimrod settled in Shinar (or Sumer), built bricks, and burned them, and later built the tower with its top in the heavens to make a name for themselves. This tower angered God and He dispersed the builders before they could finish it. It is also the Akkadian name for the Mesopotamian city of Babylon, which covers over 2,000 acres, making it one of the largest

---

81 Windsor, Rudolf R., *From Babylon to Timbuktu: A History of the Ancient Black Races Including the Black Hebrews* (Atlanta: Windsor Golden Series, 1988), p. 19.

ancient sites located along the Euphrates River in an area where it approaches the Tigris River in what is now modern Iraq.[82]

PISHON RIVER

The Pishon passes through the entire land of the Havilah, and the land was full of gold, symbolizing its richness. Genesis 10:7 mentions that one of the sons of Cush was Havilah. It seems that Havilah could be one of the sons of Cush. We also know that Cush was the father of Nimrod, and he was later reported to be a mighty warrior on Earth, according to Genesis 10:8. There is confusion about where the land of the Havilah is situated. Some believe that this land could be located in Zimbabwe and southern Rhodesia, if we corroborate this information based on the scientific argument that the origin of humanity is in Central Africa. In addition, there are also sources that pointed it as coming from the Arabian Peninsula as detailed below:

A son of Cush, the son of Ham (Genesis 10:6-7). Many scholars view the name Havilah in this text as also representing a region, and the name may well have come to be applied to the area settled by the descendants of this son of Cush. Since the majority of Cush's descendants appear to have migrated into Africa and Arabia following the breakup at Babel (Genesis 11:9), it is generally suggested that the descendants of the Cushite Havilah are to be connected with the region called Haulan in ancient Sabean inscriptions. This region lay on the southwest coast of Arabia to the north of modern-day Yemen. Additionally, some suggest that, in course of time, migrants of this tribe crossed the Red Sea to the area now known as Djibouti and Somalia in Africa, the ancient name possibly being preserved there in that of the Aualis. (*A Dictionary of the*

---

82   Achtemeier, Paul J:.*HarperCollins Bible Dictionary* (San Francisco: Harper Collins, 1996), p..97

Bible, edited by J. Hastings, 1903, Vol. II, p. 311) It is equally possible that the migration took place in a reverse direction – that is, from Africa to Arabia. The strait of the Red Sea, called Bab el-Mandeb, that separates Arabia from Djibouti in Africa, is only about 32 km (20 mi) wide.[83]

Genesis 25:18 explains further that the land of Havilah extends to or near the Sinai Peninsula. The nomadic Ismaelites were also looking after their goats and animals in this region, across Arabia and into Mesopotamia. It's very clear that the Israelite King Saul also conducted some activities in that space during his reign (I Samuel 15:7). The land could extend even closer to Egypt.[84] There was good gold, which was precious, as well as plenty of aromatic resin and onyx.

GIHON RIVER

The Gihon River is one of the four rivers claimed to have branched out of the Garden of Eden. It was reported to have encircled the entire land of Cush, as stated in Genesis 2:10-13. Many have tried very hard to identify this river with confidence, but they couldn't. One assumption was that it could be the River Nile, and modern Ethiopians have already constructed a hotel named after it, the "Gihon Hotel." The reason why it is not possible to locate this river is that reading geography is difficult. If Gihon is the river that passes through the land of Cush, and the Garden of Eden is around the Iraq of today, then it is supposed to flow out of the Garden, not into the Garden, as it is now. We are sure that Cush is the land of Sudan, as recorded throughout the Bible. If that is the case, then there are some issues that we need to pay more attention to. Many have assumed that the Cush being talked about here is the land of Sumer, where Nimrod built

---

83 Jehovah's Witnesses, op. cit.
84 Ibid.

the Tower, and where languages were confused. The Araxes River (the modern Aras River) has been associated with Gihon. This in particular comes from the mountains near Lake Van and has an outlet in the Caspian Sea. Some lexicographers associated the land of Cush with the Akkadians, who currently occupy some areas in central Asia.[85] Every single person analyzing this issue of rivers has their own interpretation. The Sudanese interpretation is that there is not any other Cush land beyond the current geography of Sudan. Cush has been associated with the lands of Nubia, and Ethiopia in Africa. Much of this confusion has been blamed on ages of flooding and environmental degradation.

EUPHRATES RIVER

The Euphrates River is also called Fırat Nehri by the Turkish, and in Arabic, it's called Nahr al-Fur t. Its exact location is in the Middle East. It's one of the longest rivers in southwest Asia. It is about 1,740 miles (2,800 kilometers) long. It rises in Turkey and flows southeast across Syria and through Iraq. It was formed in the Armenian islands with the confluence of the Karasu and Murat rivers. It descends between the major ranges of the Taurus Mountains to the Syrian plateau.[86]

TIGRIS RIVER

The Tigris flows out of the Taurus Mountains in Eastern Turkey, and it is about 1,750 kilometers long. It is very close to the Euphrates River. They are only 30 kilometers apart from each other. It flows for 400 kilometers through the Turkish border. It's one of the rivers that pass-through Iraq, as mentioned in the Bible.

---

85 Ibid.

86 *Encyclopedia Britannica*, "Euphrates River": https://www.britannica.com/place/Euphrates-River

ADAM'S FIRST WIFE, LILITH

Some literature suggests that there was a woman named Lilith, who was created before Adam as his first wife. Due to a misunderstanding between the couple, she was later banished and disappeared out of creation and out of the Garden of Eden. There are a lot of stories tied to her claiming she went to the underworld and became a demon. She was rejected because she did not listen to and obey Adam, aa the role of a woman was to listen to her husband. That did not happen to Lilith. After she was banished, Adam's rib was removed, and Eve was created. The Bible is not specific on this, and the story of Lilith was removed out of the books that were assembled some hundreds of years ago to make the modern Bible. It has been said that "the traditional Bible has gone through many religious filters to ensure that it loses some of the important sections and pieces. However, there is a part that has been left in it that suggests God created not only a man, but a woman at the same time instead of later as it has been suggested in the Bible when the rib was taken from Adam."[87] The King James Bible, in Genesis 1:27, says, "So God created man in His own image, in the image of God created He him; male and female created He them." This could be translated as God creating both man and woman at the same time, and could be proof of Lilith's existence before her banishment. Lilith had been created equal to Adam by the same God who created him, and it could have been the same God who ordered her banishment. Her strength was compared to that of Adam, which means she was strong enough, and this could have translated into the idea that led to her disobedience to Adam.

Some religions, such as Catholicism, censored the apocryphal texts because they exposed things that could divert the attention of believers. Lilith had a firm character. She was intelligent and seemed to have

---

87   Disclose TV, "Lilith Was Adam's First Wife, Not Eve, But the Bible Kept It Secret": https://www.disclose.tv/lilith-was-adams-first-wife-not-eve-but-the-bible-kept-it-secret-315540

strength equal to Adam. But Adam was more dominant in character and had a carnal appetite. During intimacy, she wanted Adam to be on her, and at certain times, she could also be on him. But Adam refused. This generated conflict, which led to the departure of Lilith. During their argument, it was reported that Adam asked "Why should I lie beneath you? I was also made with dust, and therefore I am your equal." Adam tried to force Lilith to obey, so she angrily pronounced God's name and left and never seen again.

After she fled, it was stated that she ran straight into the arms of the devil – this was when all living creatures lived in the Garden of Eden, including demons. But the demons were not allowed to mingle with other creatures. Lilith left Adam and went to Samael, which was one of the demons, and bore him offspring. This is difficult to find in the Bible. After God banished Lilith, He realized that Adam was alone. This was when He started to make him a companion and later named her Eve, the mother of all the human beings on Earth.

JOHN MILTON'S PARADISE LOST

We have heard about the war in Heaven, the war of angels (good and bad ones), where Satan and his angels were defeated in their rebellion against God. Satan means "the light bearer", from when he was still a special child of God. In Pandemonium, the kingdom built after losing their battle and stronghold, the fallen angels had a council to strategize whether to return to the battleground against God. They did not agree, and instead "decided to explore a new world prophesied to be created, where a safer course of revenge can be planned."[88] While taking on the mission, Satan encountered at the gate of Hell his offspring, Sin, and Death, who opened the gate. While flying up, he saw the new universe being created floating near Heaven, bustling with glory. The Creator was aware of Satan flying to the new world

---

88   Milton, John, *Paradise Lost* (London: Samuel Simmons, 1667).

and saw the fall of man. Once Satan was in the universe, he flew to the sun and tricked the angel Uriel to direct him toward the new home of man. This is how Satan escaped on Earth.[89] While he was flying, scanning the vast and empty universe, he learned the location of the Garden of Eden, gained access, and saw Adam and Eve enjoying the beauty of it. He was jealous of the life Adam and Eve were living, and he heard them say that they should not eat the forbidden fruit. The gate of Paradise was being guarded by the angel Gabriel, and the angel Uriel, who Satan had tricked earlier, warned Gabriel and his angels that Satan was near and that they needed to be watchful. Satan was caught in the garden by Gabriel and the angels and was banished. Because God had seen the intention of Satan, that he was jealous and wanted to destroy Adam and Eve, the angel Raphael was sent by God to warn them. Satan later returned to the Garden of Eden as a serpent and found Eve alone and convinced her to eat the fruit of the forbidden tree. Adam did the same. This is how Paradise was lost by Adam and Eve.

In modern times, scientists are still struggling to locate the Garden of Eden. Some believe it was around the area of Mesopotamia, or present-day Iraq, while others believe it should be in the areas between central and east Africa where scientific discoveries placed it. Many pastors and priests who have studied the Bible believe that all human beings are the children of Adam and Eve, and the Nilotic people were the direct descendants of Nimrod, Cush, and Noah. They were directly created in the Middle East. They think, like other theologians, that creation took place in the Middle East. The Garden of Eden and the Tower of Babel (which will be discussed further) were products of the Middle East, and it was the black Nilotic people who stayed in those locations. There is a belief that Noah and Adam were the people that everyone else was created from.

---

89   Ibid.

JOURNEY OF GILGAMESH

There are stories about how the ancient gods are related to one another. For example, King Gilgamesh, who ruled in Uruk and was rumored to be the strongest man in the whole world, was created by the gods with strength, beauty, and courage. Uruk is another name for the city of Erech, which was located in ancient Mesopotamia. The Sumerian list of kinds puts this time around 4500 BCE. Gilgamesh was reported to be two-thirds god and one-third man. As the king of Uruk, he built its great walls and temples. Gilgamesh was described as an arrogant and harsh ruler. His famous documented journey into the wilderness was to find the legendary Utnapishtim, who was one of the survivors of the Great Flood that wiped out all human beings at one point in history. Utnapishtim also was granted immortality by the gods. Walking for days, crossing mountain ranges around the Mesopotamian border that no man ever crossed, Gilgamesh arrived at the Garden of the Gods. He met Siduri, who was the tavern-keeper of the underworld, and she warned Gilgamesh that he might not cross the sea. He was doing all this to seek immortality, and when he arrived and met with Utnapishtim on an island and told him that he was looking for eternal life, he was informed that he would not get it. Utnapishtim told him a story that years back, in the city of Shurrupak, the god Enlil got tired of the human beings who lived in the city because there was a lot of noise coming out of it. He decided one day to end the noise by creating a flood to destroy all the human beings. The god Ea told Utnapishtim in a dream that he should build an enormous boat and "sure enough, the flood came, and Utnapishtim, his family, his animals, and his craftsmen were safe. They all stayed at sea until a bird they released did not come back to the ship, having found the shore. The gods criticized Enlil for punishing humanity too harshly, and in return, he granted Utnapishtim his immortality."[90]

---

90   Glasserman, Ethan. "The Epic of Gilgamesh Plot Summary," *LitChart* (LitCharts LLC, May 9, 2016, retrieved . August 14 2018).

If we look at this story, it is so similar to the Biblical story of Noah, who was instructed by God to build a huge boat because God was determined to destroy mankind on Earth by sending a flood. Because God had mercy on Noah, he took his family into the boat along with other animals of different kinds. This is how mankind was preserved, and the Earth has filled again. This story is similar to the story told to King Gilgamesh, and we may not be sure how it found its way into the Bible. We are sure that there was no Bible during the time of Gilgamesh, and it was much later when Moses had a vision and wrote Genesis. There is more than this similarity alone; there was the Garden of Gods, visited by Gilgamesh in his epic. This was similar to the story of the Garden of Eden, as documented by Moses. It cannot be proven further who borrowed from whom in the similar stories in the book of Genesis and the Epic of Gilgamesh; what I can say is that something so suspicious requires further study and has to be looked into to give a bright side to reality.

CHAPTER 2

THE PROGENIES OF THE EMPIRE

"Considering how thorough-going was the capture of the minds of the Blacks, it is not surprising that so many Negro scholars still faithfully follow in the footsteps of their white masters. I was convinced that what troubled me and what I wanted to know, was what troubled the black masses and what they wanted to know. We wanted to know the whole truth, good and bad. For it would be a continuing degradation of the African people if we simply destroyed the present system of racial lies embedded in world literature only to replace it with glorified fiction based more on wishful thinking than on the labors of historical research."[91]

INTRODUCTION

Some scholars argue that the ancient civilization of Mesopotamia was initiated by the black people who came from Africa long ago. If we look back to 7,000 years ago, we are sure that the traces of early migration are very scanty, and we are left with very few historical records which still direct us to the origin and migration of black people.

---

91   Williams, op. cit.

Though scanty, there are still traces which have been buried deeply for thousands of years by the races who happened to dominate the black kingdoms for centuries. They started destroying what the ancestors of today's black people built by burning their records and destroying their monuments to erase history. For instance, when I visited Egypt in 2017, the noses and lips of monuments to the ancient pharaohs and the Sphinx were all dislocated. This was an indication of people trying to erase the things that show it was the ancient black kingdoms that developed the civilisation. Even the names of the ancient pharaohs are being changed by giving them Arabic names, to communicate that it was the Arab civilization that established the civilization (see more in Chapter Three).

The Ethiopians who have had "civilization attributed to them are inevitably located in the heart of Negro [Black] countries in the southern part of the northern hemisphere: Egypt, Arabia, Phoenician, Mesopotamia, Elam, and India."[92] Even during the Second Millennium BC (101 BCE), which was the period that marked the transition from the Middle to the Late Bronze Ages, black civilization has been in existence.

It is believed that the land of Cush was at one time visited by Noah before he took rest in the city of "Atlantis," which was built for him by Nimrod. Before this time, he was visiting all his grandchildren, including those that were in Libya, Egypt, Ethiopia, and Canaan[93]. Even the architectural design that Nimrod used for building the Tower of Babel (Genesis 11:1-19) was taught to him by Noah. Noah was given this technology by the angels, who authorized him to build a boat that would accommodate different species that were chosen to survive during the flood. Perhaps even the first stone used in the construction of the Pyramid of Giza could have been laid down by Noah, who constructed the Ark (Gen. 6:16).

The Bible talked about this, and history has discussed it openly too. Legends have it that the city of Atlantis was built by Nimrod himself,

---

92   Diop (1974), p. 152.

93   Achala, op. cit.

and most of the era's monuments, such as the famous Pyramids of Giza in Egypt, were attributed to him. If legendary stories and myths are correct, we may find his body in a tomb either in Ethiopia or around the Egypt-Libya border. Though social scientists do not believe this, since there are no traces or records that support the narrative, one emerging debate in the world of Egyptology is that the Pyramid of Giza is older than expected. Some maintain it was built long ago, and if proven, this could support the notion of ancient builders.

Ham was mentioned in the Bible as one of the sons of Noah, who became one of the survivors of the Flood. Noah gave birth to three children, one of which was Ham; Ham himself gave birth to four children whose presence was felt in the ancient world. His first son was Cush, followed by Mizraim, Put, and Canaan. it was Cush "who founded the kingdom of Ethiopia; Mizraim, his second son, founded the kingdom of Egypt; Put, his third son, founded the kingdom of Nubia; and Canaan, Ham's youngest son, founded the land of Canaan."[94] The current Israel and the Muslim Holy Land was located in the land of Canaan, which, through invasion, the Israelites and Arabs had controls over it (Genesis 15: 18-21; 26: 3, and 28: 13, and Exodus 23:31). After carefully analyzing the narratives about the land of Canaan, the last-born of Ham, the ongoing fight over the land of Canaan may not have an end soon, because neither of the two communities (Arabs/Philistines and Israelis) own that land. They both know it was the land of black people, the land of Canaan who was forced out by the Israelites immediately after their return from Egypt where they were hosted by their Canaanites cousins for 430 years. It had been a Biblical narrative, and now science has some findings on the ancient monuments and excavations that show descendants of Ham dominated the entire Middle East and the Levant for thousands of years.

The Bible has a fantastic narrative about Ham, who was the descendant of black people who settled in Sumer and gave birth to his four children – namely Cush, Mizraim, Put, and Canaan (Genesis

---

94   Ibid., p. 56.

10:6). After the expansion, these children over time migrated to Africa and established kingdoms. These ancient names could be felt currently in Africa. Children of Cush extended their settlement and established the Cushite kingdom in the current location of Sudan in east Africa. stretching to current Ethiopia, Djibouti, Somalia, and Kenya and some parts of the Great Lake Region. Mizraim went on to establish a kingdom in Egypt and maintained that northern corridor for generations; Put's descendants established their place in Libya, and due to their presence, there are whole debates about whether the word "Africa" may come from their tongue and influence. The last-born of Ham, Canaan, went forth and established himself in Canaan and had places in Philistine and the current Israel, Lebanon, and Syria. The Bible talked about this, and how they were black. They were the last to be displaced to Africa and integrated within the interior of east and central Africa. These kingdoms survived for a long time before the Arabs took them over and established their presence in North Africa. It is a sad fact that all of the original homelands of the blacks, and it is sad that their descendants were displaced leaving the monuments which have a special relationship to the people. In fact, the current children of Israel were the descendants of the children of Cushites through their father, Terah and Abraham (see further explanation below).

The Bible confirms that Noah, with his children, lived to see his grandchildren, and after the Flood, he lived for 350 more years (Gen. 9:28). One of grandchildren that Noah loved most was Nimrod, who was the firstborn of Cush. Nimrod, when he earned the name "The Great One of God," attained the height of his greatness by expanding his civilization around the face of the Middle East. Most of the historical cities that were built around the Middle East and North Africa were part of his great work[95]. The kingdom of Ethiopia, Egypt, some areas in the Middle East, and Canaan were his work. We are aware that the kingdom of Sheba, which was located in present-day Sudan, was previously known as Ethiopia, as discussed in the Biblical text (Isaiah 18).

---

95 Achala, op. cit.

After the Great Flood that wiped out nearly everyone as the Bible narrated, the descendants of Ham ignited the ancient civilizations and had them for thousands of years. One of the grandchildren of Ham who expanded this civilisation was Nimrod. It was mentioned that "Nimrod was instrumental in the initial planning and building of the Jebu, the name of the city of the Jebuscites which was later changed to Jerusalem. Nimrod had helped with planning and building it before proceeding to build the ancient city of Nimrud in Syria and later Nineveh."[96] Jerusalem was the land of Canaanites, and it was the Israelites, under the kingship of David, who displaced the Canaanites, claiming that it was their God who gave the Israelites the land of Canaan. This was the time when the Israelites left Egypt and were led to Canaan. The Israelites committed atrocities against the Canaanites. They castrated children and enslaved women, and the survivors escaped to Africa and joined their cousins (the other children of Cush, Mizraim, and Put, who migrated long ago to Africa). It is believed that even the current people inhabiting Israel, who claim to be Jewish and Israelites, may not be Jewish or Israeli by blood. Most of them have no connection with the Jewish people. Theories like this are circulating widely and portraying some trends depicting realities around a highly-charged political debate. There was no reason whatsoever that the Jews should turn against those who had been helping them for the 430 years they spent under black people's protection in Egypt when Jacob escaped hunger.

The origin of Israel is connected to Abraham, the son of Terah, who was Chaldean by tribe. The Bible mentions that half of the tribes of Israel were of African origin. Judah had a twin son with Tamar, who was a Canaanite woman (Genesis 38); Joseph married an Egyptian woman named Assenath and bore him children called Ephraim and Manasseh (Genesis 46:20). These people are important because they extend the bloodlines of their fathers and mothers, and this means that Israelites carry African blood. Abraham gave birth to

---

96   Ibid, p. 58.

Isaac, who gave birth to Jacob and Esau, and Jacob with his children migrated to Egypt and seek refuge and became the shepherds of the pharaoh's flocks. After 430 years, they left and occupied the land of Canaan, who was cousin to the black people of Egypt (Exodus 12:40). Moses, who took the Israelites out of Egypt, was trained and brought up by the Egyptians, and he was born 80 years earlier. Jethro's daughters mistook Moses for Egyptian because of his skin color when he helped at the well, and the daughters explained to their father that "an Egyptian delivered us out of the hand of the shepherds, and also drew water enough for us, and watered the flock" (Exodus 2:19). The name Moses was given to him by an Egyptian pharoah's daughter, and this makes it an African name; the Bible confirms that "Moses was learned in all the wisdom of the Egyptians and was mighty in words and in deeds" (Acts 7:22). Moses even married a black woman: It was said that "Miriam and Aaron spake against Moses because of the Ethiopian woman whom he had married: for he had married an Ethiopian woman" (Numbers 12:1).

The life and manners he had were purely the result of black people's courageous trainings and blessings and allowed him to succeed. At the time when they were in Canaan, the people of the Kingdom of Cush had been helping them against their opponents for thousands of years, including taking thousands of men to protect the city of Jerusalem from invaders. Black people opened their doors to the Israelites even at the time of the Babylonian Empire; when they were displaced, Babylon opened its doors.

Jesus Christ, the son of God, who is believed by Christians to be their saviour, came and took refuge in Egypt when he was born among the black children of the Egyptians. There is no reason true Israelites should repay the descendants of these black people with negativity, as we see today. Most of the ones inhabiting Israel today are not Jewish, based on their erroneous behaviour toward black people. There are beliefs that only 40% of the occupants of Canaan's land are actual Jews, and the majority of them are those who want to control the world using religion as a tool.

It is not a surprise that Mesopotamia (Babylon), Philistine (including part of Lebanon), Southern Arabia, Egypt, Libya, and Ethiopia were ancient kingdoms of the descendants of the people we today call Cushites – Mizraim, Put, and Canaan, who constructed the ancient Kingdom of Cush in Sudan, as well as the Egyptian civilization, Philistine and Libya. It has further been noted that when the prophet Mohammed was born, Arabia was a black colony with Mecca as its capital. It was around 560 CE that it was further invaded by an Ethiopian army of 40,000 strong men to crush the Arab revolts. The Ethiopians used elephants as their means of transportation.[97]

BLACK CIVILIZATION IN MESOPOTAMIA

Mesopotamia is a Greek word meaning "a land between two rivers", namely, the Euphrates and the Tigris. Both rivers divided the land into two. Before the arrival of the Greeks, the land was called Sumer, and its biblical name was Shinar. It is believed the civilization that sprung up in that area emerged before 3000 BCE. The people who lived during that period were Sumerians, who were jet-black. During that period, there had never been people of any color apart from the blacks to inhabit Sumer.

The term "Sumerian" was an exonym to apply to the Chaldeans as black-headed people, and their land was located at the southern part of Mesopotamia. This land was referred to as the "land of the civilized lords" by their neighbors, the Assyrians and Semitic communities living around them. Their original name could have been Sumer, and the Bible refers to them as Shinar, which is more less the same. The black people who lived in southern Mesopotamia were also called Akkadians, from their main city of Akkad before the building of Babylon.

---

97 Diop (1974), op. cit.

They settled in that flat region bordering Turkey at the southern tip of current Iraq. This was believed to be the ancient Garden of Eden, known in the Bible to be the place where the first human beings, Adam and Eve, were created. This indicates that Adam and Eve were from the same area and were created black, contrary to what the world portrays in its books.

As I pointed out earlier, the black people who lived in Sumer had different names applied to them. One of them was Sumer; Akkadians and Chaldeans were all black people, etc. Of all humans that dwell on Earth in 3500 BCE, Chaldeans were the first that had civilization before imparting it across the region and the world. While the rest of the inhabitants of the other continents were in a barbaric state, the Chaldeans made discoveries and established governance in their region.

Rudolf Windsor is an internationally known author and speaker in the areas of history. He is the author of many books, including *From Babylon to Timbuktu*. He argues that the people who lived in the lower part of the Tigris River were Ethiopians, and black in complexion; and this, he thinks, means there were two distinct groups of Ethiopians at the time. He thinks that there were Ethiopians in southern Mesopotamia, and another group which bordered Egypt in Africa. What Windsor failed to understand is that there were not two main Ethiopian groups in ancient times. In fact, the Chaldeans of Akkad, dwelling in Sumer and Babylon, went and occupied the land known as Ethiopia after migration into Africa. Those he refers as ancient Ethiopians in different lands were, in fact, the same people, and it was only the names that changed as they migrated. They came to acquire the name Nilotic as they moved along the Nile.

Sir Henry Creswicke Rawlinson was a Major-General, 1st Baronet, GCB, FRS, and a British East India Company army officer, politician and Orientalist. He wrote extensively about the Middle East and is sometimes referred to as father of Assyriology, which is "the science or study of the history, language, and antiquities of ancient Assyria and Babylonia". Assyrians were the ancient rivals and neighbors of the Babylonians, who lived alongside them.

Rawlinson lived from around 1810 to 1895, and he found that the people who established civilization in Babylon were of Cush and Cushite origin. The people who once inhabited Akkad and Sumer were both black people, and they called themselves *Sag-gig-ga*, which means "black-headed people". This name was given to them by the neighboring tribes, who were Semitic people. Akkadia was one of the lands that were occupied by the black-headed people for generations and conquered by force.

John Denison Baldwin was an American politician, Congregationalist minister, newspaper editor, and popular anthropological writer who wrote a book titled *Prehistoric Nations*, published in 1869; he specified that those early colonists who occupied ancient Babylonia were the same race of people then occupying the Upper Nile region in Sudan. These people were later called Nilotic and made the Upper Nile their home. He referred to them as colonists because, at one point, they migrated out of Africa, which is believed to be the cradle of man, to venture out to find a better life and a place to live. They occupied the land of Sumer and settled there.

Researchers who conducted investigations obtained evidence and positioned their views conclusively that it was the Cushites or Ethiopians that were the originators of the Chaldeans of Babylonia. The traditions and cultures of Babylonia have a connection to the early times of Ethiopia and Southern Arabia (southern Arabia was also inhabited by black people) and cities of Lower Euphrates. The Ethiopian (Cushite) names such as Makkan and Mirukh (Ethiopia) have a very close connection to the cities of Ur and Akkad. Cushites were the first to build along the Euphrates River, and the pronunciation of the names of their leaders are connected to Ethiopia in a way that cannot be accidental. Such evidences are recorded in inscriptions, and Rawlinson, in his essay "Early History of Babylonia" talked about this conclusive evidence.[98] Baldwin further mentioned that investigators should try very much to be neutral in providing judgment of

---

98   Baldwin, John D. *Prehistoric Nations* (New York: Harper & Brothers, 1869), p. 192.

the past so that history can be told freely, away from bias, and made the following statement:

> If every competent investigator would allow himself to see and comprehend the country which the ancients designated as Ethiopia and the Land of Cush, there would be no failure to recognize Arabia as the mother country of Chaldea; and there would be a more intelligent appreciation of the large amount of ancient tradition which brings the Cushites into that part of Asia, and sometimes describes it as a part of Ethiopia. It was Ethiopian in race, language, and civilization, and constituted a portion of the wide-spread territory occupied by the Cushites, from the extremity of the east to the extremity of the west.[99]

In Southern Arabia, the ruins of materials found belonged to the great ages of Cushite supremacy, though they are so old, there was no proper excavation conducted, since there was less interest from archeologists to dig them. The language of Arabian inscriptions found is believed to be related to the ancient Chaldeans.[100] These old Cushite tongues are still being spoken today in some districts of Arabia and eastern Africa. It was when wars of displacement from Assyrians intensified against the Cushites led to the mass migration to Africa that they settled in Eastern Africa. Baldwin further stated that in Chaldea, there were about 163 kings who reigned, and if about 20 years of leadership and if about 20 years is allowed for each to rule, then we can estimate how far their kingdoms spread before they were disposed of. Their kingdoms would have gone beyond 4662 BCE, and this would make Chaldea as old as Egypt; due to political changes, their kingdom was disposed of. He further believed that based on the research, it seemed all the kings belonging to this era reigned at Erech, and the kingdom of Chaldea, just like

---

99   Ibid.

100 Ibid., p. 193.

any other Cushite nationalities, could have been a union of municipalities, each having a local government or prince of its own, as can be seen in the Arabian kingdom of Oman. Each one of them decided the rules of his own city.

The Egyptians refer to Chaldeans as *Ki-en-gir* or Hittite, and all of these could mean Sumer. It has been considered that Mesopotamia is the cradle of civilization and the genesis of all the civilizations that followed. Some of the reasons that led to the Sumerians' move to Egypt included wars, and the land becoming dry and very humid,

Image depicting the colour of Jesus Christ and his disciples after his resurrection. It was bought from Nicholas Kyrodos from Greece in the 18th century.
Courtesy to Coptic Church, Cairo, Egypt. 2018

which resulted in very little rainfall. It was very cold during winter, and the mountains were covered in ice, resulting in the over-flooding of the two main rivers. Though this flooding every year carried silt, which is fertile, and deposited rich soil on the bank of the river, the Sumerians felt the need to move and look for a new colony, and this resulted in their migration back to Africa. They had to cross to the northern tip of Africa, which happened to be Egypt. As mentioned, wars in Sumer added to their migration, and forced them to move to the southern part of the kingdom, toward Africa. A majority of them went to the areas where the children of Ham had been going in a mass migration over time.[101]

It has been discussed that Abraham's father, Terah, who is one of the fathers of the twelve tribes of Israel, came from the land of Ur of the Chaldeans. This has been written in the Bible (Genesis 11:26-28), and history narrates that the land of Ur belongs to Chaldea and is located at the southern tip of the River Tigris. Chaldeans, as we know them, are one of the many tribes of Cushites, and we are made aware by the Bible that Cushites are black. By this narrative, Terah was of the Chaldeans, and he was a black man who fathered some of the tribes of the current Israelites (through his son Abraham married Sarah, who was his half-sister from Lot who lived in Harran City). Thus, the descendants of Abraham, who later became the Israelites, were the descendants of the black people of the tribes of the Cushites. According to the Song of Songs 1:5-6, which is a dialogue between an unnamed woman and unnamed man in which the woman represents the Jewish people while the man represents God, Jesus said "I am black, but comely, O ye daughters of Jerusalem, as the tents of Kedar, as the curtains of Solomon. Look not upon me, because I am black, because the sun hath looked upon me: my mother's children were angry with me; they made me the keeper of the vineyards, but mine own vineyard have I not kept." This could be another proof that Jesus was black, as were most of the Jewish people. We can also state that

---

101 Achala (2011), p. 230.

Moses and Paul were also taken for black people when they were in Egypt (Acts 21:38). Moses grew up with the children of the pharaoh, and he could not be differentiated from them. Moreover, Jesus was brought to Egypt when King Herod wanted to kill him. This is because Egyptians and Israelites were the same people of the same skin, and one could not differentiate between them. When Jesus grew up, he had the traits of the what people called blacks, including thick lips and woolly hair.[102] There was no point in taking baby Jesus to a black country if the boy was brown. You cannot bring an Israeli child of today to Leer town in South Sudan and expect him to grow up there as easily as anyone else.

It has been further mentioned that Canaan, who was the last born of Ham, established his kingdom in Canaan and was later displaced by the Israelites 430 years ago. This was after the Israelites were allowed by the children of Mizraim to live freely in Egypt. After so many years, they decided to go to the land of Canaan, because their God instructed them so. They fought with the Canaanites for years, and even Goliath was from the descendants of Canaanites. This displacement happened because Noah, who was the father of Ham, cursed him, and the curse went directly to his last-born, which happened to be Canaan. For the curse to be true, the land of Canaan was given to Israelites who had no land and were wandering around the region without a fixed place. Names such as Philistine and Jerusalem (from one of the children of Philistine named Jebucite) were purely black names, and this is in association with the early expansion of children of Ham when Canaan left Babylon for the land he named after himself. The names Philistine and Jebucite were some of the children of Canaan. They came and occupied some parts of Kenya and central Africa.[103]

---

102 Whitakre, Robyn J., "Jesus Wasn't White: He was a Brown-Skinned Middle Eastern Jew. Here is Why That Matters" The Conversation, March 28, 2018 (https://theconversation.com/jesus-wasnt-white-he-was-a-brown-skinned-middle-eastern-jew-heres-why-that-matters-91230).

103 Achala, op. cit.

After displacement, the Semitic groups who were bordering Philistine encroached onto the land and mixed with the remnant of the black people of Canaan who did not escape. They intermarried and lived with them in Philistine, and this is why the name still exists today. This also explains the reason why the situation in the Philistine state will not easily be settled. The Israelites believed that their God gave Philistine to them and it is their religious duty to take over the land (Genesis 15: 18-21, Exodus 23:31) while the Philistine maintains that the land was for their ancestors and Israelites have no rights to take the land away from them. The Israelites think all the Philistines were displaced to Africa, and the remnant is not pure black people; and it is the Semitic groups that have occupied the land of Philistine and are claiming that they were the owners of the land.

The Cushites are the current Nilotic tribes, the ancient people who occupied Babylon, part of Arabia, and Ethiopia. It is beyond a reasonable doubt that the ancient nations of Babylon, Akkadia, and Sumer were inhabited by the Chaldean tribes. These Chaldean tribes, after thousands of years, can be traced into the Nilotic group of South Sudan today, and one of the tribes could be the Naath people of Africa inhabiting South Sudan and Ethiopia. Some of the tribes have moved to east Africa due to their migration to find a suitable place to live. The Nilotic tribes that inhabit eastern Africa are the descendants of the group of black tribes that lived in Mesopotamia. The Naath can be traced to the ancient Chaldeans people of Babylon, and after years of migration, the name changed to Naath.

Through tracing the pages of history, the present-day people called the Naath are believed to be the direct descendants of the ancient people of Chaldea. This is supported by their migration and their ancient cities such as Harran City, which happened to fall within the borders of the territories of Turkey and Iraq. The ancient architectures of the Nuer buildings can be seen standing today. Tourists flock to have a look at it. The only problem is, the credit is not given to black people; instead, the Turkish people think it was their ancestors who built them.

Harran City is one of the ancient places where the Chaldeans used to live. It is located in southeastern Turkey (Upper Mesopotamia). The villages are made of beehive-style houses and occupy about 300 acres of ruined land. This was one of the ancient places of the Harran people – namely, Chaldeans. It was located in a fertile area, and the residents traded in textiles. It was also a holy city where the moon-god named Sin was worshiped. The Naath term "Han-ran" came from that ancient city; Hanran means "I am a human being," and this was the name of the city during ancient times. The Naath who are currently in South Sudan still use the term "Hanran," taken from the name of the city of Harran in Babylon. Throughout the generations, the meaning and the spelling have both have changed. Harran became an identity to the Naath, to inform people that they are from the city of Harran city in the Sumerian region of Babylon. If you look at their ancient beehive buildings which are still standing even today, you can tell that it is the same style of building that the Nilotic have presently in Sudan. It was in the late Third Millennium BCE when Harran City was abandoned after so many wars occurred in its territory and the Chaldeans were displaced to Africa. It was taken over by different regimes until its history was lost. Some Naath people occupying islands in India are believed to be part of the Nilotic community. Moreover, there are some Naath people in continental India living there permanently as a result of the dispersal, and they still maintain their culture and tradition.

After a long time, they changed their name from Sumerian and took the name Naath; this was why the ancient Egyptians referred to them in this way. After some thousands of years living along the Nile Valley, they were given the name Nilotic. Their movement did not stop in Egypt or Sudan; the descendants of Ham proceeded to the interior of Africa and east Africa. This migration is believed by many people to be a return after the early phase of migration from central and east Africa, where Black people were believed to have originated as is very vocally affirmed by science. William Chancellor affirmed "the Sumer legend that there was a conversation between the old man and the traveler. The traveler asked the old man, 'What became of the Black People of Sumer? For ancient records show that the people of Sumer were Black. What happened to them?' The old man responded. 'Ah,' the old man sighed. 'They lost their history, so they died.'"[104] A race is considered lost when they have forgotten their language and their history, and this is what has happened to the black people who came from the Middle East. Naath, in particular, could be categorized in this situation. They have lost their history, their language, and their landmarks, and are not sure of their origin. Without your history and language, you could be considered lost. The old man's conversation is right, and since the blacks have lost their history, they are no longer conscious unless their history is traced back, and that is when they will have a sense of direction and sense of ownership.

Along the stretch of the Tigris and Euphrates Valley, people who were full of energy, known as Sumerians, built the world's first cities more than 5,000 years ago. They were the first to invent a system of writing and were also the first to use wheeled vehicles. It is mentioned in the Bible that it was the descendants of Ham (Africans) that built and occupied Mesopotamia, and they were called the Sumerians.

The word *Cush* came from the Cushites. *Cush* means the elder son of Ham, and is literarily referring to the ancestor of the black people who inhabited east, north, and some parts of west Africa such as Senegal; it is also another name for Ethiopia, which comes from Greek word *Aithiop* meaning "black" or "burnt face." Archaeological sources state that Cush is another name for the Upper Nile or ancient Nubia.[105] It is the area that extends from Sudan to the Horn of Africa, up to the eastern side of the Red Sea. The occupation of this region dates to about 3800 BCE, and has the oldest known agricultural tradition, occupying almost the same geographical place as that of the Sumerians.

---

104 Williams, op. cit.

105 United Nations Educational, Scientfic, and Cultural Organization, "Archeological Site of the Island of Meroë": https://whc.unesco.org/en/list/1336,

It is stated that "Sumer is the government of Nimrod and people were called Sumerians. In Naath, Sumer could be translated as *Ruel*, which are the months starting from April-June. This is the time when Nimrod established his kingdom in that region."[106] This reflects the area where Nimrod built his tower along the swamps of Shinar, which resembles the name Dapany in Naath. The features of the Sumerians have been mentioned by Sir Henry Rawlinson as dark chocolate or dark-complexed, long stature but sturdy frames, oval faces, stout noses, curly hair, and a full head, just like the ancient Egyptians. There were wars since 2300 BCE; a man named Sargon the Great of Akkad conquered the Sumerians and ruled over the city of Kish, which was situated in part of ancient Mesopotamia. He was from the Semitic desert group of nomads who later settled in Mesopotamia just north of Sumer. He ruled from 2334-2279 BCE. Widely read books such as the Bible mentioned that it was the Ark of Noah he designed with the help of the angels that set off the civilization, followed by his sons. This skill was imparted by Noah to his grandchildren, as stated below:

> Noah was able to train his sons, his grandsons, his great-grandsons including some great-great grandsons himself before he died. It is clear that Noah was the one who used God's architectural knowledge of the Ark to build the kingdoms of his four grandchildren, namely Cush who founded the kingdom of Ethiopia, Mizraim who founded Egypt, Put who founded Nubia, and Canaan who founded the land of Canaan.[107]

As can be seen, all the descendants of Africa belong to Ham, who had all the four children that are believed to have migrated to Africa; and some of his descendants are currently occupying the Middle East, southeast Asia, and southern Arabia. Cush is the name of Ethiopia,

---

106 Chuol, Stephen Kuony, Moderator for the Presbyterian Church of Bentiu, South Sudan (personal interview, April 3, 2017).

107 Achala, p. 59.

and the people called themselves Cushites; this name was retained after the dispersal from the Tower of Babel and Babylon. The name Cush also appeared in India, and it is believed that it could be one of the Cush's sons that retained that name there. For an instant, there was a tribe named Gaetuli who were in North Africa; they were the descendants of Havilah, who was the son of Cush. Prior to this, Havilah settled in an area which is currently Arabia, so he may have migrated from there to part of North Africa as the result of persecution from the descendants of Shem. Arabia was taken over by children of Abraham and Ismeal, who became the descendants of the current Arabs and Israelis. Taking over the land caused most of the people that were in the Middle East to migrate to Africa, which was populated by their cousins and brothers.[108]

According to the Bible, it was Ham's son Cush who is credited for founding the Babylonian Empire, and his empire goes back before 3500 BCE. After Cush, it was his son Nimrod who continued building the city and extended his rule to conquering his neighbors, taking over Uruk, Akkad, and Calneh (all these towns are in the modern geographical location of Iraq).[109] In Assyria, the cities of Rehoboth, Nimrud, and Resen were also taken over by Nimrod. He also founded Ninevah, and was the first emperor after the Flood. It was during his fall when the Babylonian Empire crumbled and led to the migration of the black[110] people out of Mesopotamia. Before the world was divided into its current shape, the children of Ham enjoyed peaceful domination in construction, prosperity, hunting, and seafaring, and new kingdoms were constructed for his children and relatives such as the Philistines. Nimrod himself was considered a great one because he

---

108 Hodge, op. cit.

109 Every Child Ministries, "From Babel to the Beginning of Egypt, 5000-4000 BC to ca. 3300 BC" (http://ecmafrica.org/teachingforafrica/sites/default/files/II%20Babel%20 to%20Rise%20of%20Egypt.pdf).

110 Ibid.

this all took place at the height of his civilization.[111] It could have not been a mistake when it was said that descendants of Ham were the first to forge a civilization since the time of the well-documented Great Flood, before the Earth took its current shape. Ham was the father of the African nations. Cush was the father of the Cushites, who are a black nation. Nimrod was a Cushite who founded Babylon, which was a Cushite empire.

The descendants of Ham include Cush, Mizraim, Put and Canaan. Cush had the following children: Seba, Havilah, Sabtah, Raamah, and Sabtechah. The sons of Raamah were Sheba and Dedan. Mizraim had the following children: Ludim, Anamim, Lehabim, Naphtuhim, Pathrusim, and Casluhim, from whom came the Philistine and Caphtorim. Canaan had the following children: Sidon, his firstborn; Heth, the Jebusite (from whom the word Jerusalem came); the Amorite; the Girgashite; the Hivite; the Arkite; the Sinite; the Arvadite, the Zemarite; and the Hamathite. Around 1550 BCE, the family of Canaan was dispersed around the world. The border that constitutes Canaan includes Sidon as you go toward Gerar, as far as Gaza; then, as you go toward Sodom, Gomorrah, Admah, and Zeboiim, up to Lasha. These sons of Ham had one language and one skin color, which was black.[112] Put established similar kingdoms in the open land of northern and western Africa and created kingdoms in what we know today as Libya, Chad, Niger, Nigeria, Cameron, Algeria, Mali, Morocco, Guinea, etc. History had it that Mavulis, who is the descendant of either Cush or Mizraim, sailed to Australia and founded the tribe known today as Maoris. Some of them moved to west Africa and established the place that became the country of Mauritania.[113] People such as aborigines, who are living in Australia today, were the waves of those who got displaced and moved further to that far land.

---

111 Achala, p. 57.

112 Hodge, p. 30.

113 Achala, pp. 67-68.

As mentioned, the descendant of Canaan, the Jubusite, established a city and named it Jebu; it later was renamed by King David when he occupied the land as "Jebu Salem" (Genesis 14:18-20). He was in the process of naming it Jerusalem to make sure that the name Jebu disappeared after a long period of time. Prior to their displacement, the Jebusites named one of the hills on which the soldiers were guarding the city Zion. This is the place where a castle was erected against invading enemies. Zion had been under the control of the descendants of Canaan until they were overrun by King David. This was also mentioned in I Chronicles 11.5.[114] The original Zionists were the descendants of Canaan, who was the youngest son of Ham, and he was black. They lived in that land undisturbed for more than a thousand years, and built for themselves kingdoms, from the time of Great Flood until the destruction of Tower of Babel. In addition, "the Canaanites and the rest of descendants of Ham that were escaping from being killed in the Holy Land, Ethiopia, Egypt, and Nubia (Sudan) by invaders started migrating toward the South of the Sahara. The largest movement to Africa started with the arrival of the twelve tribes of Jacob after 1100 BC, the time when the land of Canaan was occupied."[115] The influence of the children of Ham was felt far and wide, and they were in control. Edwin Sammy Achala is a researcher with a Biblical viewpoint that the descendants of Canaanites who escaped persecution are the current tribes who are occupying Kenya today such as the Luhya and Nyika. Some of their names include Samlah, Mukuba, or Mulukoba, and others have a prefix that indicates the city of Jebu, such as Jebuduli, Jebusaga, Jebuses, etc.[116] They came to join their relatives in Africa escaping from the persecution.

Based on Cushite traditions, Nimrod was celebrated under different names as one of the greatest personages in the early history of the Chaldeans. Inscriptions informed us that it was Nimrod who recon-

---

114 Ibid., p. 68.

115 Ibid., p. 70.

116 Ibid.

structed Chaldea politically and took control of the cities, becoming a supreme authority throughout the country.[117] It was after the closing period of the old kingdom of Chaldea when the city of Babylon became famous and important. The date when the astronomical observations started in that city is the oldest beyond expression. The Cushites or Chaldeans started astronomical observations in 2234 BCD and founded Babylon. This was also mentioned by Callisthenes, who wrote to Aristotle that the period "began with this date, therefore Chaldean history must begin with it; no monument of that land must be more ancient; the dynastic list of Berosus must not be allowed to reach farther back into the past; we must reverently accept this date as the chronological limit of human inquiry, beyond which there is nothing but thick darkness haunted by a few shapeless phantoms of fable."[118]

The Bible described Nimrod as a great hunter who liked to dress up with his trophies of the hunt, which included leopard skin and horn headdresses.[119] Even today, most African cultures, particularly the Naath and the Jieng people, still use leopard skin for their rituals and sacrifices, just as their forefather Nimrod did in Babylon. Horns are still being used as trumpets for war. It is mentioned in different historical texts, including the Bible, that Babylon was the empire where the languages of the world were distributed after the fall of the Tower of Babel, which was built during the leadership of Nimrod.

Different writers who base their interpretations on the Bible put Nimrod in the negative side of history, and they refer to him as evil and as a "Satan reincarnation," which means he was the source of the practices of divination in use throughout African culture and tradition. There is a practice of such activities in Africa, but the culture does not associate this with Nimrod. Some theologians decided to associate this claim with Nimrod, yet the Bible is open about how great Nimrod was

---

117 Baldwin, p. 202.

118 Ibid.

119 Ibid., p. 1.

in the ancient world. Such documents were written through the lenses of Biblical philosophy, and the use of this 'good and evil' perception was taken to explain Nimrod and his kingdom. It is hard to share such claims with individuals who attempted to impose biased views upon Nimrod:

> Nimrod was a tyrant and a dictator who desired to wrest the people's loyalty from God so that all power would rest in him. The Bible describes Nimrod as a great hunter. He dressed up in trophies of the hunt. His emblem was a spotted leopard's skin, and this is the origin of leopard skin as the chiefly symbol of the Bantu tribes [and Nilotic people]. He was known to the Greeks as Nebrod, the spotted one, since he wore spotted robes. He also wore a horned headdress, and so was called 'the horned one'. It is believed that he subdued leopards and horses for use in hunting. Some feel his name comes from *Nimr-*, leopard, and *rad-*, to subdue. (Sometimes leopards are still used for hunting in India.) Nimrod was most definitely a wizard, and some feel, Satan incarnate. The practice of divination before the hunt undoubtedly originated with him. Some have said that the proposition in Genesis 10:9 translated 'before' in the King James Version can also sometimes mean 'against.' That is, he hunted against the Lord, not only animals but also the souls of men by witchcraft. There is evidence that he warred on those who remained faithful to God, especially on the line of Shem.[120]

Nimrod was praised throughout the Bible, and his presence and innovation and leadership were felt. He was credited with the ancient empires in the Middle East and Africa. We can still see the ancient practices of the Nilotic people, especially the Naath and Jieng tribes, such as hunting, even in South Sudan. Naath has the Kuarmuon (earth master) and Kuarhok (cattleman), who use leopard skin for their powers, and the Dinka have their own names for the same practices.

---

120 Every Child Ministries, p. 1.

Even the use of leopard skin as a means of divination is being currently practiced by the Cushites, or the Nilotic people. However, we cannot guarantee that it was Nimrod who originated divination, or what others considered Satanic rituals. They may have seen practices contrary to their beliefs, but that was how the black people communicated with their god. The lineage from Cush through Nimrod has a powerful connection with the Africans and the Nilotic people, mainly the Nuer and the Dinka people of South Sudan.

Whether the practice of divination began with Nimrod is what is not clear in the practice of the traditional beliefs of the Nilotic community. We could not say Satanic reincarnation practices began with him or he had something to do with it. What we are sure of, however, is that everyone has their own story to tell, and that there is someone who blames him. He was seen as a symbol, channeling the negative side of good and evil, and had to endure discrimination. Flavius Josephus further complicated the account of Nimrod by saying that it was Nimrod who tried very much to build his tyranny among men, and it was he who offended God by turning away. He stated that:

Now it was Nimrod who excited them to such an affront and contempt of God. He was the grandson of Ham, the son of Noah, a bold man, and of great strength of hand. He persuaded them not to ascribe it to God, as if it was through his means they were happy, but to believe that it was their own courage which procured that happiness. He also gradually changed the government into tyranny, seeing no other way of turning men from the fear of God, but to bring them into a constant dependence on his power. He also said he would be revenged on God if he should have a mind to drown the world again; for that, he would build a tower too high for the waters to be able to reach! and that he would avenge himself on God for destroying their forefathers![121]

---

121 Josephus, Flavius, *Josephus: The Complete Works* (Harrington, Delaware: Delmarva Publications, 2016), p. 62.

It is assumed that a large number of people started to follow the lead of Nimrod when he was establishing his kingdom in Shinar and expanding it to Uruk, Akkad and Calneh cities, conquering them by force. Despite being referred to as someone who was against God, he also made a name for himself and for humanity by building a structure whose top reached the clouds. The building of the Tower of Babel was later confirmed by archaeologists as an astrological tower dedicated to the stars of heaven, and this was linked to what is being said in Revelation 18:13, as those stars are often associated with angels and evil spirits. We can assume that the beginning of star worship that came from Nimrod's tower to Egypt and hence to Sudan today was something that began in ancient Babylon, knowing that the descendants of Cush were there. Concrete sources or accounts we could believe to carry truth, such as the Bible as well as ancient scholars, mentioned that there is no question that a major portion of the Middle East was established by dark-skinned Africans, and such people are related to Nimrod through his grandfather Ham. No one with common sense could describe Nimrod as different from the black Africans.[122] In some locations in the Middle East, there are many black tribes and people who still believe that they are Africans but did not migrate to Africa during that period.

The question to ask is, what happened to Nimrod? As a great leader with such initiative, how did he die, and where? No concrete evidence exists as to this valuable information. Other sources mention that when people moved out of Babel after the Tower crumbled, he was caught inside and died. Others claim that he was ordered executed by Shem, whose children Nimrod had been persecuting. Still others state that when Nimrod ruled with tyrannical powers which entailed witchcraft, all the close tribes scattered and, without their former

---

122 Black History in the Bible, "Nimrod: The Grandson of Ham, the First World Leader, and the Builder of Babel" (http://www.blackhistoryinthebible.com/the-hamites/nimrod-the-first-world-leader/).

leader, were unable to cooperate among themselves.[123] The account of Nimrod being left in the Tower of Babel seems to hold water. It could be speculated that when the Nilotic people came to Africa thousands of years ago, they were moving differently, lacking cohesion. The reason why the term "Nuer" came to existence was that they had to develop different laws, since the rest of the other tribes migrated and camped in their own places. There was no leader to unite them.

At the Tower of Babel, Nimrod had his own life. He was reported to have fallen in love and married another man's wife and her own mother – Cush's wife, a beautiful woman. Though others say that she could have been his own mother, there is no proof of this. The one practice that the current Nilotics possess is that no matter what, you cannot sleep with your own mother, who gave birth to you. Such sources and accounts cannot be justified as truth. The name of the woman he married was Semiramis, who had a perfect female beauty, and who was one of the most wicked women who ever lived but was referred to as a demon-possessed witch. It is also said that Nimrod and Semiramis gave their bodies and souls to Satan.[124] Semiramis was credited with the building of the Tower of Babel, and it was said that without her, it could not have been accomplished. She reportedly said she was a virgin, but she was instead seen as a harlot and had made Babylon a center of ritual prostitution and adultery. The below narrative also tried to specify the beginning of the worship of other cults mentioned in different books:

After Nimrod's death, she could not give up her privileged position of power. She later gave birth to a son; whether by harlotry or by witchcraft is not clear. She claimed that she, being a virgin, had conceived by a sunbeam, that her son Tammuz was the savior, the promised Christ, and the reincarnation of Nimrod, whom she said was the sun god. In life, Nimrod was honored as a hero; in death,

---

123 Every Child Ministries, op. cit.

124 Ibid.

Semiramis, of course, was deified too as the virgin mother of the son of God, and developed a cult in which she and her son were worshipped, with herself as Queen of heaven, the virgin mother of god, eclipsing the son.[125]

According to this statement, it seems Nimrod was worshipped as a god – a sun god, in particular – during the time he was ruling in Babylon. In addition, Semiramis was also known by ancient people as a goddess of fertility, the great earth mother Rhea or Gaia. Tammuz and Nimrod's deaths were undocumented, and this could be because they both lived on in each other. Legend has it that Tammuz met his death in the wild, killed by a wild boar at the age of 40. His mother, the woman of Babylon, wept for 40 days, one for each year of his life. Another account claimed that Tammuz was executed by having his body cut into different small parts which were taken around the town to show to people, to sever him from society. It is further said that "[t]he dismemberment of Tammuz was the origin of the heathen practice of cutting oneself, and possibly the origin of the African practice of decorative citracization, the cutting of dots and tribal marks in the flesh. It also provides the motivation for the development of embalming in Egypt, for a great imperative was defined by the reconstruction of the dismembered Osiris. The body of the god-king had to be preserved intact in order for him to attain mortality".[126] After the death of Tammuz, the whole of ancient Babylon wept for seven days, mourning his death. It was believed that Tammuz made a ritual out of the worshipping of the seven stars, which were signs of the zodiac. There is a story which says that one of the kings who was there at the time was ordered by Tammuz to worship the zodiac, and when that king refused, Tammuz ordered his execution by throwing him to the animals in a den, where he was torn into pieces. After the death of Tammuz, all the images on Earth came alive and wept the whole

125 Ibid., p. 2..
126 Ibid., p. 3.

night, and in the morning, they went back.[127] Because of the constant weeping, it was said that his mother managed to resurrect Tammuz, as narrated below:

> Semiramis claimed her son was mystically (not physically) raised. Annual weeping for Tammuz became a ritual in Babylon as a part of annual fertility rites. It was believed that Tammuz went into the underworld and was mystically revived in the spring through the weeping of his mother. The Egyptian version of the resurrection legend says Osiris once ruled Egypt until he was killed and dismembered by his jealous brother Seth, but faithful Isis collected the pieces of his body and patched them back together, thus resurrecting him.[128]

In Egypt, the mother-and-child cult, also known as that of Isis and Osiris, had been preached abundantly in the temples. Similarly, to the Naath people of South Sudan, there was Ngundeng, a prophet whose mother was named Buk, and together they are called "Deng Buk," just like Osiris and Isis in Egypt. The distinction in this is that at the end of the day, they believe in the moon, the sun, and the stars. While he was in Babylon, Nimrod was deified as Baal, the horned god. It was from the priests of Baal where cannibalism emerged, in which parts of the body are eaten when being sacrificed. Moreover, Tammuz became known as the fire god, whose name means "purity by fire." He had a custom where children were passed through the fire. People walk on fire as well, and it is in Egypt where the death of Tammuz is commemorated in an annual festival where some pictures show his sign of the sacred tau – the letter T – symbolizing Tammuz.[129]

The fire festivals where prophets walk on fire are also seen in Naath society. In Dok land, a man named Liah Wal, with his spirit,

---

127 Ibid.
128 Ibid.
129 Ibid.

could walk on fire. It was seen as an impossible thing to do. He could perform other miracles, including burning metals and walking on them. This divination could be associated with the Tower of Babel and the practices of Nimrod, as stated in different texts. Furthermore, Isis in Egypt was seen as the goddess of fertility, while Nimrod was also associated with Baal and represented by phallic symbols, of which the obelisk is a common version. Semiramis was represented by eggs and female figures. She was associated with astrology, and the Egyptian Isis was represented as standing on a crescent moon with stars around her head.[130] In Babylon, there was a religion that spread across the land, and when Greeks and Romans adopted Christianity, most of its ancient practices were incorporated into their religion. During the Flood, there was only one god that was worshipped, but this practice changed with time. There was the question of the Holy Trinity, where there is God the Father, God the Son, and God the Holy Spirit – and in this sense, we can read Nimrod, Semiramis, and Tammuz, respectively. Believing in polytheism, in which it is thought that the reincarnation of demons' spirits can be witnessed, became a common practice among Africans, including the Nilotic people.

TOWER OF BABEL

The name *Babel* or *Ba-bel* has a mysterious origin. Researchers found that it was not an English, French, Hebrew, or Greek word. These were languages from which the name could have emerged; these languages were famous and are still influential. It is possible that the word could have come from the languages that were discovered during the destruction of Babel, when communication was confused.[131] If Babel is from none of these languages, then where did it come from? Throughout the ages, there were different pronunciations created and

---

130 Ibid.

131 Hodge, op. cit.

attributed to Babel. We know that "the best point that can be made on this is that people are still affected by language division that occurred at Babel, and this is the case, to a lesser degree, with the word Babel. Moreover, after the events at Babel, it was probably pronounced a multiple of ways, and they were all correct".[132] The Naath believe that Babel could be their language, and this is due to the meaning and spelling of the word at the same time.

Image of the Tower of Babel as illustrated by an artist.
Courtesy of Google.

The word *Babel* in Naath means 'to blame,' and elders from the community believed that the name was created when their forefathers were constructing the Tower and some of them were afraid that it was too high and God might not approve it. They convinced themselves that they were to blame for this, and indeed, it was as if they saw it coming. The second name associated with the Tower of Babel is the *Dapany* or *Dak-pany*. This was the name the forefathers gave to the

132 Hodge, p. 16.

Tower after God destroyed it. The Nuer's recent spiritual leaders, such as Kulang Ket, Latjor Duach and Tang Kuany, among others, used it consistently.

The intention of the construction of the tower was to be a remedy for the Flood that nearly wiped out every single living organism on earth during the time of Noah. Bodie Hodge mentioned that the city that marks the last construction was Babel, and this was after Nimrod and his team completed building most of the famous cities. "After building the capital of the kingdom of Sheba east of the Nile River, he proceeded to do the same for his uncles in Egypt and Sudan (Nubia). He then proceeded to do the same for his uncle Canaan where he helped to build the capitol of Jebu and then elsewhere."[133] Once he finished, Nimrod decided to go to Syria and help plan the building of Damascus and the ancient city of Nimrud, and after that, he came and established his kingdom, which was marked by the Tower of Babel.[134] Nimrod, the son of Cush, grandson of Ham, was the first world leader who brought architectural design to the ancient cities. The kingdom of Babel became Babylon, and many years later, it is now called Iraq. What remains are the ruins of the ancient city of Babylon, which are used as a tourist site. The people who live there at this time are Arabs and other communities who later occupied the land when the children of Ham left for Africa.

Archaeologists dug up evidence that shows the spot of the Tower of Babel. Their findings indicate that the Tower of Babel was real, and its construction did happen, though their speculation on what purpose it was meant to achieve is not clear. Some think it was meant to be a place for astrology, or where things of heaven such as the moon, stars, and the sun would be worshipped, because it was very high in the sky, and that was why God's anger was provoked. In ancient Babylon, the spot for the ruined building believed to be the Tower of Babel was found. It was 153 feet high with a 400-foot base. The building

---

133 Achala (2011), p. 61.

134 Ibid.

materials included dried bricks in seven levels to correspond with the outer planets. The lower part was black, the color of Saturn; the next orange, for Jupiter; the third, red for Mars; and so on.[135]

At the peak of the tower were the signs of the zodiac. According to Dr. Donald Barnhouse, an expert on Roman tribal customs, "it was an open, definite turning to Satan and the beginning of devil worship. This is why the Bible everywhere pronounces a curse on those who consult the sun, the moon, and the stars of heaven".[136] Whatever happened at the Tower of Babel is not of interest here; the point is that the early civilization that established the Tower of Babel with dried bricks, and built the tallest building then in existence, was the work of a black civilization, the direct great-grandfathers of the Cush – the Sudanese people who live in the Upper Nile Basin today.

We are also informed by the same Bible that when God's anger was provoked because of people's worship of the glory of heavens or the things that were created by God to beautify Heaven, he made them fall and changed their language, distributing different languages among the people. Initially, there was only one language that they used to speak. Dr. Henry Madison Morris, the young-Earth creationist, was quoted stating:

> As each family and tribal unit migrated away from Babel, not only did they each develop a distinctive culture, but also, they each developed distinctive physical and biological characteristics. Since they would communicate only with the member of their own family unit, there was no further possibility of marrying outside the family...was necessary to establish new families composed of a very closed relative, for several generations at least. It is well established genetically that variation takes place very quickly in a small inbreeding population.[137]

---

135 Willmington, p. 35.

136 Ibid.

137 **Ibid.**

In the Biblical story of Noah and the Flood, God sent the Flood because "the wickedness of man was great in the earth", and "every imagination of the thoughts of his heart was only evil continually" (Genesis 6:5); "the earth was filled with violence" (Genesis 6:11). The Flood killed almost everything on Earth, with the exception of a few people who were taken into the ark as instructed to Noah by God. The ark that was constructed accommodated 35,000 vertebrate animals on board. It was because of God's help that this ark was constructed by Noah to accommodate such a huge number of species. It was "approximately 450 feet long, 75 feet wide, and 45 feet high. It had a deck total of 97,700 square feet, or the equivalent to more than an area of twenty standard college basketball courts. Its total volume was around 1,500,000 cubic feet, and the gross tonnage exceeded some 14,000 tons".[138] Noah's ark was one of the biggest boats ever constructed on Earth. A leading American taxonomist estimated that 3,500 mammals, 8,600 birds, 5,500 reptiles and amphibians, and 25,500 worms of different species were accommodated.[139]

The idea of building the Tower of Babel was taken from the story of Noah. God sent a flood to wipe out all humans, with the exception of Noah and his people. The ark of Noah was reported to have rested on Mount Ararat in Armenia. The meanings of Armenia and Ararat are 'high ground'. Nimrod started to build a tower, and his purpose was to protect his kingdom from any natural calamities that may have befallen it. He instructed his workers to build a giant tower that would reach the heavens. God came down and saw that they had succeeded in building such a tower. God reasoned that if these people could unite and build something wonderful, it was because they understood each other, and there was nothing impossible for them to do. The same innovation through which Cush and his son Nimrod constructed cities in the past was being used by his descendants to build Egypt and Northern Sudan.

---

138 Ibid, p. 29.
139 Ibid.

The pyramids that were constructed could have been taken from the idea of building the Tower of Babel. Before the Arabs came to Egypt, there were the Cushites, who were living in that part of the world. The pyramid was a symbol of unity that brought people together to amalgamate their strength; it was also a signal of preparedness for future threats. The pyramid was built for several reasons: first, because it would be the place to worship Deng Kur. It was also a sanctuary where those who were lost could find the meaning of life and be given gifts to survive. The people also knew Ngundeng Bong for his generous support during the time they paid a visit to the Mound of Deng Kur. The god of Ngundeng Bong may have seen the future, and he could have predicted the coming of white people and how they were going to colonise the the rest of South Sudanese people and maybe kill them. As it happened, the mound and the other relics helped the Nuer people to survive the all-out war between the colonizers and the Nuer people. The Nuer prophet Ngundeng Bong's pyramid was constructed with the unity of the people. After its completion, it was used as a consultative venue for the people as well.

Naath elders stated that the Tower of Babel is what is called Dapany, known to be the dwelling place of gods. The Western Upper Nile prophet Kulang Ket, who was possessed by the spirit of Maani, was believed to have been carried to Dapany. He talked about it in his songs and speeches that were carried on through word of mouth. The family of Chieng Wan, who came to the possessed people in Nuer land, was believed to have come from the same place, and they were connected and related to one another. There is an entire family of divinity that has lived among the Nuer for generations. It has been talked about in the writings of the British, and it has been very clear through their directives to the people that their presence among them was seen to be normal. The Tower of Babel was not a place where human beings originated, but a place where they established a coping mechanism against a flood that might have arises. The word Babel, meaning "gate of God", was believed to be coined by Nimrod himself, as elaborated below:

Nimrod became very instrumental in the construction and expansion of not only the four kingdoms but also of many more other kingdoms. He was a hunter, engineer, builder, warrior, and sailor. He had gained knowledge out of the whole region that we know today as the Middle East. Nimrod was gifted and had what we could term as a natural knowledge. Instruction to build the ark that was given to Noah by God himself was important, and Noah passed this on to his family, especially to Nimrod his grandson. Nimrod was instrumental in the initial planning and building of Jebu, the name of the city of the Jebusites which was later changed to Jerusalem. Nimrod had helped with planning and building it before proceeding to build the ancient city of Nimrud in Syria and later, Nineveh.[140]

The sunken city of Atlantis in the Mediterranean Sea was constructed by Nimrod himself. The city of the Atlantis is believed to be the home of Noah when he was alive 350 years after the Great Flood had swallowed it. It is unfortunate that most of the cities that Nimrod built by his hands were conquered one by one, and almost none survive today. It was his knowledge that was used during the sophisticated engineering and construction of the Egyptian pyramids and the ancient sites of the Ethiopians. There are narratives that state Noah lived with his grandson Cush in Ethiopia, as he did with his grandson in Egypt too. He moved around the kingdoms inhabited by his grandchildren, providing blessings and seeing his skills being utilized by them. In reference to his home, the city of Atlantis city that sank in the Mediterranean Sea, it was through his work that he laid down all the plans and gave it to his grandchild Nimrod to build. As we know, "it will not be surprising to find his tomb in Egypt, in the caves of Ethiopia or in Nineveh, the city that was carefully built by Nimrod, Noah's great-grandson. Nimrod was a respected person and had a close relationship with his great grandfather Noah. Perhaps it was he

140 Achala, p. 58.

that had the responsibility to bury Noah, Shem, Ham, and Japheth, possibly in Nineveh where he had finally set up his headquarters."[141] A possible location for Noah's burial could be as noted above, inside the pyramids or somewhere in the caves or ancient buildings of Ethiopia.

The Tower of Babel was changed to mean "confusion" when translated to Hebrew. It was after the confusion when the place was later named Babylon. In fact, the location of the Tower of Babel is, in fact, Babylon. My own assumption is that it was built against floods that they had experienced long ago, or that their forefathers, such as Noah, had endured. Building a tower was meant to get them away from the experiences they had. On the religious aspect of worshipping heavenly bodies, as stated above, some writers think that the intention of the builders was to get closer to the heavenly bodies and worship them. This may be true, given their drawings and the places they were putting up. It should be recalled that even the Nuer at this point in time still mapped the zones of heavens and known stars by their appearance. They knew which star to guide them when doing certain things.

Anu M'Bantu and Gert Muller, in *The Ancient Black Hebrews and Arabs* (2013), have examined lengthily the quotations in the Bible that mention black, or Cushite, people. Ham in the Bible is taken to mean "dark" and, in addition, is associated with ravens, the darkest bird. In Song of Solomon 1:6, the word *sha-char*, or "shiny black," was also used. In the Naath language today, black is "*char*" and is widely used for names of people and for naming black things, including animals.

---

141 Ibid., p. 59.

CHAPTER 3

KEMET,
THE LAND OF THE BLACKS

"...all Africa is the homeland of the Blacks and the Asiatic peoples who occupy North Africa, even though they may have been there for centuries, are no more native Africans than are the Dutch and British who likewise occupy and control the southern regions of the continent."[142]

INTRODUCTION

Egypt, as a country, is one of the oldest civilizations, whose history has been told in different forms and genres. It's unique because of the indisputably ancient civilisation that developed within the Nile valley; Egypt became the epicentre of that civilisation, of which visible traces are still being enjoyed by subsequent generations. One of these remnants of the ancient world is the Pyramid of Giza, which has been designated the one of the Seven Wonders of the World. Tourists and academics visit Egypt every year to continue the interpretation of this

---

142 Williams, op. cit.

ancient civilization . However, it is the considered view of the author that, across the years, what has been written about Egypt and its early civilization by those who claim to be custodians of knowledge has not been based entirely on empirical evidence. It should be noted that some of the images that have been painted of ancient Egypt are not accurate at all. These were largely the result of aligning ancient Egyptian civilisation to Asia and the Middle East rather than an African civilisation. Cheick Anta Diop and Chancellor Williams talked about it openly, proving that it was an African civilization. The traces are very clear; even when visiting the Cairo National Museum of Antiquity, you will see that ancient Egypt could not be mistaken for having anything but an African origin, unless one has the intention of dissecting it from Aits frican origin. The origin of human beings and the migrations and settlements of various groups of people in Africa, as discussed in Chapter 1, shows that Egypt became a gateway due to its proximity to the Mediterranean Sea and the Middle East. It acted as a bridge between the Middle East and Africa. The knowledge that Ancient Babylon and some areas in the Middle East were black people's kingdoms made Egypt what it is. When black people returned to Africa, they used the corridor of the Sinai Peninsula. It was the same situation as when the ancient human species left Africa to colonize the planet; the area around the Sinai Peninsula was one of the main gates used for migration. Some of the inaccuracies, as shared by some Western-based authors, the media, and various internet-based platforms, lead one to believe that ancient Egypt was not a black civilization. This chapter aims to highlight, clarify, and correct some of these inaccurate historical narratives.

An analysis of material written by Westerm scholars suggests a complete collaboration between such scholars and the foreigners who took total control of the land, using instruments of oppression and imperialistic manipulation. The current reality is that the histories of an ancient people have been stolen by dominant white discourse and scholars. A case can be made that the people of the West have always come to Africa and claimed to be experts who know more about Africa than the indigenous Africans themselves. As Westerners arrived in Egypt, they connived with Middle Easterners to both erase and negatively re-shape most of black history since the Mesopotamian civilization. As noted by Williams, some black authors have also wholeheartedly taken as gospel truth the information contained in books written by the these Western academics over the accounts of indigeneous authors, wrongly implying that those accounts represent the true history of Africa. This has since been seen as a gap in African education, which is mostly a copy-paste from Western education. The mindset of interpreting African history is almost the way Westerners interpret Africa, and they see it through their own lenses. It has been a traditional practice in Africa that those with resources decided to study in the West, where the educational curriculum is designed based on Western tradition, yet Africa is a completely different continent with different values and beliefs.

It is unfortunate that the younger generation of African academics does not appear keen to reclaim the history of the land. Instead, they seem to largely agree with the skewed Western views of the history of Africa. This has also increasingly undermined the study of the origins of black civilization. One of the authors who has kept track of this spiteful act has stated that "for about one thousand years from the time after the great floods to events of the Tower of Babel, Egypt was ruled by dynasties that descended from Ham. After the one thousand years of peace, Egypt was attacked from time to time by outsiders until it fell to others, including Alexander the Great. Later and after the death of Mohamed, it fell to Arabs and much later to British who again turned it back to Arabic rule that continues to this day".[143] The Nubians who were left by black people as they escaped persecution from all the outside forces who came to invade the country have always been treated cruelly and denied both a democratic space and a voice. They were made to believe that the black race was inferior to others, and hence ranked lowest among humans. Further, they were

---

143 Achala, p. 119.

associated with the devil and the gorillas and monkeys in the jungles of Africa. This is exactly the same way the Westeners who came to Africa have described Africans, as they considered them an inferior race. The biases of those who committed such historical falsifications have been described thus:

> The line of ill-intentional Egyptologists, equipped with a ferocious erudition, have committed their well-known crime against science, by becoming guilty of a deliberate falsification of the history of humanity. Supported by the governing powers of all the Western countries, this ideology, based on a moral and intellectual swindle, easily won out over the true scientific current developed by a parallel group of Egyptologists of good will, whose intellectual uprightness and even courage cannot be stressed strongly enough. The new Egyptological ideology, born at the opportune moment, reinforced the theoretical bases of imperialist ideology. That is why it easily drowned out the voice of science, by throwing the veil of falsification over historical truth. This ideology was spread with the help of considerable publicity and taught the world over because it alone had the material and financial means for its own propagation. Thus imperialism, like the prehistoric hunter, first killed the being spiritually and culturally, before trying to eliminate it physically. The negation of the history and intellectual accomplishments of Black Africans was cultural, mental murder, which preceded and paved the way for their genocide here and there in the world.[144]

It is no exaggeration to say that anthropologists and Egyptologists intentionally hid the truth of blacks being the ancient developers and innovators of the ancient civilizations from current black Africans. They were well aware of what they had found in their studies of the ancient sites and monuments, but they did not want to reveal that knowledge, which shows the Nile Valley was occupied by black races

---

144 Diop, op. cit.

who generated its civilization. Just like the story of the traveler and the old man, black people have lost their history, and now they are being physically tortured and murdered to the point of annihilation.

One such case is the current characterization of the Nilotic group. Most writers position Nilotic origins either to east Africa or along the Nile Valley, which does not point to North Africa. But emerging evidence from the monuments indicate that they were in Egypt, north Sudan and even in Babylon and the Middle East. April 2018, I interviewed Mansour Khalid, one of the leading voices of writers in Sudan, q diplomat and lawyer by profession. He was from one of the early Arab tribes who are currently inhabiting Sudan, and he mentioned "the Nilotic were reported to have come from central Africa and stayed in Tanzania, Kenya, and Uganda for a long time; and because they are pastoralists such as the Nuer (Naath) and Dinka (Jieng),, they moved along with their cattle to follow the Nile upstream toward South Sudan." To him, the Nilotic people never stepped foot in north Africa. This indicates that all the ancient records of Africa that mention black people's movement and settlement were all hidden. No one seems to mention the ancient records of the Nilotic people, despite their also being narrated in the Bible, one of the oldest books in history. It is instead postulated that they likely originated along the Nile.

To gain a clear understanding of the black kingdoms that ruled Egypt, Chancellor Williams wrote that the history of black Africa must start with the rule of Thebes, because it was a region ruled by blacks. This provides important evidence that blacks built the earliest civilization in Chem, which was later called Egypt.[145] Historically, this civilization dates back to earlier than the Stone Age era.

Hugh Trevor-Roper, the British historian, claimed that "Africa had no history prior to European exploration and colonization...there is only the history of Europeans in Africa. The rest is darkness." What happened in the past is "the unedifying gyrations of barbarous tribes in picturesque but irrelevant corners of the globe," as Hugh Trevor-

---

145 Williams, op. cit..

Roper put it in is book *The Crisis of the Seventeenth Century*. Georg Wilhelm Friedrich Hegel also belittled Africa by saying that "Africa is no historical part of the world; it has no movement or development to exhibit" in his 1858 book *The Philosophy of History*. In his 1930 book *Races of Africa*, C.G. Seligman doubted whether African civilization could be associated with any black races of Africa. He bluntly stated that "civilizations of Africa are the civilizations of the Hamites, its history is the record of these peoples and of their interaction with the two other African stocks, the Negro and Bushmen."

These authors need to be critiqued for their misrepresentation of African history. Certain authors of no credible repute shamelessly skewed their research findings in favor of questionable information that implied that Arabs who occupied Egypt at a much later period had ancestors who built Egypt from the earliest of times. As Africans, the truth attributing successes and failures to ancient black people must be accepted, bad or good; it has to be taken into consideration as part of the history that makes up Africa as a whole. Egypt is an important gateway to the rest of the continent, and blacks battled for thousands of years to keep invaders such as the Hykos, Assyrians, and Persians at bay. They fought for many years and should be honored and have their history attributed to them. The truth must be revealed and inconsistencies straightened up. These were brave men and women who stood their ground for generations to maintain their territory. Pressure must be sustained in erasing historical Western efforts to undermine the origins of black civilization; otherwise, degradation of the black African population will continue unabated. Black African universities need to have a curriculum in schools that is designed to convey that these ancient civilizations were fathered in Africa. It is through studying these ancient civilizations that Africa will earn its place in the world.

We must uncover the truths and elaborate the true history of the African continent. There might be people who have personal views on the way history should have been written, but for the common man and the descendants of the first inhabitants of Egypt, it is a good thing to acknowledge the ancestors' role in protecting and maintaining the gate to Africa for generations. Rudolf R. Windsor reminded us the Biblical records show Ham is one of the three children of Noah, and he is the one who fathered the black race. Many of Ham's descendants then migrated from the Middle East, mostly around Babylon and the land of Canaan and southern Arabia, and traveled to Africa and made themselves a home. No records so far show that other humans ever inhabited this part of Africa before then. At this time, there were no Semites or Indo-Europeans in the land of Ham (Africa).[146] The Bible is one of the oldest books and has attracted the attention of many people so far, and these people believed in it. Yet these narratives of history have some accuracies. Africa was purely inhabited by people of black origin who were scattered around the jungles of Africa and called it home. It was their next Garden of Eden to inhabit.Credible sources must be consulted to determine who the ancient Egyptians were. These include scientific sources, which are derived through anthropological work such as the study of ancient human remains preserved by the dry climate. Others include iconography, which involves the examination of historical visual images made long ago, including drawings, paintings, bas-reliefs and statues, or monuments created by the former inhabitants of the Nile Valley and the rock dwellers. Linguistics is yet another important source, which helps to determine the writing and language used at the time and enhances our understanding of the origins and ethnic makeup of a group. Finally, there is the ethnological technique, which involves the comparison of sources as well as the characteristics of other ethnic and cultural groups of the time.[147] The problem here is that those that have the power to interpret and analyze evidence obtained from these sources are, and were, mostly non-black people, and oftentimes they made these inter-

---

146 Windsor, op. cit.

147 UNESCO (1979). The Peopling of the Ancient Egypt and Deciphering of the Meroitic Script. Proceeding from the Symposium held in Cairo from 28 January to 3 February 1974. http://unesdoc.unesco.org/images/0003/000328/032875eo.pdf

pretations through their own racial lenses, imagining themselves as part of the ancient civilization – epsecially Arab-Egyptian civilization. One example is the Dr. Zahi Hawass, Egyptian chairman of the Supreme Council of Antiquity, who was vocal about Israel claiming that the pyramids were built by the slaves, and in this sense, the Jews who took refuge in Egypt for 430 years. He claimed that "the opening of the sarcophagus and that skeleton that we found shows the importance of the discovery and this completely discards the theory about the pyramid built by slaves because slavery cannot build something genius like building the pyramid and I will tell the public that everyone who tries to talk against the Egyptians should shut their mouths."[148] To Dr. Hawass, the slaves were the Jewish people who stayed in Egypt for 430 years (starting in 1208 BCE) at the end of Bronze Age. It was during this period it is believed they were taken as slaves and made to build the pyramid. Dr. Hawass, when he referred to the Egyptians, was not thinking black Africans. Instead, he was talking of the Arabs. He could not even consider the Nubians who were there and persisted throughout the mistreatment and slavery of the Arabs who took control of the country in 646 AD. To him, black Africans being part of Egypt is something that did not exist. Despite evidence shown by monuments and dug by archeologists, he decided to cover it up. This is a piracy against black people, a cultural atrocity. It is a daylight robbery.

African history has often been integrated or told through a Hellenistic worldview, which combines the Roman and Byzantine empires. These developments gave rise to the Islamic dominance of Egypt and had a great bearing on the way historical events were presented, particularly given the Arabic view of Egyptian history. These days, it seems one cannot write the history of Africa without looking

---

148 Bauval, Robert, "Jews Did not Build the Pyramid, says the Chairman of Antiquities". *Egyptology and Anti-Semitism* (2002): http://www.robertbauval.co.uk/articles/articles/hawass1.html.

at the Greeks, Romans, Turkish, Indians, Arabs, and central Africans as the genesis of civilization, which is not true; Africa was a convergence of all the nations who came to seek wisdom and to benefit from the rich resources of the land, but this does not mean that their history and civilization should be shared and attributed to all visitors. What was learned from Egypt and the rest of Africa, which included architecture, mathematics, geometry, languages, and religion, aided Roman civilization, which is still admired and respected around the world. Writing an independent history of Africa requires a lot of research and correct interpretation based upon landmarks, oral narratives, bones, paintings in mountain caves, artifacts, and ancient writings about the land. The truth is that:

> The characteristic [of the] ancient and medieval sources are literary writings. The evidence they give is for the most part conscious, whether they be annals, chronicles, travels or geographies; whereas from the fifteenth century on, archival sources – unconscious evidence – became abundant. For another thing, while until the fifteenth century classical and Arabic sources predominate, after that even our Arabic sources peter out, and we suddenly find evidence from a different provenance: the European document (Italian, Portuguese, etc.) and, for black Africa, the autochthonous document. But this shift in the nature and provenance of sources also represents a change in Africa's real historical destiny.[149]

Autochthonous sources are not limited only to written sources, as stated above; they range from oral history to the memories of older generations. There is a knowledge gap in documenting the history of black people, mostly Nilotic sources, due to the lack of written sources. Older generations of black people moved from one place to another in search of new settlements, and such experiences stuck with

---

149 Ki-Zerbo, Josep, editor, UNESCO *General History of Africa* (Oakland: University of California Press, 1999), p. 88.

those who moved with their cattle; yet these were difficult to verify through written sources. When told as fireside stories, details will be exaggerated by an old man intentionally to hold the imagination of children. Thus, the stories that do survive are exaggerated over time. It is unfortunate that the most public ancient document of the past is only written down the visitors to Africa. Though we had Egyptians, Ethiopians, and Nubians who wrote down their history, most of them are not popularly used and taught in public universities as sources of ancient language. It was not until the 11th century that permanent relations were cemented by black people, with the establishment of Islam in the sphere of commerce and religion. A lot of things, such as religion, commerce, the environment, and names of places changed, including the way in which information was documented. Records became quantitative, plentiful, and varied.[150] It has to be noted that "an objective historian has no right to make value judgments on the basis of his documentary material. But neither has he the right to neglect what it has to offer on the grounds that it might possibly be misleading".[151] Whatever is available for a historian to document, there are always people who will be stakeholders to history that has been recorded in whichever way. The way the Arabs came to Africa and wrote the history of North Africa, adding their biases into it, has really made a negative impression on the ancient history of the continent.

An excavation carried out at El Omari in Nubia concluded that the population of Egypt during the Neolithic period was a mix of races, including blacks, Mediterraneans, and people with features reminiscent of Cro-Magnon man, as well as those who were a mix of all three.[152] The excavation also proved that Arabs and people of

---

150 Ibid.

151 Ibid.,p.. 91.

152 Ki-Zerbo, Joseph, editor, "The Peopling of the Ancient Egypt and Deciphering of the Meroitic Script: Proceedings from the Symposium Held in Cairo from 28 January to 3 February 1974" (New York: UNESCO, 1979): http://unesdoc.unesco.org/images/0003/000328/032875eo.pdf

the Middle East could have come as traders into Africa and Egypt in particular. Some of them moved in as nomads with their animals. This excavation was carried out using the examination of artifacts and monuments and showed the past life of the people who lived in that area in that period of time. However, the results were limited because of a lack of capacity in the form of manpower and tools, which led to poor data analysis. The data analysis indicating Arabs were part of the population could not be measured well, whether they were grazing their animals in that area for a certain period of time or permanent inhabitants. During the first wave of settlers to ancient Egypt, such a diverse population may not have been likely due to the occupation of the ancient black people's settlement and influence in the area. However, later, when Egypt was overtaken by other forces and inter-marriages between races were more common, this may have been the case. This is contrary to the belief that Arabs were the occupants of Egypt. Yet, since history was written by Western scholars who were known to suppress black views, such as Seligman and Hegel, certain inaccuracies and biases may have been introduced.

It is not a secret anymore that the ancient country of Kemet, which is now known as Egypt, was a completely African civilization and had no influence outside of black Africans. Though some archeologists and Egyptologists who conducted investigations and obtained discoveries from the tombs of mummies avoided accepting the fact that it was an African civilization, other archeologists and Egyptologists such as Bauval, Thomas Brophy, and Graham Hancock are now being honest and writing volumes of material about it. In one of their books, *Black Genesis: The Prehistoric Origin of Ancient Egypt*, Bauval and Brophy summarize their research by stating that strong evidence exists to suggest the origin of ancient Egypt can be traced to black Africans who lived thousands of years before the emergence of the Pharaonic civilization. The publication of their book has helped to set the record straight on an issue that has long beleaguered historians and pre-historians for a long time, though some of their works attributed ancient monuments, such as the Pyramid of Giza, to the intervention of extraterrestrial support. Nevertheless, their understanding of the ancient civilization of Egypt is based on the same findings they shared with me when I first visited the Museum of Egyptian Antiquities in Cairo. Most of the things they were exhibiting as ancient materials are still used in Nilotic communities even today. I can still recall seeing a lot of things used today, such as the spears used in hunting, the walking stick for aged men, the smoking pipe, and even methods of preparing food. Simply putting Egyptian civilization as African by origin is something most Nilotic communities are pretty sure about. The oral stories across Nilotic communities always place their origin to the Middle East and North Africa. This could not be a coincidence, but an actual migration that took place over thousands of years. Both writers stressed that the book is the result of "a deep and strong desire to use the best of our intellect, knowledge and abilities...in spite of many clues that have been in place in the past few decades, which strongly favor a black African origin for the Pharaohs, many scholars, especially Egyptologists, have either ignored them, confused them, or, worse still, derided or scorned those who entertained them."

A few African scholars such as Cheikh Anta Diop and Chancellor Williams, have noticed the bias and prejudice against Africans with regard to the origins of the Egyptian civilization, and they have been critical about such biases. Similarly, Williams acknowledged the displacement of Nilotic group that took place thousands of years ago in North Africa, particularly in Egypt and Sudan, when the different powers were at play in the Pharaonic land of Kemet.

The Blacks who are under pressure today in Bhar el Ghazal, the Upper Nile and Equatoria are still fighting for survival against the all-conquering Colored Arabs just as their fore-fathers fought five thousand years ago, from the Mediterranean in Lower Egypt to where they are now making a last stand...they have been massacred by the hundreds and villages left in ashes, but they fight on. This-all Black region is kept isolated and cut off from the developments and higher levels of life seen in the Arab-dominated Sudan. These

Southern Sudanese have remained 'primitive' and 'pagan,' just as their brothers elsewhere were made to remain under similar circumstances".[153]

After occupying the Upper Nile, the black people were shielded from invaders by the Sudd swamps of the River Nile. These invaders would have enslaved and annihilated the black people if it were not for the swamps, which were difficult to penetrate using their boats – though, after thousands of years, they managed to penetrate into Equatorian lands around Juba. Even the in the recent conflicts in South Sudan, the Sudd swamps have sheltered the South Sudanese from the watchful eyes of killers; they have become a haven for black people who escaped death and persecution in the Middle East and North Africa. During this period of instability, a few tribes among the black people proceeded to West Africa. The web of migration came to superimpose itself in the West African Sudano-Senegalese region through north-south migration, with the first wave of migrants arriving around 7000 BCE.[154] After several attempts in Lower Egypt by the black pharaohs to retake it, they managed to recapture Lower Egypt. To drive the Asians out of Lower Egypt, the black pharaohs instead opted for integration with the invaders such as Polycrates, the Greek general who was in the Egyptian Army; in later years, the blacks were chased out of Egypt to Upper Egypt and North Sudan under the King Psamtik III. The Asians never settled in Egypt, but instead, followed the black people to Upper Egypt and North Sudan and fought with them there, but ran out of supplies and returned to Egypt. There have been traces of evidence found in burial grounds indicating that certain settlements in Meroë were attacked and wiped out completely. These graves are visible along the Sudanese and Egyptian borders, and for many years Egypt was divided by the two races: Asians in the Lower Egypt and

---

153 Williams, p. 194.
154 Diop (1981), p. 183.

black people in Upper Egypt.[155] It was the Nubians who remained in Egypt, and such attacks resulted in the migration of the Nilotic groups, who moved to central Sudan and South Sudan.

The Egyptian Pyramids are among the wonders of the world. It is painful to note that credit is hardly given to the black people who built them. Both the Bible and history have confirmed that there was a great civilization of black people in the Middle East and in Africa. We can see that most of the areas currently occupied by Asians and Europeans in Africa were once purely black lands, and this was the case for generations. When the invasion took place from the Asians, Greeks, and Romans, it was then that Black civilization declined and the work of black Africans was erased from world history. Blacks were used as slaves and treated as subhumans compared to the white and Asian races. In fact, both European and Asian races have participated immensely in undermining the humanity of black people through enslavement and occupation of black territories.

Egypt had suffered successive displacement of its people and fell under the domination of the foreign powers for thousands of years. The independence of the country was lost centuries ago. It was the Persians who conquered Egypt in 525 BCE. The Persians were the force that made it unstable for the first time, until other powers took advantage of the country. After the Persians, Macedonians under Alexander took it over in 333 BCE; in 50 BC, Romans under Julius Caesar took it over; Arabs invaded it in the seventh century, the Turks in the sixteenth century, the French with Napoleon, and finally, the English at the end of the nineteenth century.[156] By the look of things, you will realize that a country that has suffered from different invasions could easily fall beyond repair. This is why it is very rare to see any African-ness in the people of Egypt. It has become part of their policy that they would rather have Middle East relations than the with the African states. Even at the moment, the Egyptians think Egypt does

---

155 Williams, p. 61.
156 Diop (1974), op. cit.

not belong to Africa; they think it's part of the Middle East, and of the Arab world in particular. One example is that when they are traveling to one of the black African countries, Egyptians will say they are going to Africa. This is the mindset of the people in Egypt. The Nubians who are citizens of Egypt at the moment have been squeezed into the southern part of the country and their land lack development and is marginalized.

Present-day Egyptians are biologically said to be 60% Eurasian, such as the Arabs who took over the country, and 40% black Africans, whom they displaced. Thousands of years ago, in the period that is referred to as ancient Egypt, the entire country, from Lower to Upper Egypt, was inhabited by black people. After years of war, that ended in the conquest of the inhabitants by the Persians, who first took control, the the Greeks who remained there for years, and the Romans, who later were displaced by the Arabs, who maintain control up to this day. There has been a lot of change in which group of foreign powers maintains authority. Although the 40% African genetic make-up of Arabs makes some difference in certain characteristics, such as the skin, hair, and language, the overall physical body is still black. Noticeably, there has lately been more migration of Arabs and Europeans into Egypt to increase the population. Egyptians are currently introducing a policy of refusing to allow their daughters to cohabit with blacks; they prefer light-skinned men who are closer to their complexion.

THE ANCIENT LAND OF KEMET

The ancient land of Egypt was called Kemet, which in short form is "Kmt" and means "the black land." This refers to the black, fertile soil that supported the black civilization for thousands of years. This name was given by the ancient Egyptians themselves. Within this land, the longest river in the world, the Nile, transverses the arid waste of the eastern Sahara of Egypt. Egypt also "refers to the long and narrow fertile strip running from the border of Sudan in the south to the shores of the Mediterranean in the north."[157] The length of the River Nile is about 4,000 miles (10,300 kilometers), which flows to the Mediterranean Sea, watering the desolate desert and generating life for its dwellers. The ancient people were not aware of the source of the river, and the pharaohs believed that it may have come from the underworld.[158] Regarding the people who lived in this land, it was stated that the "people who inhabit it today are called not only 'Egyptians' but also 'Arabs.'"[159] If we are talking about Egypt today, we definitely consider the population to be Arab, descendants of those who came to occupy the country a few millennia ago. It is further stated that "It thus often comes as a surprise when one is told that these names are not original or even native to this country. Many people gave the land of Egypt different names such as the Land of the Nile and Melting Pot of Culture, and it is known as the Chem from which the word Kemet came about. For us to understand better, we need to define the name 'Egypt.'"

Egyptologists stress that the name Kemet itself stemmed from the inhabitants, who associated it with the "color of their skin"; this provides strong evidence that ancient Egypt was the home of dark- or black-skinned Africans. This is further supported by the presence of the Nubians who live in Upper Egypt today.[160] Without a doubt, Kemet refers to black land and black people; the discovery of rocks in Gilf Kebir and Gabal el Uweinat with drawings made by prehistoric black-skinned people in the Egyptian part of the Sahara affirms this to be true. Investigations by archaeologists about certain signs that were discovered in these areas led them to admit that the word meant "land of the black-skinned, or

157 Bauval, Robert and Ahmed Osman, *The Soul of Ancient Egypt: Restoring the Spiritual Engine of the World* (Rochester, Vermont: Bear & Company, 2015).

158 Fagan, Brian M., *The Rape of the Nile: Tomb Robbers, Tourists and Archeologists in Egypt* (New York: Basic Books, 2009).

159 Bauval & Osman, op. cit.

160 Ibid.

it could mean black country."[161] In The Soul of Ancient Egypt, Robert Bauval and Ahmed Osman agree with the explanation that the early inhabitants of the Nile Valley were Negroid Africans that settled in the area about 5,000 BCE. Finding the correct meaning of "Kemet" would help black Africans trace the roots of their migration and also attest to their presence in the pharaonic civilization, and hence avoid conflicting theories about Egyptian civilization. The ancient drawings seen from Gilf Kebir shows the connection of African animals that were seen in drawings, and this could easily inform one about the ancient inhabitants. Some excavated artifacts, such as the mummy of the child found at the border of Egypt and Libya, have a lot to tell.

It has been argued that the human technology of what are called primitive tools began in South Nubia before it spread to the north of Egypt. This statement is a pointer to the origin of humanity. Another observation considers "the likelihood that the Nile Valley was peopled by a progressive descent of the black peoples from the region of the Great Lakes, the cradle of Homo sapiens."[162] Some evidence of early migration, as discussed in Chapter 1, has shown that pre-historic people who became natives of Egypt during the Stone Age were Africans, who migrated from the south.[163] Gabal al Uweinat, a great mountain located at the border between Libya and Egypt, is famous for the incredibly ancient drawings discovered there. They have been described thus:

> The animals are rudely drawn, but not unskillfully carved. There are lions, giraffes, ostriches and all kinds of gazelles, but no camels, the carvings are from half to a quarter of an inch deep, and the ages of the lines in some instances are considerably weathered... they were the work of the jinn [demons]...what man can do these things now?"[164]

---

161 Ibid.
162 Diop (1991), op. cit.
163 Ibid.
164 Bauval & Brophy, op. cit.

The belief that the drawings were the work of demons indicates their sophistication as well as the great mystery associated with them. Drawings in caves remind us that ancient peoples populated such places before the discovery of tools.

The word "Egypt" was coined by Greek colonists in the fourth century CE, and Egyptologists believed that it was a corruption of the word "Koptos," which also came from "Gebtu," the ancient name of the area south of the country. The word has been in existence for since at least 3000 BCE.[165]

The Greeks also named the city of Menes (Memphis) *Aigyptos* and referred to it as the whole country, because it was one of the most well-developed cities, and also the seat of their god; Memphis was also called *Hikuptah*, or the mansion of the soul of Ptah, who was the god-protector of the city. Before the black king (Menes), who was the first black king of Egypt, there was no Egypt; there was only the land inhabited by black people. That area was called *Kemet*, which is another name indicating that it was black people who lived in this part of the land.[166] After whites and Asians managed to conquer the land, they started to rename the places according to their own terminologies, making them suit their definitions. The Greeks were coining names that they could easily pronounce, and since they had dominance in the region, things changed. In the 12th century BCE, at the tomb of Ramses III, a genetic table found there indicated that Egyptians perceived themselves as black. The genetic table was in the form of a written document. During that time, Egyptians did not shy away from their representation as black people – Nubians and Naath. This was because of the reference they had of themselves, referring to themselves as Nahas (Naath). According to Cheik Anta Diop, Karl Lepsius, a white scholar from Germany, was surprised to discover that the evidence he was digging up was of a people who were purely black;

---

165 Bauval & Osman, op. cit.
166 Williams, p. 65.

he was expecting to see white people's corpses.[167] It proves that Egypt was not established by a race other than black Africans. As indicated, the civilization, from the Mediterranean to the borders of Sudan, was predominantly black. Diop wrote that "the former predominance of the Black Civilisation around the Mediterranean region is attested to by the unexpected existence of the pre-Hellenic Black virgins and goddess, such as the Black Demeter of Phigalia in Arcadia, the Black Aphrodite of Arcadia and Corinth, the black virgin of Saint Victor of Marseilles, and the black virgin of Chartres, who once was honoured as under lady under the earth".[168] This goddess predominantly inhabited the Mesopotamian region before the displacement.

Foreigners have been visiting Egypt for thousands of years. Archeologists discovered that black people who were living in Egypt were visited regularly by people from outside Egypt. This was indicated by the discovery of materials buried in the ground made from exotic materials that were not indigenous. The black people who were living in Nabta Playa with their animals also lived some time in Gebel Ramlah, and had the most encounters with people from the Middle East by trading with them. While they were herding their cattle, the traders would pass through their area, and had with them trade goods brought from the Middle East.

Arabs named the land south of Egypt "Bilad as-Sudan," which is translated as "The land of the black," and Kemet means the same. This statement is supported by discoveries made recently in the Egyptian Sahara, in artistic work done on rocks by prehistoric black-skinned people found in caves in the remote mountain regions of Gilf Kebir and Gabal Uweinat, or "land of the black-skinned" or simply "black country." This strengthens the claim that the earliest settlers of the Nile Valley were black Africans who came from the Sahara around 5000 BCE. The "prehistoric herdsmen, focusing on archeology," Diop argues, that:

---

167 Diop (1981), op. cit.
168 Ibid., p. 21.

Anthropological and forensic analysis show two different populations – Mediterranean and sub-Saharan--coexisted here at [Gebel
Ramlah near Nabta Playa]...the people who inhabited the shores
of the Gebel Ramlah were not cut off from the rest of the world.
Their contacts sometimes stretched very far, and it is evidenced by
unearthed objects made of raw materials that were not to be found
in the vicinity and must have been brought in from outside. The
best example of such long-distance imports is a nose plug made
of turquoise, the closest sources of which are located 1000 km to
the north of Sinai Peninsula. Shells were brought in either from
the Nile, 100 km away from the Red Sea much further to the
east...Ivory was brought from the south, since elephants, which
belong among the Ethiopian [Sudanese] fauna, could not survive
in such dry savanna...the typical beliefs of the ancient Egyptians
[to preserve the body so that the spirit could rest in peace in the
afterworld] may indeed have originated with the Neolithic people
inhabiting the ever drier savannah in what is today the Western
Desert, only centuries prior to the emergence of ancient Egypt. In
the basin of the dried up Nabta Playa lake, located only 20 km
away, the same people who left behind the graveyards at the foot
of Gebel Ramlah erected gigantic clusters of stelae, extending over
many kilometers...perhaps it was indeed these people who provided
the crucial stimulus towards the emergence of state organization in
ancient Egypt.[169]

These people were the herdsmen who moved with their cattle across the
borders of Sudan, Egypt, and Libya as they steered their cattle. Diop
believed that the ancient Egyptians were Africans and commented on
the routes ancient Egyptians took when they faced difficulties, or when
they had no water for their animals, or even wanted a better place
to settle. They always faced to the south, as it was the land of their
ancestors. He continued: "We understand better why the Egyptians

---

169 Bauval & Brophy, p..48.

turn toward the south, the heart of Africa, land of his origins, land of ancestors, and land of the Gods."[170] It has been further stated that "Egypt was African in its writing, its culture and its way of thinking,"[171] and so it is the duty of those who uphold the true history of Egypt to affirm this. Black people have completely ignored their origin of civilization despite the fact that their ancestors were the guides of all human civilizations that developed along the Nile Valley, including the agriculture, animal husbandry, toolmaking, and craft and construction. About 1000 BCE, the decline of Egypt started, and it ceased to be a major imperial power even as it still remained the northern gate of Africa. It was gradually conquered, and its power base was weakened by Assyrians, Persians, Nubian kings, Alexander the Great, etc.; yet its civilization and theology remained intact until Roman times.[172]

Many books cited here agree on the common front that black Africans were unhappy with the erasure of the black African origins of ancient Egyptian civilization. Powerful races went on to write falsified stories about Egypt while sitting on useful evidence, claiming it was their own. They went further by annexing African history to the Arab world.

"Not one of the many modern texts is authentic that mentions the term 'blacks' as if it had ever been used by the Egyptians to distinguish themselves from Negroes. Whenever these texts relate some facts reported by the Egyptians about 'blacks,' it is a distortion... strangely enough, the word 'Cushite' becomes incompatible with the idea of 'blacks' as soon as it refers to the first inhabitants who civilized Arabia before Mohammed; the land of the Canaan, prior to the Jews [Phoenicians], Mesopotamia, prior to the Assyrians [Chaldean epoch]; Elam, India, before the Aryans."[173]

---

170 Diop (1991), p.108.

171 Lisapo ya Kama: African History, "The Ancient Egyptians Were Black" (2016): http://www.lisapoyakama.org/en/the-ancient-egyptians-were-black/

172 Fagan,op. cit.

173 Diop (1974), p. 168.

Chancellor Williams and Cheikh Anta Diop argue that part of the Pharaonic civilization was brought from sub-Saharan Africa, and it was indeed the black African civilization that had its roots in central Africa. It is possible that even Imhotep, the great African himself, came from the same race and had roots in central Africa. This might be clarified when the burial ground of Imhotep is discovered and his mummy examined.[174] Discovering Imhotep's tomb is regarded as sensitive, and the government of Egypt has so far restricted excavations. Perhaps there is a fear that Imhotep's DNA may reveal something unexpected by the Egyptians.[175] Ancient Egypt is an African homeland and it was built to prosper, as Williams argues: "The study of the Blacks must begin in Egypt because most of their indestructible monuments are there; and, further, because many of the artifacts archeologists have been uncovering during the past seventy-five years as 'Egyptian' are in fact African".[176] The French writer Constantin François de Chassebœuf, Comte de Volney, traveled around Egypt between 1783 and 1785, during which time slavery was at its peak and most black people had already moved to the areas still occupied by Nubians today (Upper Egypt and north Sudan). He could not see many black people in Egypt when he was around Cairo. This was due to the expulsion of blacks out of Lower Egypt to north Sudan by the different forces that occupied Egypt for thousands of years. Now there are only very few people from the Nubian ethnic community of black Africans who still inhabit Upper Egypt. At that time, black people had almost lost the entire land of Egypt to the foreigners that are still occupying it today. De Volney made the following observation of what he called the Negroes:

> [By stating that] all of them are puffy-faced, heavy-eyed and thick-lipped, could be termed as real mulatto faces from their statues.

---

174 Bauval, Robert & Thomas Brophy, *Imhotep the African: Architect of the Cosmos* (New York: Disinformation Books, 2013).

175 Ibid.

176 Williams, p. 44.

He was tempted to attribute this to the climate change until, when he visited the Sphinx, the look of it gave him a clue to the enigma. [Beholding a head that was characteristically Negro] in all of its features, he recalled the well-known passage of Herodotus which reads: 'for my part, I consider the Colchoi are a colony of the Egyptians because, like them, they are black-skinned and kinky-haired.' Just to say again, the ancient Egyptians were truly Negroes of the same stock as all the autochthonous peoples of Africa, and from that datum, one sees their race. After some centuries of mixing with the blood of the Romans and Greeks through intermarriages, most of them have lost the full blackness of the original color but retained the impress of its [original mold."][177]

In other words, it is not that Africans had lost the original color. Instead, they were driven out of Egypt, and only Nubians were left to camp on the outskirts of Upper Egypt that borders Sudan. Such description was part of the testimony of a visitor to Egypt who encountered a land that was inhabited by a race of people different from those depicted in the monuments and statues of that same land – depictions, in fact, of the very race of people who were being enslaved at the time. When de Volney was in Egypt, he thought at first that the land was an Arab country, and when venturing out to look at the monuments, it gave him a different understanding of the thousands of years of history painted on the sculptures and monuments.

Perhaps it has been unhelpful to debate who has and does 'own' the land of Egypt; almost all early visitors mention in their writings that it was the land of the "Negroes", as this was the term that was applied to black Africans at the time. This is why when you see the monuments and sculptures, you should know that they are not related to the people who lived in Egypt.

Another proof is that de Volney also wrote of the star-worshipers, a group of Nilotic people who were occupying the Upper Nile. He noted

---

177 Ki-Zerbo (1999), p. 26.

that these Nilotic people were of the black race, as he described the ways in which they organized their complicated system of worshipping the stars. Still, these same people must also be recognized for their contributions to the land in which they lived, especially their efforts in agriculture.[178] In conjunction with his statement that the people he characterized as "puffy faced, heavy-eyed and thick-lipped" were inhabiting Egypt, and that these people had introduced agricultural systems and worshipped the stars, de Volney goes on to mention that these people were also living in the Upper Nile basin. He captures it this way: "It was, then, on the borders of the upper Nile, among a black race of men, that was organized the complicated system of the worship of the stars considered in relation to the productions of the earth and the labors of agriculture; and this first worship, characterized by their adoration under their own forms and natural attributes, was a simple proceeding of the human mind: but in a short time, the multiplicity of the objects, of their relations, and their reciprocal influence, having complicated the ideas and the signs that represented them, there followed a confusion as singular in its cause as pernicious in its effects."[179]

Today, the Upper Nile basin is inhabited by a Nilotic group that was displaced from Egypt thousands of years ago, as mentioned by Williams and Diop. Most people know that it was in ancient Babylonia, and later Egypt, that star-worshipping first emerged; yet a set definition of who was an ancient Egyptian has been lacking throughout early writings.

The Bible varies from this version of history slightly; there, it is written that star-worshipping did not start in Egypt, but at the Nimrod's tower in Mesopotamia (Deuteronomy 4:19). Further, those engaged in star-worshipping were thought to be turning to Satan with their embrace of the zodiac symbols. Here it must be recalled that Nimrod was the son of Cush who, after thousands of years, crossed to

---

178 Diop (1981), p. xx.

179 De Chasseboeuf, François, Comte de Voney, *The Ruins, or, a Survey of the Revolutions of Empires* (London: J. Johnson, 1796), p. 123.

Egypt and made his home there. However, he later moved to what we now know as Sudan.

Dr. Riek Machar, the Chairman of the Sudan People's Liberation Movement in Opposition, a highly educated South Sudanese politician who has a PhD in Philosophy and Strategic Planning and is an elder of the Nilotic Naath people, commented in a conversation on Egypt that "It was truly an African country." By African, he meant that it was a black country, before invaders took it over. He argued that "some Egyptians are dark-skinned, and this shows that the genes of the black ancestors who were left behind or taken as slaves still appear after generations of intermarriages." There are myriad of accounts, such as that of Herodotus, that suggest Egypt was originally ruled by black people.

Cheikh Anta Diop has stated that the black population of Upper Egypt began to retreat after a period of Persian occupation. Diop also strove to avoid using the term "Negroid" in his works, as he found it unnecessary and derogatory. Greek and Latin writers such as Herodotus, Aristotle, Lucian, Apollodorus, Aeschylus, Achilles Tatius, Strabo, Diodorus Siculus, Diogenes Laertius, and Ammianus Marcellinus all wrote that the ancient Egyptians were Negroes, with characteristics such as thick lips, kinky hair and thin legs. Unfortunately, some writers today refuse to make use of these earlier works, and instead write in their own interests, shifting the argument from a black-ruled Egypt completely. The mathematician James Lowdermilk documented several instances of ancient Egyptians keeping part of their ancient astronomical sciences secret, and refusing to allow others to learn it. They gave much to the students of other races and wanted to reserve some of it to themselves. In the 2nd century BCE, the geographer Strabo made mention of Plato's and Eudoxus's studies in Egypttwo hundred years prior, and stated that Egyptian priests intentionally did not teach them about fractions of the day and night which run over and above 365 days. They were secretive and slow to impart that knowledge.[180]

---

180 Thomas Brophy, *The Christmas Code: A New Astronomy of Christmas and How It Came from Ancient Egypt* (Oxford: Transcendental Realist Press, 2012).

THE COMING OF THE ARABS TO EGYPT

After unpacking the origins of the word Kemet (Egypt), it is necessary to do the same for the term "Arab". It has been stated that:

> The term 'Arab' has vague origins...it should only denote the people who inhabit the Arabian Peninsula. Today the term is used to encompass most of the Middle East and the Levant. The Arab League, the Middle East's equivalent of the United Nations, officially defines an Arab as being 'a person whose language is Arabic, who lives in an Arabic-speaking country, and who is in sympathy with the aspirations of the Arabic-speaking peoples.' Modern Egypt has an Arabic-speaking population of eighty-six million people, making it by far the most legitimate candidate, if one goes by the Arab League's definition, to be regarded as the quintessential 'Arab State'. This is in any case reflected by the official name it has given itself: The Arab Republic of Egypt (A.R.E)...defining Egyptians as 'Arabs' and Egypt an 'Arab State' can only be historically correct after 642 CE, i.e., after the Arab/Muslim invasion. Let us note that it is after 642 CE that the name of the country was changed to Misr. The terms 'Misr' and 'Misrayin' come from the Hebraic name 'Mizraim' found in the Bible and used for Egyptby people of the Levant and the Arabian Peninsula. Foreign early civilizations and nations in the Middle East referred to the land of the pharaohs as Musri, Musur, or Misri. Even the Biblical text personifies this name by associating the Egyptian civilization with a legendary eponymous founder named 'Mizraim' – the son of Ham and grandson of Noah – the Hebrew -im being a plural ending used to indicate 'tribe of or 'descendants of'".[181]

Edward William Lane, who wrote the *Manners and Customs About the Modern Egyptians*, holds the view that the most significant

---

181 Bauval and Osman, op. cit.

attribute of modern Egyptians is that they are Muslims of Arabian origin and they have, for centuries, made up the population of Egypt. Egypt's laws, languages, and general culture were completely changed from the ancient African culture to a more Arabian one. This made Egypt seem as if it was originally a land of the Arabs. The constitution of the country is Islamiicized, and the national language has become Arabic; there is nothing African that you can see at the moment except the ancient monuments which they are giving Arabic names. In fact, centuries ago, long-existing buildings were converted into Arabian centers of learning. When Arabs established their dominance over Egypt, they unearthed the construction stones for the sun-god temples and used them to build mosques and houses, and converted the ancient temples into places of worship. When a land is captured, the existing structures will be converted according to the colonizers' design. The same occurred in Sudan. When the Arabs took it over, most of the Christian churches were either converted into mosques or museums, or were destroyed to pave the way for Islamic structures. One of the churches where Charles George Gordon, a British Major General killed on January 26, 1885, in Khartoum, Sudan, used to pray was converted by the Arabs into a museum, with posters portraying Gordon's head when he was killed during the Mahdi's war. There were also reports of destroying churches for Christians in Khartoum.

The Arabs started pouring into Egypt from Arabia, and in 639 CE, Amr ibn al-As led his forces into Egypt and defeated Theodorus at the Heliopolis, driving the Romans out[182]. It has been stated that:

In 641 AD Babylon had fallen, and Alexandria was besieged. Terms were then agreed upon, and in September 642, Alexandria was surrendered, and Egypt passed under the domination of the Arabs. Their immediate success cannot be credited wholly to religious fervor. A proportion was no doubt inspired by the new

---

182 MacMichael, H.A., *A History of the Arabs in Sudan* (London: Cambridge University Press, 1922)

faith, but many were with equal certainty animated by purely material considerations, and their task was the easier in that they were freeing from a foreign yoke; a country in which numbers of the population already consisted of their own kith and kin".[183]

Throughout this section, it has been highlighted that even before the Islamic movement; Arabs were in North Africa. They came in through the Port of Sinai in Egypt, then into Libya through southern Syria, and then there were influxes through Sudan via Abyssinia; the famous route of the Mid-Red Sea coast led to the Thebaid. After the seventh century, Arabs were all over northern Africa and even populated Sudan.[184]

Masr, or Cairo, is regarded as the first Arab city in Egypt, and the manners and customs that prevailed within the city were associated with those of the inhabitants of Arabia, Syria, north African Arabs, and to a greater degree, Turkey. There is no other African country that is more Middle Eastern than Egypt. We have other countries within northern Africa, but Egypt is more Arab in style than the rest of them. Maybe this could be its close proximity to the Middle East. Modern Egypt's Muslims are a mixed race which, at a certain point, descended from various Arab tribes and families that settled in Egypt at different periods in time. It all occurred soon after the country's conquest by Amr ibn al-As, who was later named as the first governor. The Arabs who came to Egypt were mostly desert tribesmen who abandoned nomadic life to cultivate crops and practice agriculture on a larger scale. After a certain period of time, they intermarried with the Copts and their descendants became Muslims. Their descendants had some resemblance to the ancient Egyptians, who were black.[185] Egyptians today are not regarded as 'true' Arabs by Middle Eastern Arabians, but as half-caste and lacking the true blood of the Arabs. Some tribes,

---

183 Ibid.,. p. 11.

184 Ibid.

185 Lane, Edward William, *The Manners and Customs of the Modern Egyptians* (Cairo: American University at Cairo Press, 1836).

such as Bedouin, Berbers, and Beja from Arabia came a long time ago and established themselves in the area. Different tribes are currently occupying Egypt whose ancestors came to Egypt a long time ago. Many of them married female slaves from Abyssinia and Oromo. The blood of their black ancestors still appears among Egyptians today due to such intermarriages. As a result, many look more African than Arab. In the south of Egypt, they also mixed with the Malayans, Indians, and Africans.

As stated earlier, the term "Arab" refers to those who speak the Arabic language and are only designated to the Beja tribe. When referring to a tribe or a small number of people, the word "Orban" would be used ("Bedawee" in the singular). In Egyptian cities and towns, the distinction of tribes is almost lost, and it is only the farmers and those who live in the villages who still use the same terms to create distinctions among themselves. Yet, the Egyptians still have some tribes and families who descended directly from the Arab tribes and who avoided for centuries intermarrying slave women or other people who did not have Arab blood.[186] This practice still exists at present in Egypt. It was a practice that was kept up thousands of years ago and is still being practiced. The Egyptians Arabs fear that when intermarriages with black people happened, it might color the children that would be born and they might have black features.

The Sudan Handbook, which is written by a group of anthropologists and historians, describes certain ethnic characteristics of the people who inhabited the northern part of Sudan around the Suez Canal, as well as further into Egypt. This was during the period before the Mohammedan rule in Egypt, when the country fell to their leadership in 639 AD. According to Eivind Heldaas Seland, before the Islamic period, Arabs had been crossing into Egypt and Sudan in large numbers to work and to trade as merchants[187]. Internal power

---

186 Ibid.

187 Seland, Eivind Heldaas, *The Indian Ocean in the Ancient Period: Definite Places, Translocal Exchange* (Oxford: Archaeopress, 2007).

struggles over the control of wealth and power during the days of Ptolemy saw the Arab traders of Egypt fall into oblivion. Many major tribes in Arabia then distanced themselves from the African coast, and the only presence was that of Indian traders. Only one Arab tribe, named the Bedouin, maintained their presence and established itself in the old land of Cush.[188]

During the seventh century AD, Islam came to Egypt and unleashed more destruction on the temple and sepulchre of Heliopolis, which was the temple of the sun god. Amr ibn el-As, the soldiers' poet, was commanding small Muslim army which took control and expelled the Byzantine viceroy Cyrus of the Nile. He wrote his observations, stating that he captured a very wonderful city that contained 4,000 palaces, 4,000 baths, 400 theaters, 1,200 greengrocers and 40,000 Jews. The war that destroyed the country have been going for two and half centuries before the main library in Alexandria was destroyed. When Egypt was captured by the Islamic army, it was used as a hub for spreading Islam to the entire south of Egypt and heading to Sudan and central Africa. Islam was being spread by following the Nile valley. This conquest brought in more Arabs, who came and worked as agricultural settlers and bureaucrats and occupied the land. The Islamic scholars also came, and took over the learning sites and legacies of the displaced black people and changed some writings to suit Islamic ways of teaching. In 870, Ahmed Ibn-Tulun, governor of Egypt, declared it an independent state and located its capital at Al-Qata'i. He also declared it separate from the rule of the Abbasid caliph, who was stationed in Baghdad, knowing that Baghdad was also governed from Egypt at the time of the Islamic invasion. Despite the volatile rulers, Cairo flourished and became the center of Islamic civilization. [189]

The Bible states that Joseph, the son of Jacob, was sold by his

188 Schoff, Wilfred H. *The Periplus f the Erythræan Sea: Travel and Trade in the Indian Ocean* (New York: Longmans, Green and Company, 1912).

189 Fagan, op. cit.

brothers to merchants travelling to Egypt. The route they used was very common, and it is thought to be the same route that the Arabs used to travel to Egypt: the Sinai Peninsula. During that period, trade was based around aromatic gums, ivory, and gold that were ferried from Arabia to the ports of Egypt, Sudan, and Abyssinia. After successive trade for hundreds of years along the African coast, foreign traders settled along these trading centers. A very famous route known as the Hamamat ran from east to west between the Red Sea and the Thebaid. This route was commonly used for taking goods into the interior of Sudan.[190] Commenting on this route, Professor Elliot Smith has stated:

> From the records inscribed upon the rocks along this route we know that there was some traffic along it in the times of the fifth dynasty: but it is such an obvious means of access from the Nile to the sea that we can be sure it must have been a trade route even in predynastic times, or at any rate, a highway where the Arab and the Proto-Egyptian met and intermingled. The widespread occurrence of marine shells, presumably from the shores of the Red Sea, in the predynastic graves of Upper Egypt and Nubia is positive evidence of the reality of such intercourse.[191]

It is clear that in the early dynastic days (3150-2613 BCE), Arabians entered Egypt peacefully and in large numbers through different routes, including via the Eritrean coast. They then settled south of the Egyptian frontiers and also in Sudan[192]. While they were trading, there was a vast population of black Africans who were occupying these areas far into Egypt. It was during this period of settlement, especially when the Arabians came through Abyssinia, that led to the colonization of that part of the region. It was the southwestern Arabians

---

190 See *History of the Sudan.*

191 MacMichael, p.4.

192 Ibid.

who colonized parts of Abyssinia in approximately 1500-300 BCE.[193] Along the coast of the Red Sea and Abyssinia, goods were coming into Sudan or Ethiopia, which then were taken west and north along a corridor known as the Straits of Bab-el-Mandeb. This coincided with the movement of the Nilotic people into the Upper Nile basin, after they were pushed out of Egypt into Sudan, and further south into the Sudd swamps.

In 3150 BCE, it was migrants from Asia who occupied the eastern frontiers of Lower Egypt. The Asians had attempted to invade Egypt, but they had been expelled by the then-black rulers from the rich delta region in 2040 BCE. The Asians returned again with their colleagues, who had traveled to Africa to trade and settle.

After the leadership of Egypt was taken over by the Arabs, the Asians became aggressors and were used by the Arabs, invading Sudan as they enslaved people and destroyed kingdoms along the border. It was during this period when the Asians worked together with the Arabs who used their forces to defeat the blacks that the leaders took in these raids and "enslaved many Blacks and marched them to Egypt – men, women, and children".[194] After some time, the black population withdrew from Lower Egypt in large numbers in a bid to escape from the settlers.[195] Most of the black population fled to join others already settled in Nubia, while some traveled along the Nile Valley further south.

There is an old island on the Red Sea which was used as a commercial town a long time ago when the Arabs were crossing into Africa through the sea. The island was used as a trading center, and years after as a learning site, both by those coming out of Africa to go and trade and those migrating into Africa. It was one of the stop-overs used later by those who were going to Mecca for Islamic pilgrimage. At different points in time, foreigners controlled this island, including

---

193 Ibid.
194 Williams, p. 79.
195 Ibid.

Greeks, Romans, and Turks, particularly because of its strategic location. The island, named Suakin, was at this time a center of learning where Arab control was dominant. The Arabs also travelled through Eritrea, Sudan, and Egypt.

Ethiopia is one of the ancient countries named after thousands of years as part of Sudan; one should not confuse it with Abyssinia. What we know today as Ethiopia was known as Abyssinia then, while the current Sudan was known as Ethiopia in the past. This confusion developed due to the writings of early explorers, historians, and those who wrote the Bible. The word "Ethiopia" comes from the Greek word *"aithops"* (which means "black faces") and could refer to the entirety of Africa as well as India. Some early Greek historians thought that Africa and India were joined and thus were one.

When a group of 70 people sat together to write the Septuagint translation of the Bible in Alexandria, Egypt in the third century, they instead used Ethiopia, as it was the general term in Hebrew that was used to refer to Cush. As mentioned earlier, the name Cush was used to refer to the specific country immediately south of Egypt which was situated along the Nile. This confusion was picked up by other translators, who translated the Bible from the original Greek version. In addition, Cush in the Bible refers to the whole area that encompasses the south of Egypt, all of Sudan, and the neighboring countries. It is also known that, even in historical terms, ancient Ethiopia was called Abyssinia. Therefore, there should be no confusion at all.[196] Now we are aware that Abyssinia and Ethiopia were two different countries. Abyssinia becomes the Eritrea of today, while ancient Ethiopia has been taken over by current Ethiopia. Cush, on the other hand, remains Sudan. This is because the entire area that covers Egypt, Sudan, Eritrea, Ethiopia, etc., comprised all the lands inhabited by black people, who welcomed merchants with open arms to trade and live with them side

---

196 Werner, Roland Werner, William Anderson, and Andrew Wheeler, *Day of Devastation, Day of Contentment: The History of the Sudanese Church across 2000 Years* (Nairobi: Paulines Publications Africa, 2000), p. 21.

by side for generations. This kingdom had survived since 1070 BCE.

In 305 BCE, the Kingdom of Ptolemy was established by Ptolemy I Soter. He later took power and considered himself the Pharaoh of Egypt after the death of Alexander the Great in 323 BCE. Ptolemy I Soter's kingdom became extremely powerful as he exerted his control over a vast expanse of land ranging from Syria to Cyrene, as well as the southern part of Nubia. The capital of his kingdom was the city of Alexandria, where there was a lot of trading among merchants from other kingdoms. As this was happening, in the second century AD, Arab settlements were established along the coast of Bab-el-Mandeb.

Another well-known trade route was the Sinai Peninsula, also used by invading Arabs. There is evidence that the eastern side of the Nile Delta was used by nomads from Sinai and Syria. As I mentioned above, with the encroachment of the Arab nomads, the Sinai Peninsula was occupied by the Arabs. This suggests that the pharaoh who was ruling in Egypt had a very strong connection with the Bedouins, an Arab tribe who came to Egypt as traders long ago. Their presence could be felt in Egypt at the moment, and in northern Sudan. They were the sand dwellers of the mining region of Sinai for generations.[197] During the Twelfth Dynasty, which was about 2,000 years before the coming of the Christian era, there existed monuments and statues carved out of rocks that suggested traces of trading with Bedouin to Clinton Bailey[198]. The Bedouin people are Arabic-speaking nomads who live in the Middle Eastern deserts of the Arabian Peninsula, Syria, Iraq, and Jordan, and after that came as traders to Egypt and North Africa. Their ancestry can be traced back to either the Qays of northern Arabia or the Yemeni, who are of southern Arabian origin. These Arabic-speaking traders are said to have been expert blacksmiths, tinkers,

---

197 MacMichael, op. cit..

198 Bailey, Clinton, "Dating the Arrival of the Bedouin Tribes in Sinai and the Negev" (Leyden, the Netherlands: *Journal of the Economic and Social History of the Orient*, January 1, 1985).

artisans, and entertainers.[199]

Thutmose III ruled Egypt from 1479-1447 BCE, and during this period, he fought against the Syrians as he traded along the Nile Delta. Inscriptions found on the tomb of Horemheb, who ruled during the period from 1350 to 1315 BCE, indicate that Arab settlement in Egypt had been taking place for years. There are also indications of Arab settlement from accounts of a fugitive from Palestine who came to Egypt and begged the pharaoh to give him asylum.[200] In addition, during this period, "the Shasu or Khabiri, the desert Semites, including Arabs, Hebrews, and Aramaeans, were inundating Syria and Palestine, until, in the reign of Ikhnaton (1375-1358 BCE), they became paramount on the eastern borders of Egypt".[201] During the reign of Seti I, which is estimated to have occurred around 1313 BCE, there had been constant fighting under the previous rule of Rameses II with the foreigners who came from the Middle East and the indigenous black people. Ramesses was fighting the Hittites from 1292-1225 BCE. After his death, a good number of Arabians were captured and pressed into service as serfs and mercenaries in Egypt. It was during this period that the power of Egypt began to decline due to Arabs occupying places and gaining power, and black people retreating toward the south of Egypt. The Libyans overran Egypt in 950 BCE during the rule of the Twenty-First dynasty of the Egyptians.[202] The strength of the Libyans came from the Arabs, who travelled through the Abyssinian and Red Sea corridors and joined forces to overrun Egypt. After most people were displaced, there were intermarriages with indigenous Egyptians who persisted. Ivan Van Sertima further described the rulers of Egypt when he stated that:

Here lay the Black Princes of the Twenty-Fifth Dynasty, who

---

199 Encyclopedia Britannica, "Bedouin" (https://www.britannica.com/topic/Bedouin).

200 MacMichael, op. cit.

201 MacMichael, p. 5.

202 Ibid.

from circa 751 to 654 BC threw their shadows across the length and breadth of the Egyptian empire, from the shores of the Mediterranean to the borders of modern Ethiopia, almost a quarter of the African Continent. They were among the last of the great sun kings of the ancient world.[203]

Along the border of Egypt and Sudan, there lived a complete dynasty which had different kingdoms, which is not part of the Egyptian dynasty. Van Sertima states that "these are the graves of the forgotten Kings of Cush, the Black Valhalla through whose ghostly fields may still be heard the distant din of wars, the clash of Nubian and Libyan, of Nubian and Assyrian, over the ailing body of Egypt."[204] When these Kings of Cush were buried, the tradition of Ancient Egypt was followed, and it dictated that kings be buried with their material objects such as silver and bronze. The Kingdom of Cush was attacked by the Libyan army. The black army of Cush fought hard to protect their country from invasion, ultimately bringing Osorkon III – a Libyan king of Upper Egypt – to his knees and crushing a rebellion within Egypt. Wars were also fought to control the power within Lower and Upper Egypt, rescuing them from the Assyrians. The Cush army also held the great powers at bay for nearly a century, until they were eventually overpowered by armies with heavier iron weaponry.[205] The ancient technology of primitive weapons was in common use during that time. This led to the slow downfall of the Cush Kingdom.

Psamtik I, also known as Psammetichus, was a governor in Ancient Egypt who later became King and reigned during the period of 664 to 610 BCE. During this period, he fought the Assyrians and pushed them out of Egypt. Herodotus, the Greek historian, described him as one of the twelve co-rulers with the Assyrians of Egypt who secured

---

203 Van Sertima, Ivan, *They Came Before Columbus: The African Presence in Ancient America* (New York: Random House, 1976), p. 125.

204 Ibid.

205 Ibid.

the support of Greek mercenaries in order to become the sole ruler of the kingdom. In 663 BCE, he conspired against the state and carried out an abortive rebellion against the Assyrian rulers of Egypt when he was a governor. He formed an alliance with King Gyges of Lydia in Asia Minor to gain military support. Such alliances helped him to defeat the Assyrians during the period of 658 to 651. Psamtik I established his capital city at Sais in the western delta and succeeded in removing the remnants of the king of Cush.[206] After his death 60 years later, his successor, Cyrus, founded the Medo-Persian Empire, and in 525 BCE, the King of Persia, Cambyses, occupied Egypt. The Persian rule over Egypt lasted for 200 years, during which period settlements of Asians and Arabs increased.

The involvement of the Arabs in Egyptian political systems was not new during the leadership of Alexander the Great. For example, Cleomenes of Naucratis was appointed the governor of Arabia with the title of Arabarch and was given more responsibilities[207].Cleomenes was a Greek of in ancient Egypt and was appointed by Alexander III of Macedonia as nomarch of the Arabian district of Egypt. He received of the tributes from all the great names of ancient Egypt and the neighboring part of Africa.

During Ptolemy's reign, the Arabs are said to have provided Antigonus, a Macedonian nobleman and general under Alexander the Great, with caravans of camels for successive missions against the Syrians[208].

At the corridor of the Red Sea and Abyssinia, where trade between the Arabs and Abyssinians flourished, there was a very good link between the Qahtanites and Himyarites of southern Arabia and the Negro population of Abyssinia, who worked together to invade the Nile Valley. Sheddad, who was the Himyarite king of the ' dites, invaded Egypt during the days of Ashmun, the grandson of Ham, who

---

206 Encyclopedia Britannica, "Psamtik I" (https://www.britannica.com/biography/Psamtik-I).

207 MacMichael, op. cit.

208 Ibid.

was in turn the son of Noah. After him, the Yemeni King, Abd Shams Saba, the founder of Ma'rib, invaded Egypt during the Nubian period through the southeastern corridor.[209]

There was also an incursion into Sudan by the Yemeni King El Sa'ab 'Dhu el Karnayn' that went as far as the Maghreb. This was an expansion of his Himayaritic tribe's expedition into Sudan through Abyssinia.[210] Afrikus, also referred to as Ibn Afriki, invaded northern Africa around 46 BCE, after which there were two distinctive Himyaritic settlements in the interior of Africa.[211] Most of these Himyaritic tribes settled in western Egypt among the Libyan tribes and multiplied under the common name of Berbers. These were Himyaritic tribes from Yemen who had successfully traded with the Aksumites of Abyssinia. Aksum was one of the trading centers in this region, located at the northeastern portion of contemporary Ethiopia. The city was situated next to the Red Sea, and it existed even before the birth of Christ. It had thrived because of international trade, was one of the earliest Christian sites in Africa, and had become one of the holiest sites of the Ethiopian Orthodox Church. There are reports indicating that the Ark of Covenant is hidden there. As a busy trading center for ivory, exotic animal skins, and gold, Aksum civilization dated back to 100 BCE.

During the third century, Aksum established its own currency and started manufacturing coins. It was the first city in Africa to use money as a medium of exchange.[212] The two races (Himyaritic and Abyssinian) were united by a common religion when in 330 AD, Aksum converted to Christianity and the faith spread to the interior of Abyssinia. Yemen had been converted to Christianity half a century earlier in 100 BCE and remained Christian until 500 AD, when King

---

209 Ibid.

210 Ibid.

211 Ibid.

212 Tesfu, Julianna, "Axum (Ca. 100 B.C.E.-ca. 650 A.D." (*Black Past*, http://www. blackpast.org/gah/axum-ca-100-b-c-e-ca-650-d)

Dhu Nuwas, a descendant of Abraham, adopted Judaism.[213] Within six centuries, Persian power increased in northern Egypt and also in Yemen. The Persians put pressure on Egypt until 616 AD, when the countries in Asia Minor were finally freed from the control of the Romans. When this conflict heated up, the Persians joined the Syrians and other Arab tribes in Egypt, thus showing sympathy and giving support to their kith and kin[214]. When the Persians took over, their rule lasted for ten years, after which they lost the support of the Arabs as a result of the Islamic movement.

HERODOTUS OBSERVATIONS IN EGYPT AND ETHIOPIA

Herodotus, a Greek historian, wrote extensively about Egypt and its black population that lived almost 2,475 years ago. His writings are some of the oldest known today. His work is a fair representation compared to what Strabo the geographer has written in its discussion and observation of what he witnessed during those years, focusing on the black-skinned people he interacted with as they discussed their daily social lives and their lifestyles. Over time, the information collected did not come from the black-skinned people alone; there were immigrants who came to Egypt and settled, and were also giving details about blacks in Egypt.

Herodotus's research was driven by his love for Africa, and he was so balanced in his writings because he did not want his own cultural biases to influence his understanding of the country he was visiting. This is noticeable by the way he divided the world by race, identifying the continents as Europe, Asia, and Libya (which indicated Africa). He was also keen on the use of language which did not carry negative stratification, despite referring to Greeks as barbarians. Although the

---

213 MacMichael, op. cit.

214 Ibid.

term "barbarian" may not be considered polite today, during that time, it was a far better word than what others used, such as "Negro". He made reference to people with black skin and applied terms such as "Ethiopian" to black-skinned people living in Upper Egypt. Cheikh Cheikh Anta Diop states that:

> Undoubtedly the basic reason for this is that Herodotus, after relating his eyewitness account informing us that the Egyptians were Blacks, then demonstrated, with rare honesty (for Greeks), that Greece borrowed from Egypt all the elements of her civilization, even the cult of the gods, and that Egypt was the cradle of civilization...archeological discoveries continually justify Herodotus against his detractors.[215]

Diop continued to say that Herodotus came to Egypt in the fifth century BCE. He found the Egyptian civilization had existed for the last 10,000 years, and it was the black race who created that civilization. It was a mistake of Pharaoh Psammetichus to give the defense of the country to foreign troops. Under the Twenty-Sixth dynasty, the Greeks were officially established at Naucratis, a port used for trading. When Alexander the Great conquered Egypt under the Ptolemies, crossbreeding between the Greeks and the Egyptians took place, which encouraged the policy of assimilation. This is why we have a good portion of Greeks in Egypt at the moment who call themselves Egyptians.

Herodotus viewed Egyptians as black and confessed that he took them to be people with black skin and woolly hair. He was in Egypt approximately 75 years after the Persians had already displaced the blacks, but before the Greeks, Romans, and Arabs came and took it over. He made his presence known in the country by traveling from north to south, observing an advanced civilization in the south compared to other communities in the north of Egypt. He carefully

---

215 Diop (1974), p. 4.

recorded his observations, focusing on the status of the black people. He stated that it was the Egyptians and the Ethiopians who were black-skinned, but they were more civilized than the Arabs and Greeks who were there. He also made note of those who had white skin in Egypt by mentioning Scythians and Celts. There were also groups of people who were light-skinned, such as the Greeks, who probably got part of their color from the black-skinned Egyptians. He observed that the black-skinned people were the most beautiful and handsome.

Herodotus wrote about Cambyses, King of Persia, who captured and ruled Egypt in 525 BCE, periodically sending spies to the King of Ethiopia, who was living at the border of Upper Egypt. The Persian king's intention was to attack Ethiopia. His spies observed that the Ethiopians who lived in that area were the tallest and handsomest men in the world. Their customs and traditions differed greatly from the rest of the community. They had kings and performed rituals such as burials differently than the Libyans and other black people. They chose their kings differently, based on the man who happened to be the tallest and the strongest among the citizens. This is contrary to how the Egyptians did it. The Ethiopians lived long, sometimes a 120 years or even more, from the findings of Herodotus. The secret foods that helped them live long consisted of boiled flesh or meat and milk from their animals. This is because they were also pastoralists who moved with their herds while the rest of Africa did not have cattle. Their minerals included copper, which was considered to be the most precious and valuable metal used for trading.[216]

The King of Ethiopia also captured Egypt and ruled for many years. The ancient Kings of Cush ruled an empire that stretched along the Nile River. Pharaoh Taharqa, one of the most famous rulers of the 25th Egyptian Dynasty of Napatan Cush, reigned from 690 to 664 BCE. He was also ruler and King of Ethiopia at the time. Taharqa later decided to abandon Egypt voluntarily. Herodotus stated that:

---

216 Strassler, Robert B. (editor), *The Landmark Herodotus: The Histories* (New York: Landmark Books, 1996), p. 125.

The Priest said that the Ethiopian king finally fled and disappeared from Egypt because he had a vision in his sleep in which he thought he saw a man standing over him, advising him to assemble the priests of Egypt and to cut them all in half. He said that through this dream, the gods seem to be hinting that he might be about to commit a sacrilege, for which he would then suffer some disaster from either gods or men.[217]

When referring to Ethiopians, Herodotus was not focusing on the Nubians alone. He was also referring to the community of black people living in the southern part of Upper Egypt. He also mentioned their capital, which was located at the mother city of Meroë in the Sudan. Herodotus referred to Ethiopians as civilized, but not on the same level as the Egyptians. He observed that these Ethiopians once ruled Egypt, and they were the pharaohs before abandoning Egypt due to the dream Taharqa had. He classified Ethiopians into two categories: the long-living Ethiopians, and the cave-dwelling Ethiopians. The long-living Ethiopians were the ones that fed on boiled meat and drank pure milk from their animals. It could be that the current people who inhabit the southern part of Sudan and are referred to as Nilotic are the ones who were feeding on boiled meat and pure milk from their animals and lived for over 120 years because of their good diet.

Regarding the kings of Ethiopia who invaded Egypt in 712 BCE, another king named Shabaka ascended in Egyptian throne after disposing Bocchoris. He was highly welcomed by the Egyptian people, who saw him as regenerator of the ancestral tradition, and they had hope that he would bring back the link between the Egyptians and the black Ethiopians in terms of that tradition and other cultural practices. Ethiopia and the interior of Africa had been considered by the Egyptians as the Holy Land, where their gods originated and dwelled. The black dynasty that came from Ethiopia was received with joy by the Egyptians, and it came from the land of Cush (Sudan). The

---

217 Ibid., p. 180.

black lands ranged from central, east, and north Africa. Central Africa was seen to be the origin of black people than the east and north Africa. Always, black people looked at central Africa as the source of life, since it has evergreen forests just like the Garden of Eden.

There are other Ethiopian people that Herodotus talked about, too. The Asian Ethiopians, or Dravidians, had the same look as Ethiopians but had straight instead of woolly hair. They served in the Persian army in their own divisions as part of the Indian contingent. They resembled the current people who are occupying Ethiopia, Djibouti, Eritrea, and Somalia. Another group of people were the Colchians, who lived on the eastern side of the Black Sea and had black skin, woolly hair, and practiced circumcision, but were grouped with the Egyptians. The other group Herodotus talked about was comprised of short men, or pygmies, that were found living around the Niger River, somewhere near the west coast of Africa. These people were part of the blacks who never moved out of Africa. As their knowledge and skill increased, they built cities and practiced sorcery and divination. They wore clothes made from palm trees. This is another group of black people who dwelt in the lands of the current Sudanese.

Herodotus' main aim was, as he mentioned in his writings, to accurately report on what he saw and heard as he documented. Perhaps his writings could be disputed by some, but given his time, he was clearly reporting on what he observed. He may not be wholly accurate, but some of his writings are still relevant even today. In ancient times, four sources documented the lives of the black race. First, as mentioned above, there was Herodotus, who wrote about the skin color of ancient Egyptians. Aristotle also referred to the ancient Egyptians as Ethiopian blacks, and the Egyptians referred to themselves as Kemet, which is translated as "black", and to the land that they hand come from as the place with elephants and giraffes. Another important source is the Bible, which referred to the children of Ethiopians and Egyptians as children of Ham. It has been noted that Ham was a very dark person and was often compared to the raven, the darkest bird.

Herodotus, who was a Greek historian and lived in the 5th Century BCE, and Flavius Josephus, whose original name was Joseph Ben Mathias (37-100 AD), a Jewish priest, historian, and scholar, both concurred on the origins of the practice of circumcision. Both historians concluded that the Colchians practiced circumcision in their culture. They had picked up this practice from up the Egyptians.

> The only people who were circumcised in their privy members originally, were the Colchians, the Egyptians, and the Ethiopians; but the Phoenicians and those Syrians that are in Palestine confess that they learned it from the Egyptians. Moreover, for those Syrians who live about the rivers Thermodon and Parthenius, and their neighbors the Macrones, say they have lately learned it from the Colchians; for these are the only people that are circumcised among humanity, and appear to have done the very same thing with the Egyptians. However, as for the Egyptians and Ethiopians themselves, I am not able to say which of them learned it from the other.[218]

The practice of circumcision spread to the Middle East, including Syria, but in Palestine, men were not allowed to be circumcised. Years later, after they returned from Egypt to Canaan, they learned about the practice from the Egyptians and accepted it. Although Herodotus confused the Palestinians and the Syrians to a certain degree, they are two different groups of people. The Palestinians were earlier called the Canaanites, who were descendants of Ham, and after their migration to Africa, the Syrians took over their land. The descendants of Ham shared common culture and traditions, but a key ritual among them was that of circumcision, which was adopted by the Semitic communities who came to Egypt and lived there.

Southern Egypt today, from Qena to Aswan and stretching all the way to lower Nubia from Aswan to Abu Simbel, covers almost 450

---

218 Josephus, Flavius, Josephus: The Complete Works,(Grand Rapids, MI: Christian Classics Ethereal Library, 2018)

kilometers of the Nile Valley; it has been suggested by Robert Bauval and Thomas Brophy that the first civilization may have started from there and then spread to the entire region.[219] It was after a long time that certain practices, such as circumcision, were abandoned by the Nilotic people and instead, the removal of the lower teeth was introduced as a remedy to certain diseases by those who abandoned circumcision. Vital texts that have survived, such as Greek writings, provide rich details crucial to researchers of today. For example, Herodotus further describes the ancient Ethiopians thus:

> They are religious to excess, far beyond any other race of men, and use the following ceremonies: They drink out of brazen cups, which they scour every day: there is no exception to this practice. They wear linen garments, which they are especially careful to have always fresh washed. They practice circumcision for the sake of cleanliness, considering it better to be cleanly than comely. The priests shave their whole body every other day, that no lice or other impure things may adhere to them when they are engaged in the service of the gods. Their dress is entirely of linen, and their shoes of the papyrus plant: it is not lawful for them to wear either dress or shoes of any other material. They bathe twice every day in cold water, and twice each night; besides which they observe, so to speak, thousands of ceremonies. They enjoy, however, not a few advantages. They consume none of their own property and are at no expense for anything; but everyday bread is baked for them of the sacred corn, and a plentiful supply of beef and of goose's flesh is assigned to each, and also a portion of wine made from the grape. They are not allowed to eat fish; and beans – which none of the Egyptians ever sow, or eat, if they come up of their own accord, either raw or boiled – the priests will not even endure to look on, since they consider it an unclean kind of pulse. Instead of a single priest, each god has the attendance of a college, at the head of

---

219 Bauval and Brophy (2013), op. cit.

which is a chief priest; when one of these dies, his son is appointed in his room."[220]

There were certain foods which were not permitted by ancient religions of Egypt to be eaten – for example, certain types of fish. Ancient texts by Egyptians, such as *The Book of the Dead* or the texts in the pyramids, revealed that those who occupied the Nile Valley had knowledge about the beginning of time and creation. These concepts were discussed in their history.[221] The ancient Egyptian's concept of the beginning of time is called *"zep tepi"*. This was linked to Sirius and Memphis, which are connected to the Sothic Cycle and had become part of their religion. Prohibition of some foods and the beginning of time were also featured in the practice of their religion. Those who have studied ancient Egyptian texts on *zep tepi* have calculated that the beginning of the world, according to the ancient Egyptians, may have been 11,451 BCE.[222] This particular date has been openly opposed by Egyptologists and archaeologists around the world, who believe that ancient civilizations are no older than 3100 BCE. Whichever is the case, these dates indicate an incredible timeline with regard to civilization.

Herodotus further observed that the only land route leading to Egypt from the Middle East passed through the desert, connecting people from Phoenicia at the boundary of the city of Gaza and the land belonging to Palestine. This was the route the Persian King Cambyses came through and attacked Egypt. If an army had crossed the desert, many soldiers would have died of thirst. However, a strategy was designed where jars full of water were buried in the sand along the route, and those who traveled along the same route would dig out the jars and drink the water to quench their thirst. This route was also

220 Rawlinson, George, *History of the Herodotus Vol. 2* (Boston: D. Appleton and Company, 1885). Book 2, Chapters 5 – 99.

221 Bauval and Brophy (2013), p. 17.

222 Ibid.

used by traders who transported goods to Egypt from Phoenicia and Hellas, especially wine in jars.

ROBBING THE ROYAL MUMMIES

As a result of looting and pillage of generations of irresponsible visitors, the artifacts and artistic achievements of the ancient Egyptians are scattered all over the globe, some of the most beautiful and spectacular of them stored or displaced thousands of miles from the Nile.[223]

Athanasius Kircher was a German who lived from 1602–1680 AD and fled from his homeland in Germany to Italy while escaping from war. He had an interest in the ancient Egyptian hieroglyphs carved from Egyptian obelisks, which were brought to Rome by the past emperors. He studied the Egyptian arts in Italy and made the conclusion that Egyptian religion was the source of Greek, Roman, and Hebrew religions as well. All the ancient philosophies, including the Hebrew kabbalah, were taken from Egyptian teachings as written in hermetic or mystical writings. All the symbols on the obelisks that were taken and placed in the Catholic churches in Rome were symbols of the sun, and coincidentally, it was the god of the sun which the emperors once served that had such symbols and structures.

The obelisk that stands today at the worship center of the Catholic Church in the Vatican was once kept at the Heliopolis in Egypt, the city of the sun in the ancient world where they worshiped the god Ra. It is one of the 12 obelisks that can be seen today in Rome. The obelisk in the Catholic Church of Saint Peter's Square was brought to Rome under the orders of Emperor Caligula in 12-41 AD. It was transported across the Mediterranean Sea in a special ship. The ancient obelisk was raised in the heart of Vatican City on September

---

223 Fagan, op. cit.

27, 1588, and one of the Bishops exorcised it by stating "I exorcise you, creature of stone, in the name of omnipotent God, that you may become an exorcised stone worthy of supporting the Holy Cross, and be freed from any vestige of impurity or shred of paganism and from any assault of spiritual impurity."[224] According to some schools of thought, the exorcism did not make any difference or change anything; the obelisk, as it stands now right in the center of the Roman Catholic Church in Rome, is still viewed as a relic of the god of the sun as was the case in ancient Egypt. The artifacts that are today seen in London, New York, Paris, etc., include many of the obelisks that were stolen from Egypt and taken to foreign lands. So far, the ancient temples in Egypt have crumbled and are almost empty today compared to ancient times. Most of the artifacts were stolen and incorporated into places of worship by the Europeans who came to Egypt thousands of years ago. All the powerful sun gods, such as Amun of Thebes, have disappeared within a short space of time in history. Even the Nilotic community, who used to worship such gods, forgot them, and their generations thought of these gods as foreign because their ancestors never informed them about them.

Massive public monuments were built by ancient Egyptians to honor their pharaohs, who were buried with their treasures in their mausoleums after they died. The Egyptians' New Kingdom existed during the period from 1539-1075 BCE. During this period, the Valley of the Kings became a burial ground for the pharaohs, hence the name. Pharaohs like Tutankhamun, Seti I and Ramses II, as well as their queens, high priests and other noble elites of the 18th, 19th and 20th dynasties were buried in the Valley of the Kings.[225] Despite the commitment of the priests and government officials to protect the dead

---

224 Bauval, Robert, "Under the Pope's Nose: The Architect, The Astronomer and the Vatican" (RobertBauval.co.uk, 2006: http://www.robertbauval.co.uk/articles/articles/underthepopesnose.html).

225 Handwerk, Brian, "Valley of the Kings: The Gateway to the Afterlife Provides a Windows to the Past" (*National Geographic*, retrieved June 4, 2019, https://www.nationalgeographic.com/archaeology-and-history/archaeology/valley-of-the-kings/).

by moving the royal mummies from tomb to tomb and sarcophagus to sarcophagus, the tombs were emptied and looted of their riches. In particular, the tombs of Seti I and Ramses II were moved several times, hidden in increasingly safer places to evade the robbers. The tombs remained safely hidden for 3,000 years until 1881 AD when things changed by exploration of the tombs by researchers, after which these tombs too were found by treasure robbers and looted.[226]

Some of the tomb robbers were caught and forced to explain how the robberies were carried out. One said, "They came to me and told me 'come out' and 'we are going to take plunder for bread to eat.' They took me with them and opened the tomb and took away shrouds of gold and silver. We brought baskets with us, and we filled them."[227]. Uncovering royal tombs and stealing the treasures had been a lucrative business for thousands of years. This did not just start with the coming of foreigners; it existed even before foreigners invaded the land. It began in ancient Egypt during the early dynastic period, and it is still happening even in modern times. The visitors were only good at robbing African of its treasures and cultural artifacts, including mummies of dead bodies, thus disrespecting their burial rites.

The reason for "burying the Kings with their wealth was to prepare them for ascension into the afterlife; a preparation for the next world, in which humans were promised continued life and especially pharaohs who were expected to become one with the gods."[228] It became lucrative for poor Egyptians to loot the tombs of the royal and wealthy pharaohs as a way of claiming a share of the wealth. However, the penalty was death when one was caught looting the dead. Looting tombs was not just done by the poor, but even the priests of the prayer houses were implicated;.priests and corrupt officials would be bribed by the robbers before they ransacked the tombs.[229] The Valley

---

226 Fagan, op. cit.

227 Ibid., p. 5.

228 Handwerk, op. cit.

229 Fagan, op. cit.

of the Kings was notorious for such robbery. Measures to safeguard the tombs were put in place and included filling the tombs' hallways with debris to prevent access by thieves. However, the tombs were still broken into and looted, including taking the mummies of kings.[230] Brian M. Fagan argues that

Most of the royal tombs of the Valley of the Kings had probably been opened illegally by professional thieves by the end of the 20th Dynasty. The predations of these robbers were so severe that most of the royal treasure vanished forever…the tombs and great monuments of ancient Egypt have been under siege ever since they were built. The Egyptians themselves used them for building stones. Theban tomb robbers were followed by religious zealots and quarrymen who eradicated inscriptions and removed great temples - stone by stone.[231]

When Alexander the Great came to Egypt, he rebuilt some temples that had collapsed; many of these survive today. The ancient Egyptians considered their land the "image of heaven", in which all the powers that operated in the afterlife also operated in Egypt. It was believed that the whole cosmos revolved around the land of Egypt.[232] This shows how much ancient Egyptians held their land in awe. Max Rodenbeck states that:

Muslim masons of the eleventh century found that decorative blocks from Heliopolis slotted nicely into the inner ramparts of the Cairo city walls… nearly every column in all the hundreds of

---

230 Mark, Joshua J., "Tomb Robbing in Ancient Egypt" (The Ancient History Encyclopedia, July 17, 2017, https://www.ancient.eu/article/1095/tomb-robbing-in-ancient-egypt/).

231 Bauval, Robert and Ahmed Osman, Breaking the Mirror of Heaven: The Conspiracy to Suppress the Voice of Ancient Egypt (Rochester, Vermont: Bear & Company, 2012), p 77.

232 Ibid.

medieval mosques in the city were recycled from some pagan temple. Other ancient columns were sliced like loaves of bread into discs and inserted into stone marquetry of paving and walls. Mosque thresholds too, were often choice pharaonic plunder, placed so that the faithful could trample on the beliefs of idol worshippers...while engaged in quarrying ancient sites. Courtiers had convinced the prince to tear down the smallest of the three main pyramids of Giza...and sell the stones to contractors.[233]

The Arabs in Egypt are responsible for not only bringing down ancient Egyptian monuments to put up their mosques and buildings, but also for giving artifacts as gifts to foreigners, especially the French and the Romans, to cement their relations. It seems they bought the land with the gift of the monuments of their predecessors. The Luxor Obelisk was given to France by Pasha Mohammed Ali, and in return, France gave Egypt a large clock which is now placed on the mosque tower at the summit of the Citadel of Cairo. Transportation costs for moving these items from Egypt to France was as high as 2.5 million francs, but this was worth it when one considers the value of the Obelisk. Tomb robbery became a business that encouraged the mutilation and export of other monuments of ancient Egypt. Looting the tombs for jewelry, mummies, and other important artifacts became a thriving illegal trade from the time it started until recently, when the National Museum of Egyptian Civilization was established 100 years ago. There was also a belief that the powder from mummies made good medicine for treating several diseases. Arab Egyptians ransacked the temples and pyramids to obtain this item. Their buyers were Europeans. There were even reported cases where traders "bought the corpses of unclaimed criminals and the indigent, as well as sometimes even exhuming bodies from modern cemeteries, to create mummies, which they sold to credulous foreigners."[234]

---

233 Ibid., p. 99.
234 Ibid.. p .101.

There have been many instances where the Jews have been unfairly blamed for such crimes of looting the tombs and buying the mummies. Perhaps a more critical debate has revolved around the question of who constructed the pyramids in the first place. Robert Bauval and Ahmed Osman state that:

> The discovery of the tombs of the workmen who built the pyramids was tremendously important to Egyptians because it proved that the greatness of Egypt lay in a project of both Egyptian genius as well as Egyptian labor. It is especially important vis-a-vis Israeli claims that it was their Jewish slave ancestors who built the pyramids, but also vis-a-vis theorists who would have that the pyramids were built by Atlanteans or aliens.[235]

Such debates are still ongoing and add to the practice of falsifying history by writers. Not much regarding ancient civilizations has been attributed to black people even when evidence points to their immense contributions. Many writers and leaders have fed the machinery of institutionalized racism when they support the misconception that nothing good can be created by the black race.

Prior to his election, American business magnate Donald Trump, demonstrated deep disgust for Africans by stating that they are poor and hungry because when it rains, they only think about lovemaking instead of farming. After his election, he continued this racist rhetoric by stating that those Africans who settled in the United States of America illegally were to be deported because they were lazy. He further referred to some African leaders as thieves who steal from their own people and invest the loot in the developed countries.[236] After such derogatory statements from Trump, the African Union, the

---

235 Ibid.

236 BBC, "Donald Trump Must Apologize for Comments – African Union" (British Broadcasting Corporation, January 12, 2018, https://www.bbc.com/news/world-us-canada-42670715).

body that coordinates African affairs, stated their disappointment that the "remarks dishonor the celebrated American creed and respect for diversity and human dignity...while expressing our shock, dismay, and outrage, the African Union strongly believes that there is a huge misunderstanding of the African continent and its people by the current Administration...there is a serious need for dialogue between the U.S. Administration and the African countries."[237]

As observed earlier, the poor turned to treasure hunting by digging up the tombs and destroying the great monuments of ancient Egypt, thus holding the country hostage for thousands of years by violating the burial rights of the kings. The stones from the tombs were used by the poor ancient Egyptians as building blocks for their houses. Religious zealots and quarrymen also learned from the tomb robbers, and even erased the inscriptions from the treasures, destroying great ancient temples stone by stone, just for commercial gain. They could dig up stones with inscription and take them for sale.

Many visitors to Egypt wanted to go back with something of historical value so that they could use such items to tell the story of Egypt and its rich history. When they were back in their countries, they would carry something like a trophy to show to their fellow countrymen of the treasure they found in Egypt. They joined the tomb robbers and benefited from the looted artifacts of Egypt. The looting and robbing of treasures was not confined to the items in the royal tombs; robbers even took the mummies out of their coffins and used them as medicine to cure diseases. It was Arab doctors who introduced this practice, and between the 6th and 7th centuries AD, the mummies had become very expensive in the drug black market. After the peasants realized that stealing and selling the mummies was a lucrative business, they decided to hunt for the tombs and collect what they could find, flooding Cairo with the corpses of mummies. A narrative from an Arab writer stated that people had made a pile of human corpses, and when they were caught and brought before

237 Ibid.

the provost, they were tortured in order to confess. Most of them then confessed the corpses had been removed from the tombs. Brian Fagan describes how the dead bodies were boiled in water until the skin peeled off and the oil on the surface of the boiling water would be collected and sold to for 25 pieces of gold.[238]

DESTRUCTION OF ANCIENT MONUMENTS: THE GREAT SPHINX OF GIZA

Graham Hancock and Robert Bauval referred to the Sphinx as "Horizon Dweller." I was reminded of this when I first visited Egypt, and the term "Horizon Dweller" came to mind when I faced the Sphinx looking into the Nile. The Sphinx looks like a man lying on his belly, worshipping the rising sun. This may not be far from the intention of the pharaoh, who carved the Sphinx and created its purpose because the ancient Egyptians' god was Ra, the sun god. My translator informed me that the Sphinx was designed to worship his father, who died long along. He was bowing down to him while giving him gifts and presenting them in a humble way. It is a gigantic statue with a lion's body and the head of a man looking down upon Egypt. It was carved out of the limestone bedrock of Giza. Many theories were attached to Sphinx, and it was believed to be an eternal god of the ancient Pharaohs. Thousands of years have passed since when it was carved out and "then amnesia ensnared it, and it fell into enchanted sleep. Ages passed: thousands of years. Climate changed. Culture changed. Religion changed. Language changed. Even the position of the stars in the sky changed. But still, the statue endured, brooding and numinous, wrapped in silence."[239] It was a magnificently built creature for a purpose hidden from the world and generations.

238 Fagan, op. cit.

239 Hancock, Graham and Robert Bauval, *The Message of the Sphinx: A Quest for the Hidden Legacy of Mankind* (New York: Broadway Books, 1997). p. 3.

*The Great Sphinx looking at the Nile and rising sun and the
Great Pyramid behind it.*

Courtesy to Google:

The Great Sphinx, which is located in Giza, Egypt, dates back to the reign of King Khafre, c. 2575 -2465 BCE, and is held to be one of world's largest sculptures. It is also the most famous landmark in Egypt. The sculpture has now deteriorated a great deal, and the body parts have been weathering off with time since the reign of Thutmose IV (1400-1390 BCE). The surface of the sculpture has suffered the most erosion, while its face has been vandalized and the nose removed. Napoleon's troops are said to have shot off the Sphinx's nose with cannons as they practiced their shooting skills. However, some do not believe that Napoleon's troops did this because other figures of black people suffered the same fate; they couldn't have done it all. It is still believed that the current Arab race who is occupying Egypt could have done this on purpose to deface them and avoid the characterization of ancient Egypt as a black civilization. In addition, according to Robert Bauval, an Egyptologist said Muhammad Sa'im al-Dahr, a notorious Sufi Muslim fundamentalist, mutilated the statue of Sphinx in the 14th century, giving the reason that people had started worshiping it.[240] This could be the typical behavior of a Muslim fundamentalist who viewed ancient monuments as objects of the gods. Whether al-Dahr was punished for this is not clear even now, and has never been revealed. Some claim that he was disciplined for this act, while others mentioned that nothing was done to him.

When I visited the Sphinx in August 2018, I was surprised by the work of the ancient Egyptians, and it was my first time seeing them. The monuments, structures, and the images of the ancient Egyptians were all amazing sights. Despite the destruction that has taken place since those early years, remnants of the ancient monuments still stand today as a testament to the ancient work. The Sphinx is one of the Egyptians' most beautiful monuments. It has the glory, the mystery, and the splendor that stand with time and still proudly graces the land of Egypt. Despite destruction committed by different invaders, the statue still looks intact as it stands facing the Nile, giving the impression that it is the river's guardian and protector. If defacing the Sphinx is attributed to foreign regimes, then what would be the explanation for defacing the black pharaohs that had been carried out? When I was in the Cairo museum, I got surprised that almost all the statues of black kings were disfigured almost beyond recognition. The thick lips and the African noses that would make them recognizable as black and not Asian were completely disfigured. This distortion is obviously associated with the Egyptian archaeologists and Egyptologists who have attempted to erase the immeasurable contribution that black people made to the Egyptian civilization. it was archaeologists who dug them up and Arabs in Egypt who are now occupying the land; they committed this fraud just as they want to get rid of all blacks in Egypt.

---

240 *Encyclopedia Britannica*, "Great Sphinx of Giza" (https://www.britannica.com/topic/Great-Sphinx).

Robert Bauval mentioned that the colony of Canaanites who lived around this area in the early second millennium BCE worshipped the Sphinx. They came from the sacred city of Harran and may have been on some pilgrimage. In fact, the people who came from Harran City were not Canaanites. Canaanites were living in Canaan, and Harran was situated at the border of Babylon and Turkey. As I mentioned in Chapter 2 of this book, the people who lived in Harran City were Chaldeans. They were the ones that came to this place. It is further believed that the people from Harran City gave it the name "Hwl," which is an Egyptian term for "place." The real meaning attached to it is "Hor-em-Akhet," which is translated as "Horus on the Horizon," and this could not be far from the truth.[241]

Monuments of ancient Pharaohs in Cairo.
National Museum of Antiquity

---

241 Hancock and Bauval (1997), op. cit.

The defacing of statutes, especially the removal of noses and lips and the stealing of relics of our prophets, has taken place even in recent times such as with the prophet Ngundeng in Upper Nile South Sudan. Foreigners came to steal other resources that were left in Egypt by black people; this is an indication of how desperate the world was and still is, in taking away the creativity, ancient works of art, and even current resources of black people as has happened for centuries over.

The ancient Egyptians were seafarers and used their boats to navigate the Red Sea, the Mediterranean Sea, and the Nile corridors. They also had very good battleships. The battleships were well designed in order to protect those that were rowing by having extra layers to protect from incoming objects. Ramses II had a fleet of 400 boats on the Arabian Gulf, and some of them were very large. One of the battleships carried 4,000 rowers, 400 sailors, and 3,000 soldiers. This fleet was used to bring precious goods such as exotic wood, spices, slaves, ivory, and gold that were widely used in Ancient Egypt.[242] These socio-economic and political activities brought much development to the land, and ancient Egypt was considered a powerhouse to reckon with.

Some archaeologists are searching for the truth using scientific techniques to unveil evidence that would support their conclusions on the ancient civilization being attributed to black people. Works by some early historians and explorers, such as Herodotus and Ptolemy, have been retranslated to help uncover the truth of black civilization of Egypt. The statues and monuments contain convincing evidence of a black population, yet the existence of blacks in Egypt was nearly completely erased. Through the destruction of certain statues and pyramids in Egypt, black people almost lost their contributions to Egypt. Some of the artifacts depicting the existence of Black people in Egypt were not taken to museums, but hidden from the researchers by the Arabs and kept somewhere, destroyed, or left to an unknown fate. In other cases, deliberate damage was done to change the appearance

---

242 Gosse, A. Bothwell, *The Civilization of the Ancient Egyptians* (London: T.C. & E.C. Jack, 1915).

of these monuments to erase any black characteristics. The account below indicates how some Egyptian statues got lost or stolen, only to appear later in foreign lands:

> The appropriation of Ancient Egyptian culture by non-African cultures...the Washington Monument is in the form of an ancient Egyptian obelisk and was built to commemorate George Washington...it is used here to illustrate how easily an Egyptian symbol can be used out of its original context and by a culture that had no direct link to the original source. Many cultures that had no connection to Ancient Egypt have used Kemetic symbols for their purposes, to try to connect to a powerful ancient civilization.[243]

The Luxor obelisk was taken from Egypt to France and erected in Place de la Concorde in Paris in October 1833 by King Louis-Philippe I. This is one of the two obelisks that once graced Luxor Temple, built by Ramses II in Egypt.[244] There are many more monuments in Europe today that were in fact stolen by different Western countries under the pretext that they were given as gifts. When the Arabs occupied Egypt by overthrowing the blacks, the value of Ancient Egyptian monuments was not known to them. The Arabs therefore looted and destroyed the tombs and monuments that they found in Egypt as a way of exerting their power. It was not until recently that many visitors have gone to see the various wonders of the world, with the Egyptian pyramids probably being the most visited – 14.7 million visitors a year, followed by France with 8.2 million yearly. When the Arabs started to reconstruct the city of medieval Cairo in the 7th century AD, the remains of the temples of Heliopolis were systemat-

---

243 Ashton, Sally-Ann, "Why are the Noses Missing from Egyptian Statues?"(Kemet Expert, February 5, 2016, http://kemetexpert.com/why_are_the_noses_missing_from_egyptian_statues/).

244 Archaeology Travel, "Luxor Obelisk" (https://archaeology-travel.com/france/luxor-obelisk/).

ically ransacked and looted. The stones were used to construct other buildings.[245] It could be that under Islam, these ancient monuments and symbols were not considered religious. National Geographic reported the destruction and bulldozing of ancient monuments in Iraq and Syria by the Islamic State in Syria (ISIS). It was an attack on cultural heritage:

> The so-called Islamic State released a video that shocked the world by showing the fiery destruction of the Temple of Baalshamin, one of the best-preserved ruins at the Syrian site of Palmyra. Explosions have also been reported at another Palmyra temple, dedicated to the ancient god Baal; a United Nations agency says satellite images show that larger temple has largely been destroyed. The destruction is part of a propaganda campaign that includes videos of militants rampaging through Iraq's Mosul Museum with pickaxes and sledgehammers, and the dynamiting of centuries-old Christian and Muslim shrines. ISIS controls large stretches of Syria, along with northern and western Iraq. There's little to stop its militants from plundering and destroying sites under their control in a region known as the cradle of civilization.[246]

I recalled in Chapters 1 and 2 that the Middle East, including Syria, Canaan, Lebanon and parts of Turkey and southern Arabia, were ancient civilizations of black men, and the ongoing destruction is the cultural annihilation of the traces of black people in the name of religion.

The modern government of Egypt claims ownership over artifacts, yet their ancestors never labored in building the monuments, and neither did they know of their use. Probably even in modern times,

---

245 Bauval and Brophy (2013), op. cit.

246 Curry, Andrew, "Ancient Sites Damaged and Destroyed by ISIS" (National Geographic, November 5, 2017, https://www.nationalgeographic.co.uk/history-and-civilisation/2017/11/ancient-sites-damaged-and-destroyed-isis).

some Egyptians do not want to acknowledge that Egypt should be considered part of Africa instead of wanting it to be associated with the Middle East and Arabs. This is very clear in the Arab League, which Egypt does not and want countries like South Sudan to join. Whenever Egyptians want to visit a black African country, they often tend to say that they are going to Africa. There still remains a mentality that modern-day Egyptians are only occupiers of Egypt, and Africa is not their continent. The country is within the geographical location of Africa, yet the citizens are associated more with the Middle East, and Arabs in particular. The ruthlessness and brutality that they used to push black Africans out of Egypt are the same that they so authoritatively use against black visitors to Egypt today. When I visited the National Museum, I was approached several times by many people who asked me to take photos with them. Some told me that I look like the pharaohs, while others told me that they had never seen a black man closely and they wanted to touch my hair and skin. Friends that were with me who were from Egypt and have experienced this racist attitude were uncomfortable. The ancient monuments that were built long ago and the people owning and using them today are incompatible. Even visitors who go to Egypt notice this mismatch. If you closely look at the Sphinx – the thick lips, the nose, and the shape of the head – you will, you will be convinced that the builder was not an Arab.

FIGHTING OVER ANCIENT KEMET MONUMENTS

There is an ongoing conflict between Arab Egyptians and Israelis, as both believe that ancient Egypt is the foundation of their roots. The Israelites believe in what is written in the Bible: that "thousands of years ago, according to the Old Testament, the Jews were slaves in Egypt. The Israelites had been in Egypt for generations, but now that they had become so numerous, the Pharaoh feared their presence. He feared that one day the Israelites would turn against the Egyptians.

Image of Joseph and Mary taking Jesus to Egypt escaping King Herod's wrath.
Courtesy of Abu Sergia, Cairo, Egypt. 2018.

Gradually and stealthily, he forced them to become his slaves. He made the slaves build grand 'treasure cities'".[247]

Because the current Egyptians are not confident that their ancestors built the pyramids, they have often accused the Israelis of conducting piracy because their ancestors were once believed to have been slaves in the land of Egypt, as defined clearly by the Bible. Some of these accusations have taken place in social media. The Egyptian government has made baseless claims that the Israelis have attempted to rob the country of its monuments just as they robbed Palestinians of their land. Dr. Zahi Hawass, the Chairman of the Supreme Council of Antiquities, on September 17, 2002, was hosted live by the FOX television network in America. He was vocal in delivering his message on the concerns over Jews or slaves who were portrayed to have built the monuments in Egypt: "It was not 'slaves' who built the Pyramids,

---

247 British Library, *The Haggadah*: "Enslavement of the Israelites" (https://www.bl.uk/learning/cult/inside/goldhaggadahstories/enslave/enslavement.html). Retrieved June 26, 2019.

he stated with pride, but the 'great Egyptians'." He was informing his audiences and listeners to be careful about attributing what the Egyptians have done to others. The 'slaves' referred to here were the Jews/Israelites, who, according to the Bible, took refuge in Egypt for 430 years. Robert Bauval supported Dr. Hawass' position by stating that:

> To be fair to Dr. Hawass, it is true that there once did exist a belief in some Western countries that the 'Jews built the Pyramids'. This goes back to the 1860s, when Charles Piazzi Smyth, the Astronomer Royal of Scotland, published a book, *Our Inheritance in the Great Pyramid*, claiming that the Pyramids of Giza were built by Jewish slaves under divine inspiration. And although it is also true that this absurd theory was popular with the 19th century evangelical Judeo-Christian movements such as the British Israelites and the Jehovah's Witnesses, the truth is that for many decades now, nobody – at least nobody with an elementary knowledge of ancient history – takes such an absurd idea seriously, and this 'Jews built the Pyramids' theory has long been dumped down the crackpot bin of pyramidology. Anyone publishing such nonsense today would simply be laughed at. To put it bluntly, the 'Jews built the Pyramids' theory is as dead as a dodo.

Such theories have no basis in reality, just like the way the modern Egyptians think Egypt was the result of their ancient ancestors' labor, though according to researchers it had no connection with the Arabs whatsoever.

The Egyptians may think that the Israeli's claim to have built the pyramids when they were slaves is without merit. A few individuals within the government have even referred to Israelis as "pirates who are committing robberies."[248] The situation will definitely be uglier when black people begin to claim the history and civilization of

---

248 Bauval and Osman (2012), p. 63.

Ancient Egypt. I think the Arabs may not like it, given that in Egypt, the ancient monuments have become the greatest source of income and cultural heritage in the country.

Currently, there are reports from researchers that the Egyptian government is refusing to allow DNA tests on mummies. During my recent visit to the National Museum in Cairo, I visited a room in which mummies were kept, and I realized that most of the mummies were black. The strangest thing was that people were not allowed to take photographs or videos. The room was heavily guarded, and this left the author wondering about what was being protected, or if they were providing extra protection measures.

One could definitely see that the Egyptians were caught between two scenarios when they were preventing people to take photos. First, they want money, since tourism fetches a lot of foreign exchange, which they badly need for the economy. Secondly, and perhaps more critically, they are afraid that if photographs and videos of mummies are taken, evidence that the mummies were black will surface and prevent others making profits. This would generate more debate and further discussion on this topic, which seems to have been closed off for generations.

Dr. Hawass, who was educated in the West, once went on the offensive against the Israelis and the Jews, stating in the media that the pyramids were not built by the slaves, but by great Egyptians. By using the term "slaves", he was referring to the Israelis who were held captive for 430 years by the Egyptians. He was not referring to black Africans either, who after a millennium, were forced down the Nile Valley and acquired the name Nilotes and Nubians. Instead, Dr. Hawass reinforced the notion that it was people of Asiatic origin who built the Pyramids. With other Western media campaigns supporting the view that Jews built the pyramids, Egyptian authorities, including Dr. Hawass, who had been made one of the guardians of the monuments, strongly refuted these reports, hence his verbal attack on the West and the Jewish people. On his website, Robert Bauval quoted Dr. Hawass as he addressed the Egyptians after examining the skeleton of a 4th

Dynasty Egyptian that had been found in the Giza Pyramid. In his address, Dr. Hawass told the Egyptians not to listen to the propaganda regarding the people who actually built the Pyramids. He said:

> "I want you to learn that these are the fingerprints of the workmen; the Egyptians who built the pyramids! This can shut the mouths of all these idiots who talk about lost civilizations and all of this kind of nonsense. This man does not exist; he's a skull dating back to the time of the 4th Dynasty when mummification was very rare."[249]

The Egyptian minister of culture, Dr. Farouk Hosni, was quoted as saying that he was ready to "strike back at pyramid theorists" and to wage war to protect the pyramids and the Sphinx from those who were campaigning to help Israel steal the monuments. He further said that:

> "Israeli allegations that they built the Pyramids...triggers a crisis with Israel! This is piracy! Our history and our civilization must be respected, but the Israelis want to take over everything! We must counterattack with full strength...they keep on saying Palestine belongs to them and now they are doing the same with the Pyramids."[250]

The Arabs in Egypt would do anything, including going to war, against any country that claims ownership of the Egyptian civilization. This is analogous to the way they have been controlling the waters of the Nile; warning countries downstream not to make any attempts to divert the waters for their use. The war over the Nile water has been brewing for a long time, with Egypt monitoring it closely and crossing swords with any country that might interfere with the diversion of the Nile Water.

---

249 Bauval, Robert (2002). "Jews Did Not Build the Pyramids, Says Egypt's Chairman of Antiquity" (http://www.robertbauval.co.uk/articles/articles/hawass1.html)

250 Ibid.

It is often said the next world war will be fought over water, and there are few places as tense as the River Nile. The BBC reported that:

> Egypt and Ethiopia have a big disagreement, Sudan is in the middle, and a big geopolitical shift is being played out along the world's longest river. There's been talk about a dam on the Blue Nile for many years, but when Ethiopia started to build, the Arab Spring was under way, and Egypt was distracted. 'Egypt was the gift of the Nile,' the pharaohs said, and they worshiped the river as a god. For thousands of years, and more recently buoyed by British colonialism, Egypt has wielded political influence over the Nile. But the ambition of Ethiopia is changing all that. There are few African countries with a plan to deal with the doubling of the continent's population over the next 30 years. Yet despite its political challenges and its limited freedoms, industrial parks are being built as Ethiopia seeks to transform itself into a middle-income country, and so it needs electricity.[251]

Apart from the Ethiopian dam, the Sudd swamps is one of the areas that has been attracting the interest of Egypt for years. The Sudd swamps have valuable socio-ecological functions which support the lives of those around it. Now, overgrazing of animals and loss of vegetation has resulted from overflooding during the wet season.

Just as the ancient pharaohs thought Egypt owned the River Nile, the modern-day government in Egypt thinks the river solely belongs to them. During the South Sudan civil war which started in December 2013, undocumented sources mentioned a secret deal over water has been drafted and signed by the Kiir administration, the incumbent presidency of South Sudan, with the Egyptian government. The deal capitalized on the use of water by the South Sudanese, limiting it only for consumption purposes rather than for agriculture. It should be a

---

251 Leithead, Alastair, "The 'Water War' Brewing Over the New River Nile Dam (BBC, February 24, 2018: https://www.bbc.com/news/world-africa-43170408).

right of the indigenous people who lives along the Nile to use water for variety of reasons. Such reasons should not be limited to local consumption and agricultural purposes. The terms that were agreed upon were not made public at the time this book was written, but an insider from Kiir administration talked about it and claimed it as one of the main discussions between the Egyptians and the South Sudanese government. When the digging of Jonglei Canal failed in 1983 due to civil war, the Egyptians have been trying very hard to do anything to get the water around the Sudd swamps, which is one of the largest swamps in the world and hosts a huge ecosystem. Whether this is a project that will be executed or a political scam is not clear for now. The underlying factor is that Egypt can do anything to get the water of the Nile for its own good, even going to war with any country that will tamper with the Nile Water. When Sudan was one country prior to South Sudanese independence, Egypt had outpost units in different towns of Sudan, monitoring the Nile water and reporting back to its government. Since South Sudan seceded from Sudan in 2011, there has never been any source of electricity for the country except oil refineries. There was an establishment of generators which do not supply to the entire country, but only few government institutions and individuals. There have been plans to build a dam, but unfortunately, the government of South Sudan and Egypt refused to execute that plan. The entire country was in total darkness for generations. Egypt is ruthless in gaining the resources of any country by force. Arab elites did just that to the ancestors of the Sudanese, who came to the Upper Nile by taking over their monuments, and they are still doing it with their water. Robert Bauval and Ahmed Osman commented critically on Dr. Zahi Hawass's views:

What was very ironic about all this was that the theories of West, Hancock, and myself not only support the idea that it was ancient Egyptians who built the Sphinx and pyramids, but also provide ancient Egyptian culture with an older pedigree and thus give it precedence over other cultures. Indeed, in many of our books we advocate that it was the Egyptians who taught the arts and the sciences to the Greeks, and not the other way around as Egyptologists claim. So, either Dr. Hawass is deliberately twisting our theories to suite his own political agenda, or he simply does not understand them. Having admitted publicly that he does not read our books, this is perhaps not surprising. But we have made our views abundantly clear to him on numerous occasions, as well as to the people who support him in his 'attacks' against us. But nothing doing whenever Dr. Hawass gets the opportunity to link us to an imaginary 'Jewish plot;' there he goes again and brings out 'the Jews built the Pyramids' theory and links it to us.[252]

Due to the complexity of the monuments built in Egypt, other theories exist which argue that it was the work of an advanced civilization of black Africans, who were the descendants of the original and first peoples on Earth, that built the pyramids. Flavius Josephus states clearly that it was Nimrod who built the Tower of Babel, and the latest scientific discoveries indicate that there is evidence to support this view. Flavius Josephus had this to say:

Now the multitude were very ready to follow the determination of Nimrod, and to esteem it a piece of cowardice to submit to God; and they built a tower, neither sparing any pains, nor being in any degree negligent about the work: and, by reason of the multitude of hands employed in it, it grew very high, sooner than anyone could expect; but the thickness of it was so great, and it was so strongly built, that thereby its great height seemed, upon the view, to be less than it really was. It was built of burnt brick, cemented together with mortar, made of bitumen, that it might not be liable to admit water.[253]

---

252 Bauval and Osman (2015), op. cit.
253 Josephus, op. cit.

I cannot see a real reason for the continued speculations on who built the pyramids, since there are documented sources which are objective about it. If the pyramids were the work of other races, they would have already talked about it openly without denial. Herodotus stated that he was told by an Egyptian priest that one of the pyramids took one hundred thousand men and 20 years to complete. This priest was one of the guardians of the records of their temples. Dr. Hawass claims to have discovered the tomb of the pyramid builders, but the tomb that was excavated contained 600 skeletons. This could not have been the tomb of the pyramid builders because there would surely have been more than 600 laborers on such a vast project. There are theories stating that the technology that was used to build the pyramid was hidden completely. The workers that were used for building the pyramid were killed after the completed the building. It was quite a huge construction, and many laborers were involved. Maybe the book used as the blueprint for constructing the pyramid is yet to be discovered inside those structures.

Most of the black Egyptian pharaohs ruled well, their dynasties were powerful, and Egypt flourished under their care. It was these pharaohs the Nilotic people believe they are descended from. The Naath people believe strongly that their fathers worked extremely hard in Egypt and that they built the pyramids. The current pyramid shape of their cattle byres and huts were taken from the shape of the pyramid. In the 18th Century AD, the Naath prophet Ngundeng Bong Chan built a pyramid in the Upper Nile. It was later destroyed by the British with explosives. It is part of the oral history of the Nilotic people that their journey came through the northern part of Sudan, and even today there are places such as Khartoum and Tuti island they think were part of their migration.

Different groups in the Nilotic community present their views on how they are connected to Egypt. This is told in an oral history, and one community that wrote their version and understanding of how they are connected to Egypt is the Kalenjin community. Kipkoeech

Araap Sambu states that "The Kalenjin people have a tradition that their ancestors in antiquity were part of ancient Egypt, which they variously call Tto and Misiri."[254] The Kalenjin are among the darkest-skinned people of the Nile Valley. They share the same characteristics with the rest of the Nilotic people, such as the Naath, Jieng, Lou, Murle and Acholi. Sambu further made some assertions that it was the oral traditions passed down from generation to generation that indicated their tribe came down from Egypt, and this is told to children generation after generation.

The pharaohs of black origin were Lord Tera-Neter; Narmer or Menes; Djoser, the pharaoh of the Third Dynasty; Cheops of the Fourth Dynasty; the Pharaoh who built the Great Pyramids; Mycerinus of the Fourth Dynasty, who built the third Giza pyramid; Pharaoh Mentuhotep I who found the Eleventh Dynasty; Pharaoh Sesostris I, the founder of the Twelfth Dynasty; Pharaoh Ramses II; Pharaoh Thutmose III, son of the Sudanese woman who founded the Eighteenth Dynasty; and the Sudanese Pharaoh Taharqa. Also, King Tut is passionately talked about by Naath people as their direct descendant who lived in Egypt and was a king. The boy king ascended into the throne at the age of 10, and nine years later, he died mysteriously. He took over power from his father around 1361 BCE. There was speculation that he was murdered. Medical examination of his mummified remains shows that he did not die of disease.[255] His mysterious death was narrated as follows: "Tutankhamun had met a violent death by hanging as his head and neck were found separated from the rest of the body...a possible assassin...the young king was killed by Pa-Nehesy, the high priest of his father, the heretical king Akhenaten".[256] Though individual Egyptologists still believe that Tutankhamun was murdered, authorities in Egypt do not want to

---

254 Sambu, Kipkoeech Araap, *The Kalenjiin People's Egypt Origin Legend Revisited: Was Isis Asiis?: A Study in Comparative Religion* (Nairobi: Longhorn Publishers, 2007), p. 1.

255 Bauval and Brophy (2012), op. cit.

256 Ibid.

accept this fact even after proper examination. King Tut was the pharaoh who ruled around the Eighteenth Dynasty. In 1922, when the tomb was discovered by a group of scientists, it had riches with 50,000 artifacts to be used in the afterlife. King Tut came from a royal family, and his father Akhenaten ruled Egypt for 17 years and had abolished the gods of Egypt and encouraged the worship of only one deity – Aten.[257] Before King Tut was given his current name, he was called Tutankh-Aten. This used to be the practice, where someone was named after his god. Aten was their god; they deposed the rest of gods and prepared him for worship.

Some of the literature written before King Tut ruled was assumed to have been destroyed, as stated below:

> A good part of Egyptian literature prior to the reign of Akhenaten was destroyed after his religious reform. The narrative songs and legends were all recorded after the Eighteenth Dynasty, and some of them describe a period a period prior to Egyptian History. They were often written in a prophetic form. The composers of these texts claimed to have lived in an earlier period. They predict the coming of an era of disasters, with prolonged darkness, thunder, storms, floods, a solar eclipse, pestilence, political change, and the arrival of savior and a good pharaoh who will save his people.[258]

The Naath people of Sudan claimed Egypt and King Tut, saying that he was the *Ran* who ruled during ancient times. *Tut* is a Naath term frequently used to name people or animals. It literally means "male". This could be a male cow or a male human. The male cow is called Tut. The practical meaning is that it is mostly given to a male child of the family after birth. The Naath believed that a long time ago, during the time when blacks were living in Egypt, the Naath were part of the management of that country, and this led to the Naath having a king

---

257 Ibid.

258 Diop. p. 82.

called King Tut Kang Muon. The Naath talked openly of their past related to Egypt and could speak proudly about it.

Descriptions of Ramses II being a black man and son of Seti, who was the fourth king of the Nineteenth Dynasty and ruled between 1292-1225 BCE, portray him to be "pure black, had thick lips and a broad nose like the people of the western Sudan today. He was a warlike Pharaoh, industrious and energetic; ruling Egypt for sixty-seven years."[259] During his reign, Ramses II engaged Hittites and fought their army for years until they accepted peace. He maintained his forces on the Mediterranean coast for years. The description of all the pharoahs listed above suggests that the ancient Pharaohs were mostly black prior to invasion by other races. There is a lot of information to suggest that many Ancient Egyptians travelled to western and southern Sudan, ultimately forming the Nilotic group. Today, the Shilluk and Anuak people still maintain the kingdom system, which involves the burial of people in leadership such as the king and respectable old men inside their huts. This, for them, is the pyramids, copying the concept in ancient Egypt. The Naath, Jieng, and other Nilotic groups abandoned this form of kingdom a long time ago, and elders even the most respectable ones are buried openly. But the Naath and Jieng still build their dwellings in form of pyramids.

Around 1657 BCE, the Hyksos invaded Egypt. They were foreigners who came to rule Egypt during the 15th Dynasty. The term "Hyksos" means "rulers of foreign countries" because they were ruling Egypt. This was the start of a long history of foreign rule in Egypt. Some narratives suggest that the Hyskos were either of Hittite or Arabic in origin, and there were also speculations that they may have had some links to the Bedouins, who had already established themselves in the region as they conducted business and trade in the Sinai Peninsula.

---

259 Windsor, p. 69.

ANCIENT KEMET CONTRIBUTION TO SCIENCES

In August and November 2018, I visited the Coptic Area in Egypt to understand and learn from the early Christian history of this part of Cairo. I had a chance to visit the Abu Sergia cave, where Jesus Christ was hidden by Joseph and Mary after they ran away from King Herod in Bethlehem and came to Egypt under the guidance of angel, as stated in the Bible (Matthew 2:13-23). As one approaches the cave, there is a drawing of Mary and her Son riding on a donkey, with Joseph leading the way. Although this drawing is placed at the entrance, it is visible from afar. One can clearly see from the drawing that the cave is located along the Nile. The cave recently came to be called the "Cavern Church of the Martyrs Sergius and Bacchus, Known as the Abu Sergia." The small location hosts different churches named

Cavern Church of Martyrs in Cairo, Egypt.

after the saints who lived in that area for years. As one goes further inside, the cave divides into two compartments in which the Holy Family was accommodated for three months. One can see the stones that they used to sit on, a pot carved out of stone for their cooking, and other hallowed spaces carved inside the rock. Also placed in the cave are drawings of Jesus Christ and Mary. The structure seems to be supported with burnt bricks and pillars to prevent it from collapsing. These are renovations are not part of the original structure. At the entrance, there is a well that was used by the Holy Family. The well has been adequately preserved with transparent glass on top. The inscription on the glass reads: "The Well from Which the Holy Family Drank." The tour guide informed me that the water is still considered holy, and sometimes sick people come to visit it expecting to be cured.

The Holy Family stayed in Egypt for three years and six months before they returned to Bethlehem and then Jerusalem, as I was informed by the priest who took me around and gave me lectures on the tour. These years were spent in different parts of Egypt. Churches have been built on the various locations in which they stayed. Most of these churches are Coptic churches and synagogues, and they all talk of Jesus Christ and give him honor. A Western traveler named Franciscus Pipinus de Bononia described the area in 1320 when he visited the city of Babylon in Egypt. He stated that he was shown the cave where the Blessed Virgin and her Son lived when they fled from Canaan. Above the cave, there was a beautiful old church called Saint Mary of the Cave, and under the main altar of the church, which looks directly onto the main gate, there was a covered chapel, which the priest said was where the glorious Virgin Mary lived with her Son and Joseph while they were hiding. Their journey has further been described thus:

> The Egyptian Christians fervently believe that the Holy Family received sanctuary at Heliopolis. The canonical gospel of Matthew in fact says that the Holy Family sought refuge in Egypt from King Herod's campaign to kill all baby boys in Palestine...to this day,

just few hundred meters down the road from El Massalah, the small Church of the Holy Family stands, its interior walls decorated with scenes of the family entering on a donkey into the semi-ruined city of Heliopolis.[260]

It is possible that today, we have reached a point where traditional mythology has been incorporated into Christianity in ways that make it very difficult to distinguish facts from fiction, star worshipping being one of the ancient practices that was not limited to ancient Egyptians. Flavius Josephus informs us that Nimrod built the Tower of Babel as a place where stars could be worshipped until God was annoyed with Nimrod, which resulted to the destruction of the Tower and the distribution of languages. Basing our argument on the Bible's version of events and historians' interpretations of the events, we can say that after the destruction of the Tower of Babel, people migrated to different locations. Today, the traditional practice of worshipping of the stars remains in the Middle Eastern culture and in other parts of the world: "Yet other astronomical observations, such as the crescent and the star, are so common in the later cultures of the Middle East."[261] And while the migration took place, the worshipping of the stars spread. The Naath people worship the stars, sun, and the moon even today.

At the cattle byre of Ngundeng, the Naath prophet of South Sudan, the sun, moon, and some stars were allocated cattle. These cattle were not supposed to be given for marriage or killed. They represented the spirits of the sun, moon, and stars, and they thought the spirits were within the cattle appointed. Ngundeng had been looking at sun, moon, and stars as his point of contact in case he encountered challenges. They were always there to assist him. One example I was given when I was conducting research in his village in 2014 was that whenever Ngundeng wanted to go to a certain village, he would summon the

---

260 Bauval and Brophy (20193), p. 9.

261 Hancock, Graham, *Magicians of the Gods: The Forgotten Wisdom of Earth's Lost Civilization* (New York: Thomas Dunne Books, 2015), p. 304.

sun and ask it to allow him to pass. The clouds would cover the sun, and he would go, and the same thing would happen again upon his return. Once he arrived at his destination, he would ask the sun to go back to its duties. This indicated that he had full control over the host of the heavens, and they all listened to him. There are some prominent quotations mentioned in Ngundeng's songs, and one is that "I will light to the end of the world. Sun and moon, you are the cornerstones of God, you are the cornerstones of our Grandfather, the morning star is the cornerstone of our Father."

Thereafter, people began to migrate out, including the ancestors of today's Nilotic people, who first traveled to the Middle East then later returned to Egypt before scattering to other parts of Africa.

Ancient Egyptian civilization laid the groundwork for civilization in the modern world. Ancient people did not just bring worldly civilization, but they also taught us the meaning of the stars, the moon, and the sun. Their deep understanding of the planets above them guided the way they lived their lives. The cosmos mattered greatly to the ancient people, influencing their belief systems to a large extent. Their temples were littered with images of the cosmos, which added their understanding of the universe by interpreting actions in the cosmos. For example, the flooding of the Nile is experienced during a certain period when a certain star appears. Monuments such as the pyramids, cities, and ritual centers such as Heliopolis were astronomically organized and aligned with the cosmos. Their buildings and streets were also planned according to the cosmos.[262] Many of the brilliant minds in the time of Greeks and Romans were educated in Egypt and then spread their knowledge to other lands. Above all, they used such knowledge of the stars to invent technologies upon which we still rely on:

The most famous University of antiquity was at Heliopolis, the City of the Sun. As a seat of learning, it was the most popular of all and it was noted for the profound wisdom of the priesthood. They

---

262 Bauval and Brophy (2011), op. cit .

were called the 'mystery teachers of heaven.' The high priest was the royal astronomer; he wore a sacred leopard skin over his robes, spangled with stars. All his titles designated his high office: 'he who is great in regarding'; 'he who sees the secret of heaven'; and 'privy councilor of heaven'. The great subject of this college was applied mathematics, with its two chief branches of astronomy and physics. The student devoted his attention first to geometry; this was tested by mensuration, surveying, and volumetric problems. Only afterward did the higher branches claim his attention. The temple courts were crowded with foreigners eagerly seeking the benefits of the magnificent library and thorough scientific training. All the masterminds of antiquity seem to have been educated here, and the university rolls present a brilliant galaxy of names. Moses there became learned 'in all the wisdom of the Egyptians.' Solon, the great lawgiver, owed his system to the teaching of the priests. Plato followed, and has left the records of his debt for us to judge how great indeed his alma mater was. Thales of Miletus received his education in science here, and as a result gave to the world the knowledge of electricity. Later on, the library and the university were transferred to Alexandria, and then we find Euclid in charge of the mathematical department."[263]

It was further mentioned that Ctesibius, who invented the force-pump, and Hero, the pioneer of the steam engine, at least once in his lifetime, came to Egypt for instruction in mechanics. Another person named Hypatia, renowned for inventing the hydrometer, also studied in Egypt, and afterward rose to fame, becoming a lecturer and teaching a number of students. Archimedes, who was considered to be the greatest mechanical genius of his time, also developed a wonderful invention there. It was mentioned that he was very young when he arrived at the university. It was there that he learned the fundamental principles on which it was based. His other inventions included the

263 Gosse, p. 20.

hydraulic press, cog-wheels, and pulleys, which are all attributed to him as the result of his studies in Egypt.[264] It was further stated that

> Considering the marvels displayed by this race in hydraulic engineering, and in the transport and erection of gigantic masses of stone, we cannot but think that all this mechanical knowledge was in existence, and that these great men only carried the inventions to the outer world, no doubt improving and developing them. Had they remained in Egypt we would probably never have heard of them. It is their work at the Courts of other nations, whether they carried the learning of the Egyptians, that has handed down their fame to posterity.[265]

Egyptologists believe that Heliopolis existed before the pyramids and it was called Innu by the ancient Egyptians, while the Greeks gave it the current name "Heliopolis,", which means "the city of the sun", as it was dedicated to the god of the Sun.

This is one of the main reasons why some countries and powerful nations who invaded Egypt were coming: to learn and steal the innovations Egypt had for 10,000 years while the rest of the world was steeped in barbarism. It taught the West and the Middle Easterners who came to Egypt for pilgrimages to drink from the cup of scientific, religious, moral, and social knowledge until they acquired it. Other than Babylon, Egypt was the anchor of all human civilization on Earth.[266] The practice of teachers wearing leopard skins, as described in Chapter 2, has its roots in Nilotic beliefs. The Naath have many important totemic animal symbols and speak of those who have the "spirit of lion" or "spirit of crocodile," the significance of which was described by the ethnographer, Evans Pritchard, thus:

---

264 Gosse, p. 20.

265 Ibid.

266 Diop (1974), op. cit.

"The Nuer [Naath] have explained to me the distinction between totem and totemic spirit by comparing the relationship of a man to his totem with that of their leopard-skin priests to leopards. Leopard-skin priests respect leopards, they said, but only in the sense that they will not kill them: 'there is no spirit (*kwoth*), they respect (*thek*) only its body (*pwonyde*).' It is by reference to the contrasting terms kwoth, Spirit, and *pwony*, creature, that the Nuer most clearly indicate the difference between totemic spirit and totem.[267]

The power of the leopard skin-wearing priest in Nuer culture includes the ability to cleanse a killer of his sins and perform rites to terminate blood feuds. He would speak directly to God.[268] The Naath called the ritual master who wears leopard skin "*Kuarmuon*," or "leopard skin priest", the one who presides over most rituals. Just like the ancient Egyptians referred to the teachers as "they who see the secrets of heaven," the Naath also bestowed on them the same responsibilities, believing they were closer to God and knew the secrets of Heaven.

According to Graham Hancock and Robert Bauval:

The world view of the ancient Egyptians, which they appear to have inherited intact and fully formed at the very beginning of their historical civilization some 5000 years ago, was profoundly dualistic and cosmological. The foundation of Pharaonic theocracy, the unification of the 'Two Lands' of Upper and Lower Egypt into one kingdom, the notions that they had of their own past and ancestry, their laws and calendrical measures, the architecture of their temples and pyramid complexes, and even the land of Egypt itself and the Nile – all these were cosmological concepts to them. Indeed, they saw their cosmic environment (the Sky, the Milky Way, the Sun and the Stars, the Moon and the Planets, and all

---

267 Evans-Pritchard, EE., *Nuer Religion* (London: Oxford University Press, 1974), p. 78.
268 Ibid.

their cycles), as being bound together in perfect duality with their earthly environment (their land and the Nile, their living King and his ancestors, and the cycles of the seasons and epochs).[269]

Years of Ancient Egyptian observations and science by priests such as Imhotep contributed to the astronomy and geometry of today. The priests were able to calculate the exact period when the Nile would flood, for example, and to do this they would observe the movements of the stars, the moon, the sun, and other planets in the sky. Such calculations required complicated mathematical knowledge. It is also believed that the modern calendar is based on, or almost the same as, that of the Ancient Egyptians.[270] Following the overflowing of the Nile, some embankments were re-surveyed, requiring lines and angles to be redrawn for land purposes, leading to the creation of geometry, which was then applied to the construction of buildings. Heliopolis was a holy city, the City of the Sun, where the ancient theology that helped the development of medicine, geometry, and astronomy was developed. It was the place where study of medical, botanical, zoological, and mathematical texts were practiced. Philosophers around the world such as Plato, Pythagoras, Democritus, and Thales of Miletus travelled to Egypt to become students at great Heliopolis to study that knowledge and become acquainted with the wisdom and learning of ancient Egypt.[271]

It was the most respected and honored center of learning of the ancient world. Egyptologists believe that this center existed before the era of the pyramids era. The ancient Egyptians called the city "Innu," Hebrew gave it the name "On," and the Greeks gave it its current

---

269 Hancock, Graham & Robert Bauval, *Keeper of Genesis: A Quest for the Hidden Legacy of Mankind* (New York: Crown Publishing Group, 1996).

270 Gatulak, James: Personal interview, Juba Protection of Civilians site, 14 August, 2016, , Juba, South Sudan.

271 Budge, E.A Wallis, The Dwellers on the Nile, or, Chapters on the Life, Literature, History, and Customs of the Ancient Egyptians (Mineola, NY: Dover Publications, 1883).

name, "Heliopolis". The modern Egyptians gave it the name as "Ain Shams" which means "Eye of the Sun.", Heliopolis still maintains respect among the Egyptians because of its legacy and what it gave to the ancient Egyptians. It was headed by a high priest or chief observer whose name was Imhotep, and his function was to observe the night sky and the motion of stars. The name Imhotep means "he who comes in peace." He was respected and regarded as the father of medicine, and also regarded as historical figure because he was able to teach things that were difficult for people to understand.[272]

Imhotep was an Egyptian architect, physician, and statesman. He lived in the 27th century BC and was the architect, astrologer, and chief minister to Djoser, who ruled from during the period 2630 to 2611 BC. He was considered to be, and was worshipped as, a god of medicine in both ancient Egypt and Greece. He is thought to have been the architect who designed the "step" pyramid at the Necropolis of Saqarah in the city of Memphis. This pyramid had six steps and was 200 feet (61 meters) high.[273] The step pyramid was designed to allow the deceased to mingle with the stars that every night linked Heaven and Earth. The significance of Heliopolis and the university which was located there cannot be overemphasized. Plato and Eudoxus were educated there and later become teachers in the same school of philosophy. The fate of the City of the Sun is summarized below:

> Heliopolis was considered by the historian Herodotus to be the oldest center of learning in Egypt. It is very difficult to reconstruct the history of this ancient city, despite the fact that in size, it rivaled Thebes and Memphis and its temples and cults fascinated the learned men of classical antiquity. Schools founded by Plato and Eudoxus flourished here for a long time. The fate of Heliopolis was in many respects even more tragic than that of Memphis, for the City of

272 Diop (1974), op. cit.

273 *Encyclopedia Britannica*, "Imhotep" (https://www.britannica.com/biography/Imhotep). Retrieved June 27, 2019.

the Sun was almost completely robbed of its grand monuments in several successive waves of pillage. The locations of all the cult sites in Heliopolis and what remains of them continue to present a great archaeological puzzle, which may never be wholly solved. Although archaeologists have not yet been able to thoroughly investigate the oldest cult site in Heliopolis and form a more precise idea of how the original sun temple might have looked, evidence from elsewhere in Egypt helps to define the possibilities. Heliopolis was probably the oldest religious center in Egypt.[274]

Egyptologists have theorized about why Egypt was a renowned center of learning in the ancient world. Heliopolis was the "chosen seat of the gods" and "the horizon of the sky". There are even those who believe that the family of Jesus Christ came to seek sanctuary in Egypt, and that the current Coptic believers residing in Egypt are descendants of the followers of Christ. Others hold the belief that Jesus taught in Egypt, while others go further to state that the Jewish faith has roots in ancient Egyptian religion. Moses, the author of the first five books of the Bible – Genesis, Exodus, Leviticus, Numbers, and Deuteronomy – received his complete education in Egypt. It was Moses who wrote the Torah, what are called today the Pentateuch, or Five Books of Moses. Moses also was trained militarily and fought in the Egyptian army before God commanded him to lead the children of Israel out of Egypt to their promised land. Moses, having been cared for by the daughter of the pharaoh, was able to learn the wisdom of ancient Egypt. This was concluded by Stephen the Martyr.[275]

When the Israelites entered Egypt, they were chased by famines from the land of the Philistines, and Cheikh Anta Diop noted that they were "attracted by that earthly paradise, the Nile Valley."[276]

---

274 Verner, Miroslav, " See Temple of the World: Sanctuaries, Cults, and Mysteries of Ancient Egypt (Cairo: The American University in Cairo Press, 2013).

275 Budge, op. cit..

276 Diop (1974), p. 5.

This valley has been attracting foreigners for generations, including the merchants from the Middle East. When Israelites entered Egypt, only 70 pastoralists from the family of Jacob were grouped in twelve patriarchal families, and they had no industry and culture. They settled in the land of Goshen and became shepherds of the pharaoh's flocks. When Joseph died, the hostility between the Egyptians and Jews grew. The Bible is very vocal about what they were doing: They were employed in construction for the city of Ramses as laborers. Egypt had control measures on the Jews to making them stop giving birth, and male children were killed as a remedy to avoid population growth. After 400 years, they left Egypt as a population of 600,000 strong men, women, and children. They took with them the religion of monotheism, and Egyptian culture.[277] It was also indicated in the Bible that after a period of time in in wilderness, the Israelites grew tired of monotheism and went back to worshiping their gods, in the form of a golden calf designed by Aaron and located at the foot of Mount Sinai.[278] When they were in Egypt, it was at Tell el-Amarna in 1400 BCE, during a period where Amenophis IV (Akhenaton) was trying to bring back the worship of one god – monotheism. It is believed that Moses was probably influenced by this reform before taking the children of Israel out of Egypt. The worship of one god was also borrowed from Meroitic Sudan, home of the Ethiopians in the ancient world. The Sudanese supreme deity was seen as the only generator of the sky and the Earth and was not gendered.[279] The current Naath and Jieng of South Sudan referred to the god Amun as Deng, who lived in the sky, and Deng is still being worshiped today.

One of the synagogues which was built around the cave where the Holy Family hid was dedicated to Moses, and is called the Synagogue of Moses. This was in order to remember him as someone chosen by God to lead the children of Israel out of Egypt. It was built on

277 Ibid.

278 Ibid.

279 Ibid.

a mastaba stone or slab. This was believed to mark the spot where Moses stood when he was negotiating with pharaoh to "let Israel go." A mastaba is a solid stone block which has a rectangular shape and a carved top. The area is considered very holy, and the stone was covered with clothes and tapestries to protect it.

CONCLUSION ON THE SCIENTIFIC EVIDENCE OF BLACK GENESIS IN KEMET

There are many who have been complicit in the distortion of ancient Egypt's history, thus robbing blacks of their civilization. These include some mainstream Egyptologists, anthropologists, historians, and movie-makers. Cheikh Anta Diop dedicated his life to researching the denial of the black man of his rightful place in history. He wrote powerful critiques of the Eurocentric and Arab-centric views of precolonial African culture, in which the black roots of ancient Egypt are denied.[280] As mentioned throughout this chapter, some people continually choose to ignore "the overwhelming evidence that indicates ancient Egypt was built, ruled, and populated by the dark-skinned African people."[281] Diop discussed evidence that places black Africans in their rightful position in history.[282]

This evidence proves that the Ancient Egyptians were black and that they built the most powerful civilization that ever existed. Diop, who was known for his work as both an anthropologist and a radiocarbon physicist, redefined the way we look at the origins of civilization, and

---

280 A. More (2013). 10 Arguments that Prove Ancient Egyptians were Blacks. Atlanta Black Star. http://atlantablackstar.com/2013/10/25/10-arguments-that-proves-ancient-egyptians-were-black/11/

281 A. More (2013). 10 Arguments that Prove Ancient Egyptians were Blacks. Atlanta Black Star. http://atlantablackstar.com/2013/10/25/10-arguments-that-proves-ancient-egyptians-were-black/11/

282 This conclusion summarizes the evidence from Dr Diop's book, *Origin of the Ancient Egyptians*, as well as other articles and books written by authoritative bodies.

the work that must be done to reclaim what has been taken from Africa by others. Diop worked exhaustively until his death in 1986, writing extensively and published many books; he left behind vast amounts of information in the form of volumes of documents that maintain his fighting spirit and vision. Below are the main and undeniable points of his research that puts Africa at the center of human origin.

First, Diop investigated the physical, anthropological evidence that guided his arguments and findings. After reviewing scientific literature that supported his thesis on ancient black civilizations, he realized that the skeletons and skulls of ancient Egyptians had clear similarities to those of black men – specifically the modern Black Nubians and other people of the Upper Nile and east Africa. As this chapter has stated, the people of the Upper Nile, such as the Naath, Jieng, and Shilluk, were once also Nubian. This conclusion was drawn by Diop based on the examination of skulls from the predynastic period (6000 BCE), in which there were differences when the Nubians and the Nilotics, both of which show black characteristics, are compared. He pointed out that blacks existed in Egypt and did not just migrate there. When creation happened in central and east Africa as verified by science, there was a period of migration to different parts of the world, so blacks were the first to be created and they populated the earth. The latest discoveries around the world of ancient peoples show significant evidence of this fact. In fact, recent reports from the United Kingdom reveal that the first Briton had "dark to black" skin, following DNA analysis of human remains of a person who lived around 10,000 years ago. One of the humans that was discovered in Britain was the Cheddar Man, who lived around that period.[283] Analysts believe he had blue eyes, dark skin, and curly hair. He was reported to have lived after the first settlers arrived in Europe toward the end of the Ice

---

283 Devlin, Hannah, "First Modern Britons Had 'Dark to Black' Skin, Cheddar Man DNA Analysis Reveals" (*The Guardian*, February 7, 2018, https://www.theguardian.com/science/2018/feb/07/first-modern-britons-dark-black-skin-cheddar-man-dna-analysis-reveals).

Age.[284] The emergence of such evidence suggests that it is only a matter of time before Diop's work will be accepted across the world. The older generation of Western anthropologists and archeologists will have to unpack the institutionalized racism upon which their work has been conducted and interpreted. If Diop's research is accepted, it will change the way people write history.

Further evidence of the arguments contained in this chapter are grounded in the results of what is called a melanin dosage test.

> ...invented a method for determining the level of melanin in the skin of human beings.... Melanin is the chemical responsible for skin pigmentation, and it is preserved for millions of years in the skins of fossil animals...conducted the melanin test on Egyptian mummies at the Museum of Man in Paris, and determined the levels found in the dermis and epidermis of a small sample would classify all ancient Egyptians as 'unquestionably among the Black races'.[285]

The Melanin Dosage Test was developed by Cheikh Anta Diop. It is a simple test in which phenotype can be determined once the test is conducted, and is done by examining the melanin content of the skin. The test involves specimens which consist of few square millimeters of mummified skin. Ethyl benzoate is coated and exposed to ultra-violet light. It then renders the melanin granules in the skin specimen fluorescent and allows them to be counted.[286] After the test is conducted, the result shows skin color and ethnic affiliation by subjecting results to microscopic analysis in the laboratory.

---

284 Ibid.

285 Moore, A., "10 Arguments That Prove Ancient Egyptians Were Black", (Atlanta Black Star, October 25, 2013, http://atlantablackstar.com/2013/10/25/10-arguments-that-proves-ancient-egyptians-were-black/11/).

286 Narkive Newsgroup Archives, "Melanin Dosage Test – Phenotype of Royal Egyptian Mummies" (https://alt.history.ancient-egypt.narkive.com/63EK7IRt/melanin-dosage-test-phenotype-of-royal-egyptian-mummies, retrieved July 25, 2019).

Cheikh Anta Diop narrated how he conducted the melanin dosage test. He stated that "We then applied the method to a few Egyptian mummies preserved in the anthropological laboratory of the Musée de l'Homme in Paris...We used the technique of thin sections observed in ultraviolet or natural light...the results speak for themselves: first of all, contrary to widespread opinion, mummification processes do not destroy the epidermis to the point of rendering the method inapplicable in most cases. In particular, it would make it possible to analyze the skin of all the royal mummies of the Cairo Museum in perfect state of preservation: Thutmosis III, founder of the XVIIIth dynasty, the conqueror of all Western Asia; Sethi (Seti) I, the founder Of the XIXth Dynasty; his son, the famous Rameses II. The game would be worth the candle, and that's why I tried to get samples to analyze. The curator of the Cairo Museum, Dr. Ryad, had promised to send them to me, but I have been waiting for more than a year. I am surprised, however, that such an analysis has not already been attempted and carried out by other researchers for a very long time. In any case, we can say that such an examination undoubtedly reveals an unknown melanin level in leucoderm races and undoubtedly classifies ancient Egyptians among Africans of Black Africa".[287]

The UNESCO conference of 1978 was where a consensus was reached at the Cairo Symposium that there was no evidence that the ancient Egyptians were white, and that Egypt was not influenced by Mesopotamia and the people of the Great Lakes region of inner equatorial Africa. As has been mentioned, mountains such as Rwenzori and Kilimanjaro were called by the indigenous people mountains of the moon. Mount Kilimanjaro, the tallest mountain in Africa with a height of 18,340 feet, is the second major contributor

---

287 Diop Cheikh Anta, "The Melanin Dosage Test", *The Awakening* (https://keyamsha. com/2017/04/10/the-melanin-dosage-test-by-cheikh-anta-diop/, April 10, 2017).

to the Nile water, since it flows toward Sudan and Egypt. Both mountains contributed a lot in providing life to Egypt through early migration.

Bauval and Brophy were astonished by the level of bias and prejudice against the African origins of Egyptian civilization. They both recommended the work of Diop to all those seeking the truth of the origins of Egypt and urged them to learn further from his work. Both authors mentioned that, after Diop presented a series of works to the world, he was not given a good reception by the Egyptians when he sought to use radiocarbon dating and biochemistry to back up his research on melanin dosage. Had he been allowed to apply a melanin dosage test, Diop may have uncovered vital proof of his arguments. However, the Egyptian authorities refused his request to examine the mummies. It could be speculated that Egyptians were motivated to conceal the truth that could have been revealed by the test.[288] Perhaps the facts, and hence the truth, that has been concealed will resurface in time.

Thirdly, there is osteological measurement, or the analysis of bones used in physical anthropology for classifying races of people. It was reported that German archeologist Karl Richard Lepsius did such a study at the end of the 19th century. His findings were also indicative of the role of black Africans in Egypt. His conclusion showed that the "ideal Egyptian" had short arms and was of Negroid physical type. These may not be accurate findings, but at the time, these were the leading results and had some grains of truth.

Blood typing of DNA is a technique that has also been used to provide important evidence. Some research has been done using this technique with results that show that, even after hundreds of years of intermarriages, the blood type of many Egyptians today is the same as that of the people who currently occupy western Africa. More evidence from Diop, based on the examination of the Egyptians as they saw themselves, supports the black ancient Egyptians theory.

---

288 Bauval and Brophy (2011), op. cit.

The Egyptians once had a term that they used for themselves, which, translated, meant "the black." The name existed during the Pharaonic era. Diop added that the term is a collective noun, which described the whole people of Pharaonic Egypt as a black people. Most of the skeletons that belong to the Old Kingdom, which dates from 2700 to 2190 BCE, were collected and kept at a storeroom at Giza. This period was reported by Egyptologists to be the period of the pyramid builders. This argument was based on excavations done in the Giza necropolis.[289] This information is kept in important documents that are guarded by the Egyptians. Deep analyses of accounts written by Egyptian-born Egyptologists and archeologists would clarify some of these issues and point to the truth, but a lack of access has been the rule rather than the exception.

The sixth point discussed by Diop is the cultural unity of Egypt with the rest of Africa. The culture in ancient Egypt is no different from that found in the rest of Africa. Diop pointed out that "African cultural commonalities" of "matriarchy, totemism, divine kinship, and cosmology.". Furthermore, he expressed that "historians are in general agreement that the Ethiopians, Egyptians, Colchians, and people of the Southern Levant were among the only people on earth practicing circumcision, which confirms their cultural affiliations, if not their ethnic affiliation." Crucially, he added that "the Egyptian style of [adolescent] circumcision was different from how circumcision is practiced in other parts of the world, but similar to how it is practiced throughout the African continent."[290]

His seventh point is based on the Bible. It has been discussed thoroughly that:

---

289 Cross-sectional analysis of long bones in a sample of ancient Egyptians. https://ac.els-cdn.com/S0378603X15000650/1-s2.0-S0378603X15000650-main.pdf?_tid=328c6419-44f5-42f8-a715-60178046ffa7&acdnat=1519974498_e46f268f96c5fd2bdcb0cc25bb91d546

290 A. More (2013). 10 Arguments that Prove Ancient Egyptians were Blacks. Atlanta Black Star. http://atlantablackstar.com/2013/10/25/10-arguments-that-proves-ancient-egyptians-were-black/11/

The Bible tells us that 'the sons of Ham [were] Cush [Sudan/ Ethiopia] and Mizraim [Egypt], and Phut, and Canaan. And the sons of Cush; Seba, and Havilah, and Sabtah, and Raamah and Sabtechah.' To this point, Ham has been considered to have fathered the Black race which is situated in Africa and all Semitic tradition (Jews and Arabs) class ancient Egypt with the countries of the Blacks. (Genesis 10:6)

It's also important to clearly state here that even the children of Mizraim were listed in the Bible, yet the current collection of races in Egypt are not mentioned anywhere. The children of Mizraim coined and used the name as it suited them. Given the records of how they migrated into Egypt, it's not entirely surprising that generations in contemporary Egypt behave the way the look down on blacks. The eighth point listed in Diop's work is the linguistic unity between southern and western Africa. Diop highlighted the cultural unity and ties between ancient Egypt and her African neighbors. He used the example of the Wolof from Senegal, as their language is spoken in west Africa near the Atlantic Ocean. The ancient Egyptian word "kef" means to grasp or "to take a strip [of something]", and in Wolof, it means "to seize prey". In Naath, the language of South Sudan and the Upper Nile, this same word means "to hold" or "to seize prey" also.

Diop's tenth point relies on the testimonies of classical Greek and Roman history, which holds a wealth of information showing the presence of black people in Egypt. These are eyewitness testimonies by the likes of Diodorus Siculus and Herodotus. They describe the ancient Egyptians as black-skinned with woolly hair. Many noted that Egyptians and Ethiopians had a complexion that they termed "*melanchroes*" in ancient Egyptian, which they translated as "black", while others have translated it as "dark" or "dark-skinned". Some translations mention that, Herodotus wrote that a Greek oracle was known to be from Egypt because the oracle was black.

Finally, Diop lists his tenth point, DNA evidence taken from bones. DNA tests carried out through the method of Short Tandem Repeat profiles by a genome company that specializes in tracing individuals' ancestry to certain global populations found that analysis of the DNA of Pharaoh Tutankhamen and family indicated that their closest relatives should be in sub-Saharan Africa – more specifically, the Great Lakes region. The Nuer of South Sudan have always strongly believed that Tutankhamen is an ancestor. In fact, Naath mythology makes reference to King Tut. Further, DNA testing was conducted on the remains of Rameses III, and it was found that he was a match with the people of the Great Lakes region, of which South Sudan is a part.

CHAPTER FOUR

THE TERMS THAT DEFINED BLACK AFRICA

DISCOURSE ON THE WORD "CUSH"

Cush was the name given to the country along the Nile, and its people were referred as Cushites. It was also an old Egyptian name for the people living south of Egypt. The Bible talked about Cush or Cush (which mean literally the same thing) with a clear description of the Nile confluences, and the people who used to live there, who were Nilotic, have been there since 750 BCE. The description of the people who lived in this place was well-placed, and is contained in one of the oldest texts that existed. One of the chapters that talks about Cush was translated to mean "curse on the land" in the Nilotic, but it is purely a mistranslation. Most people believe that such quotations were actually meant for the Nilotic people.

Woe to the land of whirring wings, along the rivers of Cush, which sends envoys by sea in papyrus boats over the water. Go, swift messengers, to a people tall and smooth-skinned, to a people feared far and wide, an aggressive nation of strange speech, whose land is divided by rivers. All you people of the world, you who live on the earth, when a banner is raised on the mountains, you will see it, and when a trumpet sounds, you will hear it. This is what the Lord says to me: 'I will remain quiet and will look on from my dwelling place, like shimmering heat in the sunshine, like a cloud of dew in the heat of harvest'. For, before the harvest, when the blossom is gone and the flower becomes a ripening grape, he will cut off the shoots with pruning knives, and cut down and take away the spreading branches. They will all be left to the mountain birds of prey and to the wild animals the birds will feed on them all summer, the wild animals all winter.' At that time gifts will be brought to the Lord Almighty from a people tall and smooth-skinned, from a people feared far and wide, an aggressive nation of strange speech, whose land is divided by rivers – the gifts will be brought to Mount Zion, the place of the Name of the Lord Almighty.

The interpretation of this verse as recorded in different Bible commentaries varies, and most of those commentaries point at the Sudan (Nilotic), southern Arabia (ancient location of the Nilotic people) and Canaan (the Jews conquered the inhabitants of Canaan). The ambassadors were Ethiopian and went to Jerusalem as the ones that take words to their own nation.

Talking about "woe," which is seen as "God will destroy the Ethiopians," people believed that it was a mistake coming from the translation of the word "woe" itself. If you look at the Hebrew Bible translation, "woe" does not express a threat, but instead, an appeal for attention (see more in Isaiah 55:1 and Zechariah 2:6). He may not be threatening Ethiopia, but rather informing them and calling them to hear his prophetic message as their enemies will be destroyed. This was because the black Sudanese fought for a long time against Babylon, Egypt, Southern Arabia, Sudan and South Sudan, and managed to defeat their enemies. It was an alert message.

The statement "shadowing with wings" is seen clapping wings or humming, which is seen as the sound made by the wings of airplanes and ships moving in water. This may refer to the war of North and

South Sudan and previous wars fought by the Ethiopians. It also refers to the army invading the lands Ethiopians have been inhabiting. The word "river" was communicating a better side of the people. The word "shadow" in English has been seen as communicating something better or providing protection. If something is placed in the shadow, it means it has been protected from bombs and bullets or anyone coming in to attack. It could also mean that it has been constantly under bombardment from the planes who put it under its wings as they look down from the sky. But here, we talk of wings as in terms of protection, as stipulated in Psalms 91:4.

The term "beyond" refers to Meroë, which is the island between the rivers Nile and Astaboras. It was one of the ancient cities that was famous for commerce and was the seat of the Ethiopian government. It was meant to represent the entire empire of the Ethiopians which King Taharqa inscribed in the temple. The island was the seat of the Queen Candace's kingdom; this was elaborated further in Acts 8:27.

Ethiopia is literarily translated as "Cush," and this is believed to be connected with the restoration of the Jewish nation with the support of the Ethiopians, who were skilled in navigating the seas as mentioned in Isaiah 18:2, Isaiah 60:9-10, Psalms 45:15, Psalms 68:31, and Zephaniah 3:10. The Jews and the Ethiopians (Cushites) were being displaced by the Phoenicians and Assyrian armies long ago and they would speak of all the western remote lands as the mouths of the Nile, which is the land of the Cushites. The term "Cush" referred not only to Ethiopia, but to southern Arabia, Felix, the Persian Gulf, and Tigris, which were the locations inhabited by the Cushites (Genesis 2: 13).

The term "ambassador" as used refers to the messengers sent to Jerusalem when they were negotiating between Taharqa and Hezekiah when Jerusalem was expecting an attack from Sennacherib, as mentioned in Isaiah 37:9. This was also evidenced by the term "sea" on the Nile (Isaiah 19:5). It was also supported by the mention of "vessels of bulrushes," which were the light canoes made from papyrus and daubed over with pitch (Exodus 2:3). The phrase "Go, swift messenger," was the prophet Isaiah telling them to go and take back the word, which God was about to do (Isaiah 18:4) against the enemies of both Judah and Ethiopia.

The term "scattered and peeled" signifies strong and energetic, and the Hebrew word for "strong" means drawn out (see Psalms 36:10 and Ecclesiastes 2:3). The word "energetic" means sharp (see Habakkuk 1:8). This phrase definitely means Ethiopians, and Herodotus referred to the Ethiopians as the "tallest and fairest of men." The Ethiopians had "smooth and shiny skins". The term "scattered outcasts" could mean both the Jews and the Ethiopians, due to the suffering they underwent. Scattered and outcast could refer to the displacement of the Ethiopians from a different location and from their original homes and their being scattered to different areas. Some remnant of the Ethiopians is currently in southern Arabia, India, Australia, Iraq, Israel, Egypt, Sudan and South Sudan.

The term "terrible from beginning hitherto" is seen as the trouble that started from Upper and Lower Egypt where the children of Cush, or the Ethiopians, were resting. At the end, the Ethiopians would send gifts to Jerusalem and honor the Almighty (see Isaiah 16:1 and Psalms 68:31 and 72:10). This was carried out by Queen Candace, who went to Jerusalem long ago during the time of King Solomon. Recently, when South Sudan became independent, a group of Christians led by the leaders of the Churches managed to organize and seek funding through the office of the Vice-President of South Sudan so they could make a pilgrimage to Jerusalem, but it never happened. God dwells in Jerusalem and attracts worshippers from Ethiopia and Egypt. Frumentius, who was an Egyptian during the fourth century, converted Abyssinians to Christianity and the Christian churches under Abuna still stand there today.

The phrase "meted out" means to give punishment or make someone to receive unfair treatment. This shows the most powerful people, who humiliated their opponents whenever they were attacked. The Ethiopians were victorious during their time against their enemies (see Isaiah 14:25). The statement that "whose land spoiled by the rivers" talks about the Nile, which is formed by the junctions of many rivers, of which the Blue Nile comes from Abyssinia, the Astaboras (or the white river) which washes down the soil along its banks into the land of Upper Egypt, the Sobat River in South Sudan, and many other streams and rivers. "See ye or hear ye" is calling the whole world to see and hear what God is about to do. It was Ezekiel who sought support from Ethiopia and Egypt and formed an alliance with the two countries. This made their unity strong and they were able to defeat the enemies. The support sought by Ezekiel happened in 713 BCE, when the Ethiopians managed to help and back up the Jewish people. The statement that "the birds and the beasts will feed on them" signifies that the soldiers of the Assyrian army would be killed in plenty throughout the year, which includes winter and summer, and their carcasses would be left to the birds and animals to eat.

You can see from the Bible's perspective that Cush refers to Ethiopia, Sudan, and South Sudan. The people that the Bible talks about include the current Nilotic population that was pushed away from northern Sudan. Cheikh Anta Diop emphasized that the Sudanese civilization should react against the misleading use of terminology and should not unconsciously transfer ancient Ethiopia to toward the east, to Addis Ababa. The kings who drove the Libyans from the throne of Egypt in the Twenty-Fifth Dynasty around 750 BCE were in reality the Sudanese monarchs. He added that modern minds think of the term Ethiopia as it relates to Addis Ababa. If you look at the historical monuments of that land, you can see only a few obelisks and two pedestals of statues. The civilization of Axum, former capital of Ethiopia, is more a word than a reality attested to by historical monuments. When you look at the historical Meroitic Sudan, you can see many temples and pyramids. This shows that names have been falsified to provide a more or less Oriental and discreetly Asiatic origin by way of Bab-el-Mandeb for Negro-Egyptian civilization.

The civilization that sprung up in Meroitic Sudan was an ancient civilization indeed, as portrayed by Egyptian documents, indicating that there was trading as far back as 4000 BCE and commercial ties with Egypt that has been going on for generations. It was written that the first hieroglyphs were designed in Meroë and was transmitted to Egypt to begin the development of embryonic alphabets.[291]

"Cush" simply means "Sudan", and people from South Sudan (particularly in the Upper Nile) believed that it was the name of their ancestors or associated with their ancestors as the Bible described. The description suited the people of the Upper Nile, indeed. The land was criss-crossed by rivers that included the Nile, the Sobat, the Bhar el Jabal, and many other streams and tributaries. Most of them concentrated in the Greater Upper Nile and qualified the description of Cush being referred to as South Sudan.

I remember when South Sudan seceded from Sudan in a referendum which was conducted in July 2011; there was confusion over choosing the name of the country, and many people proposed different names to call it. The name that first came to mind and was supported by many people was "Cush", and this did not just pop up from nowhere; it has been part of the record that the Nilotic people inhabiting South Sudan still associate themselves with Cush and the ancient kingdoms of their ancestors. Even at the time of writing this work, debate was ongoing, particularly on how the country should be named, including the suggestion of the name Cush. Many were so proud to have that name back in their history. It shouldn't confuse people that "Cush" means "Sudan" – the land of the black people, not the land of the Arabs and mixed-race people who occupied it after the invasion of the land. The *Harper Collins Bible Dictionary* refers to the land as "Ethiopia". After looking up the word "Ethiopia", you will find that "Nubia" is also placed in brackets, which means the words means the same as thing, which coincides with the description that follows: "The ancient name of the Nile Valley region between the first and second cataracts south of Aswan." At the height of Ethiopian power, however, the name denoted an area reaching as far as the junction of the Blue Nile and White Nile at Khartoum (not to be confused with modern Ethiopia,

---

291 Diop (1974), op. cit.

i.e., Abyssinia). The Hebrew term is Cush, which the King James Version keeps, but some translations use the Greek word "Aithiopia" for "Cush," as in Genesis 2:13 – see "Gihon").[292] In addition, defining "Gihon" – "Bursting forth" – gives a perfect image of the second of the four rivers flowing out of Eden to water the Garden and flowing around the whole land of Cush.[293] Herodotus, the father of history, talked about Ethiopia (which is the current Sudan) by stating that:

> "I went as far as Elephantine [Aswan] to see what I could with my own eyes, but for the country still further south I had to be content with what I was told in answer to my questions. South of Elephantine the country is inhabited by Ethiopians...beyond the island is a great lake, and round its shores live nomadic tribes of Ethiopians. After crossing the lake, one comes again to the stream of the Nile, which flows into it...after forty days' journey on land along the river, one takes another boat and in twelve days reaches a big city named Meroë, said to be the capital city of the Ethiopians. The inhabitants worship Zeus and Dionysus alone of the Gods, holding them in great honor."[294]

The nomadic tribes of the Ethiopians were the Nilotic people Herodotus met. The term "Nilotic" did not exist by then. It was the nomadic people moving with their animals in that location. Meroë was the capitol of the ancient black people in which the Nubians, Nilotics and other black people were settling. Herodotus was giving a testament on where he manged to reach while he was carrying out his exploration. If Ethiopia could mean the current Ethiopia, the capital city shouldn't have been Meroë. Even the Queen of Sheba was a member of this beautiful kingdom called Cush. He further went on by stating that:

---

292 Achtmeir, Paul J, *The Bible Dictionary* (New York: HarperCollins, 1971), p. 313.

293 Ibid., p. 378.

294 Rawlinson, op. cit.

"Where the south declines towards the setting sun lies the country called Ethiopia, the last inhabited land in that direction. Their gold is obtained in great plenty, huge elephants abound, with wild trees of all sorts, and ebony; and the men are taller, handsomer, and longer lived than anywhere else. The Ethiopians were clothed in the skins of leopards and lions, and had long bows made of the stem of the palm-leaf, not less than four cubits in length. On these they laid short arrows made of reed, and armed at the tip, not with iron, but with a piece of stone, sharpened to a point, of the kind used in engraving seals. They carried likewise spears, the head of which was the sharpened horn of an antelope; and in addition, they had knotted clubs. When they went into battle, they painted their bodies, half with chalk, and half with vermilion."[295]

Herodotus lived from 490 to 425 BCE, and while he was touring around, he was recording the culture of the early inhabitants of Egypt and Ethiopia, which covered the entire region now being occupied by South Sudan, Sudan, and part of the current Ethiopia. Roland Werner, William Anderson, and Andrew Wheeler cited another confirmation of the location of Cush in the book of Ezekiel, when the Lord cursed Egypt after they stated that they owned the Nile. The prophecy emphasized that the Lord would punish Egypt by making the land a ruin and a desolate waste from Migdol to Aswan and as far as the borders of Cush.[296] The exact location of Migdol is towards the north of Egypt and Aswan in the south of Egypt, which lies at the border of Cush. Further, in Zephaniah, it was elaborated that the Lord focused his attention on Cush. When the Old Testament was first translated into Greek in 300 BCE in Alexandria, the term that was used by the ancient Greeks for the country south of Egypt was Ethiopia.[297]

---

295 Ibid.

296 Werner, Anderson and Wheeler (2000), op. cit..

297 Ibid,, p. 20.

The Bible mentions that "Cush was the father of Nimrod, who grew to be a mighty warrior on Earth", and the Sudanese king who ruled Egypt as one of the pharaohs led the mighty Egyptian army. It further mentions Sudanese generals who also participated in invading Judah during the rule of King Asa of Judah. This general was named Zerah, and he invaded the city with one million men. In addition, the Medianites, from which Jethro, the father of Zipporah, came, were Cushites. The Ethiopian eunuch was referred to in the Acts of the Apostles as "a man of great authority under Candace, the Queen of the Ethiopians who had charge of all her treasury". This man was baptised by Philip in 38 AD. He was actually a Sudanese Nubian, because Candace (Kandake) was the queen and ruler of the Kingdom of Meroë. The term *"Candace"* means "great woman" and is used as their royal title. Their husbands were not reflected in the historical record, but sometimes ruled beside them. Their powers were the same, just like the powers of the king.

We are aware that Cush is the name for ancient Ethiopia and current Sudan, and the people of that time were called Cushites. After the dispersal from the Tower of Babel, the progeny of the Cush survived and made up the current Sudan. Sudan was the later name given to the country that was once called Cush. In an open forum that discussed the political development of the country, Dr. Riek Machar enlightened the attendees by responding to the debate about the name of the country called South Sudan. Others, including the author of this book, were not happy with the name given to the country of the Nilotic people, which is South Sudan. The idea is that the name shouldn't have been South Sudan, because that name reflects geographical location and it doesn't give back what belonged to the Nilotic people. The name Sudan shouldn't have been left to the so-called Arabs of Sudan, who came and found black men in the land. After a referendum in July 2011, the country decided on a name that would satisfy everyone; it went that way. At the time of writing this work, the name of the country is still in question.

Dr. Machar, an elder from the Naath section of the Nilotic community shared these same feelings, just like any other person who had been feeling a vacuum in their hearts towards the naming of the country. He highlighted to the members what Sudan meant to everyone and the intention of having a new name for the nation. He narrated that the word "*Sudan*" is an Arabic term consisting of two words that were joined together: "*Dar*," meaning "home," and "*Sud*," meaning "black". When the two words are joined, they mean "home of blacks". Instead, the term would be written "*Sudar*", and because of pronunciation, it becomes "Sudan". The country name means "home of the black people", which is associated with the Nilotic descendants who came from Babylon to Egypt and found their rest in Sudan. One of the sons of Cush who was born after Babel maintained the name and carried it.

One of the sons that maintained the name was Nimrod, son of Cush, who remained in Babel after dispersal and maintained it. He later invaded Assyria (Asshur) until the area comingled with Asshur and Cush because of the invasion. The Syrians were living in areas such as Erbil in the Kurdistan region of today. They were from a Semitic group who shared borders with the Sumerians. Empires such as the Akkadian also came out of Cush and Nimrod. Akaddians are another black tribe who were part of the Sumerians, and who decided to establish their kingdom; Akkad was the great-grandson of Noah through the line of Cush.[298] After conquering nations, he was elevated into godlike status and was worshipped, and this was due to his conquering strength. It should be recognised that Cush had children who migrated away from Babel and scattered into different parts of the Middle East and Africa. Most of the children of Nimrod came to Egypt and then to Sudan, where they occupied a big geographical area. It was further stated that Nimrod conquered a portion of Asshur from the areas where they settled, north of Babel. After some years, around 722 BCE, Asshur became very strong and conquered Israel, and the Israelites were taken into captivity. Asshur was also mentioned to be in the same group of Assyrians who came and occupied Egypt and chased

---

298 See Tower of Babel.

the descendants of Nimrod into Sudan up to the Upper Nile Basin. The interesting thing here is the Naath elders and the singers of the gods have connected the Naath origin to Noah. This is really interesting considering that most Nuer believe in different gods in addition to the single creator and considering Ngundeng, Mani Wan, Teny Kuoth, and others who were present in Nuer society still believe in Noah as their ancestor. Some still think that the origin story of the Nuer has a very powerful connection to the Biblical creation story in which Adam and Eve were portrayed to be the first man and woman created by God and placed in the Garden of Eden. This Garden of Eden was not a very small garden, as we all know. It was watered by four main rivers: the Euphrates, the Tigris, and the Blue and White Nile. The Nuer still think that they are part of that creation. The majority still look at central and west Africa as the main focus areas to be included in the creation. One of the sons of Ham was Cush, who later also had sons, including Nimrod, who was praised as a hero and conquered lands. He was also a great hunter before God. He was blessed with skills and full of energy to do work that pleased God. When he was an adult, one of his first kingdoms was Babel. This was the beginning of civilization, when people no longer lived like nomadic people and instead settled. Their main purpose was to unite and live in unity, and where there is unity, there is always strength.

DISCOURSE ON THE WORD "AFRICA"

Africa is the modern name of the black continent. Before Africa, there were names that suggest and refer to the same continent; some were ancient, like Ethiopia and Nubia, while others are recent, like Sudan. The name "Africa" is believed to have been derived from the language of ancient Libya, where the land was called "*Afer*". In Latin, the word for Africa is" *Afer*," and when the Romans won the Third Punic War in North Africa, which was fought between the Phoenician colony of Carthage and the Roman Republic from 149-146 BCE, they borrowed the term Afer, calling it Apher.[299] Afer is believed to be the grandson of Abraham in the Bible and a companion of Hercules.[300] It is still a debate, and it will be very difficult to give an explanation of the defjnitive origin of the name "Africa". UNESCO's *General History of Africa* states that the name appears to have been in use during Roman rule, replacing the original Greek or Egyptian word "Libya," which means the land of the Lebu, or the Lubins as used the Book of Genesis in the Bible. At the end of the first century BCE, the entire black continent became known as Africa, a term thought to have originated on the North African coast. It has also been stated that "the word 'Africa' is thought to come from the name of a Berber people who lived in the South of Carthage, the Afarik or Aourigha, where 'Afriga' or 'Africa' denotes the land of Afarik."[301] The Berber are currently called "*Amazigh*" (plural "Imazighen"),) and they are the descendants of the pre-Arab inhabitants of North Africa. Berbers are indigenous Africans who are scattered across communities in Morocco, Algeria, Tunisia, Libya, Egypt, Mali, Niger, and Mauritania. They are from an Afro-Asiatic family belonging to ancient Egypt. Their communities were assimilated into Arabic culture.[302]

Another theory indicates that the word might have come from the two Phoenician terms "*Afar*," which means "ear of corn," and "*Pharikia*," which means "land of the fruits". This is due to the fertility of the land where the continent is evergreen with trees that produce fruits. Still another suggestion indicates that the word comes from the Latin adjective "*aprica*" ("sunny") or the Greek word "*aprike*" ("free from the cold environment"). Additionally, another origin could be the Phoenician root "*faraqa*," which seems to suggest the idea of diaspora and was suggested to indicate that Phoenicians who came to Africa considered themselves to be in a foreign land. Still, there

---

299 Windsor, op. cit.

300 Ki-Zerbo (ed.), op. cit.

301 Ibid.

302 *Encyclopedia Britannica*, "Berber People" (https://www.britannica.com/topic/Berber).

are ideas that the word had some roots in African languages such as the Bambara. In West Africa, the term may have its roots in the word *"apara"*. The Yemenite chief named Africus invaded North Africa in the second millennium BCE and settled in a town called Afrikyah, and this could have generated the term Africa. It is also believed by some to have an Arabic root, *"Ifriqiya,"* which is directly translated as Africa. South African History online states that:

> "The exact origins of the word 'Africa' are contentious, but there is much about its history that is known. We know that the word 'Africa' was first used by the Romans to describe that part of the Carthaginian Empire, which lies in present-day Tunisia. When the Romans conquered Carthage in the second century BCE, giving them jurisdiction over most of North Africa, they divided North Africa into multiple provinces, amongst these there were Africa Pronconsularis (northern Tunisia) and Africa Nova (much of present-day Algeria, also called Numidia)."[303]

All historians agree that it was the Roman use of the term "Africa" for parts of Tunisia and Northern Algeria which ultimately, almost 2,000 years later, gave the continent its name. There is, however, no consensus amongst scholars as to why the Romans decided to call these provinces "Africa". Over the years, a small number of theories have gained traction. Different writers have mentioned that the population of the African continent came from Mesopotamia, and this is linked to Nimrod's Tower of Babel, which was indicated to be the center of civilization. At least there is a basic connection between the Tower of Babel and the dispersion of languages to different locations. Most of ancient Mesopotamia is believed to have been the kingdom of Nimrod, the son of Cush, who later came to settle in Egypt and Sudan.

---

303 *South African History* Online, "Africa: What's in a Name?", May 20, 2015 (https://www.sahistory.org.za/article/africa-whats-name)

Based on the interpretations of a few writers such as Edwin Sammy Achala, Africans are the descendants of the Jews who came directly from Abraham. However, conflicting literature also exists which suggests that Abraham came from ancient Babylon, in a place called Ur. It was not Jews who existed before Africans, but the other way around. Black writers such as Cheikh Anta Diop and Chancellor Williams acknowledge that there are historians who refuse to see Africans as the creators of ancient civilization and culture. Although the proposition of ancient African civilization has flourished, the facts are denied by Western historians.[304] As a result, Africa is not seen as an important historical entity, but instead is considered incapable of making its own history.

A lack of meaningful research to amalgamate the fragments of the past into a single solid ancient epoch is the problem confronting African history today.[305] Important records about the black man in ancient Egypt and North Africa, which was the Kingdom of Timbuktu that today hosts most of the Arab population, are scarce. This scarcity of data is not because it has never existed, but because it was either hidden or history was rewritten to suit those who benefit by falsifying it. During the Arab expansion, most of the literature that was in Timbuktu was destroyed. Professor Diop, whose work is vocal on the founding of ancient Egypt by black people, concluded that "history cannot be restricted by the limits of the ethnic group, nation or culture. Roman history is Greek, as well as Roman, and both Greek and Roman histories are Egyptian because the entire Mediterranean was civilized by Egypt."[306] Different groups have conquered Egypt, and all of them had their eras during which they ruled the land. The culture of each group over time became intertwined until it became difficult, if not impossible, to separate them.

---

304 Ki-Zerbo (ed.), op. cit.

305 Diop (1981), op. cit.

306 Ibid. p. xviii.

The god Osiris was believed by the Ethiopians to be their deity, and at a certain point in time, it was this deity that brought Egypt under the colonization of the Ethiopians (Sudanese). Osiris has a strong connection with Africa and Sudan. Black civilization in the Mediterranean is supported by the existence of the Hellenic black virgin and goddesses, such as the black Demeter of Phigalia in Arcadia; the black Aphrodite of Corinth and Arcadia; the black virgin of Saint Victor of Marseilles; and the black virgin of Chartres, which was later honored as "our lady under the earth".[307] Despite evidence of successful military, cultural, and political backing for the Africans in Egypt and North Africa from the Mediterranean, Amadou-Mahtar M'Bow, who was once the Director-General of UNESCO, asserted that, "African societies have been looked down upon as people who did not have a history, and the history that does exist is based on myths and prejudices that have come to, unfortunately, define the history of Africa."[308]

DISCOURSE ON THE WORD "NAATH"

When the author was conducting interviews with elders at the Bentiu Protection of Civilians site in October 2016, he probed information from elders in order to clarify the meaning of some of the concepts and terms used by the Naath prior to 100 BCE. These terms were nearly forgotten and were getting outdated through lack of use by generations that followed. Most of the elders stressed that the language, culture, and traditions were disappearing at an alarming rate, and this worried them a lot. The elders wondered whether the author had plans to introduce interventions that could explain and clarify the problem to the "youth who speak the language of a pen." For the elders, the language of the pen refers to those who have gone to school

---

307 See Cheikh Anta Diop, Civilisation or Barbarism. P. 20
308 See General History of Africa.

and acquired Western education. Since school was introduced to South Sudan in about 50 years ago, most people decided to allow their children to study and benefit from a Western education. Thanks to this, the elders believe, children are losing the traditional education where information is passed down from generation to generation by the word of mouth. Elders cherish sitting after dinner in the evening, and an old man will tell his children things that happened long ago. They believe children have gone astray, and lost the basic understanding of Naath culture. During the discussions, most elders often preferred the use of the term "Naath" rather than "Nuer" because, they argued, it was the anchor of the community. They seemed not to believe the term "Nuer" could replace "Naath". The two terms are used interchangeably by the Nuer in their social life, but Nuer is a more commonly used term by foreigners and young people within the Nuer community. Even in the official documents of the South Sudan government, it is very rare to see the term Naath. All written material and documents related to the tribe use the term Nuer, not knowing that it is a recent term, just like the tern "Dinka" has nearly replaced the terms "Jieng".

Both terms are used differently by different age groups. The elders use Naath frequently because they know what it means clearly, and they have used it throughout their lives. Young people use Nuer, which is also used but has its limitations and is seen as the latest invention. The older generations still maintain the term Naath, and other terms which are not used by current generations because they sound old or are forgotten. The government of South Sudan uses the term Nuer in official matters related to the tribe. This includes birth certificates, national identification cards, and national passports. Within the Nuer community, Naath signifies the people who were later called the Nuer, because before the term Nuer was created, there was only the term Naath in use and it was later, with certain rituals conducted, that the term Nuer was invented based on these rituals. Both terms carry significant social importance and meaning. The words Naath and Nuer have been used for centuries, especially during the period when the Nilotic migration took place many years ago.

As discussed in Chapter 2, the Nilotic community came from ancient Babylon and moved to Egypt, then north Sudan, where they established their presence in the Cush kingdom. After displacement, they were pushed to Koat Lich, currently confined in the Unity State of the Republic of South Sudan, which is within the Sudd swamps, which kept them safe for generations. These terms are an important part of Naath historical records that should be cherished and embraced, and will require further elaboration. Most of the respondents told the author that they believed that current generations have stopped using the right terms and totemic symbols that their forefathers used and left for them. The elders think this is happening because people are living in changing times. The believe that since when the white man came to Africa in the 17th and 18th centuries AD, the lifestyle of the Naath people has been in constant change. This change is not seen as positive; they see it as a deteriorating factor that erases the Naath culture.

No evidence or traces of historical value of their ancient movement and migration can be found in the area where the Nuer community now inhabits, because the Upper Nile area turned into swamps. This is partly because the plain savannah grassland has no mountains that could have provided places to keep records and historical materials, such as artifacts and libraries. However, some documented and oral evidence has emerged that strongly links the words Naath and Nuer to the ancient kingdoms and practices, and particularly the usage of the word Nuer. There is evidence from Chiekh Anta Diop that the term was used positively, but the creation of the word "Nuer" was used negatively, as it had also been associated with words meaning "contamination" or "sin".[309]. This signifies that the word was a later creation, and the main question is why it came into use in the first place. Establishing a close link between these two terms and the Naath ancestors will lead to a better understanding of the origin of the Nilotic

---

309 Liah, Kim J., "The Dicourse on the Terms 'Naath' and 'Nuer'" *Center for Strategic & Policy Studies*, September 2017. Juba, South Sudan.

Harran village dates back to the Second Millennium BCE and these beehive buildings are still there today.

people and the past lives of their distant ancestors. The oral history that was passed down to children by elders states that the Nuer were an ancient people and could be regarded to have been, at a certain point in time, the nucleus of the black people. They are the Progenitors of Babylon, and were part of the ancient civilisation and migration.

We now have different tribes and other Black communities and nations in the continent, but Nuer could be regarded as their point of origin given that they were called the Chaldeans in Babylon and some of them were living in Harran City while in Egypt, they acquired the term Naath and move to Sudd swamps and got the term Nuer. Through the evolution of language and cultural practices, they managed to have the term Nuer, which was developed when the Naath were creating laws. Some of my informants whom I interviewed from other communities argued that, Nuer is a recent idea introduced by the elders of the Naath community, to signify the laws that govern their way of life, especially for the younger generation.

The oral history from the elders I interviewed in Bentiu mentioned that the term Naath has been used since the time of the ancient Babylonians, before the community could come to Egypt, but the widespread of the term was mainly in Egypt. Most of the Naath people who are in Sudan today believe that the term has been in existence for thousands of years. From Egypt to Koat Lich, which was the point of departure for the Naath people to spread around the tributaries of the Nile. The term has been in association with *"Ran"*, or "human". "Ran" is a singular form of "Naath". The term shares an origin with the creation of mankind and is believed by the Naath to be linked to the first man and woman, described in the Bible as Adam and Eve. The Naath called the first people Ran (Adam) and Nyawel (Eve). Through years of migration and interaction with other tribes, the language has lost a great deal of its original form and structure. This has led to some of the words and cultural practices to disappear due to the changing of time.

The current accent is attributed to the first man and woman, Ran and Nyawel, the ancestors of the current Naath, who first established their home in Koat Lich. The man, named Ran Gam, and his wife, named Nyawel Beeh, kept their family together and maintained the form and structure of the language as it is used by the Naath today. Through that line, the language has been kept alive for centuries.

The story of Adam and Eve, as recorded in the Bible, does not mention the language that they used, but it is my opinion that there was no other language that they could have used except the language that has now become that of the Naath – Thok Naath, the language of human beings. Thok Naath, the language that they were speaking, is believed to be associated with black people. This also reflects the early origin of the Naath people, when they were called Chaldeans while inhabiting the Sumer Valley of the Euphrates and Tigris rivers in those days. The concern over language is that the first humans, Ran (Adam) and Nyawel (Eve), were created black and not white. What is portrayed by historians, the media, and places of worship where you can see images of Adam and Eve and Jesus, is that they were white; this is not accurate. This idea is supported by the fact that Sumer lies in ancient Babylon, and it was exclusively the land of the black people, initially inhabited by Ham's son Cush who fathered the Cushite people inhabiting Sudan, Uganda, Tanzania, Kenya, and Ethiopia today.

Assuming science is correct that black people were the first humans to evolve, one would then ask: what language were they using at the time? Most of the oldest tongues, such as Hebrew, Arabic, and Greek, do not include any of the languages of black people. The oral traditions of most Nilotic people were undocumented and resulted in the loss of precious information. Foreigners who came with pen and paper to take inventory of the things that they observed based their interpretations on their own views and biases.

Diop expressed his disgust, at this, directly blaming black Africans for ignoring their ancestors. He pointed out that the ancestors created and developed the resources found along the Nile Valley, which had been considered the oldest indications of humankind's journey to civilization.[310] The Naath people were the last to be forced out of Egypt by the Assyrians and other forces that took over the land. Our ancestors fought for centuries to retain the land and its legacy until they could not fight anymore. It was at this point that they were pushed out and their legacy destroyed. However, there were people of Nilotic origin that remained and assimilated into the current Egyptian community; they never made it with the rest of Nilotic people to Sudan or the interior of Africa. Even some of the Nubians living on the extreme western side of Sudan near the border with Egypt have a Nilotic origin. However, those Nilotic groups were assimilated within the current communities and hence lost their roots. The oral history of the Naath people still has vivid descriptions of the war with the Assyrians centuries ago around lower Egypt. This historical event has stuck in the minds of Naath people, and they refer to it as "*Dak-mi-thil-Yiet*," or "swift defeat against the Nilotic people." It was at this time that black people were completely defeated and pushed out of the land of Egypt towards Sudan and then to the Upper Nile Region.

Most discussions of the origin of mankind are linked to Adam, who was the first person created by God, according to the Bible and the Quran. "*Adam*" is a Hebrew word meaning "to be red," and was

---

310 Diop (1974), op. cit.

associated with the color of the skin of a human being.[311] It was also the color of the soil in the Mesopotamian valley, in which the Garden of Eden is believed to have been located. However, the reference to red color in this story is to mask the fact that Adam was created black, as per the belief of the Nilotic community, which thinks Adam and Eve are from their blood. The Hebrews misinterpreted the story; the idea of Adam being red defeats the argument of a black Adam. In the Akkadian[312] language, "*Adammu*" means "to make". This could refer to the soil that was molded by God to make Adam.

In the discourse of the term "Naath", this author wrote an article and argues that it is the plural form for all Negroid (black) people, while the Egyptians stated that the singular form could be *Nahas*. The singular form of Naath is *Ran* (human), but it has changed with time by the way it is written and how it is spoken. Other related terms include "*Ram mi ran*", which is loosely translated as "the actual [true] human" and means the center of the origin of human beings. This further leads us to its plural form, which is "*Nei tin Naath*".[313] Oral history conveys that the word "Naath" has existed since the Babylonian times. John S. R. Duncan was a British diplomat who worked in the Sudan Political Service and was the last to leave Sudan on the eve of independence in 1956. He was also a British High Commissioner for Zambia, ambassador for Morocco, and High Commissioner for the Bahamas.

In his book *Sudan: A Record of Achievement*, he stated that the Naath people were present during the time of ancient Babylon. He emphasized that the Naath lived with large herds of long-horned cattle throughout their migration. These herds were trained in the traditions of the people of the ancient Babylonian Empire, 2,000 years before Christ. He mentioned that: "the [Naath] is born among them, he

---

311 *Behind the Name*: "Adam"(May 31, 2018, https://www.behindthename.com/name/adam).

312 Akkadians are one of the community of people we call today as Nilotic. Nilotics are many clusters of tribes who came together from Babylon.

313 Liah, op. cit.

grows up with them, he gets wives with them, and he dies with them. He believes not in the latest religions but his gods".[314] While in Egypt, during the migration routes to Africa, it was the same name, Naath, that was later used to refer to all the black people who were living in Egypt. The Ministry of Education, Science, and Technology of the government of South Sudan wrote that:

"The Nuer called themselves Naath, meaning human beings, and they are one of the biggest ethnic groups in South Sudan and western Ethiopia. In South Sudan, they live mostly in Unity State and the Upper Nile Province. They are located around the junction of the Nile River and the Bhar el Ghazel and Sobat River and along the Sobat across the border into Ethiopia.[315]

In fact, the location where the Naath are currently living was the campsite of the early migrants to the Upper Nile Basin, which took place in the 18th century; it was from this point that most of the Nilotic tribes dispersed. It is said that they left their leader – named Kuong, who was a descendant of the Naath people – in the present-day Unity State of South Sudan as the rest crossed the Nile to venture out into eastern part of the River Nile.

Cheikh Anta Diop asserts that "in fact, their true name is not Nuer, but Naas or Nahas, which is the term by which the Egyptians designated to Nubians and other Blacks of Africa".[316] There is no shred of evidence available or which I have come across that disputes this position. Indeed, the Naath were the ancient inhabitants of the Babylonian Empire. The UNESCO *General History of Africa* has provided an interesting angle to the debate, saying:

---

314 Duncan,, John S. R. Duncan *The Sudan: A Record of Acheivement* (Edinburgh: W. Blackwood & Sons, 1952), p. 158.

315 Briedlid, Anders, Avelino Androga and Astrid Kristine Breidlid (editors), *A Concise History of South Sudan: New and Revised* Edition (Juba, South Sudan: Ministry of Education Science and Technology, 2014), p. 77.

316 Diop (1981), p. 181

It is a remarkable circumstance that the ancient Egyptians should never have had the idea of applying these qualities to the Nubians and other populations of Africa to distinguish them from themselves. The Egyptians used the expression to distinguish the Nubians; and Nahas is the name of a people, with no color connotation in Egypt. It is a deliberate mistranslation to render it as Negro, as is done in almost all present-day publication.[317]

Here, the writer is referring to the genesis of the term *"Naath,"* or mankind, and how it was used in Egypt, as being applied to something that you can differentiate a certain race from the rest, when in fact, it is the race that existed in Egypt that had the same name. They were in Egypt and still used the same name (Naath or Nahas, which mean the same). In this case, Egyptians were referring to the black populations, including the Nubians as Naath. The argument presented suggests that there is no need to use the term "Naath" since the entire population of the people of Egypt were black and lived in that land. It is safe to say that, since the invasion of Egypt by the Arabs in seventh century AD,[318] the term *Naath* was in existence and was used extensively, reflecting the color of the people who were living in the land of Egypt. The category of the people we know once lived in Egypt and some of the blacks who live at the borders and inside of Sudan are still known as the Naath, reflecting the original usage. The pronunciation could be different, but the meaning remains the same.

Related to the term Naath is the term *"Nei tin Naath"* or *"Ram mi Ran"*, which was used to differentiate real humans from half-humans or half-bloods that the Naath considered to be *"Leet"* (or *"Let"*), or half-blooded animals. It was recognized that there were animals that had also been created and lived alongside humans, and this is what led to the usage of the terms *"Nei tin Naath"* or *"Ram mi Ran"*.

---

317 Ki-Zerbo, op. cit.

318 Gilbert, Adrian and Robert Bauval, *The Orion Mystery Unlocking the Secrets of the Pyramids* (New York: Broadway Books, 1995).

They believed that Leet could speak Thok Naath and walk like the Naath. They could also turn into carnivores that could feed on the flesh of the Naath. Further, the Naath referred to the dwellings of Leet as *"Rol-Letni,* the land of the flesh- eating animals.". An example of such flesh-feeding animals in South Sudan was in the story of Chieng-Bongbar, a clan of flesh- eating people of which Gatluak Maguel was part. Gatluak terrorized people in the lands of Dok, Gawar, Laak, and Thieng in South Sudan.[319] He was well known for his habit of eating people and was very difficult to kill. He is said to have eaten people in these areas for a period of ten years in the 1930s until 1940s. It is said that songs were even composed about these animals and mothers sang these songs to their children. Gatluak Maguel was arrested in Malakal in the 1940s by the British administrators who came to Sudan, and was locked in a maximum security prison. Currently, in Pangak town along the Nile, there is a prison named after him, and it is called Gatluak Manguel's Prison, so called because he was arrested there. He was later reported to have died in prison while attempting to break away. This is just one of the many stories of these carnivorous half-human-like animals that are still told in South Sudan today.

Most early writings by C.G. Seligman, a pioneering British anthropologist who conducted field research in Melanesia, Ceylon (now Sri Lanka), and Nilotic Sudan, indicate that the term *Naath* was widely used, and he said "the Nuer themselves speak of the tribe to the west of Bhar el Gabel as 'homeland Nuer' (*Naath-cieng*) and those east of the river as 'Naath-doar [*cieng Doar*]'".[320] This is an indication that Naath is an ancient traditional name that carries not only the personality of the people but also their identity. It traces their origin and helps others understand them. Seligman also argued that the country of the Nuer was" Kuerkwong," or "the barren place of Kwong." Here he

---

319 Nyuon Danhier Gatluak, personal Interviews. Paramount Chief of Nyuong and Door Clans of Nuer. Kakuma Refguee Camp. 14.10. 2018.

320 Seligman, C. G. and Brenda, *Pagan Tribes of the Nilotic Sudan* (London: George Routledge and Sons, 1932).

was referring to the place or point where the Nilotic people dispersed. Some of them went to Kenya, Uganda, Tanzania, and Ethiopia, while others, like the Wolof, proceeded to central Africa. The Kuerkuong, which is characteristically arid and without water and vegetation, is considered to be barren because animals cannot get good grass. It is therefore not productive, and hence people were forced to move to the swamps where they could cultivate crops and graze their cattle.[321] Seligman also talked about the practice of incest, saying that the elders, who later became ancestors, provide a solution to incest. When incest occurred, the elders would kill a bull and split it into two in a ritual that was meant to stop further incest among the communities. They believed that incest kills, and haunted children are born out of incest. This issue will be discussed in more detail later when looking at the term "*Kuarmuon*" and especially with regard to the responsibilities of Kuarmuon.

There is an oral history among the Naath indicating that the term was in use when Nimrod was building the Tower in Cush's country. The Naath think that Nimrod's face closely resembled that of the Nilotic people today. His facial features included marks normally found on the faces of the Nilotic people, such as small round dots that are used widely by the tribes to beautify their faces. These dots could have been used more than 5,000 years ago, and they are therefore significant to the ancient history of black people. The importance of cutting one's self was seen as a remembrance of the death of Nimrod. The discourse on "Naath" has been tied to the ancient kingdoms, and Naath theologians argue that it was the same language that was used during the time of Noah, Ham, Cush, and Nimrod, until most Nilotic dispersed and migrated. The Naath religion talked of migration at length from Nimrod's Tower, which the Naath referred to as Dapany.[322]

The Naath still kept their animals even when they were under the leadership of Nimrod, during the building of the Tower of Babel. This

---

321 Ibid.

322 See Chapter two on "the Tower of Babel"

could be seen when they were crossing the Mediterranean Sea, which the Naath called *"Baabdiit"* or "crossed only by birds". After the dispersal, modern languages were assumed to have originated from the one that was used during the building of the Tower of Babel. The Bible, however, does not specifically mention the original language that was used before the building of Babel.[323] It is believed by the Naath elders that "Thok Naath," or "the language of humans", may be the original language that was used before the building of the Tower. Bodie Hodge has provided three possibilities regarding what may have happened to the original language. First, it could have been one of the languages that survived after the building of the Tower of Babel was stopped. Secondly, it could have been conserved and used during the eras of Noah, Shem, Ham, and Japheth, whom the bible stated to be the anchors of humanity. Finally, it could have been completely lost at the Tower of Babel when new languages emerged. There is also the speculation that all the languages that came out of the Tower of Babel could have been combined into one original language. This original language would later become divided into the sub-languages which have populated the world. Hodge has even suggested that: "basically, everyone knew all the languages and then they were subdivided after Babel".[324]

Thok Naath could have been the language that was preserved through Ham, the son of Noah. Alternately, it could have been a language that shared much of its structure and form with the original language, which disappeared at the time of the Babel. The lack of Naath writers who could document the language and preserve it compromised its survival and spread. Hence. Thok Naath's existence completely disappeared from history. It was in the 19th century when evangelists came to Africa and got in touch with the Naath that they

---

323 See *Tower of Babel*, p. 231.

324 Bodie Hodge (2013). *Tower of Babel: The Cultural History of Our Ancestors*. (Green Forest: Master Books,

p. 232).

wrote down Thok Naath in their alphabet because the Naath alphabet had disappeared. For example, Hebrew, Greek, and other languages are the only ones that were publicly used thousands of years ago, and Thok Naath has nowhere to be heard. As we will see later, it was the other races that came to Egypt that referred to the black people as the Naath. There is strong evidence that the Hebrew language is not associated with the language that was used during the Tower of Babel. This is because Hebrew came as the result of Abraham, who was a black man from the Chaldean town of Ur and later, through his child Isaac, gave birth to Jacob, who fathered the Twelve Tribes of Israel. The Israelites were using Judean as their main language, as has been confirmed in different places in the Bible. The author is not suggesting that all black people who were in Babylon and Egypt only spoke Thok Naath.

Thok Naath has similarities with the Dinka which are believed to be cousins to the Naath, but huge differences with the Luo languages that include the Shilluk (Chollo), Anyuak, Luo, Acholi, Buuor, Belanda, Pari, Lango, and Jur, which currently cover Bhar el-Ghazal, Equatoria and part of the Upper Nile Basin.[325] Some of the Nilotic people, mostly from Luo, have extended their migration to Uganda, Kenya, and Tanzania and have become inhabitants there.

Experts such E. E. Evan Pritchard, who researched the social life of the Nuer, and Douglas H. Johnson, who researched the Nuer prophets, were comfortable with the status of the term *Nuer* but not with its usage. They realized that Nuer lacked the essence that would have associated it more closely with *Ran*, or human beings, and the purpose of creation, mainly how man is part of creation. Many elders have recommended that we should go back to the term *Naath*, which has maintained its original meaning as the name of the tribe. Some elders even suggested that the term *Nuer* should be banished from use when referring to the Naath. The Bible described an event when God's anger was provoked because of people concentrated on worshipping

---

325 Breidlid, Said, and Breidlid, op. cit.

the glory of the heavens or the things that were created by God to beautify heaven (Isaiah 40:26). He threw the people into the ground and gave them different languages as a punishment for disobeying him. It is said that Thok Naath (the language of mankind) was one of the languages that was used during the time of the Tower of Babel, and was translated by the Naath (Genesis 10: 1-11:25. One may question the rationality of this conclusion, but once again, I maintain that Adam, the first man to be created, was black and used the Thok Naath language to communicate. In addition, Cush was the father of Nimrod, who fathered the Sudanese people (who are Nilotic), so Thok Naath became one of the Sudanese languages. This links the people of Sudan to Adam and his lineage: Cush and his son Nimrod. The grandchildren of Nimrod were the ones who occupied the areas around Khartoum in Sudan, and when people moved, the major rivers in South Sudan were named after them, such as Sobat around Nasir in the Upper Nile (Sobat was one of the sons of Nimrod).

DISCOURSE ON THE WORD "NILOTIC"

Nilotic is a term driven from Latin which means "Nile." It has been cemented by those with the power to mean people who are indigenous to the Nile Valley and speak Nilotic languages. These languages are spoken in South Sudan, Sudan, Ethiopia, Uganda, Kenya, and northern Tanzania, and some parts of west Africa. It has never been clear to many scholars whether they originated from the Nile Valley or they migrated from somewhere and colonized the Nile Valley. One thing for sure is that most writers who found the Nilotics there believed that they were along the Nile and could not trace where they came from any further. Chiekh Anta Diop commented that "No Specialist can pinpoint the birthplace of the Hamites (scientifically speaking), the language they spoke, the migratory routes they followed, the countries they settled, or the form of civilization they have left." For sure, the term Nilotic carries no significant or serious content. It is not because social scientists do not know where they came from or what civilization they left behind. It is because social scientists decided to step their civilization down, and hide them for generations to erase them out of our historical legacy.

The place called Nabta Playa lies in the Nubian desert, which is located approximately 800 kilometers south of modern-day Cairo and hosts an ancient activity location believed to be the spot inhabited by the current population known as the Nilotic people. Social scientists discovered remains of giraffes, buffalos, varieties of antelopes, gazelles, and many other animals who went extinct. The place must have had enough water and savannah grass to host an ecosystem thousands of years ago. Between the 10th and 8th millennia BCE, human activities were taking place in this location. Fred Wendorf and Christopher Ehret pointed out that those who lived in this area were pastoralists who had cattle, goats, and sheep.[326] The people who stayed there were able to use and consume wild sorghum, and they used ceramic paints to decorate their living places and combs that were made of fish bones. The construction of their ancient huts during the 7th century indicate a large settlement. The huts were constructed in a row. The social scientists also found that the area was occupied seasonally. This means that when it was a dry season, the community would migrate to nearer water sources and built temporary shelters until it was rainy seasons, when they would migrate back to their Nabta Playa location. The inhabitants managed to make contact with the people of Southeast Asia and get fruits, legumes, millet, sorghum, and tubers. The deterioration of the weather in the Sahara got worse around 7,000 BCE, when it dried up. While this was taking place, equatorial Africa was a dense forest hosting the ecosystem. It was like a paradise on earth. The last black men that were living in the Sahara migrated to the Upper Nile; these were the Nilotic people. Their ancient migration routes were pinpointed in sub-Saharan Africa, and they were black Africans. It has been stated that:

---

326 Bauval and Brophy (2011), op cit.

Archaeological discoveries reveal that these prehistoric peoples led livelihoods seemingly at a higher level of organization than their contemporaries who lived closer to the Nile Valley. The people of Nabta Playa had above-ground and below-ground stone construction, villages designed in pre-planned arrangements, and deep wells that held water throughout the year. By the 6th millennium BC, evidence of a prehistoric religion or cult appears, with a number of sacrificed cattle buried in stone-roofed chambers lined with clay. It has been suggested that the associated cattle cult indicated in Nabta Playa marks an early evolution of Ancient Egypt's Hathor cult.[327]

It was astrophysicist Thomas G. Brophy who conducted the research and interpreted a stone circle that he found. The stone circles were laid down in the shape of a *luak* (the Nuer traditional hut and shade for cattle), where cattle are kept by the Nuer and the Jieng of South Sudan today. He interpreted that the calendar circle was made up of a doorway that ran north-south, a second that ran northeast for the summer solstice, and six center stones. Brophy took it to mean "first that the southerly line of three stones inside the calendar circle represented the three stars of Orion's Belt, and the other three stones inside the calendar circle represented the shoulders and head stars of Orion as they appeared in the sky. These correspondences were for two dates – circa 4,800 BC and at processional opposition – representing how the sky 'moves' long term."[328]

The Naath's use luak for different purposes, including keeping animals and humans safe. When there is a halo of light around the sun or the moon, the Naath will say "*Ci pay kie cang luak lat*" ("the sun has built a house around it"). For them it is something significant, and an omen that portrays an event that may have negative impact on the community. The megalithic stones or circles found in Nabta Playa

327 *Crystal Links*, "Nabta Playa Stone Circle" (http://www.crystalinks.com/nabtaplayasto-necircle.html). Retrieved June 29, 2019.

328 Ibid.

could indicate the emergence of star-worshipping during that early period of time.

Two main impacts displaced the Nilotic people during that period. First of all, it was the area that dried up, and the collected water went back to the seas and rivers such as the Nile. Since the lives of the Nilotic people depend solely on animals, they decided to move south and into Sudan, and gathered along the Nile. They stayed there for generations with their animals, moving from one water source to another, surviving for themselves and their livestock. The other factor was Asians and Europeans who were entering Egypt in an alarming rate, trading with the people who we called Nubians today and other Africans in Egypt. They began to push Africans from Lower Egypt and the Mediterranean Sea to south of the Sahara; most Africans were escaping the white oppression that was coming with the traders.[329]

John S.R. Duncan described the Nuer: "He lives with his great herds of cattle, the horns of which are trained in the manner of the ancient Babylonian Empire, two thousand years before Christ."[330] His perspective indicated that the Nuer or Nilotic people could have come from Babylon and Nimrod's Tower. His association of the Nuer's chief court with Babel is important to understand. He was describing the chiefs who settled community disputes, and their authority under the leadership of the English, as follows: "A Nuer court is, at first sight, Babel."[331] He was reflecting on the way the Nuer were in ancient Babylon and how their authority is seen through the chiefs as a manifestation of ancient Babylon. He further explained the behavior of the chiefs that were constituted by the British in the 1920s – that the courts used what looked like the symbol of the courts that once stood in Babel in ancient times. These courts were trying cases locally within the entire Naath land. When the British came, authority was taken away from the elders and those with divine qualifications and handed

---

329 Williams, op. cit.
330 Duncan, p. 158.
331 Ibid., p. 159.

over to chiefs appointed by the British. When the Naath arrived in Khartoum, they tried very hard to look for a grazing land in the desert sand, which was only along the Nile Valley. Tuti Island, a stretch of land along the Nile River on Omdurman, has been mentioned in different interviews I conducted with elders as the grazing field for the Naath people who migrated from Egypt to Sudan. This happened before the settling down of the current Nilotic people.

Tuti Island was seen as critical in a historical perspective where the two brothers chartered their destinies: Naath (Naath is an ancient name for the people we called today the Nuer) and Jieng (an ancient name for the people we call the Dinka today) over the divided wealth of their aged father and the cheating that follows created enmity between the two brothers for life. Despite the successive ancient civilizations set up by the Naath people, the still British thought that Nilotics were backwards people. They thought that people of the South had no imagination, and this led to them being portrayed as backward, silent, and content to smoke their pipes leisurely under a tree. Many have portrayed the black man as primitive and backwards.[332] One example that purports to show that the Naath were primitive and backwards is the below narrative. This happened before mirrors were in local shops, at the time when English district commissioners were colonizing and violating the rights of individuals in South Sudan and the Naath lands:

> The District Commissioner...had had come on trek and left his shaving mirror in the rest house. The rest house keeper went in to tidy up the place after he had left. He found the mirror, looked into it, and saw his father who had been dead for some years. He took his 'father' back to his hut – his private hut and not the hut which he shared with his wife. His wife was not allowed to enter this hut. The rest house keeper made a practice of talking to his father of an evening and his wife, hearing murmurs from the hut, grew suspicious that her husband was flirting with another woman. Relations

---

332 Ibid., p. 161.

between them grew strained. The rest house keeper flogged his wife because she had become irritable for no reason. One day when he was out, she screwed up her courage to the sticking point and entered her husband's hut. She found the mirror, looked at it, and found the girl. The next day she went to the court plus the girl mirror and claimed a divorce from her husband on the grounds that he was carrying on an affair with another girl and had not told her about it. The court, on the other hand, after due deliberation, granted her husband a divorce from his wife on the extremely logical ground that she had done the forbidden thing and entered her husband's hut.[333]

I am not going to argue whether this could be real or not, but this narrative serves two purposes. The first one is that all the are represented by a scenario taken from the Naath territory showing that the Upper Nile is occupied by primitive tribes who cannot even differentiate a real human being from a reflective image on a mirror. The second shows that these men, such as the district commissioners, were brave men who entered such a society and created a system that led to the emergence of chiefs that could be clothed and ruled over for the betterment of the white man.

It was mentioned that the Nilotic group started to emerge during the Third Dynasty and settled in Nubia as far as north of Aswan. The people who settled there possessed pure black elements, and the Nubians had mixed blood with the Arabs.[334] One of the groups that settled there was the common Bhar el-Ghazel type, which could be the Luo of today, living in Wau, the Upper Nile, and Ethiopia, with cousins in Kenya, Uganda, and Tanzania. They were characterized as short and broad-headed, and they were akin to the present inhabitants of the Bhar el-Ghazel province; they are very distinct from the invaders.[335] The Nilotic group such as the Nuer (Naath), Dinka (Jieng),

---

333 Ibid., p. 160.

334 MacMichael, op. cit.

335 Ibid.

and Shilluk (Chollo) were the occupiers of the White Nile Valley and have been in their current position since the second millennium BCE. They are now living in the Upper Nile and Bhar el-Ghazel regions and show some similarities with the Bantu people. Through their migration and expansion, Nilotics can be found among east central African peoples, and they live in South Sudan, northern Uganda, and eastern Kenya. The term *"Nilot"* refers to the area where they lived, mostly the region of the Upper Nile and its tributaries.[336] It has been further stated that the presence of the Upper Nile type of group, which could be the Nilotic which the Nuer, Dinka, and Shilluk were part of, occupied Nubia for a long time, and later, the Lower Nile type also followed and lived in the same area; that stretch of land experienced high Negroid traits[337] before they moved further into the Upper Nile region. As indicated by several authors, the black people which the Nilotic were part of managed to fight off invaders on the bay of the Mediterranean Sea for several years until they could not hold it anymore because of several factors, including the internal rivalry among people of Arab descent. The mainland of the Nilotic people was not Nubia; they were in Upper Egypt and the borders of Libya a long time ago, rearing cattle and studying stars for generations. They were the builders of Egypt and its pyramids. The blacks who could read spearheaded civilization. There were Negroid traits in Badarian populations from 4,000 BCE in Upper Egypt and for a certain time in the predynastic populations of both Egypt and Lower Nubia, which were later occupied heavily. As a result, Negroids were pushed to the south and Caucasoids to the north.[338] This began the decline and pushing away of the Negroid type of people into Lower Egypt until

---

336 *Encyclopedia Britannica.* "Nilot".(February 26, 2018, https://www.britannica.com/topic/Nilot).

337 Carlson, David S. and Dennis P. Van Gerven, "Diffusion, Biological Determinism, and Biocultural Adaptation in the Nubian Corridor" (Arlington, VA: *American Anthropologist*, September 1979).

338 Ibid.

they had to migrate to the Upper Nile Basin, where they had a heavy presence; some proceeded into the east African region.

DISCOURSE ON THE WORD "NUER"

Since December 14, 1898, when the Anglo-Egyptians made their first contact with the Nuer,[339] the use of the term "*Naath*" was in use but limited, while the term "*Nuer*" was widely used and covered all their neighbors. The Shilluk, the Anuak, and the Dinka could only know the Naath as the Nuer. The term "*Nuer*" has a recent origin which has been debated by the Nuer musician Gordon Koang Duoth, who talked about its origin in song. I have written about the origin of the terms, and concluded that "*Nuer*" came into existence at the shrine of Kuerkuong. This was based on research I conducted in Unity, Upper, and Jonglei States in 2007 and 2008. Elders narrated how these rituals were reached. This is how the term "*Nuer*" came into existence.

At the gathering of the elders at one function, a new calabash was brought and placed in the middle of the council of elders who had gathered to initiate a new beginning for the Naath. An ox was then sacrificed, calling for the higher powers, and the blood flowed into the unused calabash as the was slaughtered. Members of the council of elders also cut their bodies and dripped their blood as well as their saliva in the same calabash and mixed the contents together. The practices which indicate that saliva is a source of blessing are very common in the Naath community. An old man could spit saliva on your head and it would mean an invocation. A handshake is not very common when you encounter an old man; you only bend your head in respect. To a certain degree, it is believed that the morning saliva, which was not spat out, had more blessings than the saliva of the afternoon.

---

339 Johnson, Douglas H. (editor), *Empire and the Nuer: Sources on the Pacification of the Southern Sudan, 1898 -1930* (London: The British Academy Press, 2016).

The leader of this ceremony stressed that these activities were done in fulfillment of a covenant to agree with the higher powers to bless what they were about to do. Bad practices such as incest, unnecessary killings, and revenge killings that needed to be abolished, and good practices that needed to be introduced, were all discussed during this function. After exhaustive discussions and rituals, they selected a respected elder who had divine qualifications and gave him the responsibility of consulting a higher power. The higher power was the god of the ancestors who brought them throughout the migration until they were placed in the Sudd swamps. After lamentation and supplication, they asked God to bless their decisions and add His power to what they had agreed upon.

Before they finished, they all drank the contents of the calabash to seal their agreement with God. After these rituals, the elders agreed that death would come to whoever went against their agreement with God, and God would punish him. This agreement expressed the relationship between God and the people through the concept of "*Nguot*" or "*Ngut*" ("law'), denoting a sacred bond between the Creator (*Kuoth Chak*) and all creation, and among all people who had this agreement. Moreover, any violation of this covenant would lead to a curse or unforgivable sin as well as death. Cases related to homicide ("*nueer*"), in particular, would lead to curses and those involved would be regarded as sinners, thus generating the term "*Nuar*," which comes from the tern "*Nuer*". That word comes from the term "*Nueer*" (which literally means "contamination" or "sin).[340] "*Nuer*" is replacing the term "Naath" slowly. It is obvious now that most tribes inhabiting South Sudan at the moment know the Naath by the name "Nuer," and most of them do not know what "Naath" stands for in Nuer society.

With the coming of foreigners, certain terms were introduced into Nuer society. One such term is "*Turuk*," which the Nuer translate to mean "civilized." or someone who had lived in the city or town.

---

340 Liah, op. cit.

"*Turuk*" was a direct translation of the word "Turks," who were the first foreigners to penetrate deep into Nuer lands. Now the term has been embedded into Nuer society. Turks came to the land of Nuer in 1898, generating resistance and fighting between the two groups.

With the name "Nuer" in usage, an authority (*Kuarmuon*) was appointed and given power to preside over cases of those accused as sinners. The one appointed to perform the ritual would cleanse the sinners of condemnation and death. For example, when someone committed murder, he would automatically be contaminated ("*nueer*") until a ritual was performed to cleanse him. He would then be declared free from his own sins. Therefore, the term "*Nuer*" is strongly related to contamination and sin. Some people may look at it as a term that implies that members of the entire tribe are contaminated or sinners because of the nature of the creation of the term "Nuer," but this is not true. The term originated from the rituals associated with it, which included any thing or action that would solve any sin or contamination. The rituals, involving animal sacrifices, would be conducted by the leopard-skin chiefs. Sir E.E. Evans-Pritchard wrote a trilogy of books on Nuer in the 1940s ; he stated that "leopard skin-chiefs and prophets are arbiters...in which cattle are the issue, or ritual agents in situations demanding a sacrifice of ox or ram...another ritual specialist is the *wut ghok* , the 'man of the cattle'."[341] Most of these roles were created to solve the social problems of the Nuer, such handling murders, dealing with incest, and settling disputes.

Another important aspect of *Nuer* was the offering sacrifices to the gods with most of these sacrifices involving an offering of cows and rams. As reflected in the Nuer tradition (which is technically the Naath tradition), "cows are dedicated to the spirits of the lineages of the owner and of his wife and to any personal spirit that has at some time possessed either of them."[342] If any social problem occurred that

---

341 Pritchard, p. 16.

342 Evans-Pritchard, E. E., *The Nuer: A Description of the Modes of Livelihood and the Political Institutions of a Nilotic People* (Oxford: Clarendon Press, 1940), p. 16.

affected members of individual families, there were certain rules and steps, as originally agreed upon during the introduction of the term "*Nuer*" in Kuerkuong, which were strictly followed to deal with such problems.

When the Nilotic people arrived in Kuerkuong (the high ground of Kuong), most of the tribes from other Nilotic groups who came with the Naath migrated away from Kuerkong to seek better places to live. The Naath decided not to continue farther, because they liked their settlement. The soil of the land was heavy clay, broken by the sun into deep cracks during the dry season, and there was limited rain. However, it held water and allowed green vegetation to grow tall during the dry season, providing grass for the cattle. This is what Kuerkuong was to the Naath – a place they loved with their hearts.[343] Almost all the tribes migrated, but the Naath were left alone in Kuerkuong along with some Dinka, Shilluk, and Anuak. The elders who led the migration called a council meeting to brainstorm the laws that would govern the Naath in their new environment. It is good to put on record that most of the early migrations were led by those who were considered to have divine powers, and such people were the elders of the community. Even when the English came to southern Sudan, the elders were the ones that had the power. There were no chiefs or any form of government control. In the case of the women, there were "*teat,*" or witches, who advised the elders. The laws (or Meroitic laws, as they were used in Meroë during the kingdom) that governed them as the Nilotic people were no longer in effect since the tribes had dispersed to different locations. All witches were invited to give advice on what needed to be considered when developing laws, or "*nguot,*" as the Nuer called them.

The term "*Nuer*" reminds every Nuaar (plural form) person about the qualities he or she is required to uphold. Such qualities include cleanliness and social contact only with cannibals or the half-animal, non-man-eating persons. The leopard-skin chief is to administer

---

343 Ibid.

the newly constituted law, the one agreed in Kuerkuong, and thus avert any contamination that is likely to occur. Therefore, the Nuer emphasize Nuaar lifestyle to all members because it is pure and just. It was developed with a conscience to distribute responsibilities and to have a religion that governs the tribe. The current Nuer religion that is in practice, where the Nuer consult directly with God the Creator, is part of the initial agreement which was made in Kuerkuong. Sins committed are resolved by the leopard-skin chiefs through a ritual in which an animal is sacrificed.

Phar Ruot, an elder I interviewed in November 2016 at the Protection of Civilians site in Juba, described how incest was dealt with in the Nuer customs. He clarifies that when someone, either a man or a woman, sleeps with a relative; both of them are considered to have committed *"rual"* (incest), which is considered a grave sin. They would be taken to the Kuarmuon (earth master) to separate them ceremoniously. When the Kuarmuon separated them, he would use his leopard skin to conduct some cleansing rituals in which he would invite the higher powers, the gods as well as the elders, to help him perform the ritual. To the Nuer, elders are closer to God, and He listens to them whenever the elders call upon Him. The Kuarmuon cannot perform the rituals where he calls on God without the elders. The Kuarmuon would revoke and denounce the act of incest by lamenting some power words and asking God to forgive the sinners. He would ask God to consider the incest a spiritual insult by the people who committed it. He would ask the spirit to pardon them. The Kuarmuon would the command the *rual* to leave the two who had sinned against God. Through the Kuarmuon, the spirit that it is believed would have haunted them disappears immediately, knowing that the arbiter had sought forgiveness on behalf of the sinners and they will be asked not to make another mistake of the same kind again.[344] Par Ruot explains it this way:

---

344 Phar Ruot, an Internal Displaced Person in the Protection of Civilians (PoC) area in Juba, South Sudan. Personal interview, November 14, 2016.

If a husband is dead and he has a family, the wife will be experiencing strange dreams, which are believed to be an established communication between him and his wife. For the wife to cut that contact, the Kuarmuon will be informed about it, and he will bring a fruit of a tree known as Kuol. He will cut it into two halves for his rituals. This process will separate the dead from the living and the wife from the husband. As such, children will not be sick, and misfortunes will not come upon the family.[345]

The elders believed that it was *Nguot* (law) that had been agreed upon among the elders and God that caused the person to die if he or she falls ill, and incest will be blamed for it. However, incest could also occur in other ways. For instance, when a woman got married, before she could even be given to her husband, there were *Nguot* to be passed and announced during the handing over of the bride to her husband. It is believed that it was these *Nguot* that would haunt them if they committed *duer* (sin). Interestingly, the gods and the spirits are invited into the marriages. The spirits are given their share of the bride price when cows are brought to the girl's family, and she, in turn, is given to her husband. These contributions are made according to the initial terms and conditions (Nguot) agreed upon among the Nuer elders. To refute any violation and dishonesty that would go against the agreed covenant between God and the Naath. It has also been mentioned that:

It is believed that what brought misfortunes in incest are the cows that are used in marriages. I guess you are aware that to contact God, you have to sacrifice the blood of an animal so that you call God upon your request. This indicates that cows are useful in our daily lives. During marriages, Nguot or laws are passed and will govern the marriage contract, and it is not easily breakable, and

---

345 Gatluok Mabor, paramount chief of the Dok community in the PoC area in Juba, South Sudan. Personal interview, February 17, 2017.

if anyone violated this nguot, then the God that was invited in the marriage will haunt people. When incest is committed, Kuarmuon will conduct the ritual but not to cast it out completely even if they have the complete power to do so. The Kuarmuon wants it to happen again because they are also getting some kind of payment as a result. They would solve the current mistake but would be hoping to solve another one."[346]

When incest occurred, therefore, the Naath believed that it could kill, because it is one of the areas that has been put into an agreement between God and the people. If people who have committed incest or similar acts die, it is because of God's unhappiness. This is reflected in the initial agreement that was made between man and God. The Kuarmuon acts as the mediator between God and the persons who had violated the agreement. Sharon E. Hutchinson, who spent many years researching the Naath, was nicknamed *Nyariel* – a name associated with cows. When she went to live among the Nuer in the 1980s, she wrote *Nuer Dilemmas: Coping with Money, War, and the State* as a follow-up to E.E. Evans Pritchard's work on the Nuer, which spread across many years from 1930s to the 1990s. She examined the Naath's social, political, and economic life at length. She particularly highlighted a story that took place while she was researching a location within Naath land.

The story was about two siblings. The orphaned siblings decided to form a family, because they had no hope of getting cattle in order to marry wives. Their relationship raised suspicion within the community elders and the chiefs. Both of them were summoned to the council of elders to explain their status. They agreed that they were forming a family, and they hoped to bring forth children. They knew that it was an abomination and a taboo among the Nuer, but they chose to do it anyway. The elders and chiefs were stunned by their open frankness.

---

346 Magok Gatluak, paramount chief from the Haak community, Rubkuach Mayiendit County, South Sudan. Personal interview, June 4, 2017.

After listening to them, the elders and chiefs were unable to prevent the two from having a matrimonial relationship. However, they believed that whoever went against the agreement would be judged by God, with whom the agreement was made and sealed when the term *Nueer* was introduced. The elders prayed and asked the divinities to bless them and forgive the sin they had committed.[347] This was carried out to prevent any further consequences that could befall them. By doing this, "the council of elders was acknowledging the fact that the force of 'incest prohibitions' ultimately rested with divinity as the guardian of human morality. Although perceived notions of the trans-generational scope and relative intensity of various incest taboos provided an indispensable guide for human action,"[348] it was noted that both siblings realized that they had committed a sin, and they even wanted to die if being together would be the cause of their death. They believed that the anger of the gods in the form of plagues and pestilence would kill them. However, the elders intervened and blessed their union; thus, there was a chance that the divinities could forgive them. If such an incident really happened, it would have been the first violation of such act where the community elders intervened against the laws. In April 2018, I went to Khartoum and interviewed Tunguar Kueiguong, who worked closely with Hutchinson. Kueiguong was approaching 90 years when I met him. He was losing his memory. When I asked him about the case, because it happened in his home area and he was one of the chiefs then, he told me that he could not remember it anymore but acknowledged that certain things that went against the law happened, but elders cannot intervene in support of violations.

The link between the Nuer and homicide is also important to clarify. When a family member kills a person, the Kuarmuon must be invited to settle the case. The murderer must get a cow, kill it, and cut it in half.

---

347 Hutchinson, Sharon, *Nuer Dilemmas: Coping with Money, War, and the State.* (Berkeley: University of California Press, 1996).

348 Ibid., p. 238.

This symbolizes that the problems between the family of the deceased and the family of the person who had committed murder have been separated in order to avoid further confrontation. An agreed-upon amount of blood cattle must be paid and given to the family of the deceased through the Kuarmuon, who is the arbiter. He will go home with all the cattle and sacrifice a bull. From the slaughtered bull, a small piece of meat from the hump must be cut and roasted. The bile of the cow is also collected and littered on to the pieces of roasted meat. Everyone who is present during the occasion will be given some meat to eat. This seals the agreement that the problem between the two families has been witnessed by everyone available during the occasion and that the issue has been resolved.

Douglas H. Johnson, a historian who spent many years researching the Nuer, discusses Nuer justice in his work published in *The Journal of African History*, "Judicial Regulation and Administrative Control: Customary Law and the Nuer." He emphasized that "Nuer concepts of justice were founded on the principles of social obligation and a spiritually sanctioned moral order, where moral and social obligations often merged. The failure to honor a social obligation could become a debt due or a 'wrong,' which in turn could result in *nueer*; a 'sin.' The decision to take corrective action was supposed to be based on *cuong* or moral right, to receive either religious or social sanction."[349] The two siblings who had committed incest were not given social sanction by the elders permitted to receive moral right, but were left to go on with their lives, leaving judgment to the gods. Johnson referred to "*nueer*" as "sin", which comes as a result of the violation of the agreement. When an action is introduced to right the wrong, that action would be "*cuong*," which is the correct action taken when someone has sinned.

Wal Duany wrote his doctoral thesis on Nuer political leadership and its social organization. In his writings about "equality and account-

---

349 Johnson, Douglas, "Judicial Regulation and Administrative Control: Customary Law and the Nuer, 1898-1954" (London: *The Journal of African History*, Vol. 27, No. 1, 1986), pp. 59–78.

ability," he described what happened when someone committed a crime:

> '[E]quality is related to the Nuer concept of accountability. As people decide to hold others responsible for their actions, as they allow the same principle to extend universally, they create a particular kind of moral environment for each other. They expect each other to be held equally accountable. Their commitment to a system of reciprocal accountability gives them incentives to work out the fuller explanation of their system of governing principle."[350]

Before the coming of the British into territorial control of the Nuer, and before the British imposed the chieftaincy system, the Nuer were ruled by the leopard-skin spiritual leaders or those who were possessed by the spirit. They were believed to be guided by the power of God, who looked down on them and gave them the power to execute their orders. It was not until the 1870s that Nuer system was corrupted by foreigners by colonialists introducing a new way they wanted to rule the Nuer and control their lives. The Nuer resisted this and fought against the British, the Egyptians, and the government of Sudan, and eventually, the condominium (joint authority) rule took control of the Nuer and their land. Although there was resistance, there was also a loss of lives, and the condominium rule managed to control people. They then used the Nuer to their advantage, disrupting their social, political, and economic systems.

The creation of *nguot*[351] or laws[352] was historically the first of its kind when the Naath came to Koat Lich, also known as Kuerkuong,

---

350 Duany, Wal, *Neither Palaces nor Prison: The Constitution of Order Among the Nuer* (Jubal: South Sudanese Friends International, Inc., 1992).

351 Customary Laws in Lich State (Western Upper Nile). SSDF unpublished (ND). Tharkuer, Sudan.

352 Customary Law: Nuer of States of Upper Nile and Jonglei. Unpublished. SSDF (ND). Nasir, Sudan.

during the second millennium BCE. The second and third convergence conferences of all the elders of the Naath (Nuer) in the Western Upper Nile and the Eastern Upper Nile was conducted in Fangak. Even now, it appears in whatever the Naath are doing, they always mention the Fangak laws as a reference point. The Nuer Fangak laws, or *Nguot Fangak* as the Nuer refer to them, could have come from the starting point of Kuerkuong and Koat Leich. The laws were shared orally and memorized by the arbiters and members of the community. An exhaustive list of the laws that were to be used to govern the people was drawn in the 1990s and written down as a permanent record. This task was carried out under the leadership of Dr. Riek Machar, and were first implemented by the South Sudan Defence Force (SSDF) in the Nuer-controlled areas. These *Nguot* are still active today.

There has been a conflict between the Nuer and Dinka for generations over cattle. The genesis of the conflict between the Nuer and the Dinka has been narrated with passion by the descendants of the two groups. These ethnic groups make up the two largest tribes in South Sudan today. The descendants of the Dinka have been described as the largest tribal group in South Sudan, while the Nuer are portrayed as the second largest. Whether the numbers are based on the first Sudan Census of 1955/56 is debatable. There was a census conducted in 2008 in southern Sudan, but it was not accurate because a sizable population was not counted. Views and testimonies that challenge that position widely exist, stating that the culture of the Dinka people is to scatter their dwellings across the span of the land while the Nuer like to concentrate their people within a small area of land. This could also reflect the names attributed to them, which include "*Gaatnyaruop*," which means "son of the forest," and "*Gaatnyatuoy*," which means "son of the savannah and their father named Deng".

The First Southern Sudan Census of 2008 indicated that the Dinka were the majority, although there were challenges with the census as reported by the media. The Nuer men were said to have been influenced by traditional beliefs that insist that a man cannot report the number of children in his family, because he believes that his children will be bewitched and die. This cultural belief is contrary to that of the Dinka, who believe in exposing the number of his children anticipating future benefits. This was explained as the main factor that resulted in inaccurate statistics that showed the Dinka to be the majority. The Nuer prophet, Ngundeng Bong, in his songs, seems to admit that the descendants of the Jieng are the majority. Ngundeng referred to the Dinka as *"Pappiny"*, which means they have covered the face of the earth due to their settlement, where you can see few houses in a distance when you are in Dinka areas. With the Dinka movement, you can almost find them in any state in the Upper Nile and Bhar el-Ghazal. Long ago, few clans would go and live alone, but produced children and formed their own villages.

Within their comfortable environments, the sons of the Naath and the Jieng are intensely egocentric compared to the rest of the tribes in South Sudan. Astonishingly, a visitor would not be able to distinguish the two groups from the rest of the tribes in South Sudan. Even other ethnic groups in South Sudan find it difficult to physically differentiate the Nuer from the Dinka, except through their languages.

The conflict in South Sudan that has continued since December 2013 is categorically defined as a fight over dominance, pride, and protection of legacy. The current civil war started as a result of fighting over leadership by the elites, mostly from the Dinka and Nuer communities. It is a belief of the majority of citizens in South Sudan that the Dinka tribe wants to exert their dominance over government structures since they were the ones in charge of the country. Given their status as the majority tribe in the country, they used numbers to intimidate the rest of the tribes who did not have equal population. Most of their young men went into various posts of the army, including the police, the security sector, and the army, and they hold the most powerful positions. The Nuer, in the other hand, want to dismantle that system before it has grown roots in society. The only way to dismantle that system was through elections, and after the Dinka realized that they would lose the election, they created the conflict of December 2013 by arresting all the opposition, including the key leaders from the Nuer community. A civil war started, and the Dinka used government machinery to suppress and kill the Nuer. This is how the civil started and kept going for years. The Dinka have dominated the political and economic sectors of South Sudan Since the beginning of the rebellion against the Khartoum government in 1983, but the problem between the two tribes was not recent; it has been there for generations. It is believed that both tribes were from the same parents, and they quarreled over animals until hostility among them became their main activity.

The Dinka have controlled the economy since the father of the Naath and the Jieng distributed his only wealth among his children, and the Jieng took what belonged to the Naath. This happened because their father allocated a calf to his younger children, the Nuer, and the Dinka were given the older cow. The Dinka stole the calf that was given to the Nuer and disappeared, and the Nuer promised their father that they were going to avenge this in the future. Fighting among the descendants of the two tribes has gone on for generations. In the current political situation, the children of the Jieng have the upper hand compared to the children of the Naath. Previously, cattle were the center of the conflict, but now it has gone beyond that. It has encompassed the governance of the country, of which leadership is hotly contested. As described below, the genesis of this conflict is assumed to be the hostility that has historically existed between the Naath and the Jieng and has been passed down through generations. The Nuer and the Dinka behave as if they have gone back in history to the starting point, when their aged father distributed his wealth to his children. The current war is believed to be associated with the blessing and curses from God as well as egos and legacies that were given by the father of the brothers. As predicted thousands of years ago by their father, that Naath are in direct confrontation against the Jieng because Jieng stole the calf. It has been the descendants of the Naah who have always behaved like a big brother to the Jieng, by supporting the descendants of their elder brothers whenever they have a problem facing them. For example, in the 1870s, when the

Turks came to Nyang Machar in Rumbek, South Sudan, and took the Jieng to slavery and mistreated them, the Naath shouldered the responsibility to help them out. The Naath spiritual leader Machot Nyuon, who was possessed by the spirit of Teny Dhurgon, took thousands of the Nuer White Army to fight. The Jieng were supported in their fighting and dislodging the Turks at Nyang Machar, who had been enslaving the children of the Jieng for years. The Naath has been providing such support to the Jieng for generations. That act of kindness has never been returned by the Jieng to the Naath, despite them being the eldest brother in their family. Instead, when the Turks, Arabs and white men came along the Nile, the children of Jieng were their translators wrongly translating negative things that led to the Naath being killed in return.

THE EARTH MASTER

There is a function referred by the Nuer as "*ciel*", or "the curving of the Kuarmuon," in which different clans gather to give power to a person appointed by an elders of the clans unanimously. This process is normally conducted under a *gew* or *kat*, a traditional hut used mostly as a cattle kraal. Once that power is given, all one's children will be *Kuarmuoni*, and it becomes a family power. This is not magic, but a power invested upon someone appointed by the elders, and through that power, they are able to settle problems of the community, and their decisions will be respected by all. It is normally done under the representation of different ethnic groups, whose presence adds power to what has already been bestowed on the person by the rest of the community. A calabash is brought, and all the elders gather in one place. The discussion is centered around responsibilities that should be given to the appointed person. Saliva and other unsanitary things are put in a calabash. The purpose of the saliva is to bless or curse anybody who has done right or wrong, and finally settle disputes such as murder and incest. When confirming the Kuarmuon, cows are sacrificed to the gods to please the spirits that give power to the appointed person. Milk from the cows is put in a large container, and a broom is dipped in the milk that is then splashed on the people present. The appointed person is given a leopard skin. The leopard skin is a sign of aggressiveness, implying that they are supposed to perform their rituals without fear. The leopard skin can also be used to curse or bless people. At the end, the person who is leading the process will shout "Our spirit is going to be given to you to empower you over us." Once such a statement is given, the power will be transferred to the appointed one.

The earth master, or Kuarmuon, will have the power to settle disputes such as killings, incest, and other social evils, as originally agreed in Kuerkuong. When someone commits a murder, a cow is sacrificed by spilling its blood during a ceremony conducted by the earth master. The Kuarmuon's words are both respected and feared by the entire community. For instance, a murderer will be given some blessed water by the Kuarmuon to drink. The Kuarmuon will take a sip from the same water before handing it over to the murderer. This means that he has drunk from the same cup with the Kuarmuon, who is considered holy, a just man, and a judge over things. The purpose of drinking together is to protect the person from *nueer* that may come upon the murderer. Once they finish drinking from the same container, the healing from *nueer* begins. In addition, the killer will be taken to the house of the Kuarmuon, not to that of his family or the family of the deceased, and the Kuarmuon will spill the blood of the murderer by cutting his skin and dripping blood out. This is what the Nuer refer to as *"bier"*. This is to cleanse the killer of, which is loosely translated as *"contamination"*. Another responsibility is that when a married man dies and he leaves behind a wife and children, a fruit is known as *"kuol"* is brought by the Kuarmuon and cut in half. This separates the dead husband and the rest of the surviving family. The family believes that the dead husband communicates with the family members through dreams, and interaction with the dead isn't something the family wants. If communication with the dead makes the children sick, the family is expected to recover from their sicknesses if the family is reconciled with the dead through the intervention of the elders and the Kuarmuon. When the Kuarmuon wants to pass his power to another family member in the absence of community elders and members, a father will gather his children around and pass the powers of the earth master to one of them. His children already have power, but only one of them will be given the responsibility of solving community issues. He can delegate the matters to his brothers, but he alone possesses the uppermost power given to him by their father.

The genesis of the Kuarmuon began long ago, and this how the people living around Leer got to be Kuarmuons, and how the title was passed down to generations. A long time ago, in Darchieng Dok in the Southern Unity State around Leer, there lived a man named Muoth Diem, who had his magic powers. He lived near a river (the current Adok Port) with his spear and leopard skin. In that part of the area, there were also other inhabitants. These communities would meet briefly but would not talk to each other, and did not know each other. Around the 15th century AD, there were confrontations over issues of territorial and land control between the Dok community and the Haak community, who had both inhabited the land. The family of Kuoch Luoth, who also inhabited that part of the land, sent his men to spy on Muoth Diem and catch him if they could. After some time, he was caught and taken to the camp where cattle were kept. Kuoch Luoth asked Muoth Diem why he stayed in that part of the river alone. He stated that he had powers that kept him comfortable alone near the river. He was asked to use his powers, and he said that he had a spear and leopard skin.

Muoth Diem, on the other hand, asked Kuoch Luoth what powers *he* possessed, but Kuoch Luoth could only show a black goatskin as the source of his power. Both men tested their powers by going inside a shelter (*gew*). Long ago, a gew was constructed using flammable cow dung. The shelter was set on fire while both men were inside wearing their spiritual skins. When it burnt down, both men came out alive. After they came out, Muoth Diem told Kuoth Luoth that "You are a leader and you have power which is not suffi-cient. Now take this leopard skin, and this spear, and your power will be completed. If you want to settle any dispute on murder, you call upon the sky, and I will have my spear after you to give you more power."[353] Kuoch Luoth also gave the black skin to Muoth Diem in exchange for what they experienced. This is how power was transferred to Kuoch Luoth. When someone with the Kuarmuon's blood is murdered, the descendants of Muoth Diem, who were given the black skin, will be called to settle that dispute. No Kuarmuon shall settle disputes over another Kuarmuon. After Kuoch Luoth acquired his power, he had a son and named him Ruei Kuoch Luoth. "*Ruei*" means "saliva," like that which Kuoch Luoth drank during the conferment of power. This family is famous in Darchieng Dok and are called "*Kuaar Muoni.*"

THE CATTLE MASTER

Another important person among the Nuer is the Kuaarhok, who is also known as "*wutyɔɔk*" or "cattle master". His main focus is only issues around cattle. Every clan has their own Kuaarhok, and in the Dok community, Jaak Wamach was given the power to be the Kuaarhok who guarded their cattle. The Dok solve all issues related to their cattle through the Kuaarhok. In the Gawar clan, Matuot Peth was given the power of the Kuarhok by his fellows. He later had his son, Chat Kuoth Matuot, who was taken during raids by the Teny Dhurgon and Maani Lothpera to the Dinka communities. This is the clan of the Thep Yen War, which had the power within the Gawar clan in the Nuer community. The power is normally passed from one person to another if the person is alive. Every time the Teny and

---

353 Biel Tiep Kong, Community elder, personal interviews internal displaced persons camp Juba March 2017.

Maani raided the Dinka, Chat Kuoth was entrusted with ensuring that all the cattle did not escape or get taken away. Instead, some would be left behind at the cattle camp. Kuaarhok would perform his ritual by swinging a rope around and dropping it on the ground. If the rope faced the Nuer, all the cows would be brought to them.

During the migration from cattle to river and green pastures, the cattle are camped there. The place for camping is identified by the Kuaarhok, and it will be he who blesses the campsite by wishing diseases away from the cattle and the people, and asking his god to make the camp peaceful. Other responsibilities include positioning and drilling the pegs down during the camping of the cattle, and, in the case of girls whose marrying age has passed yet do not have a husband, being asked by the father of the girl to get her married. He will perform rituals, and soon after, the girl will find a man to marry her. The ceremony is conducted as follows: A girl is brought close to a *riek* (godly stick), and the ghee and milk of the cows and is poured on her body. This is to show that through she will be married through the cows and they will bring happiness to the family. After this ritual, the girl will either elope or be married openly by any man. The power of the Kuaarhok will draw someone who wants to marry her. This practice is always permitted by those related to the girl, and this is something agreed upon in the house when the father of the girl decides to take her daughter to him. Another example of the powers of the Kuaarhok is that when cows get lost, he will take the *dep* (hitch) and swing it around and drop it on the peg. One can then expect the return of the cows to their cattle byre. This practice still persists, and the power is considered as a gift that the Kuaarhok was given to rule over his fellow men by helping them taking care of the cows. He is therefore highly respected. When the Kuarhok dies, he is buried between the *luak* (cattle byre) and the *riek* (godly stick). This is because he is master of the cattle.

WAATHKHOR

"*Waathkhor*" comprises two words, each of which has a unique meaning. However, when they are joined together, they assume a different meaning. "*Wath*" is a Nuer term that means "someone who carries out an activity wholeheartedly and is admired for his courage and outstanding achievement". "*Khor*" simply means "war". "*Waathkhor*", therefore, is someone who goes to fight without reservation and emerges victoriously. It is a Nuer term sometimes translated as "a warrior". This is a name given to someone who leads people to the battlefields and engages the enemy directly, rather than directing from afar. He is feared in his village and hometown. Pritchard describes them thus:

> Men noted for their prowess and ability stir up among the enthusiasm of the youth for a raid against the Dinka or a fight against another tribal section, and direct what simple tactics are employed, but these men have no political status or permanent leadership. The warriors mobilize in local divisions of their own accord, for there are no regiments and companies under officers, and in fighting, they follow the most forward and courageous among them. Some of these warriors become renowned, and their reputation quickly attracts recruits for raids. Two of the most famous war leaders were Latjor, who led the Jikany tribes, and Bidiit. who led the Luo eastward. Neither had any ritual qualifications, but both were men of outstanding ability who were members of the dominant clans of their tribes.[354]

A Waathkor is not a commander and could be equal to the lowest ranked soldier in the army who organizes his unit in a war formation. During conflicts, he will use the Nuer traditional shield to show his prowess and engage the enemy fiercely. His responsibility is to lead the people who are going to fight. His traditional weapons include the

354 Pritchard, op. cit.

spear (*mutni kene bieth ke koat*). A community without a Waathkor never fights a decisive war victoriously, unless they groom one person to become their Waathkor. Every community has their own Waathkhor whom they strictly follow. It was a norm in the Nuer community that the Waathkor, regardless of a defeat by the enemy, would never be killed. The enemy would spare his life because they know that he is a Waathkhor. His spears and shields would be taken, and he would be allowed to go. This was a humiliation of the worst kind. If this happened to him, his status was reduced to that of a woman, and society would consider him powerless and helpless.

During traditional wars among the members of different villages even within the Nuer community, the action of the Waathkhor is seen. If one side is defeated and some of the members have retreated from the battlefield and taken refuge in huts and cattle byres, their enemies will not harm them. They are considered cowards when they are in these huts and are considered women. When a man runs away from the battlefield and hides among the women, they will cover him with their *yat* (skirts made of animal skins) and he will not be killed. He is also considered a coward. It was only recently when the laws of war changed, because the Nuer community has expanded through blood relations is disappearing slowly. Before the 19th century AD, when people fought, huts were not burned, children were not abducted, girls were not taken as wives, and those who ran into the cattle byre were not followed and killed. This practice has changed, and no one is spared; even your own blood relative could kill you. What I am saying is that the culture is changing rapidly, and laws of the Nuer community are not followed or considered by the people as applicable to the society.

The main traditional enemy that was known to the Nuer is the Dinka. Dinka men are assumed to possess cattle by stealing them from the Nuer. The Nuer will then conduct a counter-raid, proudly knowing that they are getting back the offspring of the cattle that had been taken by the Dinka men. At the moment, raiding of cattle is carried out by the youth, but previously it was the men who went to raid cattle in Dinka land. Raiding was embedded in the community and was justified as a cultural practice. It was not only the Nuer that conducted raids against the Dinka; the Dinka also conducted raids among neighboring communities, including the Nuer. The Dinka would secretly steal cattle from the Nuer because they were afraid. The Nuer believed the Dinka did not have the power to steal cattle from the Nuer in a face-to-face confrontation. They would rather steal them. From the 1980s onward, the situation changed drastically when guns and heavy weaponry became easily available to community members. Guns were used when raiding cattle and sometimes the Dinka would collaborate with members of the Nuer community, as long as they shared the same political interests. One example was the recent December 2013 conflict when the Nuer from Mayom County of Unity State invited the Dinka from Warrap and Parieng County and matched in huge numbers to confiscate all the cows in Leer, Mayiendit, and Koch Counties of Unity State. This was carried out based on political interests; otherwise, there was no connection between the Nuer of Mayom and the Dinka to collaborate and aid the Nuer.

There are very few people who are considered Waathkhors or warriors in the Nuer community. Waathkhor used to be a volunteer job, but now it has changed with the introduction of money. Some commanders and soldiers are hired as mercenaries and employed by anyone who wants a certain job done. The role of the Waathkhor has diminished, because winning a war now depends on which community has more guns and manpower compared to others. The use of traditional weapons such as spears and shields and sticks has also declined, while the demand for modern weapons has gone up. The imbalance of power created by modern weapons has reduced cattle raids in some areas with more weapons and increased the cattle raids in other communities who lack weapons and manpower. The laws of war among the Nuer have changed too. Killings have increased even among those who hide in huts and *luaks*, unlike the olden days when women hid them. In fact, women these days kill too. Houses are burnt down, women of the defeated community are raped and kidnapped, and the children are castrated or taken away. More tragically, old men and women are burned alive in their houses. There is much "*dak-mi-thil-yiet*", or "fleeing away from the scene of fighting." These fights are carried out by those who are within the same tribe, but against each other, such as the recent attacks by the Bul community of Mayom County against the Dok, Haak, and Jagei of Unity State. The Dinka, too, who are considered cousins to the Nuer, also commit heinous crimes against them.

Casualities from conflicts that involve guns have increased tremendously compared to the use of traditional weapons. The Nuer culture dictates that one of the most important ceremonial occasions in a male's life is his initiation into manhood. This initiation occurs with a group of boys who have come of age, and this group, who are initiated together, then become members of the same age-set. They walk together, eat together, and engage girls together. They remain in this age-set for life and united by the common marks. Initiation involves the deep cutting of the forehead, called "*gar*". "Their brows are cut to the bone with a small knife, in six long cuts from ear to ear,"[355] which can even be seen after someone is dead and the bone is exposed. The gar is significant both in a political and religious sense and marks changing social status from adolescence to manhood. During fighting, a man will not be spared, but a boy without the marks will not be killed. "Gar is a sign of the covenant before an individual, society and the god of the Nuer. As such, it brings members of different lineages into a special relationship with one another, and binds them into fellowship with people of the covenant."[356] In Nuer society, it is a general rule that all Nuer males of reasonable age (15 to 18 years) must be marked before they can marry.[357] Married life includes responsibility for, and a share in the running of, the Nuer society; initiated married men are consulted on matters affecting society and also perform sacrifices.[358]

---

355 Pritchard, p. 249.

356 Duany, W., 2005. Neither Palaces Nor Prisons: Constitutions of Order Among the Nuer. South Sudanese Friends International, p. 201.

357 Duany, op. cit.

358 Pritchard, p. 178.

KUARJUAYNI

The Kuarjuayni, master of the environment, has command over the animals that crawl on land and grass. He is called the Kuarjuayni because he abates harm that could come from the animals that crawl on people. He is responsible for controlling those animals, such as scorpions and snakes that may bite people, by using his powers to control their actions. Most people who walk on the roads must avoid snakes that bite, wild animals that attack humans, and even scorpions that attack them. The Kuarjuayni spills the blood of animals to sacrifice to the spirit of the grasses, or *Kuothjuayni*. He summons them to listen to him while offering them something in return. When he does this, they make a promise not to allow anything to happen to the people, as requested by the Kuarjuayni. The spirit of the grasses is possessed by many families.

When a child has returned home after being away for a long time, he will be made to stay in the "*wichcherei*" a distance from the cattle byre until grass and tobacco are taken and smeared on his or her body. This is a sign of welcoming the child home after a long time. Such children are considered "lost and found" and throwing and smearing water and tobacco is a sign of giving thanks to the gods who protected them while they were away. Throwing green grasses on their bodies indicates that the spirit of the grasses they walked on all those years kept them safe, and they are thankful to the gods of the environment. The cleansing process also involves the use of tobacco, water, and saliva to purify the child. This is one of the traditional activities practiced throughout the entire Nuer land.

KUARTHOAY

The Kuarthoay is the master of the river. He is the person who has the power of mastery over creatures under the water. He can control the activities of animals that were created to live in water. He further uses this power to show his gifts to other people. Such people are called *"Jithoay"*, which is a short form of *"Kuarthoay,"* the people of the Thoch. "Thoch," here, refers to the grasses that grow in water, and some can stand on these grasses without being submerged in water. They have special gifts which are unique to them. There are many creatures under the water, and the master can use his spirits to silence or summon them. There are areas in which humans are always threatened by the crocodiles, snakes, and other creatures. Certain ceremonies can be conducted to please the crocodiles so that they do not threaten the lives of people, and vice versa.

When the Kuarhoay is not happy with a member of the community, he will restrain the movement of that person from getting water from any river. Through their spirits and power, it is believed they can mobilize creatures under the water to strike against the intended target. Most of them use crocodiles as their totemic symbols, then pay respect by sacrifice cattle to them. When the Kuarthoay is required to perform a sacrifice to the gods of water, a goat is always given. The goat will be sacrificed near the river or be taken to the river in a place where water reaches the hips, and the god of the river will be called upon to take its gift. A crocodile will appear, devour the goat, and walk away. Other people who possess the power can even go to the river and nothing will happen to them. They can take hold of snakes or touch the crocodiles and hippos, but these creatures will not harm them.

DISCOURSE ON THE TERMS "DINKA," AND "JIENG"

As noted from the origin of the terms *"Nuer"* and *"Naath"*, the term *"Dinka"* refers to a people who belong to a larger group known as the Nilotic people of South Sudan today. The word *Dinka* is believed to have been invented by outsiders who had contact with the community. One thing is clear: The people now known as the

Dinka call themselves *"Jieng"*. Dinka is a later term, and the neighboring groups know the Dinka as Jieng. The origin of the term *"Jieng"* is not known and remains a mystery, although it has been used for thousands of years. The term *"Dinka"*, however, is said to have been introduced by an English explorer who came to Sudan and met a local person who was called Ding Kak around Melut. He was the chief of the area. Based on the interaction of an explorer was conducting his own research, the term *Dinka* was first used to refer to the Jieng people. When the explorer asked Ding Kak whose land is this, pointing the surrounding areas of Renk and Melut, Ding Kak said that all was his land, including the people. When he asked about the people, he said they are Ding Kak's. Due to a twist of tongue, the explorer called the Jieng "Dinka". Using this explanation, one can see why the Jieng people are believed to be part of the Nuer. Even today, when you ask a Dinka man from a village, they will never tell you what Dinka means. They only know that they are Jieng.

They were known in most parts of South Sudan and Sudan as *"Jaang"* (this term could also be spelled as *"Jieng"*). The mythology states that they were brothers to the Naath people, and Jaang was the elder son to their father, Deng. When their aged father decided to distribute and allocate his wealth among his children, Jaang stole the calf that was allocated to his younger brother, Naath. After doing this, he decided to escape and joined the rest of the Nilotic group. When he did this, their father cursed him and told him that he would be the weakest in the presence of his brother, and he would live with tricky behavior to sustain his life. His father cursed him by cutting him out of the family and blessed his younger brother to prosper. His brothers the Naath were blessed with the skills and strength. All of these happened when they were in Jabel Barkal in Sudan. Jaang decided to migrate with his stolen calf, and came to the junction of the River Nile and the Blue Nile and named it *"Kar-Tuom"* symbolizing the joining of two rivers. *"Kar"* means a branch of something. He was referring to the two branches of the Nile, the White Nile coming from South Sudan and the Blue Nile coming from Ethiopian islands. *"Tuom"* means to meet. This was where the two branches of the Nile met, and this generated the name "Khartoum". Jaang was doing this because he was in hiding from his father and his brother, who might have come to claim the calf. Hiding between two rivers gave him a refuge and shelter from their watchful eyes.

When his father pronounced him the curse, he was cut off from the family of Naath and became "*Juor*", or a foreigner. The Naath today use the term "Jaang" refer to all the Dinka, and it became their name. "Jaang" in Naath means "foreigner" and this term is used for the descendants of Dinka today. The rest of the people who are not members of the Naath are referred to as "*Juor*", also meaning "foreigner." The word "Jaang" was crafted by their father as a curse, and it has a very strong connotation that goes along with it. After hundreds of years, the descendants of the Jaang were used by the Naath to herd their cattle, and after a year, they are awarded with a cow. The other meaning of the term "*Jaang*" in Naath means "worker," which refers to someone who works for you as a maid. This came about because of the employment given to the descendants of the Jaang by the Naath. Their language changed completely when they comingled with the rest of the Nilotic communities, though their physical appearance remains the same. A foreigner or *juor* looking at the descendant of Naath and Jaang, would never differentiate them as such. Even the Naath cannot differentiate the Jaang from themselves. This is an indication that they are from the same parents.

THE NUBIANS

There is an assumption that to study the Nilotic people, you must study the Nubians. This may not be true, considering that the Nubians may be different from the Nilotics. History shows us that before the Nilotics could acquire their name, they came from Babylon and were part of the ancient Egyptian civilization. After years of migration, they came down along the Nile and acquired the name "*Nilotic*". Nubians

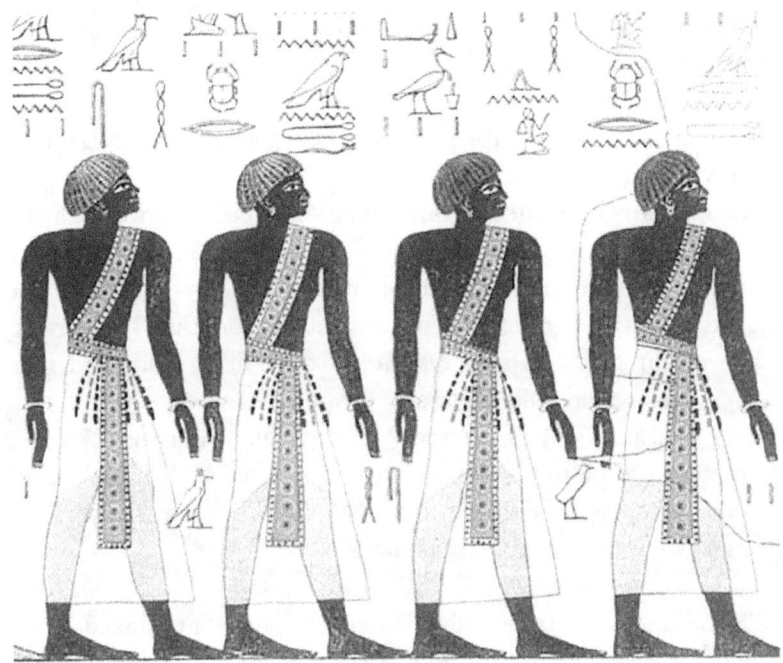

The Nubians

who are currently in Upper Egypt and Sudan were part of the ancient Egyptian people, but that does not mean that any black person present in that time and place was a Nubian. The current areas occupied by Nubians could have been the result of migration routes by the Nilotic and other black Africans. As indicated above, many confuse the terms *"Nubia"* and *"Cush"*, yet they are indeed very different. "Cush" was the name of the ancient Nile Valley civilization, while "Nubia" evolved as an alternative pronunciation of *Nobatai*, pastoralists who looked after goats. They overpowered the Cushite kingdom in the sixth century and may have been two separate ethnic populations.[359]

Most writers consider Egypt and north Sudan, in which the Cush

---

359 Omer, Ibrahim, *Ancient Sudan* – Kush, "Ethnicity"(http://www.ancientsudan.org/ ethnicity.html), retrieved July 1, 2019.

Kingdom was located, to Nubians because they persisted for genera-tions and were not displaced far from Egypt. This prompted them to stay on and intermarry with the invaders. The only other language the Nubians knows well is Arabic; their mother tongue is still in use today, but slowly its disappearing.

The Nubians were the last ones to be displaced, and through their persistence, they are still within the Egyptian and Sudanese borders. Though they faced marginalization in the country and have been annexed to Arabia through its culture and religion, they still persist.

The origin of the word "*Nubia*" is difficult to find, and much research has resulted in different etymologies which also do not provide a clear origin of the term. Eratosthenes, born in 276 BCE, was reported to be the first person to use the term "*Novfiat*", and it was later used in its Latinized form "*Nobatae*".[360] The University of Chicago's Oriental Institute, says that:

> The origin of the name Nubia is obscure. Some have linked it to *nwb*, the ancient word for gold. Others connect it with the term *Noubades*, the Greek name for people who moved into northern Nubia sometime in the 4th Century AD. For much of antiquity, the region south of the 1st cataract of the Nile was called Cush. The name is known from the ancient Egyptian, classical, and biblical texts. Whether it reflects an indigenous term is not known. The Cushites developed powerful kingdoms. The first was centered at Kerma (2000-1650 BC). The later kingdom had its capital at Napata (800-270 BC) and Meroë (270 BC-370 AD). Most of the information about ancient Nubia comes from archeological excavation, and from there, the study of monuments and rock art found there. But the art and writing of Nubians and of peoples contemporary with them also give important evidence. Records of ancient Egypt tell much about the history of Nubia, documenting a long and complex relation between the two lands. Monuments

---

360 MacMichael, op. cit.

and texts in the Egyptian language left by the Nubian kings, who became pharaohs of Egypt's 25th Dynasty around 750 BC, also provide an extensive record. Nubians developed alphabetic writing systems around 200 BC during the Meroitic periods. The Meroitic language is still not understood well enough to read more than words and phrases, but much documentation of Meroitic Nubia can be found in the art and literature of Greece and Rome, whose empires touched on the borders of the Nubia after 330 BC.[361]

As we have argued, the Nubians are the black people who have been inhabiting Upper Egypt for centuries around the Aswan Dam and along the corridor of Nile. The word "Nubia" is further claimed to mean "plaited one," which was found written on the tomb of Thutmose I. The place where it is written dates back to 1540 BCE. The Nubians were also black, and whenever we are talking of ancient Egypt, Nubians are part of that history. They share a history of that strip of land stretching from Lower Egypt towards the borders of Libya. Nubia is associated with the Negro people, as the term applies, while black people were also associated with "*Nahas*," which was the general term black people used to refer to themselves. "Nahas" was later found to be the name associated with the Nuer people of the Upper Nile today.

Cush and ancient Nubia were two different cultures and people, and this has been evident from the paintings found on their graves and sculptures and also the periods in which they occurred. Nubia's kingdom started around 3100 BCE, while Cush's kingdom was around 1070 BCE. The civilization of Nubia was a Meroitic civilization, a fusion of the ancient Egyptians and Nubian civilization. This makes sense, because most people who were in Egypt were Nubians. The Nubians were the people the Bible refers as "*Mizraim*," after the

361 The Oriental Institute of the University of Chicago, "The History of Ancient Nubia" (https://oi.uchicago.edu/museum-exhibits/history-ancient-nubiaOLD), retrieved June 30, 2019.

second son of Ham, who came first to occupy Egypt; the Cush kingdom was populated by the children of Cush, who was the first son of Ham and came before Mizraim. His descendants are the Nilotic people who occupied eastern Africa. This understanding, that Nubians were the ones that occupied Egypt, is also confirmed by anthropological studies done on fossils dug up at the border of Egypt and Sudan.

The Cushite ethnic identity, which is the Nilotic identity, was erased and disappeared when they moved out of northern Sudan to the Upper Nile valley. Then the Arabs came to Sudan, and this was followed by the spread of Arabs and Islam into the northern part of Sudan, and subsequently, in the interior of the country. They are presently a minority group in Sudan at 15% of the popuat and without any Cushite genetic identity in them. Most of the Sudanese have become Arabs with Arabic lineage, which accounts for 70% of the Sudanese population. These groups include the Jaa'lyeen, Shaigiya, Manasasir, and many others. One can recognize the difference in languages; the Nubians still maintain their mother tongue, while the rest speak only Arabic.[362] According to the *World Population Review*:

Sudanese Arabs account for 70% of the population of Sudan, with the rest of the population being Arabized ethnic groups of Beja, Copts, Nubians, and other peoples. There are more than 597 tribes in Sudan speaking more than 400 dialects and languages. Sudan is almost entirely Muslim, with most citizens speaking Sudanese Arabic. Most Arabized and indigenous tribes, such as the Masalit and Zaghawa who speak Chadian Arabic, show very little cultural integration with the rest of the population due to linguistic and cultural differences. The vast majority of the Arab tribes in the country originally migrated to Sudan in the 12th century and then intermarried with indigenous populations and introduced Islam. The Sudanese Arabs of the Eastern and Northern parts of Sudan

---

362 Ibid.

are descended mostly from migrants from the Arabian Peninsula[363] and some already-existing indigenous populations, such as the Nubian people, who share a common history with Egypt. While some pre-Islamic Arabian tribes lived in Sudan from earlier migrations from Western Arabia, most arrived in Sudan after the 12th century.

Again, it would be unfair to include the Arabs who came and settled in this land as part of the Nubia, though the Arabs have intermarried with the Nubians. Although there have been intermarriages, there is still the big distinction of who the Nubians were from the late inhabitants of the land and i the Arabs who came and occupied in the 12th century AD. There are other tribes, such as the Mahass and the Sukot, who have Arab ancestors and survived persistently among the Nubians for generations. The Kanuz and the Danagla are more Arab in color while looking African in appearance. There was persistent crossbreeding between blacks and so-called Arabs. Women from the south were also taken as slaves and sold, a practice that persisted for centuries as a result of slavery that existed in north Africa. Such women were used as wives, resulting in hybrid children – a category of people that was grouped and integrated among the Nubians.[364] Archaeologists were commissioned by UNESCO in 1960-64 to excavate the areas around Nubia. They coined the name for the ancient Nubians: the A-Group. They were part of the ancient Nubians who came from Egypt and had very strong rulers who had established the main kingdoms around the land of Nubia for thousands of years. Some of the authors who wrote various articles about Nubians referred to this process as "hybridization," due to the intermarriages of people who were found in the land. Nubians were the ones who emerged from the Neolithic cultures of the Nile Valley, and more documentation that unveiled their origin

---

363 *World Population Review*, "Sudan Population 2019" (http://worldpopulationreview. com/countries/sudan-population/), retrieved July 1, 2019.

364 MacMichael, op. cit.

and migration was unearthed from their cemeteries at the borders of Egypt and Sudan. Quite a number of the burials were intact, and intact artifacts and rocks showed their early activities. They were found along the Nile Valley around the Kubaniyya, which is one of the ancient sites believed to be their earliest settlement. The far north of the first cataract up to the second cataract, and into what is now known as the modern state of Sudan, had been named Upper Nubia.[365] The merchants and Egyptians engaged in trade to make Nubia flourish. Selling of gold from the eastern desert was one of the hot commodities attracting customers, as well as carnelian from the western desert, and exotic products such as incense, ivory, and ebony from further south along the Nile converged. They also had olive oil from the Mediterranean coast. Their totemic symbolism was used by the Egyptian pharaohs a long time ago. This A-Group flourished from the First dynasty of the Egyptian era, which was around 3800–3100 BCE, after which the Nubia was destroyed by the Egyptian pharaohs.[366] Nubia had been a land connecting different cultures – sub-Saharan Africa and the Mediterranean – and what made Nubia strong was this kind of fusion between different cultures and traditions. We are aware that there was a group of Arabs who came for trade but later merged with the Nubians. They now occupy that part of the land located in north Sudan and have become part of Nubia.

This Arab group had their culture intertwined with the Nubians, but one cannot say that they brought civilization to Nubia; instead, they learned from Nubians and became integrated. The origin of the A-Group was said to have been in the Dongola Reach in Sudan. When their graves were exhumed, corpses were found wrapped in hides made from antelopes and accompanied by ostrich feathers, which were used for insulation to keep them protected, as well as leather caps, wooden

---

365 Carlson, David S., op. cit.

366 The Orieiental Institute of the University of Chicago, "Ancient Nubia: A-Group 3800–3100 BC" (https://oi.uchicago.edu/museum-exhibits/nubia/ancient-nubia-group-3800%E2%80%933100-bc), retrieved May 30, 2019).

bowls, and other items. The graves give the impression of a lower-class group in the community. One of the cemeteries was found in Wadi Halfa in Sudan, and the graves in the cemetery ranged between 3.54 square meters and 1.62 square meters. Graves of privileged individuals were roofed with dried mud, and each was topped with stone slabs. This combination of dried mud and stone preserved the items inside. Most importantly, skeletons of goats were also found inside, and this indicates that the group was composed of herders.[367] In addition, the A-Group seems to have practiced some rituals. Broken pottery and sacrificing animals on top of graves were some of the rituals they were involved in, and this had been part of ancient Sudan.

Some of their potteries, such as jars with black tops, bowls with cross-hatchings, and geometric shapes, were part of their common culture as items of value. In addition, imported potteries from Egypt, Lower Egypt, and Syria were also used by this group and were quite distinct from the original items of the people nearby.[368] Another important group called the C-group, which was believed to have come from Egypt, was also found in the same area of the Dongola Reach. They were in that area around 2300 BCE and had settled in Lower Nubia but were associated with the Kingdom of Cush. Their culture was associated with that of north Sudan, probably from Egypt; this supports the idea of their northern expansion into Sudan. Their construction included superstructures made of cut masonry and filled with sand and gravel. The graves of the C-group were constructed of mud bricks with deposits of sacrificed animals.[369]

---

367 Omer, Ibrahuim, op. cit.

368 Ibid.

369 Ibid.

CHAPTER FIVE

CONCLUSION

After discussing the origin and early migration of the black man, and his ancient civilizations around the world, it is also important to summarize how the black man was reduced from that great civilization to a man that has no ancient records on his civilization. We will also see from the narrative below that the West has contributed strongly to creating the low self-esteem of the black man and instilling an inferiority complex. This was achieved after generations of research and investigation, and reports conducted and presented by the explorers. The mental perception of the black man has changed from a man of invention to an inferior man. The way he was classified, analyzed, and given a new class made him believe that he was that person from ancient times to the present. Education played a major factor in instilling inferiority; instead of developing further ancient hieroglyphs, which was the first writing style developed by the Cush, Egypt, and Babylon, the West took it and placed it in a museum as an artifact. Instead, they introduced their own writing style, which promoted their culture and advanced their civilization. A good example is the work of Evan Pritchard among the Nuer, when he said, "I described...the ways in which a Nilotic people obtain their livelihood, and their political institutions." Such a description was not for peaceful purposes, but instead to study the Nuer as a way to pave a path for the Sudan Condominium. His research actually did much harm to the Nuer and Nilotic people, rather than good.

The analysis throughout this book indicates that the black man ventured out of Africa and colonized many parts of the world. The remains of his ancient artistry and human remains can be traced throughout the world. Based on the analysis of geneticists and paleon-tological records, "We only started to leave Africa between 60,000 and 70,000 years ago. What set this in motion is uncertain, but we think it has something to do with major climatic shifts that were happening around that time – a sudden cooling in the Earth's climate driven by the onset of one of the worst parts of the last Ice Age. This cold snap would have made life difficult for our African ancestors, and the genetic evidence points to a sharp reduction in population size around this time."[370]

The first modern Briton, discovered to have lived 10,000 years ago, had dark to black skin, as DNA analysis revealed. The fossil of this skeleton was known as Cheddar Man and was unearth in Gough's Cave in Somerset. Cheddar Man was found to have lived shortly after the first settlers crossed from continental Europe to Britain at the end of the last Ice Age.[371] The findings were documented and aired on TV channels in the United Kingdom. The DNA testing was carried out at the Natural History Museum in London. Scientists performed DNA tests by drilling a 2mm-diameter hole into the skull and removing a few milligrams of bone powder. After this, they were able to extract a full genome, which yielded evidence of this ancient relative's appearance and lifestyle.[372] The migration route shows a Middle East origin for the Cheddar Man, but clues suggested that his ancestors were left behind in Africa. The route that the Cheddar Man took was from Africa to the Middle East and then to Europe.

---

370 *National Geographic*, "Map of Human Migration" (https://genographic.nationalgeo-graphic.com/human-journey/, retrieved July 25, 2019).

371 Guardian, February 2018, op. cit.

372 Ibid.

There were so many African kingdoms that were built and prospered, including the kingdoms of Cush, Egypt, Zimbabwe, Ethiopia, Songhai, Punt, and the Mali Empire. These were some of the most powerful ancient kingdoms, and they were a regional power which stood for over a thousand of years. Kingdom such as Cush reached their peak in the second millennium BCE, when its spread across a vast territory along the Nile. It had a lucrative business trading with Egypt and the interior of Africa. The trade was in ivory, gold, and incense. During the flourishing of the Cush kingdom, their influence was far and wide. Even today, the ancient location that was Cushite kingdom is the home of over 200 ruined pyramids.

We have also seen that black man is underrated compared to the evolving species, and this was written in books. Such perceptions resulted in negative actions employed by his fellow man against him. These negative perceptions resulted in the exploitation, occupation, and derogatory remarks against him. The Bible, as can be seen today, was interpreted and used as a tool to justify the action of men against black people. Joseph Harris framed it this way:

A most decisive derogatory racial tradition stems from the biblical interpretation of Noah's curse of Ham. The Bible did not apply any racial label, but the idea of race later became attached to the descendants of Ham. A collection of Jewish oral traditions in the Babylonian Talmud from the second to the sixth centuries A.D. holds that they descendants of Ham were cursed by being black, and this belief received even greater elaboration during the Middle Age[373]

Genesis 9:18-27 discussed the curse which Noah pronounced on Ham's last-born Canaan that "cursed be Canaan! The lowest of slaves will he be to his brothers." Despite such curses being documented in

---

373 Harris, Joseph E., *Africans and Their History* (New York: Plume, 1972), p. 4.

the Bible, Canaan was the fourth child of Ham, and at the time of the curse, Canaan was not yet born, and the curse came on him by default. Such statements were literarily taken by preachers to show that black man was cursed by the great-grandfather of humanity. It was further mentioned, with much exaggeration, that

> It must be Canaan, your first born, whom they enslave...Canaan's children shall be born ugly and black...your grandchildren's hair shall be twisted into kinks... [their lips] shall swell." Men of this race are called Negroes; their forefather Canaan commanded them to love theft and fornication, to be banded together in hatred of their masters and never to tell the truth.[374]

Reading from that chapter of Genesis, there is no mention of the children of Canaan being born ugly and black, with swollen lips, twisted hair, or kinks, and the term "Negro" is not mentioned anywhere. Such labels were the work of those who had the intention of denigrating black people. If we trace back the family of Ham, Canaan was the fourth child and not the firstborn in that family. Many people have committed genocide in the name of the Bible, and the black man became a target due to the misinterpretation of this book. We remember very well that the book of Genesis is one of the five books written by Moses, known as the Torah, after taking his children out of Egypt. During the time of Moses, the term "Negro" was not known, and Moses grew up among the black children of Egypt who were descendants of Ham. He was trained in Egypt and raised like any child of Egypt. Even the children of Jacob, who later became the children, of Israel were all raised in Egypt, in the black land of Egypt, and he grew up among them.

Certain churches also contributed to these racist ideologies. The Mormon church bought the evolutionary idea of "higher" and "lower" races of man. "The point is that these cults tried to incorporate a false racist belief into their doctrines that comes from the false religion

---

374 Ibid., p. 5

of secular humanism."[375] Because they have followers to disseminate such biases and racist statements, the whole concept spread out like wildfire, and may have resulted to the recent slavery and colonization of Africa by some white men and their governments. Other early geographers and historians – including Herodotus, who I have praised highly in this book – negatively described the people he found in Africa and used derogatory words which also helped European governments to commit crimes through complicity. The work of Herodotus, which describes some African languages negatively, should be seen as part of a bigger picture of atrocities committed against blacks in Africa and other continents. Joseph Harris described Herodotus thus:

> Although the 'father of history", Herodotus, made significant contributions to the evolution of history as a field of study, in attempting to explain African culture, which was so different from his own, he saw seeds of racial prejudice that shaped black-white images for centuries to come. He frequently referred to Africans as 'barbarians' and characterized the people of Libya by saying 'their speech resembles the shrieking of a bat rather than the language of man.' 'Barbarian' and 'savage' were terms that embodied no racial significance as such, for they were used to describe many other groups of people; but they did connote inferiority...whereas the blackness of Africans became identified with a lingered in the mind of Europeans as a badge of primitiveness. A part of this must be explained by the way in which Africans were described as animals and monsters.[376]

Comparing people to animals and insects acts to dehumanize and take away their dignity, and this led Africans to suffer from an inferiority complex. This gave a mental picture to those with evil intentions, and a majority of them accomplished their intentions. Animals are not equal

---

375 Hodge (2013), p. 134.

376 Harris, p. 4.

to human beings, and when you find people you term animals, the first thing you will have to do is to infringe on them and use them for your own purposes. When the colonization of Africa took shape, the white man came in as the master to teach Africans the way of life and to use him in the exploitation of his resources. At this, time in Africa, you could see the white man with the Bible in one hand the so-called government treaties in the other hand, and all achieving a common objective. In South Sudan, the provinces were distributed, and some countries were allocated certain locations in which the churches that supported their government came and preached 'salvation'.

Another merchant of the 25th dynasty, named Benjamin Ben Jonah, also supported the notion of victimizing Africans because of their skin color. He described people who were like animals; they ate herbs that grew along the River Nile and in the fields and forest. They were naked and had no intelligence. They had sex with their sisters and anyone else they could find, and they were the children of Ham, who were black slaves.[377] The entire continent of Africa was seen as a place inhabited by savages who are inferior to other races. This notion led to the invasion of Africa by different races who came and enslaved Africans and took over their land just as the Arabs did to North Africa, and Europeans who came and enslaved Africans and shifted them to their continent. The early geographers looked at beautiful continents and made theories undermining the people who lived there. They way Africans drank directly from the river with animals, and learned how to share resources with nature, meant that Africans were grouped as savage animals. The main thing they took back to Europe with them was referring to Africans as "monsters,"' not human beings who inhabited the continent. The continent was seen as beautiful but inhabited by savages and monsters. Their message to their governments and colleagues was that there was a continent inhabited by apes, animals and subhuman, which required it to be governed by the white race. It was a very clear message they were

---

377 Harris, p. 6.

sending to their governments. As a result of this, the Europeans had a conference in Berlin, Germany known as the "Berlin Conference of 1884-85" or "The Congo Conference" or "West Africa Conference," which regulated European colonization and trade in Africa during the New Imperialism period and coincided with Germany's emergence as an imperial power. There were no trade agreements; it was purely exploitation of Africa. What had been written by their explorers became true, and such an action led to current slaves that are now in the USA and other continents.

Some have attributed race to man's evolutionary origin. It was used to justify inhumane acts against the blacks. Race, in this context, was used against black people worldwide, where there are beliefs of 'higher and lower' races, in which blacks were seen as the lowest race in the ranking of men. The beginning of such beliefs was put forward by Charles Darwin. It was further popularized by Ernest Haeckel, who was a German. He stated that bushmen, Australians (aborigines), Polynesians, Hottentots and some of the Black tribes are at the lowest stage of human development.[378] Darwin and Haeckel believed that people with black skin color were less evolved animals and further claimed that with time, those who are not Caucasians "would inevitably be exterminated by the 'civilized races'."[379] These 'civilized' races are the white and Asian races, and they did this to Africans for the last 5,000 years. It is not surprised that Haeckel came from Germany, which later had the biggest genocide in world history, just like what they carried out against black Africans. Charles Darwin was also another contributor who played his role in depopulating Africa. His journal's remarks and the book he wrote when he was voyaging around the world stated:

> ... at some future period, not very distant as measured by centuries, the civilized races of man will almost certainly exterminate and replace the savage races throughout the world. At the same time

378 Hodge, op. cit.
379 Ibif.

the anthropomorphous apes…will no doubt be exterminated. The break between man and his nearest allies will then be wider, for it will intervene between man in a more civilized state, as we may hope, even than the Caucasian, and some ape as low as a baboon, instead of as now between the negro or Australian (aborigine) and the Gorilla.[380]

Such a frame of understanding has encouraged atrocities against the black man throughout history and has to a certain degree even been used by dictators to justify their actions. Adolf Hitler, the well-known dictator of Germany, was an atheist and an evolutionist and justified his actions by claiming they fulfilled what Charles Darwin and Haeckel had already stated. The actions of Adolf Hitler exterminated the Jews, Poles, Slavs, Gypsies and others who he thought did not belong to a pure race.[381] If he could have done such acts to his fellow whites, what would he do to the children of the black man? A book entitled *Man: Past and Present*, written by A.H. Keane in 1920, described views on the findings of the inhabitants of Africa. It is clear that the description given of the origin of the black man, or the "Negroid type" as he puts it, is essentially a comparison to a monkey living in the bushes of Africa. He didn't have a description of the role of a black man on the road to civilization. He seemed to be against the celebration of black people. He thought that if a Negro land was free from foreign influence, there would never be a true culture that could develop there – only cannibalism, witchcraft, and bloodshed. Southern Sudan was further seen as the land of the primitive, unclothed, pagans and tremendously virile men who keep much to themselves. Keane mentioned that it was a society of those who could not stand their ground in raids or fight back: they were weak, had no towns but villages, and had

---

380 Hodge, p. 18
381 Ibid.

no politicians and no newspapers.[382] The continent itself was characterized as an area of mystery and strange happenings inhabited by strange people and monsters, and this was seen as the evolving image of Africa whereby creatures less than human survived in an order less than civilized.

A good number of those who paid Africa a visit characterized blacks as unprogressive if left in their own environment and saw them as "a fine animal who in his wild state, exhibits a stunted mind, represents the cessation of all upward progress and even retrogression toward the brute".[383] Such views negate the black man and rob him of his deserved history. Africa has a rich oral history passed down to generations, and thought:

> The *Iliad* and *Odyssey* were rightly regarded as essential sources for the history of ancient Greece, African oral tradition, the collective memory of peoples which holds the thread of many events marking their lives, was rejected as worthless. In writing the history of a large part of Africa, the only sources used were from outside the continent, and the final product gave a picture not so much of the paths actually taken by the African peoples as of those that the authors thought they must have taken. Since the European Middle Ages were often used as a yardstick, modes of production, social relations and political institutions were visualized only by reference to the European past.[384]

Refusal to document the oral stories which make up a collective memory for thousands of years of African history has meant that there are few African books on the subject. The Europeans who colonized the Africans, however, wrote avidly, and these accounts are now taken

---

382 Duncan, J.S.R., *The Sudan: A Record of Achievement* (London: William Blackwood and Sons Ltd., 1952.

383 Keane, A. H., Alison Hingston Quiggin, & Alfred C. Haddon. *Man, Past and Present* (Cambridge: University Press, 1899), p. 45.

384 UNESCO, op. cit.

as the sole records of African history. This is the total opposite to what should have been accepted. Even in this modern time, in our universities, it is very rare to see Africans dedicating much of their time to studying the precious work of the ancient records. For instance, let's take a look at Kenya: Dr. Richard and Mary Leakey were not black Africans, and they travelled far to discover, in the backyard of South Sudan's garden, the ancient remains of the first people. A lack of interest and proper research is the norm, and many in African public universities are not engaged in true African history. When the Europeans began to discriminate against Africans, they started by classifying races, and described the Africans in a manner that placed them as lesser to other races. George Pouchet, who wrote *The Plurality of the Human Race*, stated that the Negro races of the Oceanic Islands and Africa had exaggerated developments around the heel-bone:

> The foot of a Nubian, and especially that of a female, shows quite different characteristics. The five metatarsi seem to rest their whole length upon the ground, without being shaped by the instep; their anterior extremities are slightly diverted, the toes having the same spaces between them, so that the foot is flat…this structure is, besides, perfectly represented in all Egyptians statues without exception.[385]

The above descriptions, where black African bodies were often measured, drawn, analyzed limb by limb in a manner likened to the assessment of a horse or of cattle, was carried out when the Transatlantic slave trade was happening. This was no less than a human harvest in Africa by Arabs and the Europeans. Descriptions given to the Negro by colonialists describe different temperaments when it came to sexuality, including suggestions that Negroes have darker blood, and that their sperm is equally dark. Dehumanizing analysis of black bodies even stretched to the development of the small labia: "Among the Hottentot

---

385 Pouchet, George, *The Plurality of the Human Race* (London: The Anthropolgical Society Press, 1858), p. 49..

women, that of the prepuce and the clitoris among the Semitic race, and even the size of the penis among the Ethiopians – such as the size that it would almost impede the union of a black man with a white woman – whilst the union of a white man with a Negress would occur without any impediment."[386] The meaning of this comes across clearly enough; the implications are that intermarriage between a black man and a white woman would not be possible, although interestingly, such an impediment did not exist for the white man who wished to take a black woman as partner. These are the perceptions written almost 200 years ago, and records and historical accounts have progressed beyond such overtly racist writing, although in modern accounts it may still be there. The mentality of authors such as Pouchet encouraged the dehumanization and classification of races, where Africans were undermined and abused beyond reasonable doubt.

Movies such as *Black Panther* are trying to bring hope to Africans, black men, and the wider black society through representation, creating black heroes for black society, young and old. This will bring back to our consciousness that which has been missing for a long time. However, a lot of work needs to be done in order to allow the re-emergence of black civilization, which was hidden for thousands of years, and this could be made possible through solid research and proper exploration carried out by open minds, free from prejudice and bias. For centuries, the black race has been exploited by its white counterpart and seen as inferior. The situation is improving and there are some historians who are studying Africa with more rigorous, objective, and open-minded approaches, while taking every step to include actual African sources. This group of historians, archeologists, and Egyptologists include the likes of Robert Bauval and Thomas Brophy, referenced throughout this book. Africans themselves have also taken the initiative to rewrite their own history and establish the historical authenticity of their society on a solid foundation.[387]

---

386 Ibid., p. 50.

387 UNESCO, op. cit

Conclusion

Below is a narrative of a description of the different types of black men who actually occupied the entire continent of Africa before the coming of other races. No matter where you go in ancient times, you will never differentiate one black from another black. It is just as if you go to Saudi Arabia, every person you will see will have the same type of nose, ears, head and hair color, just like Africa in olden times.

In some remote if undated epoch the specialized Negro type, as depicted on the Egyptian monuments some thousands of years ago, has everywhere been persistently maintained with striking uniformity...within this wide domain of the black Negro there is a remarkably general similarity of type...if you took a Negro from the Gold Coast of West Africa and passed him off amongst a number of Nyasa natives, and if he were not remarkably distinguished from them by dress or tribal marks, it, would not be easy to pick him out. Nevertheless, considerable differences are perceptible to the practiced eye, and the contrasts are sufficiently marked ... which justify ethnologists in treating the Sudanese and the Bantu as two distinct subdivisions of the family. In both groups, the relative blood natives are everywhere very much alike, and the contrasts are presented chiefly amongst the mixed or Negroid populations. In Sudan, the disturbing elements are both Hamitic (Berbers and Tuaregs) and Semitic (Arabs) while in Bantuland they are mainly Hamitic (Galla) in all the central and southern districts, and Arabs on the eastern seaboard from the equator to Sofala beyond the Zambesi. To the varying proportions of these several ingredients may perhaps be traced the often very marked differences observable on the one hand between such Sudanese peoples as the Wolof, Mandingans, Hausa, Nubians, Zandeh and Mangbattu, and on the other between all these and the Swahili, Baganda, Zulu-Xosa, Be-Chuana, Ova-Herero and some other Negroid Bantu.[388]

---

388 Keane et. al., p. 44

It has been written in different books that the Bantu and Nilotic people could easily be considered one and the same. In fact, in South Sudan today, the Bantu and Nilotic live together harmoniously, and it could be difficult to identify differences to a certain extent; but they are of two different groups with different characteristics and the same skin color. To a foreigner, they may look the same, but to the Bantu or Nilotics, the differences are obvious and important. This is why it is so crucial for black Africans to take on the task of rewriting their own histories, even when there are well-meaning white scholars attempting the same.

In Amadou Mahtar M'Bow's *General History of Africa*, the then-Director General of UNESCO emphasized that the phenomena which disservice the study of Africa's past are the slave trade and colonization built upon racial stereotyping, leading to the distortion of historiography. The classification of white and black was heavily employed by colonists to better their positions over black Africans, as they were identifying Africans by their skin color and treating them as merchandise.[389] As a result, certain racial and cultural modifications have been caused by the intentional breeding of "good" slave women, which were women of Nubia, Dinka, Fur, and Fertit heritage produced children with curly hair.[390] It has been told that the wife of Mahdi, the chosen one, was believed to be a slave that was allowed to live independently, and she was from Dinka, raided in South Sudan and taken to the region of Nubia. The unfortunate re-engagement of slavery recently in Sudan has shaped the way the South Sudanese characterize northerners as inhumane bullies. This has contributed to the way South Sudan fought its war of liberation and shifted away from northern Sudan. It was realized that inequalities based on a historical background characterized by slavery and would never end, so they chose independent South Sudan. Fatin Abbas stated his view that:

> This not only points to the kind of discrimination that South Sudanese have had to suffer at the hands of northerners, it also

---

389 UNESCO, op. cit.

390 MacMichael, op. cit.

indicates the extent to which the legacy of slavery continued to inform structures of economic, political and social inequality long after the official abolishment of the practice in 1924, and the country's independence in 1956.[391]

Although the practice of slavery has long been abolished officially in Sudan, the practice was still being carried on until the time when the Comprehensive Peace Agreement was signed in 2005. The Anti-Slavery Society documented recent cases of slavery, often conducted by the so-called Arabs. As I mentioned earlier, this misconception did not stem from nothing, it is rooted in historic inequalities. In Sudan, merchants and adventurers with private armies roamed the country and enslaved the blackest Africans, mainly those in the southern part of the country, and "the best of the slave men were taken for the army and women were sold to the officials, officers, and troops who were themselves scouring Egypt and the Turkish legion".[392] The savagery of the slave traders stemmed from the belief that Blacks were no more advanced than monkeys. The areas most affected were northern Bhar el Ghazel, southern Darfur, and Kordofan. The government was using this tribal entity to destabilize and exhaust black Africans so that they would give up chasing their dreams of liberation. The people would also submit to their rules and their religion. The benefits the tribal entity empowered by the Khartoum regime received in return included the goods they stole during their raids, which included people and livestock.[393]

In conclusion, the black man has an ancient history richer than any race in the world. He was deliberately stamped down, and all his labors were used to undermine his ancient works. Unless the descendants of black men think critically, they will always face opposition from those who have bad intentions toward them.

---

391 Abbas, Fatin, "Coming to terms with Sudan's legacy of slavery".(*African Arguments*, January 18, 2016).

392 Duncan,. P. 8

393 "Slavery in Sudan" (Cambridge, MA: *Cultural Survival Quarterly*, .September 1988).

INDEX

A

Aaron 86
Fatin 286
Abbasid 145
Abraham 72, 84-85, 92, 98,
    154, 218, 220, 233
Abuna 210
Abu Sergia 177, 188
Abu Simbel 159
Abyssinia 71, 143-144, 146,
    148, 152-153, 211, 213
Edwin Sammy 46, 100, 220
Adam and Eve 17-18, 38, 48,
    66-68, 78, 88, 217, 225, 227
Addis Ababa 69, 211
Adok 27, 256
Aeschylus 140
Afghanistan 72
African Union 167, 168
Akhenaton 198
Akkad 71-72, 87-89, 97-98,
    104, 216
Aksum 153
Alaska 54
Muhammad Sa'im 171
Alexander the Great 118, 129,
    136, 149, 152, 155, 165
Alexandria 142, 145, 148-149,
    192, 214
Algeria 11, 50, 99, 218-219
Pasha Mohammed 166
Al-Qata'i 145
Amun 163, 198
William 214

Antigonus 152
Anuak tribe 187, 241, 244
Aphrodite 134, 221
Apollodorus 140
Arabia 61, 72-74, 82, 87-89, 90,
    94, 97-98, 122, 136, 142-146,
    149, 152, 175, 208-210, 268,
    271, 285
Arab League 141, 176
Arab Spring 181
Ararat, Mount 112
Aras/Araxes river 75
Arcadia 134, 221
Archimedes 192
Aristotle 101, 140, 158
Arkell, A.J. 58, 61
Ark of the Covenant 153
Armenia 71, 112
Aryans 136
Asa 215
Assyria 71, 88, 98, 216
Astaboras river 209, 211
Aswan 159, 212, 213
Aten 186
Atlantic Ocean 205
Atlantis 82, 114
Australia 45-46, 50, 54, 99, 210
Axum 211

B

Baal 107, 108, 175
Baalshamin 175
Bab-el-Mandeb 147, 149, 211

Babylon 8, 11, 14, 17, 71, 72, 86-89, 93-95, 98-99, 101, 104-108, 110, 115, 117, 120, 122, 142, 172, 189, 193, 208, 216, 220, 223-225, 227, 233, 237, 266, 274
Bacchus 188
Baganda 285
Baggara 61
Baghdad 145
Bahamas 227
Clinton 149
John Denison 89-90, 101
Bantu 60-61, 102, 240, 285-286
Robert 123, 126, 132, 160, 167, 169, 171-172, 178-179, 182, 194, 203, 284
BBC 181
Bedouin 144, 145, 149
Beja 144, 270
Benin 62
Ben Jonah 279
Bentiu 10, 221, 224
Berber 61, 218
Berlin 280
Bethlehem 188-189
Bhar el-Ghazal 55, 233, 252
Nyawel 60
Bidiit 259
Bijie 52
Black Panther 284
Black Sea 158
Blue Nile 25, 27, 38, 61, 69-70, 181, 211-212, 265
Bocchoris 157
Napoleon 129, 170
Borneo 54
British East India Company 88
Bronze Age 123

Thomas 126, 160, 203, 236, 284
Buk 107
Bul 24, 262
Burunge 51

C

Julius 129
Cairo 117, 127, 137, 143, 145, 165-166, 168, 171, 174, 179, 188, 202, 235
Caligula 162
Calneh 98, 104
Cambyses 152, 156, 161
Cameroon 59
Canaan 72, 82-84, 86, 93-94, 97, 99-100, 110, 122, 136, 159, 172, 175, 189, 205, 208, 276, 277
Candace 209-210, 215
Cape of Good Hope 53
Carthage 217-218, 219
Caspian Sea 75
Celts 156
Chad 99
Chaldea 71-72, 90, 92, 94, 101
Chaldeans 33, 72, 87-92, 94-95, 100-101, 172, 224-225
Chartres 134, 221
Cheddar Man 200, 275
Cheops 185
Chieng-Bongbar 230
China 48, 50, 54
Cleomenes of Naucratis 152
Colchoi 138
Congo 53, 56, 61, 280
Copts 143, 270
Corinth 134, 221

Index

Croegaert 64
Ctesibius 192
Cush 6, 11-12, 18, 33, 58-60, 65,
  68, 71-75, 78, 82-83, 85-90,
  96-99, 103-105, 110-112, 114,
  139, 145, 148, 151-152, 156,
  157, 205, 207, 209-217, 219,
  223, 225, 231, 234, 267-268,
  269, 270, 273-274, 276
Cyrene 149
Cyrus 145, 152

D

Damascus 110
Danagla 271
Darchieng Dok 256-257
Darfur 25, 28, 61, 64, 287
Darwin, Charles 46-47, 280-281
David 85, 100
De Bononia, Franciscus Pipinus
  189
Demeter 134, 221
Democritus 195
Deng Kur 113
De Volney, Comte 137
Dhurgon, Teny 254, 257
Dinka 6, 9, 14, 18-21, 28-29,
  33, 59-61, 102-103, 120, 222,
  233, 238-241, 244, 251-253,
  257-262, 264-266, 286
Dionysus 213
Diop, Cheikh Anta 11, 32, 37,
  46, 53, 60, 64, 117, 127, 133-
  135, 137, 139-140, 155, 199,
  200-205, 211, 220, 223, 226,
  228, 234
Djibouti 73, 74, 84, 158

Djoser 185, 196
Dok 107, 230, 256, 257, 262
Dongola 64, 272-273
Dordogne 49
Dotog 51
Dryopethicus 41-42, 44
Duach, Latior 110
Duany, Wai 249
Duncan, John S.R. 227, 237

E

Ea 79
Ehret, Christopher 32, 35, 40,
  53, 54, 235
Elam 82, 136
El Omari 125
El Sa'ab 153
Enlil 79
Eratosthenes 268
Erbil 216
Erech 72, 79, 90
Eridu 72
Eritrea 148, 158
Esau 86
Euclid 192
Eudoxus 140, 196
Euphrates 38, 217, 225
Ewuare 62
Ezekiel 211, 214

F

Fagan, Brian M. 165, 169
Fangak 251
Felix 209
Fenton, Bruce R. 51

Fertit 286
Frumentius 210
Fur 286

G

Gabal el Uweinat 131
Gabriel 78
Gaia 106
Galla 285
Galtier 52
Gambia 33, 60
John 23, 69, 70
Garden of Eden 13, 32, 38, 49, 65-71, 74, 76-77, 78, 80, 88, 122, 158, 217, 227
Gawar 230, 257
Gaza 99, 161
Gerar 99
Ghana 59
Gihon River 5, 49, 69, 71, 74-75, 213
Gilf Kebir 131, 132, 134
Gilgamesh 5, 69, 79-80
Giza 6, 82-83, 116, 126, 166, 169-170, 178, 180, 185, 204
Sylvain 52
Gold Coast 285
Goliath 93
Charles George 142
Gorowa 51
Goshen 198
Gough 275
Great Flood 38, 79, 85, 99-100, 114
Guinea 99
Gyges 152

H

Haak 256, 262
Hadar 32
Ernest 280, 281
Ham 53, 68, 73, 83-85, 92-93, 95-100, 103-104, 110, 115, 118, 122, 141, 152, 158-159, 205, 217, 225, 231-232, 270, 276-277, 279
Hamamat 146
Hancock, Graham 45, 126, 169, 182, 194
Harran, Joseph 33, 92, 94-95, 172, 224
Hathor 236
Haulan 73
Hausa 61, 285
Havilah 71-74, 98-99, 205
Zahi 123, 177-180, 182-184
Hegel, G.W.F. 121, 126
Heliopolis 142, 145, 162, 165, 174, 189, 191, 193, 195-197
Hellas 162
Hercules 218
Herero 285
Herod 93, 188-189
Herodotus 38-39, 138, 140, 151, 154-161, 173, 184, 196, 205, 210, 213-214, 278
Hezekiah 209
Himyarites 152
Hitler, Adolf 281
Hittites 33, 150, 187
Hodge, Bodie 48, 110, 232
Homo erectus 44-45
Homo habilis 44
Homo sapiens 35, 40, 44-46, 49, 50, 52, 132

Index

Horemheb 150
Horn of Africa 43, 96
Farouk 180
Hottentots 280
Hutchinson, Sharon E. 16, 247-248
Hyksos 187
Hypatia 192

I

Ice Age 53, 200, 275
Ikhnaton 150
Iliad 282
Imhotep 137, 195-196
India 72, 82, 88, 95, 98, 102, 136, 148, 210
Indian Ocean 37-39, 50
Iran 70, 72
Iraq 7, 11, 13, 33, 49, 68, 70, 73-75, 78, 88, 94, 98, 110, 149, 175, 210
Isaac 86, 233
Isis godess 107-108
ISIS (terrorist organisation) 175
Israel 70, 72, 83-86, 92, 123, 180, 197-199, 210, 216, 233, 277
Ivory Coast 53

J

Ja'alin 61
Jaang 265, 266
Jabel Barkal 265
Jacob 85-86, 100, 145, 198, 233, 277

Jagei 20, 24, 60, 262
Japheth 115, 232
Java Man 44
Jebel Irhoud 36
Jerusalem 13, 85-86, 92-93, 99-100, 114, 189, 208-210
Jesus Christ 86, 188-189, 197
Jethro 86, 215
Jikany 15, 24, 259
Douglas H. 16, 233, 249
Jonglei 21, 59, 182, 241
Jordan 149
Flavius 103, 159, 183, 190
Juba 4, 10, 128, 245
Judah 85, 210, 215

K

Kak, Ding 265
Kalenjin 33, 184, 185
Kanuz 271
Karasu 75
Katanda 56
Keane 281
Kedar 92
Kenya 14, 33, 35, 37, 44, 50, 84, 93, 100, 120, 225, 231, 233-234, 239, 283
Kerma 268
Kulang 110, 113
Khabiri 150
Khafre 170
Manour 120
Khartoum 8-9, 17-18, 22, 24-25, 27-28, 34, 58-59, 61, 142, 184, 212, 234, 238, 248, 253, 266, 287
Kicher, Athansius 162

Kiir 181
Kilimanjaro, Mount 202
Kish 72, 97
Klasies River 57
Kuong Duoth, Gordon 241
Koat Lich 223, 225, 250
Koch County 15, 17, 60
Koko 48
Kordofan 28, 64, 287
Tang 110
Kuarhok 102, 257, 258
Kuarjuayni 6, 263
Kuarmuon 102, 194, 231, 243, 245-249, 254-257
Kuarthoay 6, 263, 264
Tunguar 248
Kuer-Kuong 14
Kuong 15, 228, 244
Kuei guong, Teny 217
Kurdistan 216
Kush 13

L

Laak 230
Laertius, Diogenes 140
Lake No 60
Lane, Edward William 141
Leakey, Richard and Mary 32, 35, 40, 42-43, 283
Lebanon 7, 84, 87, 175
Leer 22-24, 27, 60, 93, 256, 261
Lepsius, Karl 133, 203
Libya 11, 50, 82-84, 87, 99, 132, 135, 143, 154, 217-218, 240, 269, 278
Lilith 5, 76, 77
Lot 92

Lothpera, Maani 257
Louis-Philippe I 174
Lucian 140
Lucy 32, 42-43
Luhya 100
Luo 14, 33, 233, 239, 259
Kuoch 256-257
Luxor obelisk 166, 174
Lydia 152

M

Maani 113, 257-258
Macedonia 152
MacGaffey, Wyatt 64
Machar Riek 8, 29, 140, 215, 251
MacMichael, H.A. 62
Maguel, Gatluak 230
Mahass 271
Makkan 89
Malakal 9, 10, 230
Mali 59, 99, 218, 276
Manasasir 270
Mangbattu 285
Ammianus 140
Ma'rib 153
Marseilles 134, 221
Mary 188-189
Masai 33
Masalit 270
Matuot, Chot Keth 257
Mauritania 26, 33, 60-61, 99, 218
Mavulis 99
Mayiendit 261
Mayom 60, 261, 262
M'Bantu, Anu 115

M'Bow, Amadou-Mahtar 221, 286
Mecca 87, 147
Mediterranean 13, 24, 114, 117,
    127, 131, 134-135, 151, 162,
    173, 187, 220-221, 232, 237,
    240, 272
Melanesia 230
Melanin dosage test 201
Melut 265
Memphis 133, 161, 196
Menes 63, 133, 185
Mentuhotep 185
Martin 50
Meroë 14, 18, 59, 128, 157,
    209, 212-215, 244, 268
Mesopotamia 49, 68, 74, 78-79,
    81-82, 87-88, 91, 94-98, 136,
    139, 202, 219
Matthias 51
Migdol 214
Milton, John 5, 77
Mirukh 89
Mizraim 64-65, 83, 84-85, 87,
    93, 97, 99, 141, 205, 269-270
Mohammed 87, 136, 144, 166
Morocco 11, 36, 44, 50, 99,
    218, 227
Morris, Henry 111
Moses 15, 80, 86, 93, 192, 197-
    199, 277
Mosul museum 175
Mukuba 100
Muller, Gert 115
Multiregional Theory 45
Mulukoba 100
Murat, river 75
Murle 185
Musée de l'Homme 202
Mycerinus 185

N

Naath 3, 6, 17, 33, 35, 41, 53,
    58, 59-61, 94-97, 101-102,
    107, 109, 113, 115, 120, 133,
    140, 184-187, 190, 193-194,
    198, 200, 205-206, 215, 217,
    221-234, 236-239, 241-244,
    246-247, 250-254, 264-266
Nabholz, Benoit 52
Nabta Playa 134-135, 235-236
Napata 268
Nasir 234
National Geographic 36, 175
Natural History Museum 275
Naucratis 152, 155
Ngorongoro 70
Ngundeng 107, 113, 173, 184,
    190-191, 217, 252
Nigeria 99
Niger, river 54, 61, 99, 158, 218
Nile 8-10, 12, 14, 110-111, 113,
    116, 119-120, 122, 127-128,
    130-132, 134-136, 138-139,
    145-150, 152, 156, 160-162,
    169, 171, 173, 179-182,
    184-185, 188, 191, 194-195,
    197, 200, 203, 205, 207, 209,
    211-214, 217, 225-226, 228,
    230, 233-241, 251-252, 254,
    265-266, 267-272, 276, 279
Nilotic people 7, 9, 12, 14-17,
    19, 21, 25, 27, 33, 55, 58-61,
    64-65, 70, 78, 102-103, 105,
    108, 120, 138-139, 147, 160,
    184, 185, 191, 207-208, 212-
    213, 215, 223, 226, 231, 233,
    235, 237-238, 240, 244, 264,
    266, 270, 274-275, 286

Nimrod 11, 18, 68, 71-74, 78, 82, 84-85, 97, 98, 99, 100-108, 110, 112-114, 139, 183, 190, 215-217, 219, 231, 234, 237
Nineveh 33, 85, 114, 115
Nippur 69, 72
Noah 18, 78, 80, 82-84, 93, 97, 103, 110, 112, 114-115, 122, 141, 153, 216, 217, 231-232, 276
Nubia 75, 83, 96-97, 100, 110, 125, 132, 146-147, 149, 159, 212, 217, 239-240, 267-269, 271-273, 286
Nuer 6, 9-10, 12-16, 238-255, 257-265, 269, 274-275
Nuwas, King Dhu 154
Nyang Machar 29, 254
Nyasa 285
Nyika 100

O

Odyssey 282
Olduvai Gorge 32, 35
Omdurman 238
Orion 236
Oromo 144
Osiris 106-107, 221
Osman, Ahmed 37, 132, 167, 182
Osorkon III 151

P

Pakistan 72
Palestine 150, 159, 161, 180, 189
Palmyra 175
Pa-Nehesy 185
Paradise Lost 5, 77
Paranthropus 32, 43
Parieng 27, 261
Paris 163, 174, 201-202
Paul 93
Peking Man 44
Pentateuch 197
Persia 72
Persian Gulf 71-72, 209
Persian occupation of Egypt 39, 140
Peth, Matuot 257
Philip 215
Phoenicia 161-162
Pishon river 5, 71, 73
Plato 140, 192, 195-196
Polycrates 128
Pouchet, George 283-284
Pritchard, Evans 16, 18-21, 193, 233, 243, 247, 259, 274
Psamtik III 128
Ptah 133
Ptolemy 145, 149, 152, 173
Put 83-85, 87, 97, 99
Pyramids of Giza 83, 178
Pythagoras 195

Q

Qays 149
Qena 159
Quran 226

Index

R

Ra 162, 169
Ramses II 163-164, 173-174,
    187
Ramses III 133
Ran, Gaw 15, 60
Raphael, angel 78
Rawlinson, Sir Henry 88-89, 97
Reader, John 40
Red Sea 43, 54, 73-74, 96, 135,
    143, 146-147, 150, 152-153,
    173
Rehoboth 98
Renk 265
Rift Valley basin 50, 56
Rodenbeck 165
Rolnyang, Ran Gam 15, 60
Rome 162, 163, 269
Luoth 257
Rumbek 9, 254
Ruot, Phar 245
Rwenzori, Mount 202

S

Saba, Abd Shams 153
Sabean 73
Sahara 54-56, 61, 100, 130-131,
    134, 235, 237
Sambu, Kipkoeech Araap 185
Samlah 100
Sandawe 51
Saqarah 196
Sarah 92
Saul 74
Seland, Elvind 144
Seligman, C.G. 121, 126, 230-231

Semiramis 105-108
Senegal 33, 59-61, 96, 205
Sennacherib 209
Sennar 38
Seth 107
Seti I 150, 163, 164
Shabaka 157
Shaigiya 270
Shasu 150
Sheba 84, 99, 110, 213
Sheddad 152
Shem 11, 98, 102, 104, 115, 232
Shilluk 33, 65, 187, 200, 233,
    240, 241, 244
Shurrupak 79
Siculus, Diodorus 140, 205
Sidon 99
Siduri 79
Sima de los Huesos 52
Sinai Peninsula 74, 117, 135,
    146, 149, 187
Sirius 161
Smith, Elliot 146
Smyth, Charles Piazzi 178
Sobat, river 19, 211, 212, 228,
    234
Sodom 99
Sofala 285
Solomon 92, 115, 210
Solon 192
Somalia 73, 84, 158
Somerset 275
Songhai 276
South Africa 43, 49, 50, 57
South Sudan 7-9, 12, 18, 21, 24-
    25, 27-29, 33-35, 37-38, 58-60,
    64, 93-95, 102-103, 107, 120,
    128-129, 173, 176, 181-182,
    190, 198, 205-206, 208-212,

214-215, 222-223, 228, 230, 234, 236, 238, 240, 242, 251-254, 264-265, 279, 283, 286
Sphinx 6, 82, 138, 169, 170-172, 176, 180, 182
SPLA 22-25, 28, 69
SPLM 8, 22
Sri Lanka 230
Stephen the Martyr 197
Strabo 140, 154
Sudd swamps 128, 147, 181-182, 223, 224, 242
Suez Canal 144
Sukot 271
Sumer 68, 71-72, 74, 83, 87-89, 91-92, 94-97, 225
Swahili 285
Syria 7, 72, 75, 84-85, 110, 114, 143, 149-150, 159, 175, 273

T

Taharqa 156, 157, 185, 209
Talmud 276
Tammuz 105-108
Tanzania 14, 32-35, 37, 44, 50-51, 120, 225, 231, 233-234, 239
Tatius, Achilles 140
Taurus Mountains 75
Terah 72, 84-85, 92
Tera-Neter 185
Thales 192, 195
Tharjiath Lich 15, 58-59
Thebes 120, 163, 196
Theodorus 142
Thep Yen 257
Thieng 230

Thutmose I 269
Thutmose III 150, 185
Thutmose IV 170
Tigris River 5, 73, 75, 88
Timbuktu 88, 220
Torah 197, 277
Tower of Babel 13, 18, 78, 82, 98, 100-101, 104-105, 108-113, 115, 118, 183, 190, 215, 219, 231-234
Trevor-Roper, Hugh 120
Tulun, Ahmed Ibn 145
Tunisia 11, 218, 219
Lake 33, 35, 44
Turkey 70, 72, 75, 88, 94-95, 143, 172, 175
Tutankhamun 163, 185
Tuti Island 34, 238

U

Uganda 14, 33, 120, 225, 231, 233-234, 239, 240
United Nations 10, 21, 141, 175
Unity State 15, 17, 29, 60, 223, 228, 256, 261-262
Upper Nile 8, 14-15, 17, 21, 26-27, 38, 54, 55, 59, 60, 72, 89, 96, 111, 113, 127-128, 138-139, 147, 173, 182, 184, 200, 205, 212, 217, 223, 226, 228, 233-235, 239-241, 251, 252, 269-270
Upper Semliki River 56
Ur 72, 89, 92, 220, 233
Uriel 78
Uruk 69, 79, 98, 104
Utnapishtim 79